CATHERINE

Shamara

For two lovers,
there was only one sanctuary.

LOVE SPELL

$5.50 US
$6.50 CAN
£5.99 UK
$12.95 AUS

50550

9 780505 524522

0-505-52452-X

SANCTUARY

Eirene closed her eyes, looking so fragile, it took all Jarek's control to keep from taking her into his arms and evoking the most primal of reactions. He leaned back in the chair, blew out his breath. "I'll admit, I've done some things that might seem questionable, but always with good reason. I've never lied to you, not even when it would have made things easier between us. I'm just a man, with failings and shortcomings, but I try to live by a code of honor. I hope you know that."

She opened her eyes, but didn't look at him. Desperately, he searched for a way to reach her.

"*Shamara*. Do you know what that is, Eirene?"

Silence. He hadn't really expected her to answer. Her expression was cool and distant, as if she'd withdrawn from the conversation. From him.

"Shamara means sanctuary. Everyone should have a sanctuary, don't you think? A haven, a refuge from the ugliness of our universe. *Shamara*. A place to seek the light of the Spirit, to live in peace. That place might be a calm oasis on a desert planet, or a shrine in a temple, or a quiet space within ourselves. Or for some of us who are more desperate, it could lie just beyond our reach, in another universe."

He rose and paced to the portal. Endless stars glittered against a midnight infinity. "*Shamara*," he repeated softly. "That's all I'm seeking for my people. I know you hate me. I can't change that. But I need your help to find it, Eirene."

Other *Love Spell* books by Catherine Spangler:
SHADOWER
SHIELDER

Shamara

Catherine Spangler

LOVE SPELL   NEW YORK CITY

A LOVE SPELL BOOK®

September 2001

Published by

Dorchester Publishing Co., Inc.
276 Fifth Avenue
New York, NY 10001

ISBN 0-505-52452-X

The name "Love Spell" and its logo are trademarks of Dorchester Publishing Co., Inc.

Printed in the United States of America.

Visit us on the web at www.dorchesterpub.com.

This book is dedicated to two special aunts who have guided and influenced my life in countless positive ways. You have been like surrogate mothers to me, and I thank you for your encouragement and support over the years.

To Joanne Gailar— Your love of reading, your incredible writing talent, the joy and wonder you find in life, continually inspire me to find magic and stories in every situation.

To Betty Heasley— Your unshakable faith, your deep well of love and compassion for others, are a shining example of the good in this world, and a blessing to all who know you.

Much love to you both.

ACKNOWLEDGMENTS

Many wonderful people helped make this book a reality. Special thanks to Mary Gearhart-Gray for sharing her knowledge of energy and healing, and offering calming encouragement. A heartfelt thanks to David Gray for his patience in answering my technical questions, for his impressive scientific knowledge, and for brainstorming "possibilities." Appreciation and gratitude to the Lollies, Writerspace, all the "regulars" at the Monday night chat sessions, and Paranormal Romance, for their support and enthusiasm. Thanks to Angelica, Beth, and Robyn, my office cohorts; to the "musketeers"—my critique partners: Linda Castillo, Jennifer Miller, and Vickie Spears, whose talent and creativity awe me; to Roberta Brown, agent extraordinaire; and to editor Christopher Keeslar, for his attention to detail, while still allowing me creative freedom. Finally, love and gratitude to my husband, James, and my children, Jim and Deborah, for putting up with me, and subsisting on fast food. You all contributed so much. Thank you.

Shamara

Chapter One

Travan

She needed to lose her virginity—and fast.

That inane thought was Eirene's first reaction to her uncle's shattering pronouncement. Stunned, she stared at him, her heart pounding.

Vaden returned her perusal, his pale eyes as sharp as lasers, a warning of his cunning, savage character. Greed radiated from him like a malevolent aura.

"Lanrax got your tongue, woman?"

Panic clawed at her insides. "Uncle, you can't mean—"

"The Leors made a very good offer. A trade route for a virgin bride. I might have bartered you to one of those slobbering idiot Anteks, as payment for not patrolling our smuggling routes. You should show your gratitude, niece."

Gratitude? For selling her—or at least her virginity—

13

off to a Leor? Eirene's thoughts whirled, trying to assimilate this unexpected turn of events. It was true women here on Travan had no rights and served only two purposes: breeding or trading for goods and services. Yet she had hoped her healing skills would make her too valuable to be traded. She'd obviously been wrong.

"The Leor envoy arrives tomorrow," Vaden informed her. "Your future master will be with them. He wants to inspect you himself. You'll also be examined by their healer to ensure you're still a virgin."

He took a swig of his wine. His lecherous gaze swept over her as he wiped his mouth. "It's a shame I can't sample you first. You're a pretty piece. But those Spirit-forsaken Leors are damn particular about their women."

A shudder ran through Eirene, and she fought back a wave of nausea. "Uncle, I urge you to reconsider. Surely my healing abilities have some value—"

"Skills any female can learn," he spat contemptuously. "Your virginity is far more valuable."

Not nearly as valuable as the abilities she kept hidden—powers that could very well be discovered by the Leors. Desperation spurred her foolishly on. "There must be another way to acquire the trade route."

He lunged up, surprisingly agile for his age and size, and grabbed her wrist, jerking her halfway across his desk. "How dare you challenge my decisions?" He twisted her arm, wringing a gasp of pain from her. "This route is being acquired *my* way."

He released her abruptly, and she fell forward against the desk. Grabbing her chin, he forced her to look at him. Eyes the color of the morning mist—cold, ruthless—challenged her to further folly.

"I have full rights over you. You will do as I say. If you oppose me in any way, I'll take an electrolyzer rod to you. It won't leave any outside marks to alarm your betrothed. And after I shock you within an inch of your inconsequential life, you'll still do as I say. So what will it be, woman?"

Bitter defeat, laced with a debilitating sense of helplessness, burned in her chest. She should have known arguing would only make her uncle more determined to enforce his authority. She pushed herself upright, resisting the urge to rub her throbbing arm. "I concede to your wishes, Uncle." *For now.*

"I knew you'd see reason." Vaden sank back into his chair and belched loudly. "I expect your future mate to be well-pleased, especially with that hair of yours."

Leors had no body hair, and were reputed to hold a fascination for the hair common to other races. Eirene's was as black as a full eclipse and flowed to her hips. She would cut it off, find some way to make herself repulsive, she thought, battling rising hysteria.

She must find a way to circumvent this trade. She would be defenseless in the clutches of a Leor male. The race was renowned for its fierceness and cruelty—and worse, for its ability to probe minds. It would only be a matter of time before they discerned her secret. No telling what they would do when they discovered she was an Enhancer.

She showed no more of her inner turmoil to Vaden. Her fate would be far worse if he knew the truth. Besides, nothing could be gained by her protest of his decision. The system of male dominance had been in place on Travan for hundreds of seasons. A lone female couldn't battle that system. She'd been a fool to argue with him. But she would find a way out.

Her gaze dropped to the desk, cluttered with priceless artifacts Vaden personally claimed from pirating raids.

An idea took form, and she was desperate enough to try it.

"Nothing else to say, I see," he growled, pouring more wine. "I should have known you wouldn't be grateful that I traded you to someone who will keep your bed warm." He waved her away. "Return to your quarters. Tomorrow you'll be bathed and clothed appropriately to meet your betrothed."

He eyed her ragged robe with distaste, his gaze coming to rest on her breasts. Seeing her opportunity, she used her unique power, locking onto his surge of desire, amplifying it, sending the blood rushing to his groin, lust pounding through his body. A momentary diversion was all she needed to act on her idea. As his eyes closed with the overwhelming desire she'd induced in him, she grabbed two jeweled daggers, prizes from his past raids, then withdrew. She quickly fled the opulent chamber, leaving him to his raging libido.

Not that her uncle was one to suffer any desire long. "Blazing hells! Stane!" Vaden bellowed as she left, then demanded his usual consort: "Get Sarina here immediately. I need her—now!"

Once outside, Eirene stumbled back to the bleak women's compound, stunned and frightened. She had no choice but to flee. Her uncle would come after her, of that she was certain. He didn't like being thwarted, plus he'd have to deal with the Leors to whom he'd traded her, and no one crossed them. They'd be furious if the agreement was not honored. They might even hunt her down themselves.

The sudden rumble of an incoming ship caught her attention. No! Surely her betrothed wasn't arriving a day early. Her panic intensified, adrenaline flooding her body. She looked toward the orange sky. Thrusters surged as a silver ship lowered toward the landing pad. It didn't appear to be a Leor ship, but she had to be certain. Lifting her robe, she hurried closer, moving between the trees.

From the shelter of the copse, she watched the hatch open and the ramp lower. An attractive woman with flowing golden hair strode down the ramp. Eirene was both relieved and astonished. Not a Leor, but a *female*—clad in a flightsuit, no less! How odd that this woman would come here. Disdaining females as inferior, Travan men traded only with male-dominated cultures.

The men on the landing pad appeared as surprised as Eirene, turning to gawk at the young woman. Several of them strutted forward, but halted when a second female, very tall and fierce-looking, emerged from the hatch, a laser rifle in her hands.

The first spoke. "I'm Captain Celie Cameron. We're here to deliver the Elysian liquor and other supplies that Vaden Kane ordered." She tossed back her hair, her gaze sweeping the gaping men clustered in a tight group. "Is there a problem?"

The men glanced toward the second female, who shifted the rifle a notch higher. They shook their heads.

"Well, then," Captain Cameron said briskly, all business. "I'll need four of you to unload this cargo. And I'd like Commander Kane present to sign off and transfer the funds."

The men moved to do her bidding, muttering among themselves. It didn't sit well with them to take orders from a woman, but if Vaden had contracted those supplies, he'd be furious if they weren't unloaded. The woman with the rifle watched their every move as they carried the crates from the ship.

Amazed and heartened, Eirene knew she'd just found her way off Travan. She would stow away on that ship.

She didn't care where it took her. She felt inside her robe pocket for reassurance. Her fingers slid along the hilts of the two jewel-encrusted daggers she'd taken from Vaden's desk. Thank Spirit she hadn't inflicted any serious harm when she used her powers on him. After Rayna . . .

Drawing a deep breath, she pushed back the remorse. She was grateful for the daggers. The jewels in them were extremely valuable. Wherever she landed, she had the means to find her way to Elysia and pursue her lifelong dream.

But before all else, she planned to ensure her uncle's agreement with the Leors would be irreversibly nullified.

She would lose her virginity at the first possible opportunity.

Saron

Jarek san Ranul downed the glass of liquor, feeling it burn all the way to his gut, but the fire in his throat didn't come close to the pain in his soul.

"More?" Blake san Damien offered, raising the bottle.

"No." Jarek blew out his breath and set the glass on the bar. "No use drinking myself senseless. Won't change anything."

"I guess not." Blake refilled his own glass. "Sorry about your father. We've lost a good man, a great leader."

They'd lost more than a great man and leader, Jarek thought, his heart heavy with grief. They'd lost a way of life. A way of life that had been intentionally and systematically torn away from them.

Anger warred with his grief—anger that had built steadily over the past fourteen seasons, as Jarek had watched his people being decimated. Their only crime, that they were Shielders, genetically resistant to the Controllers' mind domination. The destruction came in many forms: engineered disease, Anteks, shadowers, slavers, and even Shielder traitors.

As a reconnaissance scout for his people's pitifully small militia, Jarek had seen it all—entire colonies reduced to smoldering ruins, disease-ridden bodies, the remains from mass executions. Regardless of who inflicted these atrocities, the Controllers were behind every diabolical act.

"I guess you'll be traveling to Liron to take your father's place as Council head," Blake said, breaking into Jarek's dark thoughts.

"And do what?" he growled in answer. "Tell them they might as well surrender to the Controllers and get it over with?" He hurled his glass against the opposite wall. It shattered into myriad pieces, just like the Shielder race was being splintered.

The bartender scowled and activated the vac. The little machine whirred into action, systematically scanning and suctioning the floor.

"Careful," Blake cautioned, glancing around the nearly empty bar. "We don't need to draw attention to ourselves."

He was right, of course. Ordinarily, Jarek took extreme precautions, but his riotous state of mind was impeding his common sense. He nodded, running his hand through his hair.

"How can I go back?" he demanded in a low voice. "How can I be responsible for the safety and welfare of an entire colony of people, when I can't guarantee their existence for a single cycle, much less a season? I can't

19

even guarantee Liron enough food to eat, or medicine and supplies to meet their needs."

"No one can," Blake argued. "Blazing hells, man, they're coming at us from all sides. None of us can make any kind of guarantees. But that colony needs your leadership."

Jarek clenched his fists, frustration a bitter bile in his throat. "That's not enough. We're just sitting echobirds. We don't stand a chance if things don't change—and fast."

"And just how do you propose we change things? Go openly against the Controllers in the hopes of defeating them?"

Jarek said nothing. They both know that an open assault would be suicide. Jarek hated his feeling of helplessness. He was used to action, and yet, there was very little he or anyone could do against the Controllers.

His thoughts turned to the idea that had been plaguing him for over a season. One that had become a burning obsession, haunting his thoughts, taunting him with its possibilities. If ever there was a time for desperate, foolhardy measures, this was it. "I want to check out the twelfth sector," he told Blake.

"Why? There's nothing there but a black hole."

Jarek drummed his fingers on the bar. "Maybe we'd find some sort of natural hyperspace. A wormhole—inside the black hole."

Blake looked at him as if he were crazy. "What makes you think there would be a wormhole?"

"Stories about the Enhancers, for one thing. Many believe they used a portal in the twelfth sector to travel to other worlds." Jarek sat back, awaiting his friend's reaction.

He got it: "Enhancers haven't existed for over two hundred seasons," Blake scoffed.

"But there are numerous stories about them traveling to other worlds through a vortex. We might be passing up a major opportunity if we don't check this out."

Practical as always, Blake shook his head, doubt etched on his face. "So, maybe there is a wormhole inside the black hole. But how in blazing hells could a ship enter it without being crushed to debris?"

It was a good question. "I have some ideas about dealing with that particular problem."

Blake blew out his breath. "Okay, for the sake of the argument, let's say you locate this wormhole and travel through it in one piece. Exactly what do you expect to find at the other end?"

"*Shamara,*" Jarek said softly, the word reverberating through his very soul.

Confusion replaced disbelief in Blake's eyes. "Shamara? What in the Fires is that?"

"Sanctuary. Shamara is the Shen word for sanctuary." Jarek stared at his friend, tension humming through him. "I want to find sanctuary for our people. I have to believe there's a way."

He hated to place all hopes for Shielder survival on one questionable theory. But he didn't see any other options, so he was going to do just that. And pray to Spirit that he was right.

If he was wrong, the Shielders would soon be extinct.

Massive, overwhelming culture shock. Her wildest imaginings could not have prepared Eirene for Saron. She leaned against the rough stone wall of a mercantile, staring all around her. Men and women mingled freely, like equals. Imagine that!

There was the cacophony of bustling activity: masses of people, the babble of voices in a dozen different languages, the roaring of skimmers and incoming ships. Clapping her hands over her ears, Eirene lurched away from the wall and staggered toward the center of the base.

Still, she couldn't cover her eyes to avoid the visual assault on her senses. It was all so fascinating—the brightly colored clothing; women in flightsuits and leggings instead of robes; the shops selling all kinds of products, wondrous things from all over the quadrant.

Even worse was the sensory overload. The emotional bombardment from the crush of beings swamped her. Excitement, greed, lust, anger, fear, violence. She struggled to block them out, succeeding somewhat, but was left incredibly drained.

And this was just Saron, a stop-over planet. She couldn't begin to imagine what Elysia, the trade center of the quadrant, might be like. But she was determined to make her way there, after seeing to the crucial disposition of her virginity. The odds of her uncle or the Leors coming after her were too great to put that off.

First order of business—getting currency and making a few purchases. She needed to find a jeweler and sell a stone from one of her daggers, then buy new clothing and rent a room where she could rest and clean up.

Then . . . on to the Pleasure Dome—to seek temporary employment as a courtesan. She would be safe from harm there, and she imagined that they screened their clientele. Yes, that was the best place to take care of her most pressing problem.

Drawing a deep breath, Eirene put her plan into action.

* * *

"The equipment you're seeking is very rare. So far, I haven't been able to find any." Celie Cameron sipped her drink, regret in her dark brown eyes. "I suspect if we do locate such material, it will be very expensive. I'm sorry."

Jarek gripped his drink. "I don't understand why you can't find equipment that analyzes electromagnetic distortions. Surely it's necessary to map out undeveloped sectors of the quadrant. And what about superconductors? Don't we use them in our intraquadrant hyperspace routes?"

"I don't understand, either. I thought the same thing you did." Celie leaned forward, tossing her blond hair over her shoulder. "Unfortunately, the Controllers place more emphasis on dominating the quadrant and sucking it dry than exploring and mapping new regions."

"The greedy bastards aren't exactly visionaries, are they?" Blake commented.

"No, they're not," Celie agreed. "Very little exploratory equipment is manufactured. As for our internal hyperspace, it's all artificial, and the equipment to maintain the tunnels is manufactured on an as-needed basis. All of that is done under strict surveillance."

"What about the worn-out equipment that's replaced?" Jarek asked. "Could it be overhauled and rebuilt?"

Celie shook her head. "I checked on that. The equipment is immediately melted down and recycled. Waste not, want not."

"Yeah, right," Jarek muttered. He suspected the recycled materials went into weapons. Murdering Shielders and any dissenters was high on the Controller priority list.

"I wish I had better news. I'll keep looking and contact

you if I find anything." Celie placed a slender hand on Jarek's arm. "What will you do now?"

He blew out his breath, frustration a raw ache in his chest. "I don't know. I'm not giving up, that's for sure. But I'll probably head for Liron and get everything settled there. Where are you going next?"

"Heading to Risa, first thing tomorrow. As a matter of fact, I need to get some supplies loaded on my ship. I'd better call it a night." Celie pushed away from the table and stood. Both men rose with her.

She hugged Jarek, and he kissed her on the cheek. He'd known her since she was a young girl of sixteen seasons, had watched her grow into a fine young woman. He thought of her as a sister.

"Thanks, sweetheart," he said. "Tell Moriah and that no-good mate of hers that I said hello."

Celie grinned, the expression making her look hardly old enough to be piloting her own supply ship. "I will. And I won't tell you what Sabin says about you." She turned to Blake and offered her hand. "Commander. It was nice meeting you."

"My friends call me Blake," he replied, taking her hand in both of his. He gave her his most engaging grin, the one that felled most females.

"I'm sure they do . . . Commander." Celie gently disengaged her hand and flashed Jarek another smile. "See you around. Have a good trip to Liron."

She strode from the bar, seemingly oblivious to the multiple male gazes fixed on her trim figure.

Blake let out a low whistle. "Damn, she's a looker."

"She's also very intelligent—too smart to get entangled with the likes of you. She's too young for you, anyway."

"I'm not *that* old," Blake muttered. "So, do we have the evening free before we get started?"

"Yeah, you're free until oh-eight-hundred hours standard time tomorrow."

"Great." Blake turned, slung his arm across Jarek's shoulders. "Since you won't let me flirt with the lady smuggler, I have another idea. We've been working pretty hard these past cycles. What do you say we go to the Dome for some R&R?"

Jarek was taken aback by the suggestion. He had never availed himself of the services of the Pleasure Domes. He didn't have the time or the precious miterons required for such decadent pleasures. Nor did he have any desire to purchase an act that should be given freely between a man and a woman.

He shook his head. "No thanks. I need to send some communiqués and plot our return course to Liron. You go on."

"Hey, you need some down time, too, Captain. It will do you good."

Good? Jarek no longer believed there was much that was good in this Spirit-forsaken quadrant.

He started to refuse again, but Blake headed him off. "Come on. Don't be such an old Shen." He jingled the coins in his flightsuit pocket. "I won a big pot playing Fool's Quest here at Solaris yesterday. I have more than enough for the two of us to enjoy an evening at the Dome, and still give some to the cause. Those communiqués and navigation duties can only take so long. What will you do for the rest of the time?"

What, indeed? Jarek thought. Endure another lonely night shift, filled with grief over his father and dark fears about Shielder survival?

Because of his obligations and the continual dangers he faced, Jarek never allowed himself to become involved in a relationship, much less consider taking a mate. He had nothing to offer except the strong possibility he wouldn't return from any given mission. He'd had only a few dalliances with females, and those occurred before responsibility had become such a heavy cloak.

He was sick to death of being alone, of battling heinous memories of destruction and despair. What would it be like, for once, to lose himself in mindless physical release? To find warmth and comfort in the arms of a woman without duty or commitment? Just once.

Weary and emotionally battered, he felt his resolve wavering. *Just once.* For tonight—no burdens, no accountability, no nightmares.

He nodded. "All right, let's go."

Blake whooped loudly and strode rapidly toward the bar's exit.

Jarek followed more slowly, already doubting the wisdom of his capitulation. It couldn't hurt anything, he told himself.

It was just one night.

Chapter Two

"Are you sure you're okay?" Lani asked, her high-pitched voice grating on Eirene's tautly strung nerves. "You seem jittery."

The courtesan who had been chosen to acclimate Eirene to her new surroundings was nice enough, but she seemed to be somewhat scatterbrained. Eirene drew a calming breath. It didn't help much; her pulse continued racing. Desperately, she wished her beloved mentor was still alive and here to guide her.

Rayna had recognized Eirene's rare powers when she was very young, had taught her the necessity of keeping them a secret and using them only when imperative. She'd been like a mother to Eirene, guiding her into womanhood and teaching her ancient healing techniques. But Rayna was gone, and Eirene had no one to advise her now.

"Eirene, are you all right?"

She jolted back to the present. "Oh, I'm fine. Just getting used to working in a different environment, with new clientele."

Lani giggled, the sound overly shrill, and a blunt reminder that the virginity disposal business was close at hand—very close. "Oh, sweetness, the clientele are the same wherever you go!" she trilled. "I don't think that will be any adjustment for you."

The girl fluffed her blue hair around her shoulders and her very generous breasts. The blue feathers cloaking her small frame swayed with the movement. "Where did you say you worked before?"

Eirene paused, still trying to assimilate the other woman's appearance. She'd never seen so much blue—hair, lips, feathered headdress and robe—all blue. Actually, she'd never met anyone remotely like Lani. Despite the oddity of the petite woman's appearance, Eirene sensed a good heart and kind nature. Lani harbored no malice or ill will of any sort. She had generously taken Eirene under her wing—so to speak—going so far as to share her cosmetics and perfume.

"Sweetness, surely you've got previous experience at this," Lani prompted, her gamine face scrunching in concern. "I mean, you didn't have any personal toiletries, and just that one robe. You can use some of my feathers, if you like. Most men find them very . . . stimulating. And you just wouldn't believe the things the right man can do with feathers."

"Oh, no thank you," Eirene answered hastily. "I don't usually—ah—work with feathers. As I told Madam Zandra, I don't have much with me because I managed to get a seat on an earlier transport than I planned, and my personal items are on the later transport."

Lani still looked concerned. "Have you worked at other Domes?"

"Oh, yes. I've been many seasons at 'The Tent of Women.' "

Eirene had told Madame Zandra the same thing, but the woman hadn't been totally convinced. Greed won out, however, cementing her decision to hire Eirene. The madam had clearly broadcast her hope that Eirene's striking looks would be a draw, despite her questionable credentials. Madam Zandra was a businesswoman, first and foremost.

But Lani appeared to believe Eirene. She nodded in ready acceptance. " 'The Tent of Women.' That sounds very interesting . . . very exotic."

Eirene thought of the ragged tents in the women's compound on Travan, the dust blowing through the frayed fabric. Of the women there, worn down from serving men's voracious needs, from the harsh living conditions, and from bearing too many children. Sadness joined the trepidation churning in the pit of her stomach. She vowed to herself that one day she would return to Travan in a position to make some changes.

She looked around the boudoir to which she had been assigned to perform her job as a courtesan—the place where her next actions would ensure her freedom. Its conspicuous opulence rivaled her uncle's residence. A mirrored alcove ensconced a huge satin-draped bed, on which soft pillows were artfully arranged. A plush sofa sat against the opposite wall. A vibrachair, large enough to hold two—or possibly more—sat next to a console containing Elysian wine and liquor, glasses, and a horrifying assortment of sexual "accessories." That's what Lani called them.

Having firmly assured Madam Zandra she had no exotic sexual specialities, Eirene prayed her client wouldn't be interested in using any accessories. Not that it mattered, because she intended to use her powers—just a little—to enhance the client's lust, forcing him to finish the act quickly.

She was terrified of channeling energy but more frightened of the mating act. Hopefully, if she could use just enough energy to inflame the client's libido without hurting him, he wouldn't notice her lack of experience—or her virginity.

A tone sounded and the panel by the entry lit up. "Oh, you've got a client already!" Lani sashayed over to the panel and indicated the display. "This will give you all the information you need to know about him. His name— first name only, of course—his race, his—ahem . . . personal preferences."

Oh, Spirit. Her heart pounding, Eirene walked over and read the information. A humanoid male, Jarek, had purchased the whole evening. He didn't state any unusual preferences.

"Oh, lucky you!" Lani squealed. "You got an easy one your first night here. He's human. That's better than having an alien."

"An alien?" Eirene pressed her hand against the display to steady herself. She hadn't even considered that possibility. "You mate with aliens?"

Lani shrugged, her feathers fluttering. "It's really not so bad. I refuse to take the slime-coated ones, though. And some are quite . . . nice."

Eirene shuddered.

"And your client is staying all night. That's good," Lani continued, seemingly oblivious to Eirene's revulsion. "Of course, Madam Zandra always limits it to three in one shift. She wants us fresh and perky for the next night."

Three in one night? Even more appalled, Eirene vaguely remembered Madam telling her that. Panic began to build in her tense body. Spirit, what was she doing here?

A chime sounded—her entry panel.

"He's already here. He's an eager one!" Lani patted Eirene's arm. "I'll clear out. Have fun." Balancing on her high spike heels, she strutted toward the panel adjoining Eirene's chamber with hers.

Eirene battled the urge to drag Lani back and beg her to take this client. Lani turned at the panel. "Oh, yes. There are alarm buttons by the bed, the couch, and the vibrachair. If your client gets out of hand in any way, use one to call security. Madam doesn't like for us to be roughed up or hurt. Ta-ta!" She was gone in a flash of blue feathers.

Alarm buttons? Roughed up? Hurt? The building knot of panic exploded and raced through Eirene's body. She couldn't do this. She couldn't. She didn't know anything about mating. Well, actually, she knew how it was done, but—

The chime sounded again, a death knell from Eirene's terrified perspective. *No*, she told herself firmly, willing herself to calm. This was a necessary step toward the freedom she sought. She was merely divesting herself of her most valuable *known* commodity, reducing her bartering value, and keeping herself out of the hands of the Leors. It would be far more dangerous should the fact she was an Enhancer be discovered.

Forcing air into her lungs, she opened the panel. She wasn't wearing heels, and she wasn't tall to begin with, which put her eye level with a masculine chest. Adrenaline resurged, and she froze, her gaze locked straight ahead. The black flightsuit her client wore fit snugly, emphasizing nice muscle delineation. He was solid, but not barrel-chested or overly developed like many Travan males.

"Hey. I'm up here."

His voice was pleasant, deep and quiet, but she thought she detected a hint of nervousness. Reluctantly, she raised her gaze. He was relatively young, she realized, perhaps thirty-five seasons of age. He was clean-shaven, with dark eyes and wavy hair the color of rich brown yarton wood.

He studied her in return, his gaze sliding over her face and down her body. She steeled herself, expecting the rush of lust she was accustomed to picking up from men . . . and felt nothing. At least, no emotions. He radiated energy, as did all living things. She felt the warmth of his body, and sensed a calm well of strength within him. But no emotion—no lust, no anger, or joy, or even the nervousness she had heard in his voice.

She drew another breath, trying to compose and center herself. Her fear was interfering with her powers. She couldn't control this situation if she couldn't lock on to his thoughts and feelings. And she had to be very careful, so she wouldn't hurt him.

"I'm Jarek sa—" he began, then stopped, as if suddenly remembering no last names were given at the Dome. Madam Zandra had that information, of course, along with the client's ID disk, which was held until the transaction was completed to the satisfaction of both parties.

"I'm Jarek," he finished lamely.

Eirene didn't respond, trying again to link with his mind. Why wasn't it working?

He turned his head sharply as if he heard something, his body tensing. He stared down the corridor one direction, then the other. Startled, she halted her linking attempt. He looked both directions again, then shook his head as if to clear it.

"That's odd." He took a step forward. "May I come in?"

She nodded and moved back, not used to a male asking permission for anything. He stepped into the chamber, and she backed up further. He was at least six feet tall, his build sleek and lean. Again, she became acutely aware of his vibrant life force, strong and focused. She'd only ever felt such strength from Rayna, her mentor.

The automatic panel slid shut behind him with an alarming, final thud. He glanced around the room briefly, then his dark gaze settled on her. Eirene couldn't breathe, couldn't move, like a terrified kerani caught in a snare.

He didn't move, either. Uncertainty flickered in his brown eyes, and she realized he was unsure how to proceed. Perhaps he didn't purchase pleasure at a Dome often. An experienced courtesan, like Lani, would have known exactly what to do to put a client at ease, to get on with it.

As a matter of fact, Eirene felt certain Lani would never be at a loss for words—or feathers. But Eirene had no idea what to do next, except to try to spur Jarek into lust and a mating frenzy. Once again, she attempted to tap into his psyche. Nothing. It felt as if she had slammed against a wall.

Immediately, his gaze shifted from her. He strode around her and checked the chamber thoroughly—beneath the furniture, in the lav. One hand rested lightly on one of the weapons strapped to the black utility belt encircling his trim waist. He stopped by the panel adjoining Lani's chamber. "What's in there?" he demanded, indicating the panel.

"That's another courtesan's chamber," Eirene replied, giving up her attempt to link.

Jarek scanned the room again, although he visibly relaxed. "Strange," he muttered.

"What is?"

"Ah . . . it's nothing." That dark gaze returned to her. He moved closer, halting by the vibrachair. "Sorry if I alarmed you."

She couldn't think of anything to say. She swallowed and simply stood there, trying to collect her wits.

"You're Eirene, right?"

She liked his voice, the way it resonated. She nodded, still unable to speak.

"You're very beautiful," he said quietly.

Adrenaline began snaking through her, sending her heart pounding in a terrifying rhythm. She wet her parched lips with her tongue. "Th-thank you."

This was it. She was going to lose her virginity to this man, but her plan had failed. She would not be able to cut this short by overloading his senses. She shouldn't be surprised; she'd long ago proven her ineptness at controlling her powers. Her attempts to use them had no affect on Jarek. Oddly enough, they'd seemed to agitate him, almost as if he could sense them. Which would be very dangerous, indeed. She clenched her hands and waited.

"Well, then." Blowing out his breath, he unbuckled his utility belt and tossed it onto the console. Immediately, lusty Elysian music blared through the speakers. He hastily swept up the belt and punched buttons until the racket stopped. "Sorry about that."

He grinned boyishly, and Eirene's heart skipped a beat.

There was something appealing about his clean-cut features. He didn't have the spoiled, dissipated look that accompanied excesses of food and drink and mating—the look most of the Travan men had.

He sank into the double-wide vibrachair and pulled off his boots. Muscles rippled beneath his flightsuit, indicating that he kept himself in prime physical condition. He straightened, then leaned back, his unnerving gaze fixing on Eirene.

"I guess we'd better get to it," he said, his voice low and rough. He reached for the seam of his flightsuit, began opening it. "Why don't you undress for me?"

Her mouth went even drier and it felt like her heart had leaped into her throat. She'd planned on a quick, lust-driven rutting beneath the covers, hopefully without the man realizing she was a virgin.

She had *not* considered a leisurely disrobing with the lights on. Her natural modesty came to the fore, protesting such a vulnerable act. It couldn't be any more invasive than the actual act of mating, she tried to convince herself.

Resolute, she started to open her robe. Jarek tossed his shirt to the floor, then leaned back, his full attention on her. She froze.

"Go on," he urged.

Her fingers shook so badly, she wasn't sure she could continue. She wanted to command the lights off, but Lani had told her the client chose the lighting. She would have to disrobe in the light, but she had an idea. She reached up and pulled the clips from her hair. It fell in heavy coils around her shoulders and she shook it out, spreading it over her chest and down to her hips.

A small grin tugged his mouth. "You little tease. You're going to make me wait to see you, aren't you?"

35

His obvious amusement did little to ease the tension in her chest. She nodded, then finished opening the robe. It fell into a pool around her ankles, and she stepped out of it, carefully smoothing her hair down the front. It barely covered the juncture of her legs.

Eirene sensed Jarek's heated perusal following the movement of her hands. His chest heaving, he stared at the very area she sought to shield from his view, then lurched forward, standing and stripping off his pants and tossing them to join his shirt. Surprised, she found herself thinking he was even more magnificent nude, his body lean, but solid and well honed. And he was highly aroused. Eirene might be sexually innocent, but she was a healer, well aware of how male bodies functioned.

He strode to her, masterful purpose replacing the uncertainty of a few moments before. She flinched as he reached for her, but he didn't seem to notice. With unexpected gentleness, he slid his hand beneath her hair, brushing it over her shoulder, exposing one breast.

"Spirit, but you're beautiful," he murmured. He skimmed his hand lightly up her abdomen and along her rib cage, cupping her breast.

Her legs went weak at the warmth of his hand, the unexpected rush of pleasure as his thumb rubbed over her nipple. She stumbled forward against the hot, shocking length of his body.

"Easy now." His voice was huskier, edged with tension—or was that lust?

His other arm slid around her waist, lending her support. He continued caressing her breast, and heated sensation seemed to shoot from his fingers through her body. She realized she was grasping his upper arms, but didn't dare let go. She clenched her eyes shut, trying to reclaim her equilibrium.

"Look at me, little one."

Even his voice had an odd effect on her, sending a molten warmth through her veins. Slowly, reluctantly, she raised her gaze to the heated depths of his dark eyes.

He slid his hand from her breast, up along her neck and the side of her face. Despite the roughness of his skin, his touch was gentle.

"Spirit, but your mouth is enticing." His thumb feathered over her trembling lips. "Do you mind if I kiss you?"

Would it speed things up? she wondered wildly. Nothing had gone right, and she had no control over this man. For some inexplicable reason, he appeared unaffected by her powers. All she could do was allow the mating to occur without enhancement.

"I—I'm here for your pleasure," she managed to say. "You don't need permission to kiss me."

"I figured I should ask. I don't know the correct protocol. You see, I've never done this before."

"You've never done . . . *this?*"

He grinned with utter confidence, displaying white, even teeth. She felt the force of that smile right down to her bare toes. "I've never been to a Pleasure Dome before tonight," he amended. "Although, if I'd known you were here, I would have visited a lot sooner.

"But as for *this*," he leaned down, his lips grazing hers. "I've definitely done *this* before." His mouth took possession of hers with an assured determination that clearly showed he was in charge.

Eirene knew men and women used their tongues in kissing, so she wasn't surprised when Jarek slipped his tongue into her mouth. She also knew how men and women mated, that Jarek would join his lower body with hers, much the same way his tongue was invading her mouth right now.

Rayna had explained all that to her, preparing her for the possibility that one of the males on Travan might decide to mate with her. But Rayna had never talked about pleasure.

And it was pleasurable when Jarek nibbled at Eirene's lips, then slid his tongue between them to stroke the inside of her mouth. He was slow and thorough at first, then more demanding, as his breathing grew harsher. He broke off suddenly, holding her face tightly, forcing her to look at him.

"Make me forget, little Eirene," he muttered hoarsely. "Give me a glimpse of Haven, if only for a little while."

He lowered her to the bed. The cool silk beneath her was a startling contrast to the searing heat of the body following her down. Allowing no further modesty, he determinedly swept her hair aside and looked her over to his satisfaction. Embarrassment sent a heated flush over her skin, but Eirene forced herself to lie still for his perusal.

He lowered his head, and his mouth traced a path from her neck to her breast, while his hands were everywhere on her, touching, stroking, insistent. The shock of his touch, the feel of his fingers stroking across her skin, scattered any thoughts of modesty. Yet, even through the haze of unfamiliar sensations, she sensed a desperation in his caresses, as if he were trying to lose himself in the mating.

His hands slid over her breasts, her abdomen, her legs, then between her thighs, delving into her most sensitive flesh. When he first touched her so intimately, she cried out, trying to bolt upright, but his leg across her body prevented flight. Then she no longer wanted to flee, stunned by the incredible pleasure, which lured her to open her thighs wider to accommodate his questing hand.

Then his touch was gone, and he slid over her body. His hands cradled her face, and she read the intent in his smoldering eyes, instinctively knew he was through with preliminaries. He lowered his head, taking possession of her mouth, thrusting his tongue inside. Just as he thrust below, breaching her maidenhead, surging inside her in a fiery blaze.

Agony burned through her like a laser. She arched upward, her scream captured by his mouth. Shock pounded every nerve ending as she tried desperately to assimilate, and deal with, the pain. Rayna had told her a woman's first time with a man was painful, but nothing could have prepared her for this.

Jarek jerked back, reciprocal shock reflected on his face. "Blazing hells!"

Even through the agony and trauma, she felt his attempt to withdraw. Frantically, she tightened her inner muscles, grabbing his firm buttocks to keep him anchored inside her. It hurt like Hades, but there must be no doubt about her losing her virginity.

"Son of an Antek," Jarek swore. He pried her hands away and withdrew. "What in Spirit's name is going on?"

"Mating," she gasped, trying to rein in her racing senses and clear her mind. At least the terrible burning had receded with his withdrawal, leaving only a throbbing ache. She managed to sit up. "That was the transaction."

He smoothed his fingers over her cheeks, wiping away the dampness there. "I hurt you."

She hadn't even noticed the tears tracking down her face. "Just a little," she lied.

He levered himself to the edge of the bed and ran his fingers through his thick, unruly hair. Cool air wafted over Eirene's bare skin. She reached for the cover. The movement caught his eye and he whirled, his strong fingers wrapping around her wrist.

His gaze went to her thighs. Feeling exposed, embarrassed, she tried to close them. His other hand blocked her, as he stared at the blood on the cover beneath her.

His face sharpened into harsh lines. "I want to know what's going on here."

She didn't need her powers to sense his anger. "Why are you upset? You came here to mate with me. That's what we did."

"You were a virgin."

"What does that have to do with anything?"

"Just what kind of game are you playing?" He rose and stalked to the display panel, totally unconcerned with his nakedness. She took advantage of the opportunity to slide off the bed and grab her robe.

Jarek punched the display, bringing up a listing of services. "Here," he said, jabbing angrily. "Virgins are a special commodity, available only for a very high price. The cost begins at two thousand miterons and goes up from there."

He whirled back toward her. "So, what kind of scam are you running? Hoping to trap me into paying two thousand miterons? I don't have that kind of money, lady, and I don't like being played for a fool."

Slipping on her robe, Eirene stared at him, stunned. They actually sold virginity at Pleasure Domes? Inanely, she wondered if the Leors knew about that. She had the irrational urge to laugh at the irony, but Jarek stalked toward her, his fury still evident.

"You won't be expected to pay any more than the original amount agreed upon," she said hastily.

"Damn right," he snarled. "But I still want an explanation."

What could she tell him? Eirene cast about frantically for an answer. She was about to offer something to appease him, when he suddenly whirled toward the panel, just as it slid open. A black-clad, masked figure stepped inside and raised a weapon toward Jarek.

"Get down!" he yelled. He dived to the floor, rolling toward the vibrachair. He grabbed his belt off the console. The figure discharged its weapon.

She screamed as Jarek jerked from the impact. Red stained his abdomen. He managed to get his own weapon free, and shot the intruder in the chest. The figure stumbled, then collapsed just inside the entryway.

"Jarek!" Eirene ran to him. He was curled in a fetal position, his face twisted in agony. "Let me see," she cried, prying his hands away from his abdomen. "Oh, Spirit—"

"I heard weapon-fire. What's going on in here?" Lani rushed through her panel, dressed in a blue silk robe trimmed with feathers. She stopped dead in her tracks, staring at Jarek and then the intruder. "Oh, my! I'll get security."

"No!" Jarek gasped, trying to roll up. "Don't call the authorities. Contact Captain Cameron. She's at . . . docking bay fourteen, pad number . . . thirty-eight."

"Lie down," Eirene insisted, pushing him back. He was losing way too much blood.

Lani trotted to his other side. "Captain Cameron? Celie Cameron?"

Jarek nodded, his body jerking as he struggled to breathe. "Yes . . . Celie . . ."

41

Lani's hand went to her mouth and she considered a moment. "We'll do as he says," she told Eirene. "Don't sound the alarm, or the guards will come."

Eirene wondered how Jarek was connected to the woman on whose ship she had stowed away, as well as why Lani was capitulating to his demands. "We must call the guards," she insisted. "We have to do something. He'll die if he doesn't get medical attention fast."

Lani shook her head decisively. "I know what I'm doing. Your client will be in greater danger if we call security. Stay here with him. I'm going to contact his friend." She hopped over the intruder's body to close the entry panel, then hurried back to her chamber, moving with amazing speed, considering her high heels.

Eirene couldn't believe they weren't calling for immediate medical assistance. Yet, at this point, any help might be too late. He had collapsed onto the carpet, no longer convulsing from the pain. His skin was ashen, his breathing shallow. Blood still seeped from the wound in his abdomen, pooling beneath him. Injuries like his were almost always fatal, and he'd already lost so much blood.

Too late. Almost too late, unless . . . Eirene sucked in her breath, knowing what she should do. But she couldn't—she just couldn't. Dark memories crowded into her mind, as painful as a physical blow. Rayna lying on her thin pallet, the life flowing from her . . . No!

Eirene forced her attention back to Jarek. Spirit, he would die if she didn't try to help him. She was a healer—not fully competent yet, but a healer, nevertheless. She was dedicated to nurturing life. And she was an Enhancer, even if her past attempts to use her powers had been disastrous.

She stared at the man who had taken her virginity. His dark eyes were glazed, his clean features slack as death's grip closed about him. Even in the throes of his passion, he had been gentle with her. She couldn't let him die. She had to attempt to save him. Surely she couldn't hurt him any worse than he already was.

Resigned, she leaned over him, placing her hands directly over the wound. She hadn't been able to link with him earlier, and now she feared she wouldn't be able to tap into his energy. But in his weakened state, some barrier was down, and she slipped readily into his life force.

Please Spirit, she prayed, *don't let me kill him.* Terror swept through her, and her hands shook uncontrollably. *Not like Rayna, please not like Rayna.*

Gasping, she forced air into her lungs. *You have to try,* she told herself. *You're his only chance.* Closing her eyes, she tentatively added her own energy to his, directing it throughout his body systems, all the way down to the cellular level.

She accelerated the natural healing process to many times its normal rate. She enhanced each cell's ability, stimulated the man's body to rapidly produce more blood. The energy from her hands over the wound speeded the clotting process there and formed scar tissue at an incredible rate.

She was so intent on directing the energies, she didn't hear the panel open. "What the hell are you doing to him?" roared a masculine voice. Eirene jolted back from her patient, momentarily disoriented. She stared at the blond man towering over her, belatedly realizing he had a weapon aimed at her.

"Eirene is not the one who shot him. She's just trying to help," Lani cried shrilly, punching the man's arm. "Back off, you big oaf!"

The man lowered his weapon, although his eyes remained narrowed with suspicion. Others crowded

43

around behind him. Eirene recognized Celie Cameron, and her female first officer. There was another man, also blond, but short and youthful, with freckles on his round face.

Captain Cameron dropped onto her knees on the other side of Jarek. "Spirit, look at all the blood. This is bad. Blake, we've got to get him to my ship. Chase is on the way."

The first male, apparently Blake, shoved Eirene to the side. "Move, lady. Let me get to him."

She scrambled away without resentment; she heard the concern in Blake's voice and knew he was upset. "Who is Chase?" she asked.

"A physician—one of the best," the shorter man answered, squatting beside Celie.

"Why don't you take him to the healer on Saron?" Lani asked. "He needs help fast."

"Because the healer is a known agent," Blake said bluntly. "Chase is Jarek's only chance."

What did that mean? Eirene wondered. She glanced at Jarek. He was unconscious, but his color was already better, and the bleeding had stopped. Relieved, she felt certain he was stabilized and would survive, especially if he received competent medical care quickly. Thank Spirit she'd managed to channel the energy without mishap.

The group organized quickly and efficiently, rolling Jarek onto the silk cover from the bed, so it would be easier and less jarring to transport him. Celie and Blake took him to Celie's ship, while her first officer, Lionia, and the other man—Radd, she heard him called—bundled up the body of the dead intruder and sneaked it from the Dome.

Jarek's associates had decided it would be best if the authorities knew nothing of the incident. Eirene picked up emotional currents from the group—mainly true affection and concern for Jarek, and the need for secrecy. The only conclusion she could draw was that Jarek was involved in something illegal.

She need not be concerned about that, for she'd never see him again after tonight. She felt a stirring of regret. She felt an inexplicable bond with Jarek, perhaps because of the intimacy they'd shared. She had always assumed mating was just an act, especially after witnessing how the males on Travan only came to the women's tents when they wanted a release, then walked away, hitching up their pants as if nothing had happened. They certainly never took very long.

But Jarek had lingered with her. He'd acted like he really found her beautiful; like he enjoyed looking at her and touching her. He'd appeared concerned about hurting her, although his anger over her deception was greater. Most importantly, he'd done what she needed him to do—relieved her of the burden of her virginity. She could head for Elysia now, get on with her life without the fear of being sold for her maidenhead.

Quickly, she changed from her bloodied robe back to her old, ragged one, and packed up her meager belongings. She decided against telling Lani good-bye. She didn't want anyone to know she was leaving Saron, and besides, Lani might again be with a client. Eirene shuddered, grateful she didn't have to make her living as a courtesan. She left the Dome, slipping out the discreet side entry used by the clients, and headed for the transport station.

Next came freedom and a new life.

Chapter Three

The voices woke Jarek. A female voice, obviously upset, seeped into his consciousness, and he opened his eyes with a start. Where was he?

"This can't be possible," the female said. "Do the test again."

That husky voice, very familiar somehow, came from the other side of a pale green screen standing to his right.

"I already ran it twice," came a deep masculine voice, also familiar. "The test is highly accurate. And the results are positive."

"*I am not pregnant!*"

"The medical scanner readings agree with the test. You *are* pregnant, Moriah."

Where was he? Jarek looked around the cubicle, noting an array of monitors and equipment on the wall to his left. Low beeps and hums emitted from them. Although he was groggy, he realized he was on some sort of bed, with an IV strip on his arm and silver disks attached to his bare chest. He twisted to look down at the cold, sterile tile floor. The motion sent a spear of pain through his abdomen, and he sank back. He felt his body then, really felt it, the weakness and the soreness. What the—

"How could this have happened?" shrieked the female on the other side of the screen.

"You mean you don't know?" came the dry response, twinged with amusement. "Then I obviously haven't done my job as your physician. Let me explain what occurs when a man and a woman—ouch!" The loud thud sounded suspiciously like a fist hitting a body.

"That's not funny, McKnight! Of course I know how women get pregnant. What I want to know is how did *I* get pregnant?"

"The same way." Thud, thud, thud. "Would you please stop hitting me, Moriah? This is not my fault."

"Oh, I know whose fault it is. It's that worthless, irresponsible mate of mine. He didn't get a new birth control patch—I'd bet on it. Did he come to you for one?"

"Well, no—"

"That son of an Antek! I'm going to kill him."

Jarek listened to the exchange intently, still disoriented, trying to figure out where he was. His head ached from the effort. He opened his mouth to call out, but only managed a croak.

Another voice—soft, sweet, feminine—spoke. "But, Moriah, a baby! How wonderful. Don't be upset. It's truly a blessing. You'll see."

Jarek absolutely knew that voice. His mind cleared enough that a name came to him. He tried to roll up, but it hurt too much. "Nessa," he gasped hoarsely. "Nessa!"

There was a moment of silence beyond the screen. Then a head popped around. His sister, her dark eyes wide, stared at him, a smile breaking across her delicate face. "Jarek! You're awake." She slipped gracefully to his side, placing her hand on his forehead. "Chase, he's awake."

"So I hear." Chase McKnight, Jarek's brother-in-law, strode around the screen, his large frame dwarfing his petite mate as he came up behind her. "How are you feeling?"

"I think I'll live," Jarek answered, the fog beginning to clear. If Chase and Nessa were here, then he must be on their ship, in Chase's sick bay. But why? "What happened to me?"

Chase moved around the table to study the equipment panel, then turned to run a scanner over Jarek. "You don't remember?"

Jarek tried to think. He had the vague impression of a black-clad figure with a mask, but his head was throbbing too much for him to recall more. "The details are a little vague," he admitted.

Chase looked at him assessingly. "Do you know who we are?"

"Yeah, I know you, McKnight." Jarek glanced toward his sister, who hovered anxiously on his other side. "Nessa, how's he treating you?"

A radiant smile lit her face, and she squeezed his hand. "Wonderful, as always. Oh, Jarek, I'm so glad you're all right. When Celie contacted us, she thought—" Nessa broke off and shook her head. "You gave us quite a scare, brother."

"You had a lot of people worried about you," said a low female voice. Moriah Travers stepped around the screen, stunning as always, with her bronze hair and golden eyes. "Sabin will be delighted to know you're okay—except I'm going to kill him first."

Jarek grinned weakly at his best friend's mate. "I hear you and Sabin are expecting an addition to your family. Congratulations."

Moriah snorted in disgust. "Make that one addition, and one subtraction. I call it zero population growth." She sighed. "Well, I guess there's nothing to be done now. I'm going to go break the news to Sabin—over his head." She leaned down and kissed Jarek on the cheek. "I'm glad you're going to make it. *You*, I would hate to lose. We'll check on you later."

She slipped back around the screen. Jarek tried to focus his thoughts. "What happened to me?" he asked Chase.

"That's what I would like to know," Chase answered. "I can tell you that you took a blast to the abdomen. And you didn't receive medical attention until I saw you about four hours later."

"You're telling me I survived a gut blast for four hours without treatment?"

"That's exactly what I'm telling you. I wouldn't have believed it myself if I didn't have four witnesses insisting that was the truth. But there's more to it than that— something I've never seen in all my seasons of medicine."

"What?"

"First-off, you shouldn't have survived that long with an injury like you had. Secondly, by the time you got here, the wound had closed itself, scar tissue had formed, and the blood volume in your body was almost normal. Yet Celie, Lionia, Blake, and Radd all insisted the bleeding was profuse. They did nothing but apply pressure to the wound until we rendezvoused."

"What are you saying?"

"That somehow your body miraculously healed itself."

Jarek stared at his brother-in-law, certain he hadn't heard right. "That's not possible."

"Tell me about it. I've run all kinds of tests, searching for an explanation, but there is none. Yet the evidence is there. You were definitely injured, Jarek. The wound is new and so is the scar tissue. And I can't discount the eyewitness accounts of four people I know and trust."

Stunned, Jarek closed his eyes, trying desperately to recall the events leading up to the shooting, and the actual shooting itself. He felt Nessa stroking his hand. Vague images shifted and focused. A woman, with flowing black hair and blue eyes, lying beneath him on a silken cover . . . both of them naked. The Pleasure Dome! His eyes flew open. "Where was I when I got blasted?"

Nessa and Chase exchanged glances. "At the Pleasure Dome on Saron," she said softly.

Then that part of the memory was true. But there were a lot of gaps. "How did I get here?"

"Radd's sister is a courtesan at the Dome," Chase explained. "She happened to be nearby and heard the blasts. When you asked her to contact Celie, she apparently connected you with us and did as you requested. Very astute lady. Celie and the others brought you here. It's only been one cycle since you were shot. They're all still here, as a matter of fact. Celie's ship is docked with mine, and Sabin's is docked with hers. Blake flew your ship out, and it's docked with Sabin's. We've got a full crew. Hell, we've got a space station."

Jarek still couldn't call up the details. "When can I talk to the others?"

"Rest a few more hours. Then, if you can keep down some liquids, we'll let the gang visit."

Jarek's recovery seemed to progress rapidly from there. He drank some broth, even stood and took a few steps, although his legs were shaky. The effort tired him, but his mind was alert, and bits of memory began returning.

Chase gave the okay for visitors, and Nessa, Celie, Blake, Lionia and Radd all piled into the sickbay, with Sabin and Moriah right behind them. At least Sabin had survived the encounter with his mate, Jarek thought, deciding now was not the time to tease him about his carelessness. Chase removed the screen, so the group could crowd around Jarek. He felt foolish, lying there with everyone towering over him, but accepted the fact he was still too weak to be up.

In view of his brush with death, he was glad to see his friends, who were more like family. Sabin was also a Shielder, and like a brother to Jarek. Sabin had married Moriah, a mastermind smuggler, six seasons back, inheriting a ragtag community consisting of seven women and one starship mechanic. Not just any mechanic, either—Radd was the best in the quadrant.

Celie, Moriah's younger sister, now headed up the highly profitable delivery service. The Shielders had benefited tremendously from Sabin's alliance with Moriah, gaining a badly needed lifeline of supplies and medicine. And Radd generously offered his services, keeping the aging Shielder fleet in running order.

Then there was Jarek's sister, Nessa, and her husband, Chase, a highly skilled physician. Together, they all formed an extended family, Shielder and non-Shielder, whose members were extremely loyal to each other. Blake wasn't an immediate member of the "family," but he was a good and trusted friend. He gave Jarek the once-over. "You're looking a hell of a lot better than when I last saw you."

"Considering what I've been told, that's a good thing. Fill me in, will you?" Jarek requested. "I remember someone bursting through the panel and shooting me, but not much after that."

"I hope you remember the events *before* that," Blake said. "The lady with you was a real beauty. And you were—ah—without clothing, so I assume the evening wasn't a total loss."

"And if it wasn't, I hope you have a current birth control patch," Moriah sniffed, shooting Sabin a scathing glare. Looking somewhat laser-shocked, her mate wisely moved a safe distance away.

As a matter of fact, Jarek did have some memories, which were rapidly sharpening into focus as the medications Chase had given him wore off. A pretty, heart-shaped face dominated by vivid blue eyes; a wealth of ebony hair, tangling in his fingers as he explored smooth flesh . . .

"I believe he remembers, all right," Chase interjected. "His heart rate just went up."

"Yeah, that's an interesting expression on your face, Captain," Blake teased.

Jarek forced his thoughts away from the sensual images of the woman and his shock upon discovering she was a virgin. He could sort out those events later. "Let's stay with issue of me being shot," he suggested. "The being who did it—human? Male?"

Blake nodded. "Both. I took off the mask before we disposed of the body. And there's something else."

Jarek already knew, if his recollection was correct. "He was a Shielder," he guessed.

"Yeah, the bastard was a renegade," Blake growled, fury sparking in his eyes. Blake hated those Shielders who turned against their race for profit almost as much as Jarek did. "Must have figured to sneak up on you while you were . . . occupied."

"I wasn't occupied when the attack came. I was standing near the entry panel, and—" Jarek looked around the group, urgent concern gnawing at him. "I didn't sense the man's presence until he was on me."

"That can't be right," Sabin protested. "You're the most sensitive Shielder I know. You would have sensed another one of your kind a hundred meters away."

"I picked up an unusual energy emission twice before that," Jarek mused. "It wasn't Shielder energy, but it threw me. The projection was brief both times. I wonder if it somehow blocked my would-be assassin."

"I don't like the sound of that at all," Blake said grimly. "That could mean the Controllers have found some way to neutralize our mind shields."

"I'm not sure this had anything to do with the Controllers," Jarek said slowly. "It felt like a natural energy, not a jamming frequency."

"I still don't like it," Blake persisted.

"The whole situation is strange," Celie pointed out. "What about the fact Jarek got blasted in the gut, and not only survived four hours until we reached Chase, but his wound practically healed itself?"

They shook their heads in amazement, looking toward Chase, who shrugged. "I have no way of explaining it. I suggest we give thanks to Spirit, the ultimate Healer."

"Jarek," Celie said slowly. "There's something else I need to tell you. I'm wondering if it might be related to that Shielder shooting you."

Her tone told Jarek he wouldn't like the news. "What is it?"

"The Controllers have offered a reward of ten thousand miterons for your live capture. Apparently, they want to "talk" with you before they execute you. They've offered five thousand if you're brought in dead. They've posted holograms of you on every major planet and star base, and on all agent downloads."

Blazing hells. Now every soldier and shadower and renegade Shielder in the quadrant would be looking for him. Jarek battled anger and a sense of futility. This latest development meant he was running out of time. He wasn't afraid of death, but there was so much left to do. And he could never allow himself to be taken alive—he knew too much.

"How in the Fires did they get your hologram?" Sabin asked.

"Probably when I was arrested on Intrepid five seasons back. That was the time you bailed me out, Sabin. The Controllers didn't know who I was then, but I'm sure there were plenty of renegades willing to enlighten them. Once they figured it out, they found the hologram in the file. Damn!"

"What will you do?" Nessa asked, her face pale.

Chase slid an arm around her and gathered her protectively to his side. It was a gesture Jarek had seen often, a positive reminder that Nessa was well-loved. This time, however, it only served to remind him he was utterly alone, despite this circle of family and friends. The suffocating weight of his responsibilities—the fate of an entire people—pressed down on him.

"I'll do whatever I have to," he said wearily.

Chase seemed to sense Jarek's exhaustion. "We can sort this out tomorrow," he said firmly. "No one but Lani knows Jarek is here, and Radd says she can be trusted. He's safe for now, and I want him to get some rest. Everyone out."

They all left, leaving Jarek alone in the semidarkness. He lay awake, battling the desperation and dark fears plaguing him. Everything seemed to be going from bad to worse.

The Controllers were getting more aggressive and more

violent in their attempts to wipe the Shielder race from the face of the quadrant. The only plan Jarek had for helping his people was based on nothing but pure speculation, with very high odds of failure. Assuming he lived long enough to even attempt it. And he was only one man. He needed help, from a far greater source than himself.

He sent a silent prayer to the Spirit, asking for assistance and guidance. Asking for a miracle—and fast.

Elysia was beautiful, a tropical paradise with balmy breezes and swaying palms. At first, Eirene was enthralled by its exotic beauty. The enchantment quickly gave way beneath the oppressive psychic barrage. In that respect, Elysia was far worse than Saron. The massive marketplace was ten times larger than Saron's, and packed with beings from everywhere in the quadrant.

At least Eirene had her experience from Saron to draw upon. She worked diligently at erecting a mental wall to block the bombardment of emotions, succeeding most of the time. Slavers' Square almost did her in however, the tidal waves of pain and despair from those chained, huddled beings mentally overwhelming her as she neared the vicinity. She quickly learned how to navigate around the square at a safe distance.

Since her new robe had been bloodstained and ruined, it seemed as if she were starting over, having to sell another gem and barter for new garments. This time, she bought leggings, with a slim tunic to go over them, both in a silvery blue. Feeling very daring, she had her hair trimmed to midway down her back and put a henna rinse on it. The rinse left mahogany highlights in her hair, softening its natural ebony color. Eirene was pleased with her new look.

She rented modest quarters, then located Darya and sent a transmission requesting an audience. Rayna had trained with Darya many seasons ago, and spoken often of the healer's amazing abilities. Eirene had long hoped to learn from her.

She was thrilled when the healer responded graciously to her request. Darya was willing to speak with her, but she was too busy to meet for five cycles. Eirene sold a second gem and paid for her quarters for the next seven cycles. She'd be here permanently if she could convince Darya to take her on as an apprentice.

Then, there was nothing to do but wait. Eirene explored the marketplace some, and practiced maintaining a mental wall. Even so, the effort exhausted her, and the crammed stalls of brilliantly colored goods and the loudly hawking vendors overwhelmed her senses. She learned to only go out for short jaunts, building her mental muscles a little at a time.

Physically, the soreness and stiffness from mating with Jarek was gone by the second cycle. Unfortunately, the memories didn't fade so readily. Eirene's strong visual bent worked against her, inundating her with clear images of the man who had claimed her virginity. His mesmerizing caroba-brown eyes and clean-cut features; his wavy brown hair; his lean, virile build—she recalled each enticing detail of how he looked.

She discovered she had a strong tactile bent, as well. The feel of Jarek's hands sliding through her hair, then over her bare skin; the warmth of his firm lips, his taste, his scent—all were details she seemed unable to exorcise from her mind.

Most alarming was the attraction she had felt toward him—a male, and a veritable stranger at that. She'd felt nothing but revulsion for the dissipated, selfish men on

Travan; considered herself safe from such foolishness as yearning after a man. Rayna had warned her often enough to never yield to the other sex, or to give them any power over her. Women had very few rights as it was.

It didn't matter, Eirene told herself, resolutely pushing away the images of Jarek. She would never see the man again, and in time, the details of her encounter with him would be a distant memory.

For the first time in her life, she was in control of her own destiny. She had made it to Elysia and gained a coveted audience with Darya, possibly the greatest healer in the quadrant. Eirene knew exactly what she wanted to do with her life, and how she would go about it.

No one knew she was an Enhancer, nor would anyone ever discover that fact.

She was safe, and free. No one would ever take that away from her.

An Enhancer! Jarek bolted upright in his bunk, as the realization hit him with the force of a rocket launcher. The pleasure servant Eirene had been an Enhancer. There was no other explanation.

Unwilling for his mind to be clouded, he had refused Chase's offer of pain medication, despite the acute discomfort in his abdomen. He'd lain awake most of sleep shift, ransacking every thread of memory; ruthlessly probing his mind, demanding it produce every single detail.

He focused on the events after he discovered Eirene's virginity, reliving his wounding and the hazy activities following. He now remembered the shooting quite clearly: how he had sensed the intruder at the last minute, dropped and rolled, reaching for his weapon and firing.

He recalled the blast of agony in his gut, Eirene's stricken face above him, a blue-haired woman in a swirl of blue feathers next to her. He'd kept his wits enough to demand they call Celie instead of the authorities. Then things blurred . . . He wasn't certain whether the events after that point were real or distorted by pain and loss of blood.

But he did have images—insistent images—of Eirene leaning over him, her hands hovering over his abdomen. She had closed her eyes, and then a torrent of heat and energy had surged into his body. He remembered arching upward, stunned by this assault on his already-screaming nerve endings. Oddly, it seemed the energy was flowing into both his abdomen and his head; that it sedated him even as it recharged his body. Then he felt as if he was flowing along a rapidly moving current, a kaleidoscope of colors and sensations, leaving him totally disoriented.

He had drifted in and out of consciousness, aware Eirene still hovered over him, until a strident male voice broke the energy surge, and he sank into welcome oblivion.

At least that's what Jarek thought he remembered. He hadn't eaten or drunk anything at the Dome, so he couldn't have been drugged. Add to that the amazing fact that he had not only survived a fatal wounding for four hours without medical treatment, but *his wound had closed itself*.

Jarek thought about these things for hours, considering every angle and possibility, and returning to the same conclusion each time.

Eirene had healed him. Somehow, she had channeled a special energy into his body that had healed the wound and replenished his blood supply. Jarek was an educated and well-traveled man. He'd never heard of any race of beings who could heal with pure energy, except one. The race he'd been researching the past season. Enhancers.

But they were extinct. Or were they? In his determined quest to learn all he could about the Enhancers and their possible link to the black hole in the twelfth sector, Jarek had uncovered some unusual tales. Accounts of people being born with Enhancer abilities. The occurrences appeared random and were extremely rare, and the people supposedly possessed of such abilities disappeared from sight, probably snapped up by the Controllers or powerful private factions. There was no proof of living Enhancers, yet the tales persisted.

Jarek had listened to the continually circulating stories—and he had long ago learned to trust his instincts. Right now, his every instinct screamed that Eirene was an Enhancer. If he were right, she might be able to help him navigate that black hole. He had to find her.

He struggled off the bed, cursing his weakness, although he was much stronger than he had been yesterday. Already dressed, he scooped up his boots and headed for the entry panel. It opened before he reached it.

"What are you doing up?" Chase demanded, stepping through the entry. Celie was behind him.

"I need to return to Saron." Jarek paused, unwilling to reveal more. If Eirene were an Enhancer, she'd be in danger if that information fell into the wrong hands.

Chase frowned and started to say something, but Celie cut him off. "I'm afraid you won't want to go to Saron, Jarek. Not after you hear my news."

Something in her voice caught Jarek's full attention. "What is it?"

"First, sit down before you fall down," Chase ordered, rolling up a chair. "You're too weak to be walking around."

Jarek sank into the chair, his gaze fixed on Celie. "Tell me."

Her eyes were solemn. "I've got two things to tell you. The first is good. I may have found equipment for scoping out your black hole."

Yes! Thank you, Spirit. "Where?"

"It's a rather odd situation. The equipment is on Aldon."

"Aldon? That's a Shen colony, isn't it?"

Celie nodded. "Yes. It's their main settlement."

Jarek pondered this. The Shens, whose society had evolved around a magic-based culture, didn't deal in technology. "How would the Shens have come up with such equipment? I can't imagine them interested in exploring black holes."

"Well, no, they're not into space exploration, but they're always interested in making money," Celie pointed out. "They didn't manufacture this equipment. It was apparently left on Aldon."

The situation was getting stranger by the millisecond. Jarek rubbed his forehead, wondering if his faculties were still off balance. "I'm not understanding this. Who left it there?"

"That's what's so amazing about the whole situation. Supposedly, this is equipment Enhancers used, then stored on Aldon, before they became extinct."

Enhancers? Jarek almost bolted from the chair. "Sweet Spirit. Are you sure about this?"

Celie leaned against the counter. "I got the information from Eark. He's a Shen we've worked with for over six seasons, and he's always been reliable. He says the equipment was left by Enhancers, and has been on Aldon more than two hundred seasons."

Adrenaline thrummed through Jarek. The Enhancers

were supposedly the ones who had traversed the black hole in the twelfth quadrant. And he suspected Eirene was an Enhancer. He didn't believe in coincidences. This was divine intervention. It had to be.

"How much?" he demanded hoarsely. "How much do the Shens want for that equipment?"

"Eark wouldn't give me an amount." Celie threw up her hands in frustration. "He was very vague, said it would be negotiated when the buyer got to Aldon."

"Damn." Jarek felt a sinking feeling in the pit of his stomach. The Shens were going to demand a fortune for the equipment, and his own resources were severely limited. Then something Celie said registered. "Did you say the Shens would negotiate when the buyer got to Aldon?"

"Yes. I couldn't believe it when Eark told me that."

"The Shens never let anyone visit their settlements. The locations for most of them are secret. Are you sure that's what your friend said?"

Celie nodded. "Yes. He said you could come to Aldon. I asked him again, to be sure I'd heard him right."

Even more reason for Jarek to believe a divine hand was involved. He'd worry about finding enough gold on the way. "I've got to get ready to leave."

"Wait," Celie said. "There's more, Jarek, and I'm afraid it's very grim."

He sagged back in the chair, bracing himself. "Tell me."

Celie drew in a deep breath and clasped her hands together. "Eark told me that the Controllers are amassing a huge number of troops. Word is they're getting ready to search every moon and asteroid, looking for Shielder colonies. And they've doubled the reward for all Shielders captured, and for information leading to any settlements. They're determined to eradicate the Shielders once and for all."

Acute urgency, laced with bone-chilling fear, pumped through Jarek. Could things get any worse? First the bounty on his head, and now this. They were almost out of time. Hell, they were already out of time! If he didn't gain possession of that equipment and find an escape route, they faced total obliteration.

"I've got to leave now."

"Whoa," Chase protested, clamping a hand on Jarek's shoulder before he could stand. "You're not going anywhere until I check you over."

Jarek shook his hand away. "I can't wait around to get better, McKnight. Every second counts. I have to get to Saron," Jarek insisted. He was even more convinced now that he had to find Eirene. If she really was an Enhancer, she could be vastly useful, both with the equipment and the black hole. He couldn't logically explain how he knew this. He just knew, deep inside, that he needed Eirene. Just as he knew only a miracle could save the Shielders now.

"But I thought you'd go straight to Aldon," Celie said.

Jarek spread his arms so Chase could run a scanner over him, though negative findings wouldn't deter him. "Oh, I'm going to Aldon, all right. But first, I have pressing business on Saron. I'm leaving now."

Chase drew back, frowning, but offered no further argument.

Jarek picked up his boots and headed toward the corridor. Spirit, he *was* weak. But time was of the essence.

He stepped into the corridor, Celie and Chase right behind him. Nessa hurried toward them. "We have company," she said. "The transport just dropped her off. She's on Sabin's ship and headed this way."

"Who?" All three of them asked simultaneously.

Just then, the airlock connecting Celie's ship with Chase's hummed open. A petite woman, swathed in blue feathers, stepped through the entry. Except for her porcelain white skin, everything about her was blue: her eyes, her long silky hair, her pouty lips, the ridiculous feathered headdress on her head, even her four-inch stiletto heels. She smiled brightly and wobbled towards them.

"Oh, helloooo!" she trilled. "Celie, you're looking wonderful."

"Hello again," Celie replied. "What brings you here?"

"I decided I needed a vacation, and I've come to visit my brother. I only got to see him for a millisecond on Saron." The woman turned toward Jarek, Chase, and Nessa, who all stared at her in utter fascination. "Hello there. I'm Lani, Radd's sister. Pleased to meet you."

A sudden memory jolted Jarek out of his amazed trance. He'd seen this woman before. She'd been the one standing by Eirene after he'd been wounded.

"We've met—kind of," he said. "At the Pleasure Dome on Saron."

She squinted her eyes and scrunched up her button nose. "Oh, yes! You were the one shot in Eirene's chamber. I didn't recognize you with your clothes on. My, but you recovered quickly. To be honest, I didn't think you'd survive." She sashayed up to him and ran a finger down his chest. "But then, you're quite a specimen."

He stepped back hastily. "Uh, thank you. And thank you for calling Celie instead of the guards."

"Think nothing of it. When you said to contact Celie Cameron, I realized you must be connected to Radd, which meant you were connected to Sabin, which meant"—Lani paused and lowered her voice conspiratorially—"you were probably involved in something you didn't want the authorities to know about."

"Right." Just trying to keep up with Lani's light-speed chatter was making Jarek dizzy, but he pressed on. "By the way, how is your friend Eirene? I'd like to see her again." From the corner of his eye, he saw Chase and Nessa pry their gaze from Lani to stare at him.

Lani waved a blue-tipped hand dismissively. "Oh, she didn't stay around after you were shot. I tell you, no one has a decent work ethic any more. Why, we can't keep anyone—"

Jarek cut her off before she could go off on a tangent. "Do you know where she went?"

"As a matter of fact, I do. I was worried about her. When I saw her leave, I followed her to make sure she was okay. She went to the transport station and bought a ticket for Elysia." Lani blew out an exasperated breath. "Didn't even tell me good-bye. How rude."

Jarek couldn't believe this turn of fate. Again, he was struck by the fact it wasn't coincidence that Enhancer equipment had been uncovered on Aldon, or that Lani had arrived with the information he needed to find Eirene. As far as he was concerned, it *was* divine providence. He took only long enough to kiss Nessa and shake Chase's hand, and give Blake some final instructions. Then, ignoring their vehement protests, he headed for the airlock.

He was going to Elysia. And he would locate Eirene. He was the best reconnaissance scout in the entire Shielder militia. It didn't matter how far she ran.

He would find her.

Chapter Four

The big event was at hand. Today Eirene had her audience with Darya. Meeting the great healer had been only a distant dream when Eirene was on Travan, seemingly trapped, with no options other than living her days out in servitude to the men there. Yet fate had intervened, giving her this wonderful opportunity, and she intended to take full advantage of it.

Unfortunately, she'd awakened feeling ill, flushed with fever and weak. Nothing of any concern, she insisted to herself. Just a minor virus, probably caught on her jaunts through the marketplace. She dressed with care, ignoring the shakiness in her limbs. Nothing would keep her from this audience—nothing. Too queasy to eat, she drank a little water, then set off for Darya's quarters.

Traveling through the crowded marketplace, she felt even worse, but pushed forward. The usual mental bombardment must be making her symptoms seem more pronounced. Regardless, she couldn't miss this appointment with Darya. She might not get another chance. People jostled her, and she stumbled twice, but pressed on. Nothing would prevent this meeting.

A sudden jolt of mental energy spiked through her like a knife. She swayed to a halt, grabbing a vendor's cart for support. Surely the energy burst was simply the normal emotional turmoil churning through the masses. She could block it out if she could only concentrate.

Another mental jolt speared her, staggering in its intensity and focus. This time, the energy was more definitive. An insidious, seeking force—terrifying, as its tentacles seemed to wrap around her.

Tracking her, only her.

Adrenaline shot through her body, amplifying her rising panic. Who—or what—was it? Her uncle wasn't capable of broadcasting such energy, but he might have hired a psychic tracker. Yet she should have been able to block any probes. Where was the transmission coming from? Behind? Ahead?

Her heart pounding, she pushed away from the cart and scrambled forward. She shoved through the crowd, oblivious to the protests. She had to evade her anonymous pursuer. Darya . . . she must reach Darya.

There it was! A faint mental trail, the same energy he'd sensed in Eirene's chamber at the Pleasure Dome. Not the same pattern he would pick up from another Shielder, yet distinct and recognizable. Jarek felt certain Eirene was emitting that energy. He pushed forward, scanning the crowd up ahead, the psychic trail getting stronger as he advanced. He focused all his concentration on the glimmer of energy, locked on to it. It was directly ahead of him. He was closing in.

There! A flash of silver and a glimpse of dark hair bobbing through the crowd. Eirene. Jarek speeded up, forced harder, jostling bodies aside. He'd been on Elysia four cycles now, checking every departure from the transport station, patrolling the marketplace for any sign of his prey. He would not let her get away.

She must have sensed him, because she began running, edging to the side. Jarek took off, leaping from the pathway and dodging in and out of stalls. She went faster; so did he. Fortunately, he was recovered from his injury, well-rested and in good physical condition. He gained on her rapidly.

She was just ahead of him now. Almost in reach . . . until a vendor pushed a cart into his path. He crashed into it, the hard yarton wood slamming the breath from him. The impact spun him into another stall, as he battled to regain his balance. A shelf of Saija silk halted his spin. He found himself on the ground beneath several bolts of colorful fabric.

Loud, angry voices jabbered as he managed to untangle himself from the silk and struggle to his feet. A large, bearded man, bare-chested, with gold cuffs around his bulging biceps and numerous gold hoops in his ears, shook his fist in Jarek's face. "You son of an Antek!" he bellowed. "I brought that silk all the way from Vilana. Now you've ruined it!"

Jarek backed away, his hand going to his laser. "I apologize. I'm sure the silk isn't ruined. All you need to do is brush it off and—"

"You broke my cart! And you terrified my babies," a strident female voice came from behind him. "Just look at them."

Jarek whirled to stare at the first vendor, a tall, thin woman with garish orange hair and a long, sour face.

Babies? Worse and worse. He glanced up the pathway. Eirene was nowhere in sight. *Damn!*

"Your babies?" he asked cautiously, edging the direction she had gone. A group of grim-faced merchants blocked his retreat. Great. They competed ferociously among each other for business, but were tighter than a miserly Shen if one of their own had an altercation with an outsider.

"They're everywhere," the woman sniffed, waving a thin hand toward the ground.

Jarek looked and saw them—lightspeed-quick balls of fur, chattering and darting into nearby stalls. Lanraxes. One maroon baby lanrax scampered toward him, obviously terrified, and squealing in distress. It leaped onto his leg and dug in its magnasteel-sharp claws. He winced and unthinkingly pulled the small creature off his leg.

"Here." He thrust it toward the woman. "I'm sure you'll be able to round all of them up. I'm sorry, but you pushed your cart into me." He eyed the terrain, looking for the quickest escape route.

Hissing, the woman grabbed his arm. "You'll pay! For my cart, for these babies, for—"

"And my silk!" The man grabbed Jarek's other arm. "It's worthless now, I tell you."

He had to get out of here. His Enhancer was getting away. Jarek wrenched his arm free from the woman. No such luck freeing himself from the man. The lanrax squealed and leaped to his chest, digging in and pressing against his neck. Blazing hells.

"Look," Jarek said to the woman, peeling off the lanrax so he could see, "I didn't even dent your damn cart. It's yarton wood, for Spirit's sake." He turned his burning gaze on the male merchant. "And Saija silk can be cleaned. I suggest you let me go before you regret it."

68

"He's a thief," another merchant muttered, and they moved closer.

Jarek groaned in abject frustration and urgency. He had to take desperate action, as much as he hated to do so. He drew his laser, which he kept on the stun setting, and put the silk merchant out of commission. The man sagged to the ground, sunlight flashing off his gold jewelry. The woman began to wail and scream for help, while the other merchants drew back, terror replacing their anger.

"I'm sorry," Jarek called over his shoulder, as he darted around the cart and made a run for it.

Despite the cries of outrage from behind him, no one tried to stop him. Dangerous criminals and petty thieves abounded in the marketplace, and few beings were willing to accost a possible felon. The apparent exception was the maroon lanrax, which had reattached itself to Jarek's leg and was clinging for dear life.

He ran up the pathway, skirting the masses of people, careful to avoid any more disasters. He couldn't concern himself with his aching ribs, which must have been bruised from the impact with the cart. Nor did he take time to remove the lanrax or give it any consideration. He was focused on one thing only—Eirene. Which way had she gone?

He mentally scanned for the energy pattern specific to her, but didn't find it. He picked up other Shielders in the vicinity, but not Eirene. Where was she? He searched the marketplace, despairing that he'd lost her. He finally found a faint trail, along a path that forked to the left. He veered up the path, rapidly edging along the crowd, but more cautious of carts this time.

He almost passed her in his haste. She was huddled beside a stall, arms wrapped around herself. She was trembling violently. Her head was down, her hair shorter and not as dark, and the blue robe gone. But he knew it was her. Same slight build and, more importantly, the same energy he'd sensed at the Dome. He stopped beside her. She appeared oblivious to his presence. "Eirene."

Her head snapped up, her blue eyes widening in shock. "No!" she gasped, scrabbling along the stall, trying to rise to her feet. "Go away."

He grabbed her arm before she could flee. Her skin felt hotter than the sands of Calt.

"No!" She jerked back, trying to free herself. Then she kicked at him and flailed her free arm against him. "Let me go!"

He winced as she made contact with his bruised ribs. He grabbed her other arm. "Stop this. I'm not going to hurt you."

She fought like a trapped kerani, although her movements seemed sluggish, weak. "Let me go. Let me—" She stumbled against him, her legs giving out. Her hands gripped the front of his tunic. "So weak . . . what's wrong with me?"

"I don't know," he murmured, gathering her unresisting body into his arms. He felt her shaking, and realized chills from the fever must be causing it. "But I'll take care of you. You're safe with me."

She shook her head weakly. "No. Never safe. Please . . . leave me alone."

"I'm afraid I can't do that," he said, with true regret. He needed her too badly. She was going with him, whether she wanted to or not.

She closed her eyes and sagged against him, her breathing shallow. She appeared to be very ill. Jarek felt like a real bastard as he thought of a way to turn her illness to his advantage. The idea was unethical and dishonorable, going against his ingrained sense of integrity. But ensuring Shielder survival called for desperate measures.

"Sorry, little one," he whispered, despising what he planned to do next.

She didn't respond. Resolute, Jarek cradled her closer as he turned and headed for his ship.

The images were surreal, like a dream. And she was hot, so hot. Eirene twisted, trying to get away from the burning heat. Strong hands stilled her, and a cool cloth swept across her face. She turned toward the coolness, desperate for relief.

"Eirene, can you hear me?"

A male voice calling to her . . . must be a dream. She blinked open her eyes, but quickly closed them against the painful light. Hazy images seeped through her mind, bringing a memory of being tracked, of trying to get away from— Impossible. The man who'd relieved her of her virginity was long gone, having left Saron before she did. This was just a bad dream.

The cloth drifted over her face again, bringing her more alert. This felt too real to be a dream. She forced her eyes open. Him! She jolted up with a hoarse cry.

"You *are* awake." He tossed the cloth aside and sat on the edge of the bunk, pressing her back down.

Not that she would have gotten far, she realized, feeling her body shaking. *What was happening?* She stared at Jarek, disoriented and confused. Panic fluttered in her chest, but she was too weak to act on it.

"How did you get here?" she croaked. Her throat felt parched, and she was so hot.

"You're ill," he said bluntly. "Very ill. You have to help yourself."

Bewildered, she glanced around. She was in a chamber she'd never seen before. How had she gotten here? Nothing made sense, and her muddled mind seemed incapable of logical thought.

"I don't understand," she whispered.

"I know about your abilities, Eirene. You can heal yourself. You *have* to heal yourself."

Alarm twinged through her dulled senses. "What are you talking about?"

His dark gaze seemed to bore right through her. "Your abilities. I know you're an Enhancer."

This time, the adrenaline that jolted through her cleared some of the fog. How could he know that? *How could he?*

"I don't know what you're talking about."

"Oh, I think you do." He took her hand and pressed it against her forehead. "Feel the fever. You're burning up. Feel the tremors wracking your body. You're very sick. Do you want to die?"

She *was* sick. Fear closed in, making it difficult to breathe. Yet she would never admit her secret to him, or anyone else. Rayna had pounded home the importance and necessity of Eirene keeping silent about being an Enhancer.

She turned her hand, grasping his. "Help me. Find a healer."

"You don't need a healer. You can help yourself, Eirene. Just like you healed me."

"I don't know what you're talking about."

"There's no need to hide the facts from me. I'll never tell anyone—I swear. You healed me. I'm certain you did. As I lay dying, you put your hands over my wound, and you healed me. I know you can do the same for yourself."

He seemed determined to force an admission from her. But she'd die first. There were many things in the universe worse than death. If anyone discovered for certain she was an Enhancer, her fate would be unthinkable. Controllers and other factions snapped up those with Enhancer abilities, imprisoning them and tapping into their powers.

She closed her eyes. "I didn't heal you. You were bleeding heavily, unconscious. Your people took you to a healer."

"The wound had already closed itself by the time I saw Chase," Jarek insisted. "And I remember, Eirene. You knelt by me and put your hands on me, and I felt the energy flow from you. That's how I found you—by following your energy trail."

Oh, Spirit. This man must be a psychic tracker. She should never have helped him, especially since she couldn't control her powers. She had exposed herself and now he knew—or thought he knew. Yet she would *never* admit the truth.

"Everyone has energy. I'm not an Enhancer, and I didn't heal you." She closed her eyes, giving in to the weariness dragging her down. She felt too badly to care any more. Surely Haven would be better than this world.

"Eirene! Don't let go. *Heal yourself.* I know you can do it."

"No, I can't." She drew a labored breath. "If you won't help me, then let me die in peace."

She didn't speak again, instead drifting on the silence surrounding her, shutting Jarek out. *What could he do to her?* she thought dully. Soon she'd be out of his reach.

After several moments, he asked quietly, "Would you really choose death?"

Over becoming a virtual prisoner again, over being

forced to use her powers to harm others—yes. With a great effort, Eirene roused herself to answer. "There is no choice. You've decided for me."

He blew out his breath in a big sigh. "Blazing hells. The best laid plans," he muttered.

She felt the mat lift as he stood and heard his boots clicking across the room. There was a low hum, like a panel opening, then he said, "You can come in now, Doctor."

"So you're ready to let me talk to her," came a melodious female voice.

"I doubt you can convince her to do anything," he replied.

Eirene was only halfway listening, with an odd detachment. But the whisper of sound by her, and the cool hand against her face drew her attention. She forced her eyes open. An elderly woman, dressed in the royal blue robe of a healer, smiled down at her. "Feeling better, my dear?"

The woman radiated an amazing energy—soothing, yet invigorating; warmth and comfort. Her compassionate green eyes and lined face reminded Eirene very much of Rayna. She roused herself. "I feel terrible."

The woman smiled. "You'll start to notice the effects of the medicine I gave you in about an hour."

Even more confused, Eirene stared at the woman's kindly face. "You gave me medicine?"

The woman nodded and patted her hand. "I did indeed. You have Alberian flu, my dear. Easy enough to treat, although you'll feel like you've been shoved into the Fires for a few days. But I predict a full recovery."

A full recovery? Then she wasn't dying. Eirene glanced at Jarek. He shrugged, stiff and grim-lipped. No reason she should be surprised by his treachery. He was a man, not to be trusted—like her uncle. Eirene returned her gaze to the elderly woman. "Who are you?"

The woman smiled again. "I'm Darya."

Lani finished her vigorous workout and headed for the shower. Just because she was on vacation was no reason to neglect her routine. A woman should never let herself get out of shape. Besides, being in top physical form came in handy in her line of work. That, and a high level of proficiency in the martial arts. She wished her brother would exercise. Radd met a lot of space scum in his profession and needed to be able to defend himself. Of course, he had his mate, Lionia, to protect him now.

Lani showered, then dressed in her newest Saija silk robe. A profusion of midnight-blue feathers covered the entire front of the robe. She always felt better when she dressed her best—no reason to be slouchy just because she was taking some time off. She slipped on her highest, sleekest sandals and went looking for Radd.

She stepped into the empty corridor. It was much quieter now that all visitors but her had departed one cycle earlier. Lani pondered her options. She decided to check the cockpit and see who was there, rather than barge in on Radd in his private quarters.

Celie swiveled around when Lani entered the cockpit. "Oh, hello, Lani," she said, smoothing her caroba-colored flightsuit. The rich brown matched her eyes and complemented her fair hair and skin.

Lani really liked Celie. She'd known the girl for six seasons, had watched her mature from a child into a poised young woman. Like her older sister Moriah, Celie had class, something sadly lacking in most races and societies, thanks to the Controllers and their brute enforcers, the Anteks. Lani sniffed disdainfully. What was this universe coming to?

"Hello, Celie," she said brightly. "What's going on?"

"It's pretty quiet. I think Radd is in the engineering bay, doing some repai—"

A beep came from one of the consoles, cutting Celie off. "That's my subspace transceiver," she said. "Do you mind if I take this incoming hail? Then we'll find Radd."

"Oh, no. Go right ahead," Lani trilled. She loved learning new things, and hoped she could watch Celie negotiate a deal with a client. Most people thought Lani was simple-minded, but she did believe a woman should exercise her brain as well as her body, and tried to keep up with current events.

Celie swung around and punched on the video transmitter. "Captain Cameron here."

An image formed, then sharpened. A male face came into focus, a commanding face with high cheekbones and fathomless ebony eyes. A Leor, bald and bare chested—a massive, well-muscled chest, Lani noticed with feminine appreciation. Celie sat up straighter.

"Captain," the man rumbled, his voice deep and guttural. "Greetings."

"Commander Gunnar. May a thousand suns shine favorably upon your Lordship," Celie responded, the deference in her voice unmistakable. "What can do I for you?"

Lani was excited to witness a business transaction with a Leor. She'd never had personal dealings with one, as they didn't frequent Pleasure Domes, but she had heard many stories about the fierce barbaric race. She eagerly moved to the seat next to Celie, where she could watch everything. Gunnar appeared oblivious to her presence.

"You were on Travan eight cycles ago, delivering cargo," he barked at Celie.

"Yes, I was—"

"Did you carry any passengers away from there?"

Celie's brows drew together in confusion. "Passengers?"

"A female—black hair, blue eyes."

Black hair, blue eyes? Lani had just made a recent acquaintance of a woman with that coloring. . . .

"No, Commander," Celie answered. "I didn't pick up any—"

"Yours was the only ship to leave Travan during the two cycles after she disappeared," Gunnar interrupted relentlessly. "Think very carefully before you answer, Captain."

Lani bristled at his arrogant, accusing tone. How dare he imply that Celie would lie?

"Your Lordship," Celie said evenly, her calm admirable, "I did not pick up any passengers on Travan."

Gunnar's mesmerizing gaze seemed to bore right through Celie, as if searching her very soul. "That woman was my bride, exchanged for a trade route. I am very displeased over her disappearance. Again, I warn you to carefully consider your answer."

His threat was implicit. No one with any sense crossed the Leors. They had ways of discerning the truth and dispensing swift and terrible justice. Lani noticed Celie gripping the console, her knuckles white. How dare this overgrown testosterone factory upset such a sweet, decent young woman?

"I believe she's already answered you, *your Lordship*," Lani snapped. "Why don't you go pick on someone your own size, you big bully?"

Celie gasped, as the Leor's midnight eyes pivoted to

Lani, narrowing and sparking with fury. "Who are you, to presume to speak to me in this way?" he growled.

"Commander, she is my guest and not aware of your ways," Celie broke in quickly. "I apologize—"

"I'm a citizen, with the same rights as you," Lani interjected. "And I know Captain Cameron doesn't lie. Why, the nerve of you, to accuse her of such a thing!"

"Lani, please!" Celie said. "Don't concern yourself any further. Commander Gunnar and I understand each other quite clearly." She turned back to the screen. "I did not receive a passenger on my ship. I'm sorry I can't help you."

Gunnar's narrowed eyes remained locked on Lani for a long moment before he returned his attention to Celie. "Since I have done business with your sister for over seven seasons, I will accept your word. You know the consequences of lying. I believe the woman left Travan on your ship, but perhaps she was a stowaway. Where did you go after you left Travan?"

As if sensing Lani's accelerating urge to dress the man down, Celie held out a restraining hand. "To Saron, where I stayed a little over one cycle.

"Where have you traveled since then?"

"I haven't been planet-side since I left Saron."

Gunnar considered this. "And has every section of your ship been checked?"

"Yes. I only have three private cabins, and those are currently occupied. My storage bays have been restocked and we do daily walk-throughs. There are no stowaways on my ship, Commander."

He inclined his bald head, acknowledging his acceptance of her answer. "Very well. Vaden and I will direct our search to Saron, then."

The screen flashed off abruptly. Celie slumped in her

seat and released her breath. "I've never had an experience quite like that with the commander before."

"He's too full of himself, and very rude!" Lani fumed. "I'm sorry if I got you into trouble when I jumped in, but he deserved it."

"It's all right. Gunnar can be very irritating. He's also very volatile. I must ask you not to do that again."

"I'll try not to," Lani muttered, thinking about what the Leor had said. A woman with black hair and blue eyes, fleeing him, most probably going to Saron as a stowaway on Celie's ship. Lani had always heard that Leors insisted their brides be virgins. Very interesting.

She knew a woman fitting that description. A woman who had professed to be an experienced courtesan, although she'd been extremely nervous when her first client was announced. A woman who had disappeared immediately after that client left . . . leaving blood on the bed's satin comforter.

It might have come from Eirene's robe, which had been bloodied when Jarek was shot. But, somehow, Lani didn't think so.

Not that she would ever share such information with Gunnar. She wouldn't give that arrogant bastard the time of day.

"You lied to me." Eirene slapped away Jarek's hand.

"I had to." Ignoring her hand shoving against his, he returned the cloth to her face. "Be still. Darya said this would make you more comfortable. Matter of fact, she said you needed to be sponged all over to keep the fever down."

"That will be a cold day in the Fires," Eirene snapped, protectively grasping the top of the robe she'd discovered herself wearing. "What happened to my clothes, and who put me in this robe?"

"Your clothing was covered with mud, and Darya sent me to get you something clean. She made me leave while she tended you."

Jarek paused, his dark gaze clear and direct. "I don't know why you're so concerned with modesty. You were in a Pleasure Dome, offering your body in exchange for money. And it's not as if I haven't seen all of you."

Eirene felt a hot blush sweep her face. Outraged, she tried to twist away from him. "Go away and leave me alone."

"You cut your hair." He caught a few strands between his fingers. "Changed the color. Why?"

That brought her up short. She needed to consider the possible reasons Jarek had followed her to Elysia. He could be a psychic tracker, working for her uncle or the Leors, but somehow, she didn't think so. If he had tracked her to Saron, her uncle would already be here.

She thought it more likely Jarek had been at the Pleasure Dome by pure chance. When she had foolishly used her powers to heal him, he'd guessed she was an Enhancer, and followed her, hoping to use her abilities to his own selfish advantage. He had strong mental powers of his own, making him a dangerous adversary. She could never allow him to know the truth, or let him force her.

And she certainly didn't want him to find out her uncle or the Leors were most likely looking for her. That would give him even more power over her. He already posed a serious threat to her freedom. She turned her head away, tugging her hair free.

He grasped her chin, turning her face back toward him. "Why?" he persisted.

She felt awful—achy and weak, her thoughts muddled. If she wasn't careful, she could easily say something which would make her situation even more tenuous.

"I was tired of my hair," she murmured. "Now go away and leave me alone." She closed her eyes with a sigh.

"Feeling pretty bad?" he asked, his voice sympathetic.

Probably just an act, she decided. He'd already lied to her about the seriousness of her illness, and he was a male, two strikes against him. She couldn't let her guard down for a millisecond. But, oh, she felt miserable.

"I don't think death would feel as bad," she said fretfully.

"I'm sorry." Again, he sounded sincere. He was just too dangerous. Too handsome, with his boyish charm and those dark, charismatic eyes. And obviously intelligent. She must be very cautious until she could get away from him.

She heard the sound of liquid being poured. "This will make you feel better," he said. "Let me help you sit up, so you can drink it."

His hand slid beneath her back and she forced her eyes open. She was feverish, and his hand felt cool. She tried to raise herself, but she was too shaky. He slipped his arm around her and supported her. She stared at the creamy liquid in the glass. "What is this?"

"I have no idea. Darya mixed it and said you need to drink a dose every hour."

Darya. Just thinking of the healer created a painful weight in Eirene's chest. "I missed my audience with her, thanks to you," she muttered, bitterly disappointed.

He held out the glass patiently. "You were in no condition to meet with her. She offered to reschedule your audience."

She took the glass and drank small sips, wincing with each swallow down her burning throat. Reaching deep inside, she found the courage to raise her eyes to Jarek as she handed him the glass.

"You're not going to allow me to make that audience, are you?"

He hesitated, his gaze searching hers. This close, she realized there were golden specks splashed against the deep brown of his eyes. She also saw regret and determination reflected there.

"No," he said. "I can't. I need you too badly."

Her heart leaped into an irregular beat. Oh, Spirit, how was she going to get free of this man? "What do you want from me?" she whispered.

"I want you to help me."

"How?"

"By using your natural powers. If you're an Enhancer, you might be able to help me save my people."

No. She couldn't help him if, even if she wanted to. She couldn't help anyone. Her heart surged even more, and she battled for breath. "I've already told you—I can't help you."

"Eirene—"

She turned away from him. "Leave me alone."

He didn't touch her, but she felt his words as if they were a laser blast. "I can't do that."

She rebelled at the implacable finality of his words, silently screaming her refusal to let him win. But right now, the only thing she could do was put a temporary distance between them.

"I need to go to the lav." She struggled to push herself upright and to the edge of the bunk.

"Running from me won't change anything," he said quietly, but he helped her stand.

She clung to him, appalled at her debilitating weakness, as he walked her to the panel and opened it. "Maybe I'd better go in with you."

Her eyes widened. "Absolutely not!"

He grinned at her shocked expression. "All right, little one. I'll give you some privacy. But I'll be here if you need me."

The tile floor of the lav felt blessedly cool beneath her bare feet. The closed panel gave her some badly needed space from Jarek, from the power he wielded, and her current helplessness. She was disappointed to discover there was no portal or window that might offer the possibility of escape. Not that she could get far in her condition.

She took care of necessities, then went to the sink and splashed cool water on her face. It felt so alien in here, so different from her simple facilities on Travan. Yet it was every bit as bad as Travan had been, perhaps worse.

On Travan, she had at least garnered some respect for her healing abilities. Here, she was nothing. Jarek had the upper hand, and she was utterly alone—in a foreign, hostile world.

She was sick, tired, and badly shaken. Tears filled her eyes, scorching trails down her face. Distressed at her weakness, she batted at the evidence of her emotional frailty.

Jarek apparently decided she'd been in the lav long enough. He opened the panel and strode in behind her. She turned her head so he wouldn't see her tears, her despair. But it was futile to attempt any distance from this man. She was too vulnerable and, like any true predator, he sensed it.

She cringed away from him. She didn't want him touching her, physically or mentally. "Stay away," she protested, putting out her hand as if she could stop him.

He pushed it aside and lifted her into his arms with ridiculous ease. She struggled feebly and he tightened his grip around her. "Stop fighting me, Eirene. You can't win."

She ceased her battle, knowing she couldn't best him right now. But she had no intention of surrendering.

He carried her to the bunk and lowered her onto the mat, drawing the cover over her. Gently, he smoothed the tears from her cheeks, just as he'd done at the Pleasure Dome.

"Sleep now, little one," he murmured. "You'll feel better tomorrow. We'll talk more then."

She turned her face away, shutting him out of her sight. But she couldn't shut him from her mind. Or stop the horrible fears gnawing at her. She'd escaped from Travan, and marriage to a Leor, only to become trapped in a new prison.

And she didn't know if she could escape from this one.

Chapter Five

Early the next cycle, Jarek slipped into Eirene's cabin. He steeled himself for the coming encounter, knowing she despised him, and with good reason. He had deceived her, leading her to believe she might be dying. He'd stolen her innocence—albeit unknowingly—and her freedom. He had every intention of taking her with him to Aldon, then to the twelfth sector, by force if necessary. His actions were ruthless, dishonorable and against every Shielder principle of justice. And yet, he saw no other choice.

Still asleep, Eirene lay curled on her side, her hair forming a glossy curtain across her face. Her chest rose and fell with each soft breath, pushing her breasts against the thin fabric of her robe. Jarek remembered clearly how perfectly those sweetly rounded breasts had filled his hands, how responsive they'd been to his touch. He sucked in his breath, forcing back a rush of desire.

The events in the Pleasure Dome were just another piece of the puzzle Eirene presented, one he would eventually unravel. But he couldn't let physical attraction cloud his judgment, nor would he ever force his attentions on a reluctant female. He had no doubt Eirene wanted nothing to do with him. She'd been too weak to stand on her own last night, yet she had battled him, then withdrawn mentally and physically from him. It shouldn't have bothered him, but it did.

A longing for something that could never be stirred inside him, along with the familiar, bitter knowledge that his personal wants must be subjugated. Even if he had met this woman under different circumstances, they wouldn't have a future. His commitment lay with his people.

He sank into the chair by the bunk and reached out, taking her hand. Her skin was soft and cool, the fever apparently gone. "Hey," he said softly.

She stirred, shifting to her back, her hair falling free of her face. Her features were perfect, her skin as smooth as satin.

"Hey," Jarek said again.

Her eyes opened, clear and brilliant, and he found himself falling into deep blue pools of tranquility. Spirit, she was lovely. Her dark hair and fair complexion fit the classic descriptions of Enhancers, according to his research. The serenity in her eyes gave way to loathing, as she realized where she was. She jerked her hand away.

She pushed herself up slowly, pressing against the wall. Her gaze remained on Jarek, distrustful, wary. "I had hoped you were a bad dream."

He'd far rather be her fantasy. "I'm not a dream. How are you feeling this morning?"

"Better." Challenge sparked in her blue eyes. "Well enough to meet with Darya."

They both knew that meeting wouldn't be taking place. "You look better," he responded neutrally.

She drew a deep breath, then launched an offensive. "Why are you keeping me here? I've told you I can't help you."

"How can you be so sure about that, until you hear everything I have to say?"

"Because your words won't make any difference. Nothing will. You seem to think I've got special powers. You're wrong."

She could be telling the truth, which would mean he was terribly wrong—or just plain crazy. In fact, he wondered if he had lost his mind; if his desperate search for a solution had thrown him totally off kilter. Hell of a foundation for a life-or-death strategy to save an entire race. But he had nowhere else to turn.

He couldn't discount the overwhelming evidence that Eirene had healed him; nor the unusual energy pattern he picked up only from her; nor his own instincts, which had never failed him. Every instinct screamed she was an Enhancer.

"I know you're special, Eirene. You're an Enhancer."

Her eyes flared before she looked down. Her hands clenched the cover. "I have no idea what an Enhancer is."

The denial didn't affect his plans, but eventually, her cooperation would be crucial. He had decided to tell her the truth about the Shielders, in the hopes of stirring her sympathies. It would put him at greater risk, but now that the Controllers had issued a galaxy-wide warrant for his capture, he had little left to lose.

"Just hear me out, Eirene. Let me tell you why I—why *we* need you to help us."

She looked away, clearly resistant to whatever he had to say.

"I'm a Shielder." He waited, but got no reaction from her. She didn't seem to comprehend the significance of that fact. "You don't know what a Shielder is?"

She kept her face averted, but at least she answered. "I've heard of Shielders, but I don't know anything about them."

"We have a genetic mental shield that allows us to resist the mind-domination of the Controllers."

That seemed to catch her attention. She swung toward him, eyes wide. "You have mental powers?"

"Not exactly. Certainly not like those of your people. But we're not affected by psionic brain waves. The Controllers can't dominate us. We've fought them for many seasons, attacking and then retreating to hidden bases and colonies. The Controllers declared all-out war on Shielders about twenty seasons ago. Much like they did with the Enhancers, more than two hundred seasons back."

Jarek paused, giving her time to absorb this information. "The Enhancers are now extinct, with a few, very rare exceptions—random individuals born with Enhancer genetic makeup. The Shielders are coming very close to that same end."

Eirene stared at him, her hands clenching the cover even tighter. He felt a slight energy surge from her, and pressed his case.

"The Controllers have created viruses to kill us; offered rewards for every Shielder captured, as well as for information on colony locations. Anteks routinely raze settlements, murdering all the men, women, children and animals. Any survivors are sold into slavery. Our resources are dwindling. We don't have enough food and medicine, or the weapons we need to fight back. To make matters worse, the Controllers have recently organized a major offensive to annihilate us once and for all. Antek troops are searching out Shielder colonies. I just got word this morning—"

He paused, his throat working. He closed his eyes, trying to force the grief and anger under control, trying to banish images of mutilated, charred bodies. Images which were burned into his soul. Resolutely, he opened his eyes, seeking Eirene's gaze. "Another Shielder colony was decimated yesterday—no survivors. They're coming at us from every direction, Eirene. There's nowhere for us to hide, no weapon powerful enough to defend us, and nowhere to run—or so it seems."

"How horrible," she said softly.

The compassion in her eyes shot a ray of hope through him. "I have a plan which might give us a chance at survival. We're pretty certain there's a black hole in the twelfth sector. Several ships have disappeared in that area, and one of my scouting ships picked up electromagnetic distortions near there."

He leaned forward, keeping his gaze locked with hers. "The stories about Enhancers claim that they traveled through a wormhole which was inside that black hole. A portal, if you will, to another part of our galaxy—or even to a new galaxy entirely. I want to locate that wormhole and find a way to navigate it. That's where you come in."

Apprehension chased away the sympathy in her eyes. He could feel her withdrawal. "I'm sorry about your people, truly I am, but I don't see how I can help."

"You're an Enhancer, Eirene. You might be able to

help me operate the equipment on Aldon, to manipulate the energies of the black hole, so we can traverse it."

She stared at the mat, restlessly smoothing the cover. "So you've decided I'm an Enhancer, even though I've told you repeatedly I'm not. You're just going to kidnap me and force me to go with you."

No sense caroba-coating the truth. "Yes."

Her gaze snapped back up, myriad emotions swirling through those luminous eyes. "What about me? What about my life, my dreams? I may never get another opportunity to work with a great healer like Darya. "You'd sacrifice all that simply because you think I'm one of these . . . Enhancer people?"

He knew about lost dreams, lost opportunities. However, he had chosen to make the sacrifices; Eirene had not. He pushed away the guilt and remorse—useless emotions which wouldn't save his people. "I know your dreams are important, but I'm asking you to set them aside, at least for now. The survival of thousands of people could depend on your cooperation."

She wrapped her arms around herself and looked away, shutting him out yet again. He sighed. He had given it his best shot. Time to back off, to let her assimilate what he'd told her. He understood her resistance to exposing herself, despite her genuine empathy. He didn't blame her—he had a good idea what happened to known Enhancers. Admitting her powers made her vulnerable, left her a sitting echobird to the Controllers and other private factions. And she had absolutely no reason to trust him, given his actions thus far.

"Tell you what," he said, rising from the chair. "You'd probably like to get up and move around some. While you do that, I'll go prepare something for you to eat."

She closed her eyes, leaning her head against the wall.

"I'll be back in a little while," Jarek told her.

He checked to be sure the hatch alarms were on, so she couldn't slip away, then let himself out.

Thoughtful, he retrieved the lanrax from his cabin, having resigned himself to the fact that the little creature had bonded with him and would probably perish if he ignored it. It perched on his shoulder, chattering and chewing on a piece of bread, as he fixed a simple grain dish for the morning meal. Since Darya had warned him Eirene would be weak for a few cycles, he decided to take food to her cabin.

She was sitting on the edge of the bunk when he carried in the tray. Her face was pinched and pale, and he suspected just being up had tired her.

Her attention focused on the ball of fur balanced on his shoulder. "What is that?"

He set the tray on the console beside the bunk. "It's a lanrax. They bond with the first person who leaves a scent on them. They're very possessive and dependent, but many people claim they make wonderful pets."

She stared at the lanrax in wonder. "It has four eyes!"

"Yes, it does. That's a lanrax trait. They can see extremely well in both daylight and darkness."

"We never had any pets on Tra—" Eirene stopped herself. "Any animals in my colony became food. At least the four-legged kind."

Jarek grinned, both at her apparent slur on men, and the fate common to all creatures. He could relate to the scarcity of food. "It's that way on Liron, too."

"Liron?" she asked. "I've never heard of it."

"I've never heard of 'Tra', either."

She flushed, but didn't rise to the bait. She slid back onto the bunk, settling upright against the wall. Her robe rode up with the movement, revealing shapely calves and dainty bare feet. Sighing, she closed her eyes and rubbed her forehead.

"Head hurt?" Jarek asked, pouring another dose of Darya's concoction.

"Spirit, yes. It feels better when I'm lying down." Eirene opened her eyes, spearing him with her crystal gaze. "But I can't rest well here. I want to return to my own quarters."

"Here, drink some more of this," he said, refusing to argue. He held out the glass.

She took it and drank. Jarek guessed the medicine made her feel better, or she'd resist. He was beginning to see the magnasteel core inside the woman, despite her petite, fragile appearance. But then, Enhancers didn't need physical strength, not with their mental powers. Eirene would be a handful when she was fully recovered from her illness.

She said nothing as he placed the tray across her legs and settled into the chair, shifting the lanrax to his lap. He held the silence as well, willing to give her latitude to adjust to the situation. She picked at her food, her gaze returning repeatedly to the lanrax. Jarek reached down to pet it. The animal chattered contentedly.

"It seems to really like that," Eirene commented.

"Yes, lanraxes need contact with their owner."

She ate a few bites, watching him stroke the animal, then put down her utensil. "Can I pet it?"

"Maybe. Sometimes they won't let anyone but their bonded owner touch them."

Setting aside the tray, she scooted to the edge of the bunk. Her robe slid up around her thighs, giving Jarek an eyeful before she tugged it back down. Spirit, she had great legs. His throat dry, he forced his thoughts away from that forbidden avenue.

She leaned toward the lanrax, and it hissed, digging its claws into Jarek's thigh and causing him to do some hissing of his own. However, the little creature seemed to accept her touch, gradually relaxing and chittering softly.

A delighted smile spread across Eirene's face. "It's a female," she declared decisively, stroking the soft maroon fur.

Jarek had just felt a surge of energy, and wondered if she had used her power to come to that conclusion. She probably had no idea he could pick up her energy pattern so easily.

"A female, huh?" He hadn't taken to time to verify the lanrax's gender, although he'd been around enough of them, since the one he'd given his sister many seasons ago had been very prolific in the reproduction business.

"Now how can you tell that?" he asked. "Seems to me you haven't looked in the right place to verify this little fellow's sexual persuasion."

Another smile tugged at her lips. "*She* is sweet and gentle. Not obnoxious, or bossy, like a typical male."

Jarek turned the lanrax onto its back. It squealed indignantly, but allowed a gentle examination. "You're right. She's a female. Explains why she's so temperamental."

"Maybe she doesn't like being locked up, or forced to do what you want her to."

"Oh, she loves it, because she has me," he couldn't resist teasing. "But she needs a name. What do you think we should call her?"

Eirene thought about it. "Don't you have a name you like, perhaps that of a family member?"

Jarek shrugged. "I could choose from a lot of names. But I thought you might like to pick something."

Surprise flashed across her face. "You'd really let me choose the name?"

It was such a little thing, yet she seemed excited by the prospect. Her reaction intrigued him. Hell, everything about this woman intrigued him. "Sure. Go ahead."

"How about Rani?" She paused, swallowed hard. "It's a version of a name I'm very fond of."

He'd have let her name the damn lanrax anything she wanted, just to see the pleasure it seemed to give her. "Rani . . . I like that. Rani it is." Jarek leaned back, watching Eirene. He could tell the name meant something to her.

"Where is *your* family?" he asked quietly.

She froze, her tension palpable. "I have no family."

He'd be willing to bet that wasn't true. "Where are you from?" he persisted. She'd started to name a place and stopped herself, so he didn't really expect an answer. He did get a reaction, though—a brief spiking of her energy.

"I don't think that's of any concern to you."

His instincts told him she was hiding something—or hiding from someone. Not surprising or unusual in this universe with no real justice. He took another approach. "You never told me why you cut your hair."

"Yes, I did. I told you I was tired of it."

"I meant the real reason."

Her eyes narrowed, wariness flashing through them. They were her most expressive feature, Jarek decided. She'd probably be appalled if she knew how clearly they appeared to reflect the inner woman. Not that he planned to tell her.

"There's not a specific reason I changed my hair," she told him coolly. "Although you seem to think there is.

Just like I'm not an Enhancer, but you insist on believing that I am."

The ever-present doubt nagged at Jarek, chipping away at his tentative confidence in his plan. Could his instincts have failed him? *No,* he told himself. He'd always trusted his gut feelings, and they'd always seen him through. He had to believe his strong intuitive abilities came from a higher power, and that he would receive the guidance he needed to save his people. He must believe in that. He only hoped he found a solution before the Controllers captured him.

"Perhaps changing your hair had something to do with you being an Enhancer," he speculated. Maybe he wasn't the only one who suspected Eirene's true identity. Maybe someone else was pursuing her.

She looked away before he could read her reaction. "You're wrong," she insisted. "On both counts." She shoved the tray towards him. "I'm tired. I want to rest now."

He'd pushed far enough for now. He put the lanrax down and took the tray. "That's a good idea. I'll check on you later. If you're feeling better, maybe you'd like to eat the next meal in the galley."

She didn't acknowledge him, turning away and shutting him out, as she did every time he pressed her. He took the tray to the galley, Rani scampering right behind him, and cleaned up there. Then he spent the rest of the morning in the cockpit, answering messages and dealing with the many responsibilities his father's death had thrust upon him. Rani curled in his lap and remained there as he worked. He found her presence comforting in an odd way. At least he wasn't so totally alone with her around.

At mid-cycle, he returned to the galley and prepared

some soup. Rani scrambled back to her perch on his shoulder, watching with interest, her upturned nose twitching at the scent of cooking food. After he finished, Jarek gave Rani a piece of bread and returned her to the lav in his cabin, ignoring her loud protests.

He went to check on Eirene and found her awake, sitting in the chair. She looked more rested, and some color had returned to her face.

"You feel up to walking to the galley for mid-meal?" he asked.

"Yes. I'd like to get out of this chamber." She pushed herself out of the chair. She swayed a little, but held up her hand when Jarek moved toward her. "No. I want to get around on my own."

"Okay," he agreed, but he stayed close in case she needed assistance.

She looked around as they stepped into the corridor, lightly touched the wall. "Is this a ship?"

"Yes. It's my craft. Star-class, fast enough to take us to Aldon, then the twelfth sector."

She stumbled, and he grasped her arm to steady her. Anxiety radiated from her, and she was trembling. The realization she was on a ship must have brought home the reality of his intentions. He pulled her around, bringing her flush against him. He could feel her heart pounding.

"I told you exactly what my plans were," he said quietly.

"Let me go. Please," she pleaded, panic edging her voice.

"Hush, little one. You have nothing to fear from me." He ran his hands soothingly along her back.

She didn't pull away, and he held her close a few moments, waiting for her to calm. She was so small—a petite package containing a megaton of power. As they stood there, he became aware of more than her breathing and her heartbeat. He felt her soft curves pressed against him, felt the smooth resilience of her skin beneath the robe's bell sleeves. Blazing hells. She was still weak, clearly shaken by the reminder he was forcing her to go with him, willing or not. And all he could think about was her allure.

Her innocence was so obvious now, he couldn't understand how he hadn't recognized it at the Pleasure Dome. She had no knowledge of feminine wiles or flirtations, but then she didn't need to resort to artifice. Her simplicity and her fresh, unadorned beauty were seduction enough.

He slid his hands up to cup her face, seeking to reassure her, as he willed his libido to cool. "I've told you I won't hurt you, little one. My word is good."

Despair filled her eyes. "You're forcing me to go with you."

"You're safe with me," he reiterated.

Desperation remained etched on her face. Gently, he skimmed his thumb over her lower lip. Just that one touch triggered a host of erotic images. He remembered vividly how she had tasted when he kissed her at the Pleasure Dome; how she had felt, naked beneath his hands. His body responded in a heated rush. A pull stronger than gravity and as old as creation brought his mouth to hers.

He shouldn't be doing this, shouldn't be giving in to the clamorings of his body . . . Spirit, she was sweet. All softness and warmth and inexperience as she allowed his mouth to settle over hers. He teased her lips with his tongue, grasping for control, determined not to ravage her mouth like he wanted to do.

Suddenly, she pushed against him, breaking the contact. He released her, and she staggered back. Her face was flushed; her chest rose and fell rapidly. Great. He'd really messed this up.

"I'm sorry. That shouldn't have happened," he told her. Would he be forever apologizing to this woman, he wondered, forever plagued by contrition for his actions towards her?

She braced herself against the wall. "Is this part of the deal, too? Not only am I being kidnapped and forced to travel with you, but I must submit to your sexual urges as well?"

"No! No . . . I—" Jarek raked his hands through his hair. Damn. "I know you won't believe me, but I don't make a habit of doing this, of—" Of what? Letting lust cloud his judgment? Shatter his normal magnasteel control? Eirene affected him in ways no other woman ever had. He needed to regain control—and fast.

He drew a deep breath and forced himself to meet her gaze. He saw both accusation and alarm there. Damn, now she was even more afraid of him. He didn't want her fear, only her cooperation. "This won't happen again. I give you my word."

"What good is the word of a man who would hold a woman prisoner, a kidnapper?" she shot back.

"I've explained my reasons for taking you with me. I believe you're a compassionate person. Surely you can understand that I have no other options. And I think you know, deep down, that I mean you no harm. My behavior was out of line, and it won't happen again. Trust me, Eirene. Please."

She whirled and headed for her cabin. Wanting to kick himself, Jarek let her go. He couldn't continue to mishandle her and expect her to come around and cooperate with his plans.

Not only that, but time was running out.

Eirene appeared well enough now. He'd only been waiting until he was sure Darya wouldn't be needed further. They would depart Elysia first thing tomorrow.

Eirene hurried through the marketplace, toward the transport station. The temperature on Elysia dropped considerably at night, and the air was chilly. She clutched her robe closer as she moved along the path, weaving between various beings. The marketplace never closed, as transports departed and arrived at all hours. It was amazingly crowded at this time of night, but Eirene paid scant attention. She had one thing on her mind—escape.

Fortune had been with her when she entered Jarek's cabin as he slept. The sleep state had lowered his mental defenses enough for her to merge with him and deepen his sleep even more. She'd been very careful, praying she wouldn't hurt him.

Then she'd used her powers to disarm the hatch alarm and leave the ship. That had been a near disaster. She'd overloaded the circuits and almost caused a fire. Just more reminders of her incompetence.

Relieved to be free, she'd hurried to her rented quarters and retrieved her satchel, which contained the jeweled daggers that would provide her a means of surviving.

By the time Jarek woke up, she'd be long gone. It didn't matter where—there were numerous settlements where she could learn healing techniques. He might search for her, but eventually, he'd give up the hunt. Perhaps she could even return to Elysia one day and work with Darya.

She slowed as the transport station came into sight,

thinking about the Shielder people and their horrendous plight. Her heart went out to them, and her hatred for the Controllers elevated another notch.

But she couldn't help the Shielders. She had no real control over her powers, couldn't channel them with any sort of consistency. She caused more harm than good when she tried. Pain speared through her as she thought of Rayna. She stumbled, then caught her balance.

There was more to worry about—the added threat of being discovered as Enhancer, and sold into slavery. The Controllers would expect her to use her powers on their behalf. They could torture her all they wanted, but she wouldn't be able to produce for them, either.

Jarek himself was threatening enough. He had turned her universe upside down on every possible level. Eirene wanted to curse him, but knew the blame rested with her. By healing him, she had foolishly broadcast her Enhancer abilities. She hadn't been careful enough leaving Saron, and he'd been able to follow her to Elysia.

On top of everything else, she was attracted to Jarek. When he'd kissed her earlier this cycle, her body had come alive with physical cravings she'd never experienced before. The encounter brought home the seriousness of the threat he presented.

At least it served to strengthen her resolve to escape, and she had succeeded in that endeavor. Freedom lay within her grasp.

She skirted the edge of the transport station, her destination the automated ticket terminals on the right. She would check the departure boards and choose a destination before she got in line to purchase a ticket. She glanced at the lines to gage how long it would take, and a tall male caught her eye.

A Leor. He was massively built, and was without a

shirt. His bald head gleamed beneath the huge halogen lights illuminating the area. He moved through the lines, studying every individual as if he were looking for someone. A fission of alarm shot through Eirene, and she quickly took cover behind the nearest departure board.

Leors were common enough on most planets, and this one simply might have gotten separated from a traveling companion. Yet her instincts were on full alert, warning her to be cautious. She'd stay out of sight until he left. She peeked around the board and watched the Leor, as he moved methodically through the crowds, intently scanning every face. Then another male approached him, and Eirene's heart almost stopped beating.

Vaden. Oh Spirit, what was her uncle doing on Elysia? Shock and fear clouded her thinking momentarily, and she forced air into her constricted lungs. Foolish question. She knew why Vaden was here, the same reason Jarek had been able to trace her to Elysia. Because of her carelessness. On Saron, she hadn't tried to change her appearance in any way. She'd been too shaken from her experience at the Pleasure Dome to even think about a disguise.

Anyone could have followed her to Saron's transport station. The automated ticket terminals hologrammed everyone who purchased a ticket. Her uncle had probably tracked the ship she'd stowed away on to Saron, picking up her trail there. He'd probably paid off an official to check the holograms from the ticket terminals, and discovered she had purchased passage to Elysia.

Careless. She'd been so careless!

No way she could get off Elysia now. Vaden had probably checked every departure since she'd arrived, and he'd continue watching the transport station. No telling how long he'd persist. Falling into his hands was unthinkable.

She'd seen how cruelly her uncle punished those who defied him, and she had no doubt he would be even harsher with her, a mere woman. When he discovered she was no longer a virgin, he might well kill her. Or worse. He might barter her in a trade with a race who didn't care whether a woman had her virginity. A race even more barbaric than the Leors. Why hadn't she thought of that before?

Eirene sank back against the board and willed her panic to calm. She could go to her rented quarters and lay low, but she still had Jarek to contend with. He appeared able to pick up her psychic trail, and he would try to track her down. She knew he wouldn't give up looking for her.

Maybe she should go back to him. She had escaped him once; she could do it again. She could return to his ship, and he'd be none the wiser. Her uncle wouldn't know where she was, would have no reason to follow Jarek's ship. When they reached the next destination, she'd escape from Jarek again and disappear into the cosmos. Too many planets for him to search them all.

Calmer now that she had a viable plan, she turned to slip back into the crowd and return to the ship.

And came face to face with Jarek.

Chapter Six

"Going somewhere?"

His voice was calm, reverberating with the unyielding resolve that Eirene was coming to despise. At the same time, she felt an inexplicable sense of relief. She should be devastated Jarek had caught her, and yet, she had the insane urge to throw herself against him and let him protect her from the world. The stress of the past days must have affected her more than she realized.

He had managed to wake and find her in record time. Obviously, her pitiful attempt to deepen his sleep state hadn't worked. He appeared able to track her with ease. She couldn't even shield her energy patterns. Now he stood waiting, obstinate and determined, his narrowed gaze pinning her to the spot.

"Well?" he prompted.

"No," she muttered. "I'm not going anywhere. I just came out for some fresh air." She patted her satchel.

"And to retrieve my personal belongings." She glanced furtively toward the ticket terminals, then turned to head toward the landing bays.

His hand shot out, closing around her upper arm and jolting her to a stop. "You seem very interested in those terminals."

He intended to have it out here. Eirene glanced again toward the transport station. Her uncle and the Leor had split up and were working the lines from both sides. Any millisecond, they might see her. Her heart pounded against her rib cage. Renewed panic froze her breath.

She tugged against Jarek's hold. "I'm ready to go back to the ship."

"Somehow I find that hard to believe." His eyes speculative, he looked back at the throngs of people in line. "Someone there you're trying to avoid?"

Adrenaline thrummed through her. She didn't think Jarek would hand her over without a fight, but she didn't believe he could take on both Vaden and a Leor. Besides, she had no intention of telling Jarek she was being pursued.

"Please," she said, trying to keep her voice steady. "I'm tired. Let's go back to the ship."

He studied her, far too discerning. A new fear coursed through her—not of capture, but that this man knew her every thought. Surely that wasn't possible.

"Very interesting," he mused. "You say you're tired, and by all rights, you should still be weak from the flu. Yet here you are, almost three kilometers from the ship. You look like you're holding up pretty well."

She wasn't about to admit she'd tapped into her power to give herself the energy boost she needed to get to the transport station. Fortunately, she hadn't caused herself any injury in the process. From the corner of her eye, she saw the Leor reach a line only ten meters away. The lack of oxygen in her constricted chest was beginning to make her lightheaded.

"Jarek, please. I'm ready to go back to the ship."

He glanced around once more, then turned her and started toward the landing bays, keeping a firm grip on her arm. "Lucky for me, you're more frightened of something—or someone—than you are of me. Otherwise, I'd be chasing you across the quadrant. And make no mistake, Eirene. I would follow you, and I would find you."

She was beginning to believe that.

Jarek moved at a good pace, slipping through the crowds and tugging her along behind him. As they reached the outskirts of the marketplace and the crowd thinned, he dropped back beside her.

"I noticed some interesting things," he said casually.

Eirene cast a glance over her shoulder. Not seeing Vaden or the Leor behind them, she was finally able to draw a deep breath. Her body trembled from the scare, but she felt safe now. At least from that particular threat. Jarek was another matter, and she didn't want to know his conclusions. She tried to walk ahead of him, but he pulled her back.

"Very interesting," he continued. "Like how I had trouble waking up, although I'm usually a very light sleeper. But Rani kept making noise and pawing at me, and I eventually came to."

The lanrax roused him? Amazed, Eirene slowed. "Why would Rani wake you?"

Jarek shrugged. "Maybe she knew something was wrong." His dark gaze locked on Eirene. "Maybe she sensed unfamiliar energies."

So now both Jarek and the lanrax could detect Eirene's use of her powers. Not good. "I wonder what got her

105

stirred up," she murmured, walking faster.

Jarek's grip on her arm forced her to match his pace. "That's not all. Somehow, one of the hatch alarms became disabled. It wasn't turned off at the control panel, which, by the way, requires a security code. No, the strange thing is, the alarm was short circuited—as if an energy surge overloaded it."

He stopped, looked at her again. "I guess you didn't notice anything unusual when you left the ship."

She'd botched this big time. She hadn't meant to short circuit the panel, merely to turn off the alarm. The wisps of smoke drifting from the panel had only confirmed her lack of control over her powers. Yet she had no choice but to attempt to use them, at least until she gained her freedom.

She lowered her gaze. "I didn't see anything odd," she said, praying for forgiveness for all the lies she'd uttered since meeting Jarek.

He grasped her chin, forcing her to look at him. "Eirene." His voice dropped into a deep, gentle tone that sent dread skittering through her. "You and I both know the truth. One day, you'll trust me enough to be honest with me."

He couldn't know for sure, she reminded herself. He was only speculating, only hoping. She pulled away. "I wish you would listen to me. I can't help you. I'm sorry, but I can't."

Sighing, he took her arm again. "Well, I guess we're just going to be miserable together then."

The warmth of his hand against her chilled skin sent odd sensations through her body. Miserable was an apt description, she decided. Especially if she didn't find a way to ignore the electricity sparking between them.

Resigned to enduring Jarek's company a while longer,

she walked silently beside him. The after-affects of shock set in, leaving a bone-deep fatigue, but she didn't dare draw in energy to revive herself. Heaviness weighed down her legs, and the distance to the ship seemed longer than she remembered. Finally the landing bay came into view.

Utterly exhausted now, Eirene was actually grateful to be returning to Jarek's ship, even though it represented another prison. She'd rest and gather her strength, waiting until they arrived at their next destination before she again tried to escape.

They entered the massive, well-lit bay, still a distance to go before they reached the landing pad where their ship sat. So many spacecraft here, Eirene thought, again amazed at the hugeness and diversity of the quadrant. So many designs and styles and colors.

Here, as in the marketplace and the transport station, activity bustled along constantly, with ships being serviced, or loaded with supplies, or warming up to depart. She and Jarek walked down a wide path running along the pads, ships on either side of them.

Suddenly, a blast zinged into the ship on their right, barely missing Jarek's head. He moved in a lightspeed blur, flinging Eirene to the ground, covering her with his body. His weight crushed her, driving all air from her lungs. Another blast ripped the air above them. The hubbub of voices turned to shouts of alarm.

"Don't make a sound," Jarek whispered harshly into her ear. "Do exactly what I tell you, when I tell you."

Too stunned to speak, she tried to nod, but couldn't move.

"I'm going to roll toward the ship on our left. Roll behind me, and stay down," he instructed.

He pushed off her and hurled himself toward the underbelly of the ship, yanking hard on her arm to make sure she followed. She tumbled after him, coming to rest in a heap in the shadow of a midnight-blue cruiser. He scrambled to his feet, dragging her up and pulling her with him, around the nose to the other side, just as another blast discharged.

A jolt of energy singed through Eirene in a startling rush. She felt a flash of pain and stiffened, wondering if she'd been hit. But just as quickly, the pain was gone. Jarek leaped to the walkway on the other side of the ship, pulling her with him.

"Run!" he ordered, taking off in a burst of speed.

She heard more weapon-fire, some shouts. A fresh surge of adrenaline lent strength to her legs. She hitched up her robe with one hand and ran, skirting loaders, and other beings trying to scurry out of the way. Her heart pounded and her lungs burned as she followed Jarek blindly.

Several ships down, he darted back to the right, pulling her beneath a ship and behind its sled base. Motioning her to stay there, he too pulled a blaster from his right holster, wincing and transferring the blaster to his left hand. Eirene saw blood dripping from his right arm and realized he'd been shot.

"You're hurt," she gasped, reaching toward his arm.

"I can't worry about that now." He edged toward the path they'd just vacated.

He leaned out slightly and studied the area behind them, pulling back as another blast exploded. More cries of alarm filled the air.

"Blazing hells. He's after me, all right. The bastard can see us, but we can't see him." Jarek motioned toward the right, to the path they'd originally been on. "Let's go another direction."

Her chest heaving, Eirene followed. It occurred to her that it might be Vaden shooting at her, and not at Jarek. But there was no reason to do other than what Jarek ordered. She sensed his extreme competence, realized if anyone could keep her safe, he could.

He wove in and out of ships, moving them several paths over, heading in the general direction of his own ship. Eirene gave up trying to think, as everything around her became a jumbled blur. She focused on keeping her legs moving, sucking in oxygen as fast as her tortured lungs would allow. There were no more blasts, so hopefully, they had lost their assailant—or assailants—possibly Vaden and the Leor.

They reached Jarek's ship, and Eirene sank gratefully to the floor as he secured the hatch. "No time for that," he said, pulling her up. "We have to get out of here."

Resisting the urge to groan, she stumbled after him into the cockpit. He shoved her into one of the two leather chairs. "Strap yourself in." He slid into the other chair and started flipping switches. The ship hummed to life.

Jarek hit another switch and static crackled over a speaker on the console. He requested permission to take off.

"Permission granted," came the computerized voice over the speaker. "Wait until twenty-three-hundred-fifteen hours before take-off. There are two departures ahead of you."

Jarek glanced at the timepiece in the console. "Like hell I'm going to wait that long." He punched some pads, and the engines revved loudly.

Eirene fumbled with the unfamiliar harness. She'd never been on a spacecraft until she'd stowed away on Celie Cameron's ship. On the commercial transport from

Saron, the flight attendant had attached her restraints for takeoff and landing.

"Here," Jarek said impatiently, startling her. She'd been so intent on the harness, she hadn't seen him leave his seat. "Let me." He pushed her hands away, and slid the magnetic plates together with a snap, wincing as he did so. Alarmed, she saw his arm was bleeding profusely.

"Your wound—"

"No time for that," he cut in, returning to his seat. "We have to leave *now*. Hang on. This will be rough."

It was a wild ride, all right. Jarek took off right on the tail of the first departure, thrusting his ship into the turbulence created by the wake of the first craft. Feeling as if every bone in her body was being jarred into debris, Eirene wondered how he managed to control the ship, especially with his injury.

Finally, they cleared Elysia's gravity field and veered away from the ship ahead of them, and the ride smoothed out. She unclenched her teeth, gratefully drawing a full breath.

"Sorry about that." Jarek entered information into a keyboard, then flipped more switches. Three screens lit up in the console. Leaning back, he studied them intently. "Looks clear."

His gaze shifted to her. "You all right?"

"I think so. Why did we take off so close to that other ship?"

"Because I wasn't about to wait around, giving whoever is after me the opportunity to get to his own ship and follow me."

Or whoever is after me, Eirene thought, relieved that Vaden and his Leor cohort wouldn't be able to track her.

Jarek sank back and probed his right arm, grimacing. "Blazing hells." He blew out his breath. "I don't suppose

I could convince you to use your energy to heal my arm?"

Surprisingly, she wanted to. The lines of pain etched on his tired face, the hopeful entreaty in his dark brown eyes, tugged at her like a powerful undertow. She hated to see anyone suffer, especially this man, who seemed to bear the weight of the universe on his broad shoulders.

She quickly shook herself away from the temptation. What was wrong with her? She would never—*never*—reveal her powers to Jarek or anyone else. Not only that, but with her ineptness, she might make his wound worse. At least he'd survive if she used traditional healing methods.

"I'm sorry," she said. "I can't. I don't have—"

"I know, I know. You're not going to admit you're an Enhancer. Not that I blame you. But it sure would come in handy right now if you'd just be honest."

He definitely didn't allow himself to be swayed from his convictions, Eirene mused. He was so different from the selfish, indulgent males of Travan. They only cared about having their own needs met, without concern for the women and children dependent on them.

"I can clean and bandage the wound for you," she offered. "I've had some training in healing."

Gratitude flashed in his dark eyes. "I'll take you up on that offer."

She wondered if anyone ever did anything for him, or if his entire life had been spent taking care of others. "Where are your medical supplies?" she asked.

He checked the scanners once more before he rose and retrieved bandages and antiseptic from a supply vault in the corridor. He returned to the cockpit, setting the items on a console.

"We need to do this here," he said, unfastening the

top of his flightsuit and slipping it off. "I have to set our course and monitor the screens." He sat in his chair and pivoted towards her.

Eirene stared at the broad expanse of bare chest, the pale brown nipples, and the flat, muscled planes sliding lower. Awareness of Jarek's masculinity tingled through her, and her breath caught. Once again, she couldn't help comparing him to Travan men. He was a male in his prime, fit and firm, so unlike the overweight, flabby men she'd always known.

Unsettled by his effect on her, she turned her attention to the ugly wound on his right arm. She slid her left hand behind his arm to hold it steady. His triceps was firm and smooth, his skin incredibly warm. Touching him affected her as much as looking at him had, sending tiny shockwaves through her body. Totally disconcerted now, she released the arm like it was a hot ember, scooting back.

"What's wrong?" he asked. "Is it bad?"

She drew a deep breath, furious with herself for her lack of control. It was serious enough not being able to marshall her powers, but she should at least have her own body under her command. Her self-control was deplorable. How could she ever be a competent healer if she couldn't master basic self-discipline?

She forced herself to focus on Jarek's wound. "I can't tell how bad it is yet," she managed to reply. "I need to clean it first."

She took his arm again, ignoring the feel of warm skin and muscle. The wound was still bleeding, but as she blotted away the blood, she was relieved to see the injury was fairly small. Jarek remained still, although she knew her ministrations must hurt. She worked quickly and efficiently, anxious to put some distance between Jarek and herself. She didn't like the way she continued to respond to him on some deep, primal level.

He's your captor, she reminded herself fiercely. *He only wants you here because of your powers.*

That certainly put their relationship into perspective. He might be more honorable and a far better man than those she knew on Travan, but he was still holding her against her will. And he was planning to use her to achieve his own ends.

She needed to remember that.

She had the touch of an angel. His arm burned like Hades, but her fingers were cool and gentle. They moved over his wound with practiced ease, tingles of energy pulsing through his skin in their wake. Jarek felt certain the energy flow was unintentional, that Eirene's powers sometimes manifested innately, without her being aware of it.

And, true to form thus far, her nearness affected him physically, sending an unwanted rush of desire to his lower extremities. He shifted uncomfortably, forcing himself to concentrate on her face as she worked.

She had beautiful skin, like alabaster Saija silk. Her dark hair, shimmering with copper highlights, created a striking contrast to her face. But it was her eyes that captivated him, as they had from the moment he met her. The deepest blue, like the enchanting lagoons of Vilana, they sparked with intelligence and character.

Exhaustion dulled them somewhat right now, but she still worked competently, and appeared to enjoy using her healing skills. When she was done, he leaned back, taking her right hand with his left. "Thank you."

"You're welcome." She tried to tug her hand free, but

he tightened his grip, reluctant to end the physical contact.

"You seem to have a flair for healing. Is that why you were so interested in meeting with Darya? To learn more about medicine?"

She paused, and he suspected her wariness of him made her reluctant to reveal anything, especially something as intimate as personal dreams.

But she nodded and admitted, "It's what I've always wanted to do. To become a great healer like her. I was hoping she'd accept me into her apprenticeship program."

And he had destroyed that chance, at least for now. He cursed the yoke of responsibility that necessitated uprooting this innocent woman. Plus he'd put her in danger, with every lowlife in the quadrant after him to collect the bounty on his head.

"Perhaps one day your dream will become a reality," he replied, hoping he might eventually be able to give her that.

She tugged against his hold. He let her go, and she gathered the medical supplies, refusing to meet his gaze. "I'll put these away," she murmured, turning toward the entry.

She never made it. A sudden jolt sent the ship listing sharply, and hurled her to the floor. Jarek barely managed to stay in his chair.

"Damn! Where did that come from?" He swung around and set the external viewers in motion. "Are you all right?"

"I—I think so. What was that?"

He activated the weapons console, already planning evasion tactics. "Felt like a laser blast to me." He checked the external viewers, found his worst fear confirmed.

Blazing hells. "There's a ship four hundred meters aft. No hail, just an attack."

Eirene scrambled to her feet, her face paling. "Vaden," she whispered.

Jarek whipped around to stare at her sharply. "What?"

She shook her head. "It doesn't matter. What can we do?"

Not a damn thing. Jarek quickly considered his options. "I don't know. That ship has enough armaments to destroy a good-sized planet." He spun to the main computer and activated Radd's program. It was their only chance. "Get back in your harness."

As she fumbled into the straps, the shrill beep of the subspace transceiver pierced the tense silence. It came in on the universal frequency, which meant the hail wasn't from anyone Jarek knew well. He hit the comm pad. "Who is this?"

Static crackled and a view screen to the right flickered. An image flashed on with startling clarity. A male, with a massive head, stubby snout, small glittering eyes. *Turlock.*

"Turn on your video transmitter, coward," he sneered, drool slipping down his jowls. "I know it's you, san Ranul."

"You don't know anything," Jarek countered. "Why are you attacking my ship?"

"I saw you fleeing from Elysia, like the weakling Shielder that you are. I haven't forgotten what you did to me six seasons ago, san Ranul. Only I didn't know who you were then."

Jarek narrowed his eyes, fury rushing through him. He would have finished the bastard off, if he'd had the chance. But Turlock had fled, and Jarek had been unable to track his ship.

He turned to his computer, rapidly entering information on Turlock's ship and scanning Radd's program. "You've got the wrong person."

"That's a sizeable bounty the Controllers have on your head, Shielder. I intend to collect it, then hang around to witness your execution. I almost had you on Saron, but the idiot I sent after you failed."

So the assailant at the Pleasure Dome had been after Jarek for the Controller reward. "I don't know what you're talking about," he hedged, studying Radd's data. There it was—just what he needed.

"You can deny it, san Ranul, but your hologram has been posted on every planet and star base in the quadrant. I know who you are, and I know it was you at the transport station, with that female. She's a pretty piece. She might like to keep me company while I watch you die."

A small gasp drew Jarek's attention to Eirene. She stared at Turlock's image, revulsion etched on her face. He reached out and gave her arm a reassuring squeeze. "It's not over yet," he whispered, determined to beat Turlock at his game.

Her huge eyes locked on his face, and she nodded. "I believe you."

Humbled by her obvious confidence in him, Jarek prayed her faith would prove justified. He armed his laser canon, well aware that Turlock's sensors would pick up the energy surge.

"Your pitiful weapons can't hurt me. This ship is indestructible," Turlock boasted. "You're trapped, Shielder. I would advise you not to try anything when we board."

He was right that his ship's special armor couldn't be penetrated by the weapons at Jarek's disposal. Nor could

Jarek be certain of outrunning Turlock's ship. But he could put it out of commission, if he could hit the main thruster at just the right angle.

Radd's program, which described every make and model of ship currently in use, also listed each ship's vulnerable points. A direct weapon strike to those areas could either disable or destroy the ship in question. Radd had developed his program specifically for Moriah's women, and for the Shielders.

According to the data, an armored Starblade interceptor like Turlock had was vulnerable around the main thruster. And Jarek intended to take full advantage. He would strike, then try to speed his own ship out of weapon range.

He figured Turlock would deploy a magnetic grapple to tow him in, and he had to act before that happened.

"Hang on," he told Eirene, locking the laser cannon onto Turlock's main thruster.

He discharged the laser, then gave his ship full power, moving away from Turlock's craft. His sensors, along with Turlock's bellow of rage, indicated a direct hit.

Yes! he thought, the high of victory surging through his veins.

"What did you do?" Eirene asked, her voice shaky.

"I hit his main thruster with a laser blast. It should put the ship out of commission. Turlock won't be able to go far until it's repaired. But now we have to put a safe distance between his ship and ours. Come on, come on," Jarek muttered, pushing the limits of his ship.

The ship was sluggish, and he quickly saw the reason why. Turlock's initial volley to halt the ship had done some damage to the starboard side, mainly the storage bay. Not fatal—unless they couldn't get out of Turlock's firing range.

Jarek kept the ship moving, his sensors indicating Turlock was activating his torpedoes. At least Turlock's ship didn't close the distance, so the laser blast must have done its work on the thruster. Damn! The bastard had just fired a torpedo.

Jarek sucked in his breath. "Hang on again."

He nosed his ship into a perpendicular angle to Turlock's craft, then arced around. The torpedo changed course with him. He turned at a sharp right angle, priming his cannon for another burst. As expected, the torpedo followed.

He kept changing angles, looking for the best firing position. Slowing slightly, he locked the laser onto the torpedo hurtling towards them. Now or never. He punched the firing pad, then nosed the ship a different direction.

They saw the explosion port side as they turned, and Jarek exhaled the breath he'd been holding.

"What was that?" Eirene asked.

He looked over, noticing her white-knuckled grip on her armrests. She'd been smart enough not to distract him during the crisis, for which he was grateful. She was quite a trooper.

"A torpedo," he said matter-of-factly, although greatly relieved. The adrenaline that had kept him alert and deadly focused was dissipating, leaving him shaken that Turlock had been able to find him so readily, and to sneak up on him. What bothered him the most was that Eirene had been in danger.

"Oh," she said, her voice faint.

"I'd say we're out of danger. Turlock can't follow us." Jarek studied the readouts. "But it looks like he managed to do some damage to our ship. We'll need some repairs before we can go to Aldon."

He checked the navigation unit to determine his exact coordinates. He was reluctant to return to Elysia, now that news about his identity and the bounty on his head appeared to be widespread. Any of the star bases would be just as dangerous.

He had another pressing concern—getting together the necessary resources to acquire the equipment on Aldon. That boiled down to gold miterons, the universal currency of choice. He had planned on meeting with Sabin to see if he could help with funds. Jarek knew where Sabin was, and hopefully, Radd would be there as well.

"We're heading for Risa," he told Eirene.

"Is it a star base?" she asked.

He was reminded again of how little she appeared to know about the quadrant. She must have lived a very sheltered existence up until now.

"No, Risa is a small planet where my friend Sabin and his mate live. Moriah established a settlement there for a small group of women about eight seasons ago. Now men and children live there as well. One of the men there is Radd, and he's the best ship mechanic in the quadrant. He'll be able to fix my ship."

"Has the settlement grown much?" she asked.

"No. It's still quite small. No public transports of any sort."

"Oh." She looked away, obviously disappointed.

She was transparent, unable to hide her feelings. Jarek felt certain she'd been hoping for an opportunity to give him the slip while they were there. She wouldn't find it on Risa. She wouldn't find it anywhere, as long as he could track her. The sooner she accepted that, the better.

He set course for Risa. Once they finished there, they'd be on their way to Aldon.

*   *   *

Lani leaned back in her chair, watching the interplay between Radd and Lionia. Her brother had certainly chosen an unlikely female for his mate. Lionia was a Zarian, a race of fierce warriors. She stood a head taller than Radd and exercised every day to maintain her lithe, well-muscled frame. Radd despised exercise, preferring to expend his energy repairing ships—and keeping a satisfied glow on his mate's face.

Lani thought they made an adorable couple. She was glad her brother had found someone with whom to share his life, something she never expected to have. She was too independent and set in her ways to compromise on a daily basis with another person. And she'd dealt with enough men to know few existed who measured up to her high standards. Besides, she never allowed herself to dwell on foolish hopes, although every once in a while, she did feel very alone in the universe.

None of that. Briskly, Lani rose from the table and stacked the mid-meal plates. "That was delicious," she said cheerily. "As usual, Radd, you're a genius with a replicator."

"Haveta admit, I've never met a machine I didn't like," Radd said. "Or a beautiful woman, either." He winked at Lionia, and she beamed at him. The atmosphere in the galley quickly heightened to one of a suggestive intensity.

Lani rolled her eyes indulgently. The couple acted like they were newly mated, although they'd been together over six seasons. "Why don't you two run along?" she suggested. "I'll clean up here and fix a plate for Celie. She's been working much too hard lately."

Radd and Lionia took her suggestion, departing for their cabin, with eyes only for each other. Lani sighed. True love. How rare, and how precious. She bustled around, efficiently clearing the galley in spite of her high heels and fluttering feathers. Then she prepared a plate for Celie and left it on the table. The girl needed a break from the cockpit. She could eat in the galley.

Lani had stepped into the corridor and headed for the cockpit when a strident tone chimed. She didn't do much intra-galactic travel on private spacecraft, so she had no idea what the tone was. But she loved learning new things, and would ask Celie about it.

Just then, Celie emerged from the cockpit, her face set in serious lines. "Oh, Celie," Lani called. "I have your meal ready in the galley. You need to eat properly. By the way, what is that tone?"

"It's the signal that a ship is approaching," Celie explained. "Commander Gunnar is demanding to be allowed to dock and board."

"Commander Gunnar? That arrogant Leor?"

"One and the same," Celie sighed, concern darkening her eyes. "He's never done anything like this before. I can't imagine what he wants."

"How rude. The man has absolutely no manners!"

"Now, Lani, you promised me you wouldn't antagonize the commander. The Leors are proud, and very explosive. They won't stand for having their authority challenged."

"Then someone needs to teach them a thing or two," Lani sniffed.

"I'll have to ask you to go to your cabin if you can't remain civil around Commander Gunnar," Celie warned.

Lani was instantly contrite for upsetting Celie. Celie was a genuinely nice person, and it wasn't her fault Gunnar was an arrogant brute. Besides, Lani couldn't see what was happening if she was banished to her cabin.

"I apologize for talking out of turn," she told Celie.

"I'll be on my best behavior with Gunnar—company manners!"

A small grin twitched Celie's shapely mouth. For a moment, she looked like the carefree, impetuous girl Lani had met six season ago, rather than a ship captain responsible for important deliveries. "Company manners should be sufficient," Celie said, bracing her hand against the wall. "They're about to dock. Hold on."

The ship jolted, and the airlock light flashed on. Straightening, Celie walked to the panel. Lani followed, eager to see Gunnar in person and find out what he wanted.

The light blinked off, and the panel slid open. Gunnar stepped through, followed by two more Leors, both heavily armed. In the flesh, he was much larger than Lani had expected, towering over Celie, who was tall for a humanoid female. His broad chest was bare, although he wore an open cloak that covered his arms. Snug leggings encased the most muscular thighs Lani had ever seen. My, he was quite a specimen.

Lani raised her gaze to study his face. His bald head was well-formed, perfectly suiting his rugged features. And his eyes—she'd never seen anything like them. They were impassive obsidian orbs which swept over Celie and then Lani. She couldn't see any pupils, only black bottomless pools that gave her the shivers.

Gunnar snapped his fingers, and the two Leors behind him moved around and headed down the corridor, weapons drawn. Celie's eyes widened and her mouth opened. Lani held her breath, wondering if Celie was rattled enough to speak first, an absolute sign of disrespect to the Leors. But she caught herself and waited, looking at Gunnar with a questioning expression.

"You lied to me, Captain," he snapped, stepping closer, his cloak swirling around him.

"I lied to you? About what?"

"You said you never saw Lady Eirene, my intended bride. You swore you had no knowledge of her presence on your ship."

Eirene? Lani's attention snagged on the name. So, her speculation had been right. That girl had been running from Gunnar.

Celie stared at him, her expression a mix of confusion and incredulity. "I did not lie about that, Commander. I had no guest on this ship from Travan to Saron. If I had a stowaway, I wasn't aware of the fact."

Gunnar's face hardened. "Do not play me for a fool, Captain. Eirene was seen on Elysia with Jarek san Ranul. Turlock, her uncle's associate, reported seeing them there. San Ranul's connection to your sister and her mate is well known by us. As a matter of fact, witnesses saw you and Jarek together on Saron. Do you deny it?"

Oh, this was so dramatic! With bated breath, Lani awaited Celie's reply.

She shook her head slowly. "No, I don't deny it. I met with Captain Ranul to discuss some equipment he wanted to purchase. But I had already been to Travan, and I wasn't aware of any stowaways."

"I find that hard to believe, Captain. First my intended bride travels to Saron, disappearing the exact day your ship departed from Travan—and also travels to Saron. Then you are seen with Jarek san Ranul on Saron. After that, Eirene purchases passage to Elysia. San Ranul just *happens* to travel to Elysia. There, the two are seen together by an associate of Eirene's uncle. Turlock reported that he tried to stop them, but they managed to escape."

Gunnar bent down until his face was level with Celie's.

"I do not believe in coincidence. And I do not like being lied to. We deal harshly with those who betray us."

Celie grew pale, but she met his gaze evenly. "I'm well aware of that fact, your lordship. And neither my sister nor I have ever betrayed you."

Anger started simmering in Lani, building to a boil. This man was bullying Celie, terrorizing her with his accusations and threats. Clenching her hands into fists, she took a step closer before she remembered her promise to Celie. Reluctantly, she forced herself to remain silent.

"Tell me, Captain, why I should not blow up this ship, along with everyone aboard." Gunnar spit out each word slowly, ominously.

Celie staggered backward as if she'd been struck. She pressed a hand to the wall for support. That snapped it. Furious, Lani stalked over to the oversized tyrant and punched him in the back as hard as she could. It was like hitting a ship's hull. He turned, seemingly unfazed, and she found herself eye to chest with him. Cradling her throbbing hand, she tilted her head to look up at him.

"Because she's telling the truth, you imbecile!" she shrilled. "Captain Cameron does not lie, not even to primordial slime like you. She is the most honest and loyal person I know. Why don't you go back where you came from? Or better yet, fly your ship into a black hole!"

"Lani," Celie gasped. "You promised."

But Lani was past the point of maintaining silence. She glared at Gunnar, tempted to hit him again, despite her aching hand. "I thought the almighty Leors could probe minds," she taunted. "Why don't you try that before you go around accusing innocent people? Then you'd see Captain Cameron is not lying."

"I cannot probe a mind which has undergone resistance programming, something your friend's leader,

Moriah, and all her people do. Not that I have to explain myself to you." Gunnar ran his insolent gaze down Lani and back up. "What is this?" he sneered. "It looks like a blue echobird that got caught in a rocket launcher."

Oh! One dead Leor, coming right up. Lani drew back and kicked him in the shin, digging in her sharp heel for good measure. His grimace told her she'd finally managed to inflict pain. Good!

Amazement replaced his grimace. "Only a fool would challenge me," he growled. "I think this heap of feathers needs to be taught a lesson."

Lani slipped into a crouch, raising her arms and positioning herself for her most powerful martial arts kata. "Come on, big guy. I'd like to see you try."

Celie stepped between them. "Lani! Stop it this instant!" She forcefully moved Lani back a few steps, her dark eyes beseeching. "*No more.* You're making a bad situation worse."

Her heart pounding from the adrenaline rush, Lani blew out her breath. Celie was right. She lowered her arms, forcing her fury back. "Maybe you're right. But . . . ohhh—" she glowered at Gunnar. "I'd like to put him out of everyone's misery."

"That's enough," Celie said firmly. She turned back to Gunnar. "I'm truly sorry, Commander, for all of this. I must beg leniency for Lani. She knows nothing of your ways and did not realize she was issuing a physical challenge."

"Ignorance is not an acceptable excuse." Gunnar's gaze snapped back to Celie. "You are not in a position to bargain for anyone."

Celie drew a deep breath. "We can only throw ourselves on your mercy, your lordship. As I said, Lani does not know anything about your people. I apologize for her insolence. I'm also sorry about your intended bride. But I give you my word that I never saw her aboard my ship. I have no knowledge of her whereabouts."

She held her hands out in supplication. "I ask you to consider that we have done business with the Leors for more than seven seasons. In all that time, have we ever betrayed you, or failed to deliver what we promised?"

Gunnar considered a long, nerve-wracking moment. "I know of no instance where Moriah or you have failed to honor any agreements," he concurred. "But there is now strong evidence to indicate treachery."

"The Leors are known for their sense of fairness and justice," Celie replied. "Would you judge and condemn us without solid proof of our guilt?"

By Alta's blue moons, Celie was sharp, Lani thought with admiration. Despite her youth, she'd managed to stay calm and argue her case in the face of serious threats. Lani felt a twinge of guilt, knowing she hadn't helped the situation any, but Celie appeared to be handling things quite well.

"If there is guilt, be assured I will find the evidence," Gunnar growled. "And I will not allow past associations to interfere with retribution."

The man had no feelings, Lani decided. He was just a muscle-bound, strutting automaton. But then, she knew a lot of men like that. She shook her head in disgust.

Gunnar's two lackeys returned from their search, followed by Lionia and Radd, both in a disheveled state. "We found nothing unusual, Commander," reported one Leor, "except for these two, acting like lanraxes in heat."

Gunnar grunted dismissively. Radd and Lionia both looked at Celie, and she shook her head in silent warning.

"Shall we position the detonators, Commander?" the second lackey asked.

Lani's heart lurched. Up until now, this had seemed like a grand space adventure, but suddenly it wasn't so much fun anymore. All heads turned to Gunnar.

"No," he said slowly, fixing his intimidating gaze on Celie. "I will wait until I have further proof of guilt. But, in the meantime, I will take a hostage—to be executed should I discover Captain Cameron has lied to me."

Lani blew out her breath, her legs going weak in relief. Gunnar taking a hostage was preferable to being blown up.

Celie's expression didn't waver. "Let me give my crew some instructions, then I'll prepare to leave with you."

"I forbid you to go," Lionia protested, stepping forward. "I gave your sister my word that I would ensure your safety. I will go in your stead."

"Naw, neither one of ya is goin'," Radd spoke up firmly. "As the only male on this team, it's my job to take the risk. I'm goin'."

Celie held up her hands. "I'm the captain, and this is *my* responsibility. You will follow my orders and remain on board."

"Hostages!" Lani fumed, her anger returning now that she knew the ship wouldn't be destroyed. "How barbaric!" She pointed a blue-tipped finger at Gunnar. "Haven't you got anything better to do than terrorize innocent people?"

Those soulless eyes pinned her to the spot. "I tire of your foolish tongue, female. Putting you in your place might prove to be very satisfying."

"As if you could," Lani scoffed, thoroughly incensed. "I can handle any coward who hides behind hostages."

"Coward?" Gunnar's eyes narrowed to ebony slits.

"Perhaps I should take *you* as my hostage. I would enjoy teaching you proper respect for your superiors."

"Oh, really? Well, why don't you do that, big guy? I might enjoy teaching *you* a thing or two."

"Enough!" Scowling, Gunnar folded powerful arms across his chest. "You tempt me sorely to take you with me, female. In fact, I think I will do just that."

"No," Celie protested. "With all due respect, your lordship, as the captain of this ship, it is my responsibility to go—"

"*Fine!*" Lani yelled, her gaze locked with Gunnar's.

"So be it," he snarled. Turning, he snapped his fingers. "Bring the blue-feathered woman and let us depart."

"No!" Celie interjected firmly. "I must insist that I go."

"Denied, Captain," Gunnar snapped. "I have made my decision. He pointed at Lani. "Take her."

"Get your hands off me, you big oaf!" Lani yelled as one Leor tried to grab her. Gripping his arm with both hands, she jerked him forward. She kicked his knee as she wrenched him sideways. He went down, a surprised look on his face.

Everyone looked in amazement from her to the massive soldier sprawled on the floor.

"I'm getting my things first," Lani insisted. "Then I'll accompany you, but your men are not to touch me. Is that clear?"

Gunnar watched the downed Leor struggle to his feet. His gaze flashed to Lani, cold, assessing. "As long as you understand I am the absolute authority on my ship."

"Right." She turned and marched down the corridor, feathers fluttering. She never went anywhere without her clothes and her toiletries. And her reading disks. Just because she was going to be a hostage didn't mean she could become intellectually lazy. She'd just bet Gunnar had nothing but muscle between his inhuman eyes, and wouldn't even know what a reading disk was.

Behind her, Celie again protested, "She can't go. It's my job to take the risks, and my decision."

"Seems to me the decision was made for ya, Celie," Radd answered, sounding totally unconcerned. "Don't worry. Lani can take care of herself."

She certainly could, Lani huffed silently. And in the process, she planned to teach the obnoxious Commander Gunnar and his louts some manners.

He would be sorry he had ever tangled with her.

Chapter Seven

It took four cycles to reach Risa. Eirene slept all of the first day of the trip, and part of the second. She had been pushed to her physical limits, and utter exhaustion claimed her.

Now, however, her normal energy appeared to be returning. Relieved to have escaped Vaden, she planned to do the same with Jarek—as soon as the opportunity presented itself. Unfortunately, from what he had told her about Risa, it didn't seem she'd have a chance anytime soon.

She studied the landscape as they flew over the planet's surface. It appeared desolate and stark, no hills or mountains, and only sparse outcroppings of scraggly trees. She didn't see any signs of civilization.

Then they topped a low rise, and suddenly, a breathtaking vista stretched before them. Their ship hurtled over a small forest, then over a carpet of lush, green grass at a dizzying speed. Stately trees interspersed the vivid stretch of green, then fell away as a lake came into view.

Eirene leaned forward eagerly. Travan had been an arid, barren planet, hot and dusty, especially in the women's compound. She'd never seen a body of water like this, a sparkling blue oval reflecting the sun in piercing bursts. She was disappointed that they crossed it so quickly.

Her attention shifted to the sturdy buildings, laid out in an orderly fashion, with neat pathways connecting them to each other. More trees lined the paths, along with brilliant masses of blooms. Eirene thought it enchanting.

"Do you like it?" Jarek asked.

"Oh, yes," she breathed. "It's as beautiful as Elysia. And better, without all the crowds and the marketplace."

He chuckled. "Moriah is going to take an immediate liking to you. She masterminded the transformation of this little corner of Risa, and she's very proud of it."

"Was this once barren like the rest of the surface?" Eirene asked in disbelief.

"It was. But Moriah is one of those people who thinks if you dream big enough, and believe hard enough, anything is possible."

Hearing the wistful tone in his voice, Eirene turned to look at him. "You don't believe that?"

He was silent for a long moment. "Ah, little one, I'd like to believe it. But I've been praying for a miracle for a long time. If one doesn't happen soon, my people face extinction."

She looked away, unsure what to say. Guilt tormented her. She'd been over the Shielders' situation repeatedly in her mind, but she knew she couldn't help Jarek. As well as the known risks of exposing herself as an Enhancer, she couldn't channel her powers with any sort of consistency. Worse, there were horrible consequences when she did try. She thought of Rayna, feeling the familiar pain and regret. No, she didn't dare attempt to use her powers.

A landing site came into view, with a surprising array of ships lining the sizeable pad. Two people stood watching from the ground as Jarek turned on the hoverlifts and brought the ship down. He powered down and unhooked his harness, then swiveled his chair toward her. "Ready?"

Strangely enough, she was. She'd braved the universe outside Travan, managed to find her way and hold her own. She'd proven to herself that she could survive the unknown.

She stood, smoothing down her tunic and leggings, grateful Jarek had gotten them cleaned on Elysia and returned them to her. "Yes, I'm especially ready to get off this ship."

As they came down the ramp, a woman and a man moved forward to greet them. The woman was stunning, tall and statuesque, with long coppery hair and golden eyes. Slightly taller, the man offered a handsome contrast, with his ebony hair and eyes. Their attention was focused on Jarek, and Eirene stepped to the side as the couple descended upon them.

"Jarek! It's good to see you," the woman exclaimed, her voice low and melodic. "I was worried when you left Chase's ship way too soon to be recovered. But you're looking much improved over the last time I saw you." She hugged him tightly.

"You're looking pretty good yourself." Grinning, he splayed his hand over her abdomen. "You've got that special glow."

She shoved him away. "Oh, cut it out! You *would* rub it in."

Despite her reaction and her words, Eirene sensed the woman's genuine affection for Jarek. But her emotions had sisterly overtones, rather than carnal ones.

The man stepped forward, his expression stern. "Yeah. I don't need any help from you, san Ranul. You always like to stir up trouble." His wide smile belied his accusing words, and he shook Jarek's hand heartily, then hugged him.

Startled, Eirene realized she could pick up none of the man's emotions, as with Jarek. *Why?* she wondered, studying the two men. They were about the same height, and both had similar builds—lean but well-muscled. Both had high cheekbones and well-chiseled features. Were they brothers? Or . . . were they both Shielders? She tucked the question away for future investigation, as Jarek turned towards her.

"Moriah, Sabin, this is Eirene. Eirene, meet two of my best friends in the universe."

They studied her, their expressions guarded, and she wondered what Jarek had told them. But then Moriah smiled and stepped forward, her hand outstretched. Sincere warmth and friendliness engulfed Eirene.

"Welcome to Risa. If you're a friend of Jarek's, then you're part of our family."

Eirene took the proffered hand, and knew immediately that Moriah was a woman of valor. She sensed something else—a second life force emanating from Moriah—another soul. The woman was pregnant, which explained Jarek's teasing behavior.

Eirene returned Moriah's smile. "Thank you. I'm glad to be planetside. I'm not so sure space travel is for me."

"Especially if you're cooped up with san Ranul," Sabin

said. "He's far too serious, not nearly as interesting as I am."

Moriah rolled her eyes. "Oh, please. Don't listen to him, Eirene. He's too full of himself."

"As far as I can tell, all men are that way," Eirene said.

Moriah laughed. "Oh, I like you already. I hope you'll get to stay a few cycles." She sent Jarek a questioning look.

"That depends," he said. "I have some damage to my ship from a little run-in with Turlock. Is Radd back yet?"

"Turlock? That son of an Antek," Sabin muttered. "Too bad we didn't finish him off on Saron. How bad is the damage to your ship? Radd's not here. He's with Celie and Lionia, and they ran into some trouble with the Leors. They're on the way back and should arrive tomorrow, the cycle after at the latest."

"The damage isn't too bad, but I can't go to Aldon until the repairs are done. If you don't mind, we'll hang out here."

"Don't be silly. We love seeing you," Moriah said. She linked her arm with Eirene's and turned her toward the group of buildings. "I'm glad you're staying a while. We'll get quarters ready for you. You can have something to eat and drink at the main hall while you wait."

Sabin and Jarek hung back to talk, as Moriah led Eirene toward a large building set back from the landing pad. "Let's go meet the others."

Eirene felt like she was being swept away in a whirlwind as Moriah led her into the largest building, which was apparently the main hall. The huge room bustled with activity.

Two long tables flanked by benches lined one side of the room. The tempting aromas of cooking food wafted from an open panel behind the tables, so Eirene assumed that this was a dining area.

Groupings of comfortable-looking chairs and smaller tables occupied the middle area, where two adults sat and chatted, watching a handful of children playing. More tables and benches lined the opposite side of the room, with some large pieces of equipment situated next to them. Cloth was piled on one of the tables, metal sheets and tools on another. Two women and one man were working at the tables, apparently replicating clothing and metal goods.

"This is the heart of our settlement," Moriah explained. "We eat our meals here; replicate clothing, furniture, tools and weapons here; and spend much of our free time here. There's a galley on the other side of that wall." She pointed to the open panel near the first set of tables. "Let's introduce you to everyone."

Eirene first met Marna and Tyna, crusty older women who had grown tired of delivering supplies and now took care of the cooking and laundry. Then there was Roanne, a shy dark-haired woman with a stutter, and her mate, Ardon. They had two children, and Roanne replicated clothing for the settlement's inhabitants. Valene, a pleasant young woman, assisted Roanne with the clothing production.

No hostile or anxious emotions bombarded Eirene. All the women radiated well-being and contentment. Their feelings towards Eirene were welcoming and warm. They appeared to know Jarek well, emitting excitement and pleasure that he had come for a visit.

An elderly man and woman sat in two of the over-stuffed chairs in the room's center. They were apparently in charge of keeping an eye on the four active children playing nearby. Even through the moderate emotional melee in the room, Eirene sensed a commanding power in the old woman as Moriah led her to the couple.

The woman raised clear gray eyes when Moriah and Eirene approached. Her gaze locked on Eirene. Eirene felt a strong surge of energy reaching out and engulfing her, but it was well-controlled, almost muted.

"Janaye, this is Eirene. She's traveling with Jarek san Ranul, and will be our guest for a few days," Moriah said. "Eirene, this is Janaye. She's our beloved matriarch. Just don't cross paths with her, or that yarton club she carries might accidentally connect with your head."

"Go on with you!" Chuckling, Janaye held out a hand gnarled with age. "Pleased to meet you, child."

Eirene gently took the crippled hand and returned the woman's perusal. Janaye's snowy hair was gathered into a loose, silky bun, the escaping wisps framing her lined face. Despite her years, her eyes were sharp and aglow with wisdom. She was so like Rayna, tears pooled in Eirene's eyes.

Emotion clogged her throat. She had to clear it before she could speak. "Lady Janaye."

"Just Janaye, my dear. I'm so old, the title has worn off." Janaye smiled warmly and Eirene returned the smile. Janaye turned to Moriah. "I can tell this child is weary. Pull up a chair so she can sit and rest."

Moriah laughed good-naturedly. "I will do that. But first, let me introduce her to our other elder." She gestured to the old man in the chair next to Janaye's. "This is Elder Gabe. He's from Jarek's home colony, and he's graciously offered to help us create a tracking and defense system for Risa."

"I thought his mission was to pester me," Janaye scoffed. He spends more time in his chair than at that command center you built."

"Don't need to spend much time at the center, Jannie," the old man retorted. "I can work circles around these young starsnappers." He offered Eirene his hand. "Greetings, young lady. My, you're a looker. I'm allowed to say that 'cause I'm too old to do anything about it."

"You're too old to do anything," Janaye interjected tartly.

"Eh, what's that? I can't hear a thing you say, woman!"

Thoroughly charmed, Eirene took his hand. "It's nice to meet you, Elder Gabe."

"Would suit me fine if you'd call me Gabe." He gestured to the chair Moriah pulled up. "Sit down and make an old man happy."

Eirene sank gratefully into the chair. Already tiring, she let the emotions of the group drift over her. The children put out a different sort of energy from the adults, one that was exuberant and innocent, without any real fear or concerns.

She could also sense the feelings of all the women in the room, with the exception of Janaye. She wasn't surprised by Janaye's ability to block, because of the woman's obvious psychic power. Now she had to worry about Janaye discerning the truth about her being an Enhancer. She'd have to guard her own energies very carefully around the astute old woman, assuming she could.

The odd thing was she couldn't sense anything from the two men in the room. She knew it wasn't a male/female discrepancy, because she'd always been able to read the men on Travan; had picked up on many males on Saron and Elysia.

It might somehow be related to the Shielder race, only Eirene didn't know for a fact that all the men on Risa were Shielders. She didn't dare ask, because from what

Jarek had told her, Shielders didn't usually reveal their identities to outsiders. Too dangerous, just as it was for Enhancers.

Janaye reached over and took Eirene's hand. "Tell me, child, where are you from?"

Eirene felt the power subtly probing. She sat up straight, panic stirring. What could she say, without giving away information or making Janaye suspicious? She struggled to come up with an answer, but was saved by Jarek and Sabin's entrance.

Jarek's arrival created quite a stir. Everyone but Janaye and Gabe rushed to greet him. The women hugged him and fussed over him, while Ardon shook his hand and slapped him on the back. Even the children vied for his attention, tugging on his flightsuit until he swung each of them up in the air, amid squeals of delight.

He looked so different here, laughing with Tyna and Marna, smiling broadly as he teased the children. He seemed younger, happier, as if he'd forgotten his burdens for a brief time. His flashing smile and the sparkle in his eyes made him look even more handsome.

Eirene couldn't help but stare. She'd sensed Jarek's power and fortitude, but never comprehended how truly dynamic and charismatic he was. Here, the force of his presence lit up the hall, and everyone gravitated towards him. He was a true leader, she realized, with the heart and soul and courage to inspire others to follow.

"Impressive, isn't he?" Janaye murmured.

Startled, Eirene turned to see those discerning gray eyes fixed on her. "Yes, he is," she answered honestly, suspecting it was futile to deny the truth to Janaye.

Janaye's gaze returned to Jarek. "He's destined for greatness, that one. The stars were aligned with providence the day he was born."

A shiver went through Eirene and she wrapped her arms around herself. She could easily believe that Jarek would achieve monumental things, but she knew she wasn't the one to help him reach those heights of greatness. Her powers were worthless as long as she couldn't handle them—dangerous, even.

Jarek strode toward them, and Eirene's breath caught in her chest. She tried to ignore her reaction to him, reminding herself the only reason she was with him was because he had kidnapped her. He stopped by Janaye's chair and leaned down to kiss her.

"Ah, here's my favorite lady. I'll bet you've been flirting with all the men, breaking their hearts."

"Jarek, you charmer. I can understand why mothers hide their daughters when you come around." Janaye beamed at him with genuine affection. "You're looking good, young man. When are you going to settle down and give this old woman more children to love?"

"Maybe when mothers stop hiding their daughters," he teased, then squatted beside her. "How are you feeling?" He took both her hands in his, serious now. "Did the medicine Chase sent help any?"

Janaye shrugged away his concern. "Some. I'm just old, Jarek. My journey on this plane is winding down."

"Well, we'd like to keep you around a while longer. So you take care, okay?" He pressed his hand against Janaye's face, then rose to greet Gabe.

Gabe pushed to his feet and gave Jarek a big hug. "Good to see you, boy. Sad news about your father. He was a good man—damn good!"

Eirene started at this news. When had Jarek lost his father? She watched him and saw the shadow cross his face, the sadness that filled his dark eyes. "Yeah, he was a good man," Jarek said softly. "But in a way, I'm glad he won't be around to see what's coming."

Gabe's brow furrowed. "Don't tell me it's gotten worse. Blazing hells! How much more can we take?"

"Not much. But I've got a plan, sir. I'm hoping we can discuss it while I'm on Risa. I'd like your input."

Gabe beamed with pride. "Of course, Captain. I haven't planned any tactical maneuvers in a while, but I'd love to hear what you have in mind. You're a fine military commander. We're damn lucky to have you taking up where your father left off."

Jarek blew out his breath, his shoulders slumping. "I'm not so sure about that, Elder. If my ideas don't work, I fear for our survival."

He suddenly looked exhausted. Eirene knew he hadn't gotten much sleep during the trip from Elysia to Risa. He'd remained in the cockpit most of the time, on the lookout for more attacks. A surprising concern gnawed at her. Impulsively, she stood and pushed another chair into the circle, next to her own.

"Here," she offered. "Why don't you sit down?"

He flashed her a startled look, then nodded gratefully. "Thank you." He sank into the chair, absently rubbing his right arm.

Eirene knew the laser wound still hurt him. She'd put a fresh bandage on it this morning. It was healing, but still tender. Yet he'd managed to toss squealing, excited children into the air. She wondered if he ever put his own needs first.

"I see you've met Eirene." Jarek reached out, placing his hand on her arm. "I'm hoping she'll help us with my most crucial plan."

Eirene clenched her hands in her lap. He didn't play fair. He was as relentless as the sun's rays beating down on Travan's caked ground. She couldn't help him. Spirit, she hated being torn like this—hated her incompetence. But there was more than just the fact she couldn't control her powers. If the knowledge she was an Enhancer got out, it could only lead to one thing—a living hell in the clutches of the Controllers or some other faction just as evil.

"Yes," Janaye said slowly, catching everyone's attention. She stared straight ahead, seemingly at nothing, her eyes glazing. "Eirene has her own special destiny to fulfill."

Eirene turned from Janaye to find Jarek staring at her, determination heating his eyes. Great. Already, he was swaying Janaye to his side. Weary of the emotional tug-of-war, Eirene stood. "I'd like to go to my quarters now."

"The evening meal is ready," Moriah announced from the galley. "Come on, everyone."

The children shrieked their approval and raced for the tables, the adults following at a more leisurely pace. Gabe and Jarek helped Janaye to her feet. Leaning heavily on her thick yarton cane, she laboriously made her way to the tables, Gabe at her side.

Her chest tight with frustration, Eirene turned away, but Jarek caught her arm. She whirled, longing to inflict bodily damage upon him. Her fierce reaction startled her; she'd never been a violent person. "Let me go."

"I'm simply escorting you to the meal."

She couldn't sense his thoughts or feelings. Why then, did she have such strong emotional and physical reactions to him? She took the offensive, knowing no other way to defend herself against him. "I don't want you telling these people I'm working with you. What does it take to get the truth through your thick head? I can't help you!"

141

"Come on," he said quietly, ignoring her outburst and tugging her toward the tables. "Tyna and Marna are much better cooks than I am. And these are special people. You'll enjoy sharing this meal with them."

She *was* hungry, and Jarek's skill in the galley was limited to only a few dishes. Giving in, Eirene allowed him to lead her to a table. Dishes clattered and jovial voices filled the air as food was passed and the plates were filled. Then, at Janaye's command, a hush fell over the room, and she thanked Spirit for blessing them with food. The hubbub of voices resumed, and everyone dug in.

The food was simple, but good—fresh bread, cheese, and an assortment of vegetables. Eirene ate slowly, too intrigued by the social dynamics of the group to pay much attention to what was on her plate. The relaxed atmosphere and easy bantering between the men and women amazed her the most.

On Travan, there had been total segregation between males and females, except when the men visited the women's compound to appease their sexual urges. The men ate in their opulent dining hall, their food prepared by the women. After the men were seen to, the women gathered in small groups in their drafty tents and shared a much plainer fare than the men enjoyed.

But here, as on Saron and Elysia, men and women mingled freely and equally, with no sign of male dominance. The women outnumbered the men, and the men treated them with deference and respect. All the men but Elder Gabe and Jarek were mated, and they displayed a sincere affection and caring toward their mates. Eirene sensed no tension or strain from anyone, only a comfortable air of camaraderie.

The colony members appeared to be a cohesive, supportive group. They were like a large family, something she had never experienced. Feeling more out of place than ever, Eirene envied them. Her mother had died when she was an infant, and she'd never known her father very well. She'd always hoped they would have a relationship, but he'd left, then died six seasons ago.

With Rayna's passing, Eirene no longer had any emotional attachments to Travan. She'd never fit in with the other women in the compound, perhaps because of her unusual abilities. Outside her dwindling hopes of settling on Elysia, she had nowhere to go, no place where she belonged.

She remained quiet, only answering when spoken to. Oddly enough, no one pressed her about her past or her home. When the meal was over, she rose and started stacking dishes.

"Oh, no, you don't," Moriah said, coming up behind her. "We'll put you to work soon enough, I promise, but not tonight. The children are responsible for clearing the tables after each meal, and we have a rotating schedule for the chores that need to be done. You're not on the work detail—yet."

"Okay," Eirene conceded gratefully. She was tired, probably off balance from a new environment and meeting so many people.

"Would you like to go to your quarters now? You're welcome to remain in the hall and visit. Most of the adults will be up a while yet."

"My quarters, please," Eirene answered. She needed time to herself, to regroup and plan her next course of action.

"All right. I'll take you."

They walked outside. The temperature had cooled pleasantly, and Eirene drew in a deep breath. The air was fresh and clear, scented with the masses of huge flowers growing along the path.

"It's beautiful here," she told Moriah.

"Thanks. I think so, too." Moriah inhaled, lifting her eyes to the glittering heavens. "No matter how far I travel, this will always be home."

Home. Longing reverberated through Eirene. Longing for a safe haven. For the freedom to make her own choices and to lead a simple, fulfilling life. And now, after witnessing the closeness of these people, she realized she wanted something else. A place where she belonged.

Jarek watched Eirene leave the hall. She looked petite beside Moriah, dainty, yet well-curved. The tunic she wore hugged her figure, emphasizing her generous bust line and trim waist, while the leggings outlined her shapely legs. He felt the familiar tightening in his body and mentally clamped down on the unbidden urges.

He couldn't allow his desires to take precedence over duty. He didn't understand the pull he felt to Eirene, but there was no need to analyze it. He could never act on it.

She'd been quiet tonight, her expressive eyes large as she intently watched Risa's boisterous inhabitants at the evening meal. She'd ignored him, but then that was her usual reaction when she was upset.

"So she's the reason for your odd behavior."

Jarek turned to find Sabin watching him. "What do you mean?"

Sabin shrugged. "You hightailed it off Chase's ship when you were still as weak as a baby kerani, determined to return to Saron. Yet Chase said he distinctly heard Celie say the equipment you wanted was on Aldon. I figured something or *someone* on Saron must be critical to your plans if you went there first. And here you are, with Eirene. I've never known you to dally with any female, especially when our people are in dire need. Normally, I'd be inclined to assume her presence here is not personal—except now I see you watch her like a starving lanrax tracks a krat. Something must be up."

Was his fascination with Eirene that obvious? Wearily, Jarek rubbed his throbbing arm. "Speaking of lanraxes, I have one I need to unload from my ship. She's bound to be hungry and angry at me for leaving her."

Sabin raised dark eyebrows. "Avoiding my question?"

Jarek blew out his breath. "No. As a matter of fact, I'm going to need all the help I can get from you and Moriah. I intend to tell you everything."

"Sounds like a long and interesting story."

More like inconceivable . . . impossible . . . crazy. Jarek wondered how his friend was going to react to his wild speculations. "You may think I've lost my mind when I tell you my plan."

"I seriously doubt that. You're the most centered person I know." Sabin gestured toward the chairs in the middle of the hall. "Why don't I get us a drink? You can tell me about this plan of yours."

He was back in a moment, carrying a bottle of Elysian liquor and two glasses, and took the chair next to Jarek. He filled one glass and handed it to Jarek, then filled the second one for himself. Sitting back, he raised his glass. "To friendship. And to the survival of our people."

"I'll drink to that." Jarek took a sip, admiring the smoothness of the liquor. Moriah's delivery business ensured they had the best products available.

"So, tell me about it," Sabin urged.

"Won't Moriah be joining us?"

"No." Sabin shook his head ruefully. "With the pregnancy, she fatigues easily and usually retires early. If you need her input, we'll go over it again with her tomorrow. You can't leave until Radd gets back, anyway."

Jarek downed the rest of his drink. "Well, here goes," he muttered, and proceeded to tell Sabin his theory about the wormhole within the black hole, and its possible connection to the Enhancers.

He again went over being shot at the Pleasure Dome, explaining that Eirene had been nearby when it happened. He told Sabin about his belief she had healed him, and that she was an Enhancer. He did not volunteer the information that Eirene had actually been at the Dome in the role of a courtesan, or that she'd been a virgin.

Whatever conclusions Sabin drew about Eirene being in the Pleasure Dome, he didn't voice them. But he did listen intently, and sat in thoughtful silence for a long moment after Jarek finished. "That's quite a theory," he said finally. "I've heard tales about Enhancers, but I always wondered if there was any truth to them."

"The Shens seem to think they existed," Jarek observed.

"You have a point. And Moriah has a great deal of respect for the Shens, especially Eark. If he told Celie that equipment came from Enhancers, then there's a strong possibility the stories are true. Still, that doesn't mean any Enhancers exist in the present."

"There are a lot of stories circulating about Enhancers being discovered," Jarek argued. "Too many to discount. And there's the fact that my wound was healed by the time I reached Chase. That, and my memory of *Eirene healing me*."

"Damn, this is amazing," Sabin said.

Jarek leaned back and ran his hand through his hair. "So, do you think I'm crazy?"

Sabin sighed and stared at his glass. "No," he said slowly, looking up to meet Jarek's gaze. "You're not crazy, san Ranul. At least, I hope not. Because if you are, then I am, too. I'm actually starting to believe there could be Enhancers among us—and that your plan might work."

Chapter Eight

"We can dedicate all of the profits from the mercantile on Calt to the plan," Moriah said. "And divert the majority of what we make on deliveries for the next few lunar cycles."

"I'm hoping to purchase the equipment, assuming the Shens will sell it to me, much sooner than that," Jarek responded. "I don't think we can wait much longer. With the bounty on my head, and the Controllers' latest attacks, we have to move quickly."

Uncomfortable at being present at this financial summit between Jarek and Sabin and Moriah, Eirene tried once again to slide off the bench. Jarek's hand tightened on her arm. He had insisted she sit in on the meeting, saying she was an integral part of the plan. Sabin and Moriah hadn't questioned his decision, but Eirene thought he was taking a huge risk.

He knew nothing about her, nothing—he had only a

suspicion he couldn't prove. She could be in the employ of the Controllers, for all he knew. She could lead Antek forces to Risa and Aldon, and any other place Jarek was foolish enough to mention. Of course, that would be dependent on her escaping him.

Blowing out a frustrated breath, Eirene wrapped her hands around her cup of tea. Shafts of morning sunlight streamed through the high windows, creating brilliant squares on the tables. Voices drifted into the hall from the galley, along with the clattering of dishes being loaded into sterilizers.

The children sat quietly in the center of the room, their faces furrowed in concentration as they worked on lessons given to them by Roanne and Valene.

Janaye supervised the children, although she was nodding off in her chair. Immediately after the morning meal, Gabe had gone to the command center with Ardon to work on Risa's tracking and defense system. The day was well underway.

"I'll leave tomorrow," Sabin was saying, "and pursue the felons that are in the vicinity. I should be able to collect some bounties pretty quickly."

That caught Eirene's attention. *Bounties?* "Are you a shadower?" she blurted without thinking, then felt foolish. It was none of her business.

"He is, in a way," Moriah explained. "But he only hunts those criminals who have proven longstanding records of violence against the innocent, and the money he collects goes to the Shielders."

"But aren't all shadowers under mental compulsion to the Controllers?" Eirene asked, thoroughly confused.

Sabin obviously knew Jarek was a Shielder—it had been mentioned several times this morning. And Sabin was giving money to the Shielders, instead of turning them in. Jarek had explained to her how all Controller agents underwent indoctrination, so they'd be under mind domination.

"I'm also a Shielder," Sabin answered. "We're immune to the Controller indoctrination."

"Oh." Eirene considered this new information. That might explain why she couldn't read Sabin, either. Although she didn't know for certain, she was beginning to suspect she couldn't read any Shielders.

"Anyway," Sabin continued. "I might be able to collect some sizeable bounties."

"I don't even know how much gold we need," Jarek said, his frustration evident. "The Shens refused to tell Celie what they wanted for the equipment. For all I know, they've priced it out of reach."

"Then all we can do is collect as much as possible," Moriah said calmly. "We'll pool our resources and get you what we can. If it's not enough, then we'll keep working at it."

"You're right, Mori." Jarek looked from her to Sabin. "Thanks, both of you."

"Let's get to it." Sabin swung his leg over the bench and strode toward the entry. "I'll ready a ship to depart this evening."

Moriah stood as well. "I'll contact Adya and have her stop at Calt to collect whatever gold the mercantile has earned since the last pickup. We'll schedule collections every four cycles."

"As soon as your ship is repaired, you can head for Aldon," Sabin said. "We'll meet you there and bring any gold we manage to gather."

"Good idea. I need to contact Blake and the colonists on Liron," Jarek said, rising. "Then I'll see if I can do any of the ship repairs while I wait for Radd. And I can work wherever you need me, Mori."

"You're going to be very sorry you said that." Moriah flashed a stunning smile over her shoulder as she headed after Sabin. "I've got a dozen new yarton trees waiting to be planted."

"Me and my big mouth," Jarek groaned, following her outside.

Eirene slipped off the bench, feeling very insignificant.

"I'd really appreciate it, child, if you'd keep an old lady company."

She looked over to find Janaye awake and watching her shrewdly. The old woman gestured toward the children. "Besides, I can always use some help with these scamps." She leaned forward and addressed them. "Jarek said if you completed your lessons, he'd let you play with his lanrax. And it's a beautiful day. We'll go outside when you're done."

Four precious faces beamed at this news, then four heads bent back over their scanners.

Two hours later, Eirene and Janaye sat outside beneath a huge yarton tree, watching the children running and playing. Rani, exhausted from romping with the children, was curled in Eirene's lap.

Jarek drove a skimmer loaded with agricultural equipment and several saplings into the clearing on their right. He got out and unloaded a machine and the trees. The temperature was already warm, and rising. He stopped to peel off his shirt and toss it aside, his muscles flexing. Eirene tried not to look, but she couldn't take her eyes off him.

"Tell me about your power." Janaye's voice broke into her perusal.

She whirled toward the elderly woman. *"What?"*

Discerning gray eyes stared back at her. "Your power, my dear. It's quite apparent you have special gifts."

Panic rose swiftly, and tension spread through Eirene. She'd been afraid she couldn't hide anything from Janaye, and she'd been right. That didn't mean the woman knew her exact abilities, or that she was an Enhancer, Eirene tried to reassure herself. She probably only sensed the energy.

Resigned to Janaye's perceptiveness, Eirene said, "I can sometimes pick up emotions from others."

"Ah." Janaye nodded. "You're empathic. What else?"

Eirene debated whether to deny any other abilities. But she wanted badly to discuss her fears with someone. Rayna had been her only confidante, and she felt lost without her mentor. Janaye appeared to be so wise; surely she would understand. Taking a deep breath, Eirene took the plunge.

"Lady Janaye, you must promise not to tell anyone."

Janaye reached over and patted Eirene's hand. "Certainly, my dear. I've never discussed my abilities with others. Too dangerous. Those of us who are different in any way, be they Shielders, or psychic, or energy healers, are persecuted in this quadrant. Your secrets are safe with me."

Eirene believed her. Janaye had dropped her mental shields, allowing Eirene to sense her complete honesty and compassion.

Eirene stared at the sparkling lake. "I can manipulate energy—sometimes. But it terrifies me."

"Why?"

"For one thing, I don't know where this power came from. Is it a gift of Spirit, a chance to help others, or an evil tool from the Fires?"

"My dear, power is a very strange thing. It doesn't

really matter where it comes from, because all energy is basically the same. Energy can be channeled any number of ways, for good or for evil. When all is said and done, it's not the *source* of the power which matters, but how that power is *used*. That's what determines its nature."

She'd known that on some level, Eirene realized. Yet good intentions didn't make her proficient in the use of her abilities.

"But what if someone doesn't know how to properly use his or her power?" she asked. "What if they can't control it, and only cause bad things to happen when they try to use it? Isn't it evil, then?"

Janaye looked at her knowingly. "Power can't corrupt a pure heart, child. As for learning control, that comes with time, and with spiritual growth. You need to work on developing your soul growth. Take time every day to meditate, and commune with Spirit. Pray for guidance, and open yourself to receiving that guidance. Then watch carefully, because the answers often come in unexpected forms."

Just then, a resonant tone sounded from the main hall.

"There's the call for the midday meal." Janaye pushed to her feet. "Go get washed up, children." She turned to Eirene. "Don't worry so, my dear. All will be well."

Eirene followed her to the main hall, thinking about the elder's words. She wanted to believe Janaye, but doubts still nagged her. Perhaps she could develop control over time. But, in the meanwhile, what sort of damage might she inflict?

Celie arrived just as they were finishing the evening meal. They were alerted to the ship's approach by strident exterior sirens that had the children screaming and clapping their hands over their heads, and the adults cringing.

"Again?" Tyna bellowed in her gravelly voice. "Gabe doesn't know what he's doing, the old fool!"

"I don't think the kinks are out of your tracking system," Sabin yelled to Gabe over the racket.

"I don't understand," Gabe yelled back. "It shouldn't do that when one of our ships comes in. Radd rigged them with a special signal that should trigger a lower tone." He dashed off to the command center, Ardon on his heels.

Moments later, the awful clamor stopped, and everyone heaved a sigh of relief. "I'll go meet the ship," Moriah said, heading for the landing pad. Sabin followed.

Jarek took Eirene's arm and tugged her toward the entry. "Come on, let's go with them. I want to see if Celie has any news and to find out what happened with the Leors."

Eirene thought of the Leor who had been with her uncle on Elysia. He had looked utterly cruel and very dangerous. She shivered, and Jarek's hand tightened on her arm.

"Hey, you okay?"

He was far too perceptive, too attuned to her reactions. Her skin tingled from the warmth of his hand as he steadied her. Awareness, memories of far more intimate contact flowed through her. She had to stop thinking about that night in the Pleasure Dome. She needed to steel herself against his potent charm, and focus on putting distance between them.

"I'm fine," she murmured, tugging her arm away. "Just an aftershock from those sirens."

He grinned, and her heart skittered in that odd little reaction his smiles always generated. *Way too potent.*

"Yeah, they are pretty unsettling, aren't they? Poor

Gabe. I think his electronic skills may be lacking a little. But he's an incredible battle tactician."

She liked the gruff older man, and she suspected Janaye did as well, although she seemed determined to deny it. Thinking about the way those two bickered, Eirene smiled briefly, then slowed as another thought occurred to her.

"What are Celie and her crew going to think when they see me here? I was at the Pleasure Dome when they came to get you. They might recognize me."

"I'm sure they will," Jarek agreed. "They're very observant. They have to be, in their line of work."

"And they'll remember where they saw me." She couldn't explain why that fact disturbed her, since her actions had been to ensure her new-found freedom. But she was beginning to feel a bond with these people; oddly, their respect and acceptance mattered to her.

He halted and turned towards her. "Does that bother you?"

She lowered her eyes from his penetrating gaze. "I know it shouldn't. I made the decision to work at the Dome of my own free will."

"That's something I'm most interested in hearing more about. You and I both know being a courtesan is not your calling."

Anger and embarrassment sent heat flaming her cheeks. "I'm sure Celie and her crew will share your lurid curiosity. But you'll all be disappointed, because I don't have to explain myself to you or anyone else."

She tried to move around him, but he grasped her shoulders, bringing her square with his body. "I'm not judging you, Eirene." He slipped one hand beneath her chin, raising her face and forcing her to look at him.

"Neither is anyone on Risa. Every woman here has an

unhappy past. Some have suffered abuse at the hands of men, or society in general. Moriah and Celie were abused by their father, then sold into servitude. Tyna was a slave on Odera, Roanne was a slave in a textile plant. All the other women have stories just as tough. No one will question your actions or judge you based on your past. They'll accept you as you are now."

Eirene stared into his dark eyes, reading the sincerity there. She was stunned that these happy, energetic women had experienced such suffering; even more amazed that they generated no negative emotions after their life experiences.

"I had no idea," she murmured. "They've certainly overcome the past."

"That's Moriah's doing. She's a dreamer and believer. She brought these women together, created this sanctuary for them, and takes in anyone who comes to her in need."

Eirene's respect for Moriah increased tenfold. Was it really possible, she wondered, to create a reality if you wanted it badly enough? She fervently hoped so.

"Come on," Jarek turned her toward the landing strip and gave her a gentle push. "We don't want to miss anything."

The ship landed as they arrived at the pad. They remained a safe distance until the hoverlifts and thrusters disengaged.

Celie stepped out first, tall and slender, her blond hair flowing freely over her shoulders. When she saw Moriah, she ran down the ramp, and the two women hugged tightly. The first officer, the same woman who'd been with Celie on Travan and Saron, exited the ship next, her impressive height making Celie look small by comparison. Then came the young man Eirene had seen at the Pleasure Dome. Round-faced and freckled, he didn't look old enough to be a renowned starship mechanic, much less mated.

Celie stepped back and pushed her hair from her face. Sensing the young woman's distress, Eirene knew something was definitely wrong. Moriah, Sabin, and Jarek all watched the hatch, seemingly waiting for someone else to disembark.

"Where's Lani?" Moriah asked. "Did she return to Saron?"

Celie's face clouded, but before she could speak, the young man said, "She got taken hostage."

A flash of shock from Moriah bombarded Eirene. "What?"

"Gunnar took her hostage," the young blond man answered.

Moriah radiated stunned disbelief. "Gunnar took Lani? Why in the universe did he do that?"

"Mori, you're not going to believe this," Celie said, her voice shaky. "Commander Gunnar contacted me twice, upset and hostile. The first time, he asked me questions about my trip to Travan. Wanted to know if I'd taken a passenger with me when I left there. He didn't believe me when I told him no, threatened me if he found out I was lying."

Travan? An uneasy feeling settled in the pit of Eirene's stomach. Just who was this Gunnar, and why was he asking Celie questions about Travan, unless—

"The first time?" Sabin interjected, his eyes narrowed.

"Yes, there were two encounters," Celie said wearily.

Moriah slipped an arm around her sister. "He accused you of lying?"

Realization broadsided Eirene with sickening clarity. The only Leor who could possibly be asking Celie about a passenger from Travan, so soon after Eirene had left there, had to be the Leor who had entered into the bride bargain with her uncle. The Leor who intended to marry her.

"He warned me more than once of the consequences if I didn't tell him the truth." Celie's reply sounded far away to Eirene's stunned mind. She forced herself to focus, to listen and find out how much this Gunnar knew.

"But after we talked the first time, he seemed to accept what I told him," Celie continued.

"Which was?" Sabin prompted.

"That I had been to Travan, but I didn't carry any extra passengers when I left. At least, not any I knew of."

Oh, Spirit, Vaden and Gunnar had correctly deduced Eirene had been on Celie's ship. Worse, Gunnar apparently knew Celie and Moriah, and had been able to track down Celie. The poor young woman had taken the brunt of his wrath.

"Leor males are serpents," Celie's first officer announced, her voice deep and harsh. "Scum of the universe." She fingered the handle of a dagger sheathed at her waist, a ferocious gleam in her stunning aqua eyes. She emitted waves of savage aggression. "Every one of them deserves *kamta*."

"*Kamta* is the Zarian method of carving up their enemies," the young man explained to Eirene. "Lionia says that about anyone she doesn't like. By the way, I'm Radd."

With a start, she realized she could read him. He was calm and relaxed, radiating no tension at all. She could pick up his feelings when she couldn't read the other men. He must not be a Shielder.

Celie stared at Eirene, her expression confused. "Don't I know you?"

"You met her briefly on Saron," Jarek cut in. His arms folded across his chest, he stared at Eirene thoughtfully, then returned his attention to Celie. "Did Gunnar tell you anything about the passenger he was seeking?"

The air crystallized in Eirene's chest. *No. Don't take this any further.*

"Yes, as a matter of fact he did. He said he was looking for a female who'd been promised as his bride, a Lady Eirene. A woman with black hair and—" Celie faltered as her gaze swung back to Eirene. She frowned, her brows drawing together. "Blue eyes," she finished slowly.

Everyone stared at Eirene. She stood frozen, like a kerani in a trap, her heart pounding. Oh, Spirit . . . What now? She battled the inane urge to turn and run and keep running, but common sense told her she was trapped. Even so, she sidled away from the ship.

Moving smoothly behind her, Jarek cut off her only avenue of escape. He rested his hands on her shoulders, halting her movement. "There's nothing to fear. You're safe here with us."

"I think I know where I saw you," Celie said.

"The Pleasure Dome," Lionia said bluntly. "She was with Jarek when we got there."

"Are you from Travan?" Celie asked. "More importantly, did you stow away on my ship?"

Eirene nodded. "I'm sorry for the trouble I caused you."

"I think I'm starting to get the picture here," Moriah mused. "This isn't totally your fault, Eirene. You're not responsible for Gunnar's actions. He can get pretty aggressive."

"I'll say," Sabin snorted. "Celie, what happened the

second time Commander Gunnar contacted you?"

Celie tore her gaze from Eirene. "He didn't just contact me. His battleship intercepted my ship, and he demanded I allow him to dock and board."

Moriah looked genuinely shocked. "Gunnar did that? He hasn't done such a thing since—"

"He hit my ship with a photon blast six seasons ago," Sabin interjected. "I'm not surprised by what he did to Celie. What did he want this time?"

Celie flipped her hair over her shoulder. "He accused me outright of lying to him. He said he'd determined his bride had traveled to Saron, and that she disappeared the same day my ship left Travan. At first, he'd been willing to accept the fact that this woman had been a stowaway on my ship. But then I went to Saron, where I was seen with Jarek. Gunnar tracked the woman—I mean, Eirene—to Elysia. He claimed one of her uncle's associates saw her with Jarek on Elysia, but that they got away."

Eirene felt sick inside. Her carelessness had not only left a clear trail for her uncle to follow her, but had put innocent people at risk.

"Since Gunnar knows about our connection with Jarek," Celie continued, "he decided there was too much evidence to be coincidental, and that we were conspiring against him. He was ready to blow up our ship."

Eirene's heart leaped into overdrive, even though Celie's ship obviously hadn't been destroyed.

"Oh, Spirit!" Moriah gasped, her face pale. "I don't believe this."

"I do," Sabin said grimly. "The bastard thinks like a damned Controller."

"But he didn't follow through with his plan, thank Spirit," Moriah said. "Why did he change his mind?"

"I threw myself on his mercy. I reminded him that

we'd worked with his people over seven seasons, and our dealings had always been honorable. I appealed to his sense of justice."

"Did a very good job of it, too," Radd interjected. "She handled herself like a real professional."

"I didn't do well enough," Celie sighed. "Commander Gunnar refrained from detonating the ship, but he decided to take a hostage, in the event he discovered we had lied."

"Lani challenged the serpent," Lionia explained. "Showed *saktar*, great courage. He took her as his hostage."

"I insisted that I should be the one to go." Celie threw up her hands, her distress obvious. "As the ship's captain, it was my place to take the risk. But Lani insisted on pushing Gunnar, and he chose to take her. I think he had some idea of exacting retribution for her insulting him. Poor Lani."

Lani taken hostage! Eirene felt sick inside. This was all her fault.

"Nah. Quit frettin' about it, Captain," Radd said. "Lani will be just fine. She can take care of herself."

Everyone looked at him with skeptical expressions. Eirene thought of how petite and fragile the girl was, how large and fierce Gunnar had looked. She didn't see how Lani could survive an encounter with the barbaric Leors.

"Gotta admit, though," Radd continued, "I am a little worried about Gunnar."

"You call this a battleship?" Hands on her hips, Lani surveyed the corridor in disgust. "It's filthy!"

"Warriors do not do slave's work," Gunnar snapped. "The ship will be cleaned when we return to Dukkair." He swept his gaze contemptuously down her feathered

161

form. "Perhaps you should be assigned that duty."

Righteous indignation sizzled through Lani. The nerve of this savage! She wasn't lazy, and certainly didn't think cleaning was beneath her, but neither was she a slave. "Perhaps your men could benefit from the discipline of performing necessary tasks, no matter how menial," she retorted.

Two furrows appeared above the bridge of Gunnar's nose, and his eyes sparked with anger. The lack of eyebrows and the smooth dome of his well-shaped head lent him an exotic look. Lani decided she'd have to access a computer and do some research on Leors.

"We are exceedingly disciplined," he hissed. "We insist on rigorous training and personal self-sacrifice in our soldiers. No error or flaw is acceptable."

"Then I take it cleanliness is not considered a necessary trait."

Gunnar's face hardened even more. My, but the planes of his face were chiseled as beautifully as the rugged glaciers of Atara. Lani wondered if his ancestors might have come from the ice regions.

"We keep ourselves very clean," he gritted out. "But we do not perform slave labor."

"Well, I won't live in filth. If this situation can't be corrected, then I demand you return me to Celie Cameron's ship immediately."

"You are not in any position to make demands. You are a hostage. Perhaps a stint in the brig will clarify that fact."

"What? You expect me to stay in that hole? It's even filthier than this corridor! Is this how you treat people in your charge, Commander? With rudeness and negligence and squalor?"

"*You are a hostage!*" he roared, clenching his hands

into fists. "Not a guest on the High Commander's residential ship."

"I'm well aware that I'm a hostage," Lani huffed. "But I have rights. The Intergalactic Humanities Act from the Varian Summit of the fourth millennium clearly states—"

"The Intergalactic what?"

Gunnar was obviously becoming very distraught. His face was flushed and veins were bulging at his temples. Lani folded her hands primly. She refused to respond to raised voices and inappropriate language in any way but a cool and calm manner.

"Are you finished yelling?" she asked. "When you are, we'll continue this discussion in a civilized manner."

"Civilized?" he sneered. "This from an echobird who attacks at the first provocation. I have not forgotten the fist in my back or the heel in my leg—the touch of a weakling."

Lani narrowed her eyes. "That's because you're an arrogant, overbearing brute who likes to threaten and intimidate women. I wasn't about to stand there and let you browbeat a sweet young woman like Celie. Why, the girl—"

"Cease!" Gunnar rolled his eyes toward the ceiling, pinching the bridge of his nose. "Your strident chattering is beginning to wear on my patience."

Patience? The man wouldn't know patience if it blasted him in the rear—and a nicely muscled rear it was. She was on vacation, Lani reminded herself. Time to put the job aside for a while.

She launched back into the fray. "And your chauvinistic attitude towards women is beginning to really annoy me, Commander."

"Enough!" Gunnar held up his hand. "What will it take to stop your endless carping?"

"Two of your men and cleaning equipment at my disposal."

"You expect *my men* to clean this ship?"

"That would be a very courteous thing to offer, Commander."

"Will that shut you up?"

Lani drew herself up. "For now."

He growled—actually growled—like a wild tri-horned boar about to change. The timber of his voice reverberated through her, right down to her blue-tipped toes. My, but the man was primitive. Excitement shuddered through her.

His gaze boring into her, Gunnar raised his hand and snapped his fingers. "Karr, Feron, come! You are to assist this yapping echobird in cleaning the ship to her satisfaction. Then she will cease her complaints and we can continue our journey in peace."

Both men eyed him incredulously. "You are ordering us to *clean*, sir?" the one called Karr dared to ask.

"You will not question my orders!" Gunnar roared. "Obey immediately or face charges of treason."

The two soldiers snapped to attention, each crossing one arm over his chest. "As you wish, Commander."

"Thank you," Lani told Gunnar. If he could concede to her, however ungraciously, then she should show the proper courtesy. No one had any manners anymore.

He turned away with a grunt.

"We need cleaning supplies," she told Gunnar's lackeys. They grumbled beneath their breath as she followed them down the corridor.

Lani smiled to herself. She knew something no savage warrior would ever admit—the bigger they were, the harder they fell.

Chapter Nine

Eirene slipped away while everyone was at the main hall, discussing what had happened to Celie and her crew, and what Gunnar's next move might be. No doubt they would talk about Eirene after she left the hall. She had been well aware of the curious stares, the speculation. She desperately needed to be alone, without others' emotions pressing in on her.

Once outside, she headed for the lake. She moved through the copse of trees, toward the shimmering, beckoning water. Since Celie's arrival, the little bit of peace Eirene had found on Risa had dissipated. Feeling emotionally battered and vulnerable, she sought a place to replenish herself. The water seemed to have an energy, psychic and spiritual, that drew Eirene like a starflower to the sun.

She was within ten meters of the lake now. Stepping from the shelter of the trees, she moved to the water's edge. She understood it wasn't a large lake, but it looked huge to her because she'd never seen anything like it. She sank down on the sandy strip rimming it, and slipped her hand into the blue water. Despite the dispersing heat of the day, it was cool, calming.

Closing her eyes, she swished her hand through the water, letting the peaceful sound sooth her soul. Spirit, but she'd made a fine mess of things. She hadn't thought to disguise herself or use a different name when she fled Travan, so she'd left a clear trail for her uncle.

Her actions had put Celie and her crew in danger, and led to Lani being taken hostage. And to top off a bad situation, Eirene was just as helpless, just as much a prisoner here, as she'd been on Travan. How could things have reached this point?

She longed for Rayna. Her mentor would have soothed her and shared gems of wisdom and guidance. But Rayna was gone, her life worn away by hard work and harsh living conditions—and by Eirene's foolish attempt to use her powers. Renewed grief washed over Eirene. Drawing up her legs, she wrapped her arms around them and rested her chin on her knees.

She sat that way a long time, allowing the fresh air and the water's energy to ease the edge off the terrible pain. A sudden awareness of another presence jolted her out of her lethargy. She raised her head as Jarek stepped from the trees. A small dark form scurried after him— Rani.

Why couldn't he leave her alone? The least he could do was allow her some solitude. But he gave her no respite, moving to her side and squatting down.

"Are you okay?" he asked.

She shrugged and stared out across the water. She felt rather than saw him settle on the sand beside her, stretching out his legs. She heard the deep inhalation and exhalation of his breath, felt her body stir in acute awareness of his closeness.

"Why don't you tell me the whole story?"

Her frustration and guilt boiled over. "What would it accomplish? Lani's already been taken hostage." A horrible thought occurred to her. What if Gunnar knew about Risa? If he did, then he was certain to come here, because of Jarek's connection with Moriah and Celie. That would endanger the entire community on Risa. She whirled toward him, panic churning.

"Spirit, Gunnar is probably headed for Risa."

"Possibly." Seemingly unconcerned, Jarek pried Rani from his arm and settled her on his lap. "But I don't come here that often. He's more likely to go to Liron. However, I'd venture a guess he's not the only one you have to worry about. The truth, Eirene. That's what I want right now."

She stared down at her hands. A part of her longed to rest her head on his shoulder, to feel the comfort of his arms around her. To share the burden of her fears and her guilt. Yet she wasn't ready to tell him everything. Trust came hard after a lifetime on Travan.

"If you'll tell me the truth," he persisted, "I can protect you better."

"What about Lani, or the people here on Risa? What if the truth only puts them in more danger?" *What if the truth takes away my only hope of freedom for good?*

Jarek swung around on the sand so that he was facing her. Falling onto the ground, Rani squealed in protest, and darted around to reposition herself on his lap. He leaned forward, his dark eyes burning into Eirene's.

"Knowledge is power. Ignorance only breeds disaster. If I know who is after you and why, I can plan for contingencies. Hopefully, I can keep you safe. I think I already know most of your story, anyway."

The familiar panic flared. She felt uprooted, exposed, with no safe haven in sight. Her hands clenched tighter.

"It appears you were promised as a bride to Commander Gunnar of Dukkair, probably in some sort of trade, since that's how Leors get a lot of their mates," Jarek continued. "You didn't want to be forced into marriage with a Leor. Perhaps you were afraid he would discover you were an Enhancer. You escaped from Travan by stowing away on Celie's ship and traveling to Saron."

He had an uncanny knack for ferreting out the truth. A terrifying aptitude, actually. Drawing a shaky breath, she shifted her gaze to the water.

"I just did some research on Travan," he said. "The women there basically have no more rights than slaves. They're often traded in business dealings. Is that what happened, Eirene?"

The noose around her neck tightened. The chance at freedom grew more elusive, more fleeting, with every passing moment. And yet, what was the sense in denying what he already knew, could confirm if he wanted to?

"Yes," she whispered.

"You arrived at Saron and hired on at the Pleasure Dome. I think I know why you did that."

The reminder of the Pleasure Dome flashed vivid images through her mind; Jarek lowering his body over hers, kissing her, possessing her in the most fundamental way a man could claim a woman. No . . . she refused to dwell on those events.

"The problem is, you think you know everything about me," she snapped, goaded beyond her endurance. She glared at him defiantly. "But you could be wrong, you know."

He watched her, his expression unreadable. "About you being an Enhancer? I don't think so. The more I'm around you, the more certain I am."

"None of that concerns you." She scrambled to her feet.

With light-speed reflexes, he was up beside her. "You can't tell me I'm not involved, because I damn well am."

"Only because you want something from me—something I can't give you." She tried to walk away but he grabbed her arm and pulled her back.

His magnasteel grip forced her to turn, drew her to rest against the hard planes of his body. "Look at me, Eirene."

Reluctantly, she found herself responding to the command in his voice and raised her gaze to his. Heated emotion sparked in his eyes.

"I'm involved because I took your virginity. Because you saved my life. And yes, because I need you, damn it."

The rough, honest words touched off disconcerting longings deep within her. For a brief moment, she wondered what it would be like to have Jarek need her for the woman she was, not for *what* she was—a freak who couldn't control her powers.

She silently cursed the Pleasure Dome and the necessity that had taken her there. If not for that, she wouldn't be in this predicament. "That stupid virginity caused a lot of trouble," she muttered.

Surprise crossed Jarek's face, then his lips twitched. She had the distinct impression he was battling a smile. Her heart strangely lightened by the inanity of her remark, she had to suppress her own smile.

"I think of it more as divine intervention," he said. "Let me guess. You took that job as a courtesan to get

169

rid of your virginity, so Gunnar would no longer want you for his bride."

Again, no sense in denying his conclusion. She sighed. "I didn't want my life decided for me. I still don't. And it doesn't matter what happened at the Pleasure Dome."

"It does matter, Eirene." He slid his hand upward to cradle the side of her face. "I'm honored that I was your first. I blundered it badly, and I hurt you. I'm sorry about that."

Shifting, he drew her closer. He was so solid, so warm . . . so aroused. Awareness, fueled by memories of him stroking her body, of him pressing his mouth against her bare skin, snaked through her, alluring and dangerous.

"Even so," he whispered, lowering his head, his lips hovering an atom's-breadth from hers, "I'm glad I was the first."

Spirit, but her heart was pounding. A tidal wave of desire roared through her veins, blotting out rational thought. She wanted him to kiss her. She wanted to taste him, to run her hands over the muscled expanse of his body. Wanted him to touch her like he had at the Dome.

And he knew it, too. A possessive, triumphant light gleamed in his eyes. Then his mouth settled over hers, confident and sure. He slid his arms around her, and his tongue teased her lips, slipped between them. She opened for him, allowed his invasion of her mouth. At the touch of his tongue against hers, electricity arced through her.

Her equilibrium totally blasted, she clutched the front of his flightsuit. She savored the taste of him, clean and fresh; the feel of him, the warmth radiating from his hard body. Desire surged through her, intense and terrifying, yet like a magnetic undertow she couldn't resist. Didn't want to resist—

Rani's shrill cry pierced the air. Sharp claws pierced

Eirene's shoulder as the lanrax leaped between them, protesting indignantly. Jarek drew back. "What the blazing hells—"

"Sorry to bother ya," came Radd's apologetic voice. "But I wanted to tell ya I looked over the damage to your ship."

Jarek released Eirene, and she stumbled back, dragging air into her lungs. Standing at the edge of the tree line, Radd offered a crooked grin. "Didn't expect to find this. We can talk about your ship later."

Her head clearing, Eirene was appalled at her response to Jarek, at her own behavior. What was wrong with her? She was off balance, uncertain and in a strange environment, she told herself. That would explain this momentary insanity.

She edged away from the men. "I've got cleanup detail. I need to get back to the hall."

Jarek held out a detaining hand. "Wait. I want us both to hear what Radd says about the ship. You're in on this, too, Eirene."

She started to protest that she didn't want to be in on anything, wanted nothing to do with Radd or Jarek or his ship. But, looking at Radd's inquisitive face, she clamped her mouth shut. Too many people already knew far too much about her, and she had no desire to impart further information. Blowing out her breath, she waited.

Radd stepped forward, and Rani crouched low on Jarek's shoulder, hissing. "Not much to tell," Radd said. "Most of the damage was to your starboard bay, with a little to the thruster and the hoverlift on that side. I'll get right on it, and knock it out in a few hours."

"Good," Jarek said. "I appreciate that, Radd. Then we'll be able to leave tomorrow." His gaze met Eirene's, challenging, in command. "We'll go directly to Aldon."

His statement jolted through her like a blaster. No stops for supplies or anything else. No chance to escape him. She stood silently, trying to think of something—anything—to thwart his plans.

Radd nodded, seemingly unaware of the tension between Jarek and Eirene. "I'll tell the group to start loadin' supplies for ya. And I want to donate some of my personal funds."

"Radd, you don't have to—"

"I intend to do it. No problem."

"That's great," Jarek said sincerely. "You don't know how much that means."

"It's nothin'. See ya back at the ship." Humming a little tune, Radd strolled off.

Determined Jarek wouldn't throw her off balance again, wouldn't have any further effect on her rebellious body, she started after Radd.

"I didn't take you for a coward, Eirene."

She halted, challenged by the taunt. She'd escaped her uncle, found her way in a strange world, tried to ensure her freedom the best way she knew how. She'd resisted Jarek's trickery, escaped from him once, almost fallen into the hands of her uncle and a Leor. She'd been shot at, had treated Jarek's wounds. She was *not* a coward.

Now she battled a more insidious threat—one that was inexplicable and intangible. She would not run—she'd diffuse the attraction between Jarek and herself now. She faced him.

"I'm not a coward," she told him icily. "But I refuse to fall victim to male lust."

"You think that's all there is between us—lust?"

"What else could there be?"

He studied her speculatively. "Sounds to me like negative experiences with men have influenced your thinking. Among Shielders, women are treated as equals, and with respect."

"Are they held prisoner against their will?"

"Point well-taken," Jarek conceded. Dropping Rani gently to the ground, he started towards her. She took a step back, then forced herself to stop. She refused to retreat from him. But her heart started pounding again, and when he reached her, that disconcerting warmth flooded her body. Her senses went on full alert.

He slid his hands over her shoulders, and she had to tilt her head to look up at him. His gaze, heated mahogany, bored into her. "I was out of line when I kissed you on the ship, because you weren't ready for anything like that. But I won't apologize for tonight. You wanted that kiss as much as I did."

Again, she was stunned, and appalled that he could read her so well. "You're wrong," she protested. "You can't possibly know what I feel or think."

"I know a lot more than you would like me to know. Tell you what, little one. After we complete our mission—Spirit willing that we do—I'll give you back your freedom. And then maybe we'll explore this so-called 'lust' we seem to experience when we're together. I think you might be very surprised at what we find."

This time, any response deserted her completely. She could only stare at him, shocked by his words, while her body hummed from his nearness. He stepped back, and she felt oddly bereft at the loss of his touch.

Then he was gone, striding through the trees without a backward glance. Rani darted after him. Eirene was left alone with her tumultuous thoughts and traitorous body.

She would control her reactions, she vowed. She knew she couldn't stay with Jarek. He threatened her on too many levels. She couldn't provide what he needed, and he couldn't give her the things she yearned for. She had to get free of him—not only physically, but emotionally. And soon.

Jarek breathed a sigh of relief when they cleared Risa's gravitational field. His ship was flying smoothly, his detection system showed no other craft in the vicinity, and Eirene was with him. Not that she could have escaped from Risa. Fairly certain she didn't know how to pilot a ship, but taking no chances, he'd implemented some precautionary measures. The first night on Risa, he and Sabin had installed additional override codes on all the spacecraft on Risa. There was no way Eirene could have commandeered a ship.

The skimmers had been secured as well, so she couldn't leave the general vicinity. Jarek had been confident he could find her anywhere within the colony. If anything, he was even more attuned to her unique energy, could locate and track it easily. Oddly enough, Sabin and the other Shielders weren't able to pick up on it as readily, although Sabin could sense the energy when he concentrated.

Jarek looked over at Eirene. She sat stiffly, staring out the portal, cool, beautiful, distant. She wore the deep blue robe Roanne had given her before they left Risa. Her energy fluctuated erratically, as it seemed to do when she was particularly upset—usually with him. The two of them certainly had a volatile relationship. But that wasn't unusual when emotions ran high, which they invariably did where Eirene was concerned.

He had trouble maintaining his normally cool and lucid control, both over his thoughts and his body, when she was around. Leaning back, he ran his hand through his hair. Perhaps it was best that Eirene was determined to erect emotional walls between them. He needed no distractions, especially with so many concerns pressing in on him.

The gold he had available to offer the Shens for the equipment was not a substantial amount. Sabin and Blake would be meeting him at Aldon to deliver any additional funds they'd been able to collect, but that would have to be enough. Even if they did manage to get the machinery, there was no guarantee that it would work, that Eirene would help him, or that his theory was even remotely correct.

He'd know the outcome soon enough. Grimly, he leaned forward to lock in the coordinates to Aldon. "You can take off your harness now," he told Eirene.

She undid the magnetic clasp. "I'm going to my cabin."

She wanted to distance herself from him, while he wanted her in the cockpit with him. He tried to tell himself it was so he could keep an eye on her, but he knew better. He wanted her near, wanted to feel her energy, to gaze into her remarkable eyes. He wanted to hear her voice and, Spirit help him, feel her touch.

He didn't want to be alone anymore.

His thoughts were traversing a dangerous path, one he didn't dare take. His commitments necessitated a solitary existence, and he'd accepted that fact—up until now.

He nodded his head. "Okay."

She rose and quickly left the cockpit. As the panel slid shut behind her, Rani began squealing. Maybe some good had come out of chasing after Eirene. Jarek reached down and released the lanrax from the padded pouch he'd secured on the side of the main console. Rani climbed his leg and settled in his lap, chattering contentedly. At least he wasn't completely alone. He'd never in a hundred light years imagined a lanrax might keep him from the abyss of total emotional desolation, but it was so.

Activating the automatic controls, Jarek settled back and stared out at the dark depths of space. He did this often on long trips, his gaze fixed on the stars while he mentally sifted through the many decisions he had to weigh and consider, reviewed his immediate and long-term plans, listed whom he needed to contact, what orders to issue.

He didn't know how long he'd been in his reverie when the alert went off, its harsh clanging jarring him from his thoughts. Jarek lurched forward, quickly shifting to present mode and reading the monitors. Blazing hells.

Two ships were bearing down on him, both larger than his own craft, both heavily armed. And both of them had their armaments activated. Where had they come from? He should have picked them up sooner, unless they had stealth capability. That could mean they were space pirates, Anteks, or worse, Controllers. Damn.

His subspace transceiver beeped, universal frequency. So the bastards wanted to talk to him. He activated Radd's program, although he didn't see how he could disable two ships, then punched the comm button.

"Who are you and what do you want?" he demanded.

He didn't activate the camera on his videoviewer, so his assailants couldn't see him. But his screen flashed on, revealing a man with heavy jowls and small dull eyes. Probably part Antek, like Turlock.

"Greetings," the man hissed, showing rotten teeth. "San Ranul, we presume. Turlock informed us you might hide on Risa."

How could Turlock have possibly known that? The

Leors were aware of Jarek's link with Moriah and Sabin, but that was it. Jarek made it a point to keep even his own people in the dark about his connections and activities—for everyone's protection.

He would not deny his identity this time. Even if he convinced these thugs it wasn't him they wanted, they wouldn't let him go. They'd murder him and confiscate his ship. Turlock always operated that way. Then they'd descend on Risa, looking for Jarek.

"Why didn't Turlock come after me himself?" he challenged, trying to buy time. "Afraid, after what happened our last encounter?"

"It's a big quadrant. Turlock's been looking other places. Figured you'd come out of your hole sooner or later."

Jarek studied the position of the two ships, his gut clenching. By the Fires! He was situated between them. Even if Radd's data revealed a weakness in their ship structures, he couldn't disable both of them. The millisecond he fired, they'd retaliate with deadly force. That would be preferable to capture, but there was one problem. Eirene was on board.

"San Ranul? You there?"

What now? Jarek rapidly considered possible options. He would never allow Turlock's thugs to take him into custody. And neither was there any way he could allow Eirene to fall into their hands. That would be unthinkable. He knew all too well how most renegades treated women.

"Answer me, san Ranul!"

"I'm here," he replied, still sifting through solutions. "Care to share your plans for me?"

"Glad to see you've got enough sense not to fire on us. Would hate to send you to the Fires on a torpedo."

"The Controllers don't pay bounties on debris," Jarek retorted. "Besides, I'm worth a lot more alive."

He'd sworn he'd never be taken alive. He knew too much, had information that would bring total and final destruction on the Shielders if it fell into the wrong hands. He'd taken precautions in the event he was captured, more so since the bounty had been issued on his head. If he disappeared, Liron and other colonies would be evacuated to sites known only to Jarek's chief officers. He himself didn't know those locations. He'd also undergone rigorous training to ensure his resistance to drugs and torture.

Despite the careful strategy, there was no guarantee that he wouldn't crack under torture; or that all Shielders could find a new place to hide, or reach alternate sites quickly enough. He had always planned on ending his own life if necessary. Too much risk to his people otherwise. It saddened him that he had come to this point. He thought of beloved family and friends, all that he had shared with them. And of the possible solution for Shielder salvation, so close, almost within his grasp. So close, yet out of reach.

And there was another consideration. Eirene. She was possibly the only hope remaining for the Shielders. In the event anything happened to Jarek, Sabin had instructions to find her and carry out the plan to locate the wormhole.

Jarek still had no tangible evidence to support his theory, but he knew with every cell of his being that an Enhancer would be key in operating that equipment on Aldon. Research into the little-known details on the Enhancers had indicated that their equipment had been operated on mental power, rather than artificial, or solar and wind sources.

Also, Enhancer or not, he simply couldn't bear the

thought of Eirene being tortured or raped—or her life snuffed out. Not now. Not ever.

"Yeah," the hideous male on the screen growled. "Turlock wants you alive. We're taking you to Saron. He'll meet us there."

Sabin felt the ship lurch, heard the clank against the hull. A magnetic grappler had attached to his ship. He didn't have long.

"We'll be boarding immediately, and we'll be heavily armed," Turlock's man warned. "Don't try anything, san Ranul."

Jarek turned off the comm and raced to Eirene's cabin, urgency pounding through his veins. She whirled from the portal when he entered her cabin. Her face was pale and drawn.

"There are flashing lights out there, and it feels—" She stopped abruptly. "What's going on?"

"The ship is about to be boarded. We don't have much time." Jarek grabbed the satchel containing her things and took her arm, pulling her toward the corridor. "Come on."

She stumbled after him. "Boarded? Are these my uncle's men?"

"No. It's me they're after. Hopefully, they know nothing about you."

"Then they're bounty hunters." She tried to slow, but he pulled her along.

"Yes—they're Turlock's men. And they're planning on taking me to Saron."

Jarek entered the galley and turned to Eirene. Her eyes were huge in her ashen face. The ship jolted and he grabbed her to steady her. Turlock's henchmen were docking. They only had a few moments until the airlock pressure stabilized, and they forced the entry.

"Listen carefully. We have two things in our favor. The first is that they will expect me to be alone, because I've always traveled alone. The second is that Turlock keeps the ships of his victims. He's creating a major fleet. They'll pilot this ship to Saron."

She stared at him, listening intently. Her chest heaved, and her energy spiked to high levels. Jarek wished he had time to reassure her.

"I'm going to hide you. Most of our ships have concealed storage areas, a trick Moriah showed us. There's one in this galley, and it's stocked with food and water, for a situation such as this."

He reached behind the replicator and pushed a pad. A section of panel swung out, replicator and all, revealing a compartment large enough to hold weapons, gold, supplies—or two people.

Eirene hitched a breath. "You want me to hide in there?"

"Yes, and quickly."

"But—"

"No arguments. Please, Eirene. We don't have time. Wait until it feels like the ship has landed. There's a release on the inside which will open the panel. Come out when you think it's clear. Use your powers to guide you. You'll know if others are nearby."

Her troubled gaze searched his face. "But what about you?"

"I'll be fine," he lied. He would say anything to get her safely inside.

"Jarek." She touched his face, and the force of his feelings hit him like a photon blast.

He cared deeply for her, far more than he would ordinarily ever admit. Far more than he had ever cared for any woman. Spirit, how he hated to leave her.

He tossed her satchel into the compartment. Pulling her into his arms, he held her tightly for a moment of eternity that would never be long enough. Then he lifted her chin and kissed her, brief but deep, dipping inside her mouth for a taste of her to carry with him.

The airlock tone sounded. Reluctantly, he released her, giving her a gentle shove. "Now get in there. Quickly."

She stepped inside, turned to look at him. Rani chattered, and he looked down to see the lanrax at his feet. He scooped her up and tossed her in with Eirene.

"The compartment is soundproof. They won't be able to hear you in there. But you can hear them. There is a speaker on the inside panel which will allow you to monitor anyone who might be on board."

He paused, drinking in one last look. He'd never see her again, at least not in this physical plane. "*Use your powers*. Spirit gave them to you for a purpose."

Her unwavering gaze never left him as the panel swung shut. Breathing a sigh of relief that she was safely hidden, he stepped into the corridor. He didn't want to end his life so close to where she was. Didn't want to draw Turlock's men to the galley, or for Eirene to possibly sense what was happening.

He'd have been long gone from this existence by now, if her safety hadn't been of paramount importance, but he still had time to do what must be done. He figured Turlock's men would gas his ship before they boarded, to prevent him from firing upon them. It would give his system a nasty jolt, but it wouldn't matter, because the poison was fast-acting.

He slid the tiny capsule from his front pocket. Such a small thing to be so deadly. He thought of his sister and his mother, nieces and nephews; of his best friends, Sabin and Blake; of Eirene. He felt sadness, and regret—for so many things, especially for dragging her into this situation.

No more time.

Good-bye, Eirene. Be safe.

He raised the capsule to his mouth.

Chapter Ten

The cycles spent in the compartment were the worst in Eirene's life, even though the conditions weren't that bad. Light strips provided faint illumination. She had sufficient food and water, and blankets to offer padding for sitting and resting. Rani had been content enough, as long as she was being held or petted.

But the horror of possible discovery, and an untenable certainty about Jarek's fate gnawed at Eirene incessantly. She couldn't stop thinking about how he had looked as the panel closed between them. His eyes had reflected a kaleidoscope of emotions, among them longing and desire. But it was the resignation she'd seen in those dark eyes that tore at her soul.

He knew he wouldn't survive this encounter with the bounty hunters, despite his bravado. They'd both known it, both known he was lying for her benefit. She felt certain he wouldn't allow himself to be captured alive, not with his knowledge of Shielder activities.

A hero. Jarek san Ranul was a true hero, a type of man she'd never imagined existed until she escaped the confines of Travan. In the darkness of her cramped quarters, she finally admitted to herself how much she admired and respected him, how much he'd come to mean to her in the short time she had known him. She'd never imagined she could care for any man. Her experiences on Travan and Rayna's dire warnings had entrenched distrust from an early age.

But Jarek had broken that mold, proven that Rayna's convictions didn't apply in every instance. He had captured her heart. And now he was gone.

Eirene grieved during those long, dark hours in her hiding place. She grieved for Jarek, for the Shielder race that needed his courage and vision so desperately, and for a world in dire need of healing.

Emotionally exhausted, she lay quietly, occasionally listening to the cruel, harsh voices of the two men who had boarded the ship and were now taking it to Saron. She avoided touching them mentally, as they radiated evil, insidious vibrations.

The ultimate irony of the situation was that Jarek's last act had given her what she'd wanted her entire life, what she'd wished for so adamantly while she'd been with him—a chance at freedom. With him gone, she finally understood that realizing a dream could bring pain as well as joy. She hugged Rani close as tears clogged her throat.

"Thank you, Jarek," she whispered.

The hours crawled past. She had no idea how long she'd been confined when a sharp angling of the ship and much turbulence told her they were descending. Rani squealed in alarm, and Eirene snuggled her close, remembering how the little creature had clung to Jarek's legs and arms, always anxious to be near him.

The ship leveled out, and the hoverlifts switched on in a muted roar. The ship lowered until it jolted onto the landing pad. Moments later, the engines cut off, and an eerie silence replaced the noise. Eirene switched on the speakers and listened, anxious to know when the ship would be empty, and she could leave.

"Well, we made it," grunted a rough male voice.

"No thanks to you, Keraat. I've seen a blind child fly a ship better than you."

"Shut up, you son of an Antek. We're here aren't we? And we managed to take san Ranul alive. Turlock will be pleased."

Alive? Jarek was alive? Eirene leaned against the wall, stunned and disbelieving. Her heart skittered and a thrill of happiness shot through her.

"He will, at that," the second man responded. "Alive, San Ranul is worth an extra five thousand miterons. Our take will be higher."

Jarek was alive! She had assumed he would battle his captors, that he would be killed. Surely he would have found sacrificing his life preferable to being taken alive and creating greater risks for his people.

Despite the dangers Jarek now faced, she couldn't deny her happiness that he was living. Excitement buoyed her, gave her a surge of strength.

"Wonder why he came along so easily, without a fight? Guess them stories of him being so dangerous was just rumors."

"You never know. Ardonite gas takes the battle right out of 'em, even Shielders. Balen says san Ranul is still pretty indisposed."

185

Eirene's thoughts whirled, as she considered the situation. Was there any way she could help him? She didn't know how to contact Sabin and Moriah, so she couldn't get outside help. She was on her own—assuming she was able to get off the ship without being seen. And assuming she could locate Jarek. Then she'd still have to get past the men guarding him, and find some way to get him free.

Use your powers. His final words came back to her. He'd known she would face challenges, and he'd urged her to use her abilities.

She was terrified of her powers, and with good reason. Rayna might still be alive, if not for her mistake. Eirene had managed to heal Jarek without major mishap. She'd employed her powers again to escape from his ship on Elysia, although they hadn't worked very well on that attempt. The bottom line was, as dangerous as she knew her powers to be, she only dared use them when there was nothing left to lose.

Jarek would be tortured and executed for certain if he couldn't get away from these bounty hunters. She would have to risk using her powers to help him. But first, she had to get off the ship and find him. Keeping the speaker on, Eirene settled down and waited. She heard the men shuffling around and muttering to each other.

This time she deliberately reached out, tapping into their thoughts and energies, in the hopes they would lead her to Jarek. They were dark, depraved beings, and she wanted to cringe away from them, but she persisted, although she gleaned no usable information.

After awhile, their voices faded away, as did their energy patterns. The ship was silent. She did another mental sweep, feeling nothing. They were gone.

She scrambled from her hiding place, determined to

leave quickly and follow. But she was stiff from her cramped quarters, and the galley's bright light painfully bombarded her eyes. Squinting, she groped for her satchel.

Rani chattered anxiously, and Eirene tucked the creature beneath her other arm. She briefly considered leaving Rani there, but decided against it. She might not get back to the ship, or the men might return. She made a quick stop in the cockpit to retrieve Rani's padded knapsack and slipped the protesting lanrax inside.

Eirene bolted off the ship, grateful no one stood on guard. She glanced in all directions, trying to pick up the two men. Too many ships crowded the landing bay, and a good number of beings milling around. She couldn't lose the men, or she'd never find Jarek. She closed her eyes and stood still, concentrating, reaching. She picked up a lot of energies, much of it degenerate, but she was learning to distinguish individual patterns.

There—the same tainted energy she'd felt on Jarek's ship. She whirled around, her focus honing on two walking men, already halfway across the landing bay. Eirene took off at a full run, zig-zagging through the crowd. Rani squealed in alarm.

Spirit, don't let them get away, she prayed. She ran until her lungs burned, yet still lagged behind the men. They turned up a ramp, entering a red-and-black ship several pads down. She slowed, gasping for breath, and approached the ship cautiously, Rani still squealing.

"Hush," Eirene admonished, and the lanrax calmed somewhat.

Eirene stared at the ship the two men had entered. She needed a plan. And fast.

*   *   *

Lani's high heels tapped down the gleaming corridor. She glanced around in satisfaction. The Leors employed abhorrent color schemes in their ships, either orange or red—or in some appalling cases, both. But even such an awful decor looked better when it was properly maintained. Gunnar had assigned Karr and Feron to daily cleanup detail, much to their disgust, and to snickering from the other two crew members.

The regimen wouldn't hurt them in the least, Lani thought. While the Leors were highly disciplined about physical fitness and battle readiness, they were sadly lacking in other areas. For one thing, they were uptight, pompous, and unimaginative. They never enjoyed any amusement activities, as far as she could tell.

She pursed her lips. She was utterly bored. This last part of her vacation wasn't nearly as interesting as she had hoped it would be, with the exception of Gunnar. The only time she had any fun at all was when she verbally sparred with him.

She paused outside his council chamber and smoothed her simple Saija silk shift. The Leors kept the temperature on the ship much too high. She understood the reason, having done some extensive research on them since she'd been on board.

Leors descended from a race of beings resulting from a reptilian species cross-breeding with humanoids. They didn't have internal temperature regulators, and relied on external heat sources. Their special skin absorbed heat readily, so they wore minimal clothing and kept their environment very warm. Lani found all this fascinating, but it didn't make her any more comfortable.

She'd been forced to abandon her robes and most of her feathers. She now wore her skimpiest clothing, and today, she'd put her hair up, sacrificing fashion in the interest of comfort. After all, she was highly adaptable— much more flexible than these ultra-primitive males. She sounded the panel tone.

"Enter," Gunnar called in his guttural voice.

She opened the entry and strolled in. Gunnar sat at a massive table, with Karr and Marat flanking him. He looked up and scowled. He always did that when he saw her, and it was beginning to annoy her greatly.

"You're interrupting an important tactical meeting," he growled. "What do you want?"

"There's something I'd like to discuss with you."

All three men groaned. "It will have to wait." Gunnar turned back to Karr and Marat.

She had been patient long enough. "It can't wait. I'd like to get started on my plans immediately."

"Her plans." Gunnar sat back, rolling his eyes. "Goddess spare me!"

She crossed her arms over her chest. "You might as well hear me out, Commander. Avoidance will not make a problem go away."

"It might if I jettison that problem into outer space."

"That's very childish, Commander. I expected better from you."

She knew he'd rise to her challenge. His eyes narrowing, he snapped his fingers. Karr and Marat rose stiffly, bowing slightly toward him. They departed with backward glances and snorts of disgust.

"Sit," Gunnar rumbled.

Lani took the chair to his right, and he swiveled toward her. Leors wore leggings and boots when they dealt with the more conservative races of the quadrant. But on their planets and their ships, they wore virtually nothing—just loincloths. With his magnificent physique, Gunnar certainly didn't need clothing to give him presence.

He filled a chair better than any man she'd ever seen. He leaned back slightly, giving the appearance of being relaxed, but the ripple of muscles in his bare chest and bulging biceps indicated he was alert, ready to take action at a moment's notice.

He sat with his feet planted solidly on the floor and his legs spread in a masculine stance that sent Lani's heart into free fall. His hairless, supple skin heightened the effect, emphasizing his massive, muscular thighs—and the massive bulge beneath the loincloth. *Oh, my*. It was way too hot in here. Lani snapped open her feathered fan and fluttered it near her flushed face.

"What did you come to carp about this time, woman?"

She forced her gaze back to Gunnar's hostile black eyes. He might have a body that would affect even the most jaded courtesan, but he needed to work on the attitude—and the manners.

"I hate to be rude, but this leg of my vacation has been very disappointing. Quite boring, I'm sorry to say. I haven't had anyone to talk to, and there's been absolutely no adventure, not even a small skirmish."

Gunnar stared at her in disbelief. "You expect to be amused? Perhaps you would like me to attack another ship so you can have some excitement?"

"Certainly not. But if you just happened to cross paths with an enemy, or wished to negotiate a trade deal—for a new bride, perhaps—that would be interesting."

"I am not looking for another bride," he growled. "I do not wish to experience another female's treachery. I am concerned only with protecting Leor territories and interests—not entertaining a foolish woman dressed like a bird. How many times must I remind you that you are a hostage?"

She waved a hand dismissively. "A mere formality, in order for you to save face. You know Celie wouldn't lie to you. And while it's been somewhat interesting to be a hostage, I need to get back to work. I don't have unlimited funds, you know."

"A mere formality? You have much to learn about Leor ways, woman. You will not dictate your release, or anything else, to me."

He was being thick-headed and unreasonable, as usual. "Listen, Mister Cave Dweller, you can't expect me to stay here under these dull conditions. Plus I have responsibilities, and a job to return to."

"*You* have a job?" he sneered. "I cannot imagine you possessing any useful skills. Can you pilot a ship, or defeat an opponent in combat, or replicate weapons? Can you plan tactical maneuvers, or heal wounded warriors?"

Lani was oddly stung by his scorn, although she knew the Leors valued only those skills relating directly to their way of life. Her research on the Leors had been most revealing. For the most part, developing trade routes, expanding their territories, and battling fiercely to protect their interests comprised their entire existence.

They placed a high value on honor and justice, something she admired. But, oh, they were stubborn, insensitive brutes—at least the men were. She hadn't met any Leor women, so wasn't prepared to pass judgment on them.

"No, I can't do those things," she replied. "But what I do is very important."

"And what is that?"

Lani paused, not at all certain how he'd take the answer. Oddly enough, in addition to admiring honor and bravery, the Leors also valued chastity. As a rule, they didn't engage in sexual activities until they were mated.

They looked upon abstinence as a discipline, and believed channeling their sexual energy into their physical training made them better warriors.

She happened to disagree, but questioned the wisdom of telling Gunnar she was a courtesan. Not that she was ashamed of what she did—she provided a vital service, and thoroughly enjoyed herself in the process—but Gunnar was difficult enough as it was.

"You might say I'm in the entertainment field."

He mulled this over, his forehead furrowing. "Entertainment? Dancing? Singing?"

She couldn't sing an on-pitch note, not even in a crystal echo chamber. And the erotic Elysian scarf dances she liked to perform would shock this staid Leor commander to his puritanical core.

"Among other things," she hedged. "But as I said, Commander. It's been interesting, and I've learned a lot, but I want you to release me. I need to return to my obligations."

"No."

The man epitomized the word "obtuse." Lani placed her hands on her hips. "What do you mean, 'no'?"

But it appeared she no longer had his attention. His gaze slid higher, fixed on her upswept hairstyle. "You are not wearing your hair down."

She'd been in the chamber fifteen minutes and he was just noticing that fact? "This ship is too hot for me to keep it down. I've already explained to you that the high temperature you maintain is most uncomfortable for me. I've even had to strip to my barest clothing."

"So you have." His gaze shifted downward, settling on her chest.

His expression remained impassive, but Lani had been dealing with various males too long to be fooled. The

slight tic in his jawline told her he wasn't unaffected by
her breasts, clearly outlined through the thin silk. Good—
there was nothing wrong with the Leor libido, despite his
people's foolish abstinence from sex.

She thrust her chest forward. Let him look. Maybe it
would heat his blood, and he'd turn down the cursed
temperature. Or, at the very least, a blast of desire might
shake him up a little.

A low growl rumbled in his throat, and his gaze
snapped back up. "You are a hostage. You do not give
orders, and you will remain in my custody until I am
certain of Celie Cameron's innocence."

Oh! He was insufferable. "Then you had better find
something to keep me entertained, Commander, because
I won't stay here with nothing to do. And I expect financial compensation for the income I'm losing."

His eyes turned icy, and he leaned forward, slowly,
menacing. "Woman, you have done nothing but com-
plain since you have been on board. You say the ship is
dirty, the food is bad—"

"I offered to replicate nutritious meals for you and
your men."

"You gave us *green* things—*vegetables!*"

"You eat too much meat. It's not good for you."

He slapped his hand on the table, the sound reverberating in the chamber. "The ship is too hot, we have no
manners, you want to be released, and now *you want to
be entertained*. Perhaps some time in the brig will help
you learn silence."

"Only a coward would put a woman in the brig," she
retorted, thoroughly irritated. "If you can't handle me
any other way, so be it. But only after Karr and Feron
clean it."

He grabbed the edge of the table, intense frustration

193

darkening his face. "What is it you want from me? I have done everything in my power to quiet your constant complaining. The ship has been scoured, the temperature settings reduced, *vegetables* added to the menu, my men's language censored. What more can be done to silence you, except for the brig?"

Lani leaned back in her chair. "If you won't release me, then you can talk to me."

Total shock and incredulity blazed onto Gunnar's face. "*Talk? To you?*"

Lani smiled brightly. "Yes. We'll chat every day."

Gunnar stood abruptly, his chair banging the wall. "Marat! Get in here. Put this female in the brig. *Now!*"

The weapons dealer was a seven-foot Jaccian with four tentacles, no eyelids, and a revolting odor. Dealing with it was a harrowing experience. Perhaps calling it a "he" would be more appropriate, since the creature radiated definite lascivious inclinations. Rani hated him on sight, snarling and lunging, until Eirene was forced to secure the flap of the knapsack.

"Me help you, lady?" the Jaccian shrilled in a singsong voice, leering at Eirene and trying to peer down the front of her robe.

She edged away, drawing the robe protectively around her. "I wish to purchase a stun gun."

"Ah! You have enemy? Me sell you excellent disrupter. Fry enemy's brain, then he die—slow."

He stared at her breasts, his lust increasing exponentially. Slime began oozing from the barbs in his tentacles, intensifying his horrible smell. From inside the knapsack, Rani chattered in protest. Covering her nose, Eirene was sorely tempted to take him up on his offer, purchase a disrupter, and put him out of commission permanently.

That she could have such a thought shocked her. She'd never wanted to harm anyone in her life, not even her cruel uncle or his henchmen. She'd always considered healers above such leanings.

She shook her head. "The stun gun will do."

He moved closer, his glittering, unblinking gaze sweeping down her body. "You have gold?"

Backing up, she held out a gemstone she'd pried from the hilt of one of her jeweled daggers. "I have this to trade. I expect the stunner and some miterons in return."

He snatched the gem, and she hastily wiped her hand on her robe. "Stunner for this," he intoned. "No miterons."

"That's outrageous," Eirene argued. "The stone is worth much more than a single weapon. I've gotten clothing, food, and lodging for an entire week with one just like it."

"Stunner for gem," he insisted. "Me give charger for free."

She hadn't considered such matters as charging the gun. She knew very little about weapons, and certainly didn't understand the settings on a stun gun.

Since she was anxious to get back to the landing bay to help Jarek, she didn't want to take the time to find a jeweler and haggle over a fair price for the gem. She also wanted to get as far away from this Jaccian as possible.

"I'll give you the stone if you'll trade me a weapon that's already charged and explain the settings to me," she said in resignation.

"Me show you many things," the Jaccian sing-songed, pocketing the gem.

He had a lot of things in mind, all right—all of them sexual in nature. She struggled to ignore his lust. Then he decided to wrap a tentacle around her. That did it.

Eirene sent him a strong burst of energy, overstimulating the nerve endings in the offending tentacle. She didn't even worry about her powers malfunctioning, not caring if she accidentally fried him.

When he dropped the stunner with a shriek of pain, she scooped up the weapon and her satchel and ran, Rani squealing all the way. Eirene hurried toward the landing bay. As much as it frightened her, she was about to use her powers again.

This time, to free Jarek.

Damn. He shouldn't be alive. But here he was, trapped inside a brig, like a kerani about to be led to slaughter.

Jarek leaned forward, resting his elbows on his knees and rubbing his throbbing forehead. Blazing hells. He'd dropped the damn suicide capsule. Like a clumsy fool, he'd been thrown off balance when Turlock's men blasted the secured airlock panel to force it open.

He'd hit the wall, and the capsule skidded along the floor. Through the gaping hole in the panel, vapor had jettisoned into the corridor. Closing his eyes tightly to protect them, Jarek battled breathing in the gas, fumbling for his blaster. If he could just get it out, could just raise it to his head . . . he could finish it now.

But it had taken too long to get his weapon free of its holster. His body had interceded, involuntary reflexes forcing him to breathe. Fiery flames of pain scalded his exposed skin and agony blazed through his lungs.

His last thought had been of Eirene. He'd prayed she would be spared, even as he fell to the floor, spasming uncontrollably. Even as blackness descended.

Now, here he was, at Turlock's mercy, and most likely headed for the Controller prison on Alta. He refused to think of what would happen there.

Instead he focused on Eirene, hoping that she was safe, that she'd been able to get off his ship undetected. He knew she had the means to take care of herself. He'd seen the daggers in her satchel, which he had searched one night shift while she was asleep. The two empty sockets in one dagger hilt told the story. Eirene was selling the jewels to survive.

Jarek tried to tell himself that he had covered every base, that his capture wouldn't have major repercussions. Eirene would be safe. Shielder settlements would be evacuated. Sabin and Blake would carry out Jarek's plan to search for the worm hole. Even if he weakened under torture and drugs, the information the Controllers garnered would no longer be accurate or damaging. He hoped.

So, Jarek asked himself wearily, *what else could go wrong?*

"Hey, you cretins! Lookee what I found outside our ship."

"Ooohee, looka that!"

"Hey, sweet thing. You must've come here just to see me."

"Hold on there, Webb. I saw her first. She's mine."

Jarek's head snapped up. What the—*Eirene!* She stood just inside the hatch, smiling boldly at Turlock's men. His heart stalled out. What in the Abyss was she doing here?

He leaped to his feet and strode to the entry of the brig, cursing the force field which kept him from going to her. What the blazing hells was she thinking?

All four of Turlock's men had congregated on this ship, awaiting their leader's arrival. Jarek had sized them up, memorizing their names. They were tough brutes without a shred of decency. And here was Eirene, endangering herself.

Little fool!

Just then, she looked straight at him and he felt as if he'd been gut-punched. He drank in the sight of her standing there, even as he cursed her recklessness. Her deep blue gaze seemed to hold him in its spell, the inexplicable pull between them flaring to maximum throttle. Spirit, but she was beautiful. And in grave danger.

Narrowing his eyes, he shot her a scathing look that clearly broadcasted his displeasure with her rashness, and warned her to get away—now. Tilting her chin upward, she looked back at the men.

"No need to fight over me, you handsome brutes," she cooed, her voice low and husky. "I'm woman enough for all of you." She ran a slender hand suggestively along the neckline of her robe. It had been unfastened to a precariously plunging level, providing a tantalizing glimpse of the swell of her breasts.

Where had she learned to act like this? She was an innocent—or at least had been, before Jarek blundered through relieving her of her virginity.

"Just look at them funbags," Balen said, ogling Eirene's breasts.

Leering, the four men closed around her. She shot Jarek another quick glance, and he saw the uncertainty in her eyes. She was in over her head, risking her life, most probably in the misguided notion of helping him.

He almost shouted out an offer to provide information in exchange for Eirene being allowed to leave. He stopped himself just in time, knowing his protests would only make matters worse. If Turlock or his men realized Jarek knew Eirene, and cared for her, they'd use that knowledge to their advantage.

"I'll go first." Derian grabbed Eirene, and Jarek almost forgot about the force field. Just in time, he stopped himself from touching it and receiving a nasty jolt.

"Son of an Antek!" Derian jumped back from Eirene. "My body's tingling something awful."

Jarek lowered his hands. He couldn't pick up Eirene's energy and suspected the force field blocked any transmissions from her. But she must have just used her power. He stared at her, noting her flushed face, the way she clutched her robe.

Loud guffaws filled the corridor. "Can't take the heat, eh?" Webb sneered. "Let me show you how it's done."

Eirene took a step back, slipping her hand into her pocket. Jarek had an idea. If he could get free, there might just be a chance . . .

"Balen!" he roared. "You're a coward. You and the other three scum who call themselves men. I'll bet the four of you couldn't take me."

Suddenly, a shrill chattering erupted nearby, drawing everyone's attention to a wiggling knapsack just inside the entry. Jarek realized Rani must be in there, and his voice must have stirred her up.

"What the—" Webb said, reaching for his weapon.

Eirene held out her hand, and the chattering stopped. Jarek moved quickly to distract the men. "Did you hear me, you bastards? I challenge you to a fight—me against all of you."

Balen, who had maintained a drunken state the entire trip, belched loudly. "Go to Hades, san Ranul. I'm not letting you out." He returned his bloodshot gaze to Eirene. " 'Sides, I'm about to be very busy."

The other three men growled in agreement, their attention once again focused on her.

"You won't let me out because you can't even find

your way to the brig's control panel, you idiot," Jarek taunted. "For your information, it's the black panel on the left, the green pad."

He saw Eirene's gaze dart to the panel. She started edging that way. "Let's do it, sweet thing!" Keraat hurled himself against her, pinning her against the wall.

A millisecond later, he released Eirene, clutching his chest with a cry. She whipped a stun gun from her pocket and fired at him. He slumped to the floor with a moan.

Balen lunged at her, but she managed to shoot him. Unfortunately, before she could reposition to get the other two, Webb grabbed her arm, slamming it against the wall. The stunner flew out of her hand.

"Bitch!" Derian roared, charging forward. "Let me at her."

"Eirene!" Jarek yelled, giving up all pretense of not knowing her. "Try to get me out." He didn't dare tell her to use her powers, for fear Derian and Webb would figure out she was an Enhancer.

Eirene wrestled with Webb, raking her nails over his face. With a howl her assailant released her, and she stumbled toward the brig. Derian tackled her just as she got her palm on the control panel. It wasn't enough contact to deactivate the field. Jarek watched helplessly as Derian slammed her to the floor, rolled on top of her, then hit her in the face.

She went limp, and Jarek's heart stalled again. "Eirene! Help yourself. You know what I'm talking about."

She groaned, and Derian straddled her, shoving at her robe and undoing his pants. "I'll still take my pleasure from this bitch before I kill her."

Webb leaned over them, blood oozing from the scratches on his face. "No, I get to kill her."

Jarek's gut twisted. This couldn't be happening. "Eirene, a man's most vulnerable place is between his legs," he yelled desperately. "You know what to do."

She stirred and shifted, and Derian, still trying to get her robe up, cursed. "Be still." He raised his fist. "Or I'll hit you again."

"No," she murmured faintly.

Suddenly Derian clutched his crotch and rolled sideways into Webb. "Help!" he screamed. "I'm on fire!"

"That's my girl!" Jarek called. "Now get me out."

She scrambled to her feet, barely lurching free of Webb's grasp. Her hand connected with the control panel, and the green force field shimmered off. Jarek raced through just as Webb wrapped his arm around her neck.

Jarek crashed into both of them, knocking them down onto Derian. He hated to risk further injury to Eirene, but didn't dare give Webb the opportunity to draw his weapon. She struggled against Webb's hold, which gave Jarek the opportunity he needed to wedge between them. She scrambled out of the way, and Jarek wrestled with Webb, who was trying to fumble his disrupter out of the holster.

They rolled to the side, Webb ending up on top. He was bigger than Jarek, and Jarek was still suffering the after-effects of the gas. He felt himself weakening, but battled to hold on against the barrage of Webb's punches.

Another volley of shrill squealing filled the chamber, and Rani hurtled into the air, leaping onto Webb's back and biting him ferociously. Webb jerked, managing to knock her off his back. Taking advantage of the distraction, Jarek landed a solid punch.

Fury twisting his face, Webb raised his fist to retaliate. Suddenly, he stiffened, his eyes glazing over. He fell forward, hitting Jarek with a thud. He was unconscious, complements of Eirene's stun gun.

Jarek rolled him away in time to see Eirene shoot Derian, who had managed to stagger to his feet. Derian swayed, then collapsed on top of Webb. Jarek blew out his breath. Chattering happily, Rani scampered onto his chest, and snuffled warm breath against his neck.

"I don't know how she woke up so quickly, or how she got out of that knapsack," Eirene said, her voice unsteady.

As if that mattered. She had just taken a terrifying risk—and she'd saved his life. Peeling Rani off his chest, he pushed to his feet and stared at Eirene. A huge bruise was rapidly forming on the side of her face, and she was trembling.

A flood of emotions swept through him. He wanted to shout for joy that he was alive, that he was free again— thanks to one very amazing woman. He also wanted to shake her and yell at her for her foolishness.

"Just what the blazing hells did you think you were doing?" he demanded. "You took a huge risk, lady. Do you know what those bastards would have done to you? You probably wouldn't have survived the evening shift."

Shoving her hair back, she angled her chin defiantly. "I did what I had to do. You saved my life; I saved yours. It was only right."

Damn, but she looked wonderful to him, even with her tangled hair and battered face. He struggled to hang on to his anger, but the exuberance of being alive and free, and her rebellious expression, made that almost impossible. His adrenaline slowed to a dull roar, and other emotions replaced the fighting mode.

He wanted to take Eirene in his arms and soothe away

the ugliness and pain she'd just experienced. To kiss her senseless and carry her to bed, and properly and thoroughly initiate her into womanhood. He wanted to—

By the Fires. He was through with thinking about what he wanted. Life was too fleeting to waste time wishing. He had a second chance and he intended to take full advantage of it.

He stepped over the two men. "We'll discuss your foolhardiness later. But right now—come here, you."

He swept her to him, ignoring the pain from his battered body, and cradled her head in his hands. Careful of her bruise and his own damaged face, compliments of gas burns and Webb's pummeling, he lowered his mouth to hers. Kissed her deeply, hungrily.

With a little sound that did wicked things to his libido, she burrowed against him, opening her lips for him like a starflower to the sunlight. Her tongue touched his, tentative at first, then more boldly, initiating a mating dance older than creation.

The blood rushed to his lower extremities, a throbbing reminder of just how long it had been since he'd lain with any woman other than Eirene. He didn't even remember the last one's name, or her face. Eirene permeated every thought, every cell of his being.

His. She was his, only his. He would no longer let his responsibilities keep him from his personal desires. He would find a way to accomplish both.

Needing to touch her, to claim her, he slid one hand down to cup her breast. She trembled, and he tore his mouth from hers. He stared into the crystal depths of her eyes, reading the desire there. He rubbed his thumb over her nipple, feeling it harden, feeling the breast swell against his hand, begging for his mouth to worship it.

"Jarek," she breathed, her fingers clutching his flight-suit.

Fiercely triumphant at her physical response to him, he battled the acute need to find a bunk and possess her then and there, branding her as his. They were on one of Turlock's ships, with his lackeys merely stunned, not dead. Turlock could arrive at any time.

The need for survival triggered more rational thought, although it did little to cool Jarek's ardor. Drawing a deep breath, he dropped his hand. "We'd better get out of here."

Eirene blinked, the glaze of passion in her eyes slowly giving way to reality. "Oh," she said, glancing around at the prone men. "Oh . . . you're right. Do you think Turlock is on his way to Saron?"

"I'm certain of it. Come on." Jarek took her arm and peeled Rani off his leg with his free hand.

He guided Eirene around Keraat and Balen, stopping to confiscate a blaster from Balen's belt. "We'll move my ship to another landing bay. Hopefully, Turlock will think I left Saron."

Eirene retrieved Rani's pouch from the floor. "Isn't that what we're going to do anyway?"

"We'll definitely leave within the cycle." Jarek lowered the protesting lanrax into the pouch and secured it. "But I need to check the ship to see if Derian and Keraat did any damage while they had it. I also need to inventory my supplies. They might have transferred them to another ship. Once I know everything is in order, we'll depart."

She turned to face him. "For Aldon?"

Her eyes were calm, accepting, and he felt no flare-ups of her energy. She no longer seemed upset by the idea. He began to dare hope she had decided to help him. That maybe she wanted him as much as he wanted her.

"We'll head for Aldon," he concurred. "After we check the ship—and do one other thing."

"What else do we need to do?"

He fully intended to show her. Leaning down, he kissed her again, splaying his hand across her rear and dragging her against his blatant need.

She responded, kissing him back. Her growing expertise in that area almost undid him. He ended the contact, his breath ragged, his heart pounding. Moving to her ear, he pressed tiny kisses along the delicate shell, felt her shiver.

"This is only a prelude to what I have in mind," he whispered. "If you don't want to go any further, you'd better say so now, lady. Otherwise, I plan on finishing what we started in the Pleasure Dome."

Chapter Eleven

Her hands shaking, Eirene brushed her damp hair. *This is only a prelude to what I have in mind.* Jarek's seductive words swirled in her mind, and a disconcerting warmth flooded her body. Staring into his dark, heated eyes on Turlock's ship, she hadn't been able to summon the will to object to his provocative declaration. Spirit help her, but she wanted to mate with him.

The ship had been moved to the far side of Saron, and Jarek had gone to take a shower, Rani scampering right behind him. Eirene had gone to her own cabin to do the same, both excitement and trepidation whipping through her. She'd never imagined she would want to lie with a man, would feel the intense physical cravings she felt whenever she looked at Jarek.

She didn't understand the inexplicable forces that drew her to him. Yet she felt a deep need to bond with him, spiritually and physically. Perhaps it was because of the experiences they had shared, saving each other's lives. She only knew she wanted this closeness with Jarek.

At the same time, she was terrified at the thought of such intimacy with, and vulnerability to, any man. She knew nothing about the sensual play between a man and a woman. What if she didn't please Jarek? What if—

Her cabin panel slid open, and Jarek stepped in, wearing nothing but a towel and a seductive grin. "Hey," he said.

Eirene stared at him, her mouth going dry and rational thought scattering like sand in the wind. *Oh, my.* Even with his swollen, bruised face, and the burns on his neck and hands, he was still magnificent.

His smile faded as his gaze skimmed over her, noting the tunic and leggings she'd put on after her shower. "Why are you wearing that? Change your mind?"

Her heart pounded so hard, she thought it might burst through her chest. "Well, no ... I ..." Self-conscious, she twisted her tunic in her hand. "I—I don't know the correct protocol." She wondered if he remembered saying those words to her in the Pleasure Dome.

"I see." The smile returned, confident, devastating. "I think we can solve that dilemma." He walked toward her, letting his towel slip away. "As for protocol, clothing is fine. It provides me the pleasure of undressing you."

Oh, Spirit. Of its own volition, her gaze dropped to his flagrant arousal. He was so big, so intimidating. She sucked in a breath as he reached out, skimming his hands over her shoulders and brushing her hair back. He reached for the top of her tunic.

"I don't mind clothing at all," he murmured huskily. He slipped his fingers beneath the seam, sliding it open with excruciating slowness. "As a matter of fact," he paused, pressing his lips above the open seam, "I think I'm going to enjoy this very much."

He straightened, and she gasped in surprise when he swept her into his arms. Pressed against his chest, she felt the heat of him, the solid, reassuring beat of his heart. He carried her to the bunk, lowering himself beside her.

"That's better," he rasped. "Now I can do this right." He leaned over her, peeling back the fabric one millimeter at a time, kissing her exposed flesh as he went.

She felt the air rush over her breasts as the fabric parted, then his hands and lips were there. He took one nipple into his mouth, and sensation sizzled through her. She arched upward, feeling the pull all the way down to her feminine core. Spirit, but memory had failed her. This was far more potent pleasure than she had remembered.

She moaned softly, and he shifted to the other breast to give it the same sweet attention. She could barely breathe, able only to gasp in small amounts of oxygen. She threaded her fingers through his thick hair, pressed him closer.

He made a sound deep in his chest, then moved his attention lower, kissing his way down her midriff. Raising up, he tugged the tunic free of her arms, pulled it from beneath her, and tossed it away. Then he slid his hands beneath the waistband of her leggings, his touch a brand against her skin.

"Lift your hips," he urged.

Not caring that she would be completely exposed to him, she complied, and he tugged the leggings down and off. She watched, mesmerized, as he ran his hands slowly, sensually, over her legs and pelvis, as if he were mapping her, memorizing every curve.

She'd always thought his hands were beautiful, strong and capable, yet surprisingly gentle. But now they were

marred by ugly burns, as were his neck and face. Eirene's heart ached at the pain he must have suffered. Hating the thought of him hurting, she rolled to her side, and up on her knees facing him.

He stared at her, desire flaring in his eyes. She leaned forward, took his left hand, and lifted it to her lips. She wanted to heal him so badly. But she didn't dare. She couldn't risk what had happened with Rayna. Instead, she pressed gentle kisses over the damaged flesh.

"Give me your right hand," she whispered.

He held out his hand, palm up, and she raised it to her lips, giving it the same loving tribute. Then she leaned forward, bracing one hand on his shoulder. His arms slid around her and drew her closer, as she gave the same attention to his neck. Moving to his face, she gently swirled her tongue over the swelled, bruised areas.

She started to pull back, but he crushed her to him. "Eirene," he muttered hoarsely. He slid his fingers through her hair, capturing her face and claiming her lips with his.

She hadn't realized how much she'd craved his kisses, how provocative the mating of tongues could be. She didn't know she could be so wanton, falling back on the mat with Jarek, entwined with him, pressing her pelvis against his erection.

Or that she could be more wanton still, opening her legs when his hand slid between them to claim her most intimate flesh. He launched a sensual invasion, stroking and exploring, probing her intimately, deeply.

She couldn't think, couldn't do anything but dig her hands into the mat. And still he continued, relentlessly inundating her with pleasure, until she thought she might die from it.

"Jarek," she moaned.

"Feel good?"

Her eyes jolted open, and she saw he was lying on his side, propped on one elbow, his other arm draped down her body. His gaze, filled with sensual promises, locked with hers.

"What are you doing?" she gasped.

"Watching you. Spirit, you're beautiful."

Suddenly embarrassed, she felt a heated flush creep across her cheeks. "Jarek—"

"Eirene, trust me. *Please* trust me." He leaned down, brushed his lips against hers. "I need your trust. I ask you to give me that much."

The entreaty in his voice touched her heart as deeply as he was touching her most intimate core, sparking emotions she'd never experienced. She yearned to give this man everything he needed, everything he wanted.

She framed his face in her hands. "I do trust you, Jarek."

"Then give yourself to me." He kissed her mouth, her chin, trailed his lips down her neck.

"I'm yours," she whispered, pulling him over her.

He settled between her legs, and she felt his hardness pressing against her. His tongue mated with hers as he probed below, gaining entry to her body. She felt a sense of déjà vu—flashbacks of the Pleasure Dome. This time, however, Jarek was slow and careful as he entered her. She was tight, and tensed when the initial discomfort became pain.

He held himself still and smoothed the hair back from her face. "Easy now. Relax, little one."

Soothed by his tender tone and his touch, knowing he would never hurt her, Eirene drew a deep breath, forcing the tension away.

"That's it," he crooned, rocking gently against her. "We'll take it slow and easy."

Holding her with his eyes, he moved deeper as her muscles adjusted and gave way. The effort of his restraint etched harsh lines across his face. Her heart swelled at his concern for her, his tenderness. How could she not trust this man who put the welfare of others before his own?

The fullness of him buried deep within her, his heated touch on her breasts, created a primal, instinctive need, and she began to move with him, matching his rhythm. Faster, fiercer, more urgent with each deep thrust.

"That's it, sweetness," he gasped. "Stay with me. We're almost there."

Almost where? Eirene didn't know where she was headed, only that she was rushing headlong into a glittering, surreal realm where she'd never been before. No thought, only sensation, a wild freefall that sent her heart pounding. Their harsh breathing, Jarek's hoarse encouragement, her soft cries—all merged into a sensual landscape. The tension, the energy, building, building . . .

Fly with me—now! Jarek commanded, his voice reverberating inside her head.

Jarek! She thought his name as she ignited in a fiery blaze, pleasure hurtling like a shooting star through her body. Energy sizzled and arced between the two of them.

Oh, sweet Spirit. Eirene! Jarek's voice again burst into her mind, just as he shuddered and cried out his release.

He collapsed against her and buried his face in her hair with a groan. She didn't even attempt to move. It seemed like an eternity before her breathing returned to normal, before she was capable of any rational thought.

Jarek groaned again, finally rousing himself enough to lift his head. He shook it as if to clear it, blew out a big

211

breath. "Oh, stars." He shifted off Eirene, turning onto his side and drawing her against him. He pressed a kiss on her hair. "You okay?"

"Hmmm," she murmured dreamily. "Just fine." Even now, her body tingled with aftershocks. Amazed, she thought that if mating was this pleasurable for men, then she could understand why Travan males visited the women's compound so often.

Jarek tightened his arms around her. "I heard you call out my name," he said quietly, "In my mind."

She angled her head to stare at him, not comprehending. "In your mind?"

"Yes. You communicated with me mentally, Eirene, like some Shielders do. And you hit me with a massive energy surge, right as you climaxed. That's what put me over the edge."

Spirit, no! He must be wrong. Thinking that she might have unknowingly discharged energy at a vulnerable time shook her to the core. "That's not possible," she protested. "You must have imagined it."

He shook his head. "I didn't imagine it. That was the most incredible experience I've ever had. I've never felt anything like that, not even in my most erotic dreams."

His blunt words shocked—and terrified—her. Could her power have been activated without her knowledge?

"Did you hear my voice in your head, Eirene? I spoke to you mentally when I felt the energy begin to surge."

He hadn't said those words out loud? *They'd been telepathic?* Panic evaporated the last of the euphoria. "No! I told you that's not possible!" She shoved against him and rolled to the edge of the bunk.

He grabbed her arm, halting her flight. "Hey, don't overreact. Let's talk about it."

She couldn't believe she could discharge energy and

not even know it. Eirene realized she was trembling, as Jarek drew her back into the shelter of his arms.

"It's not possible," she said again, although she knew deep down he was right.

"Many things are possible, sweetness. Shielders are resistant to psionic mind waves, and some can communicate telepathically. Shens use magic to create much of their world. Enhancers manipulate natural and artificial energy. I've seen so many unusual things, I'm beginning to believe that *anything* is possible.

She shook her head, too upset to listen. Jarek turned her so she faced him. "Eirene, I'm telling you about the telepathic communication and the energy surge not to upset you, but because I believe it's important for you to understand how your powers work, and to be able to manage them. Your safety and welfare depend on it."

So did his plan, she thought, beginning to seriously doubt the wisdom of allowing intimacy with a man who had held her prisoner against her will. She'd lived her entire life on Travan and was woefully ignorant in the ways of the quadrant.

"I don't think we can do this again," she murmured.

Jarek gave her his nova-wattage smile. "Oh, I'm certain we can, little one. I'll be glad to demonstrate, if you don't believe me."

"Let me go." She shoved against him, fear and frustration churning inside her.

His expression turned serious, and he released her. She slid off the bunk and grabbed her tunic. Keeping her back to him, she hurriedly put it on. Her emotions were all jumbled, and she was so confused. If only Rayna were here to discuss this.

She felt Jarek moving behind her. His hands settled on

her shoulders, their warmth seeping through the silk fabric to her chilled skin beneath.

"I didn't mean to make light of the situation," he said gently. "I'll wager a guess that you're afraid of your powers. Maybe you don't understand them, or don't have full control over them yet. You still haven't admitted to having them, at least not in so many words."

He massaged her tense shoulders. "What about my injury at the Pleasure Dome? You saved my life, Eirene—*my life!* This is a miracle, a gift from Spirit. What a waste it would be for you not to use it."

He didn't understand. It wasn't a gift. It was a curse.

"I know a lot of this is new to you," he continued. "Mating certainly is. I suspect using your powers is also new. You'll get used to these situations, and learn how to cope with them."

Eirene was more convinced than ever that he was wrong. How could she control powers when she didn't even know she was expending them? She closed her eyes in despair.

Jarek pulled her back against him, rested his chin on her head. "Do you regret what we just did?"

No. She didn't regret that at all. She'd never dreamed anything could be so incredible, so intense and pleasurable. And she cared for Jarek, far more than was prudent. He evoked alarming responses within her, both emotional and physical.

Even now, her body stirred in reaction to his nearness, the heat of his big body behind her, the feel of his arms around her. Even now, she again craved his kiss, his touch, the feel of him inside her. What madness was this?

"No," she whispered, unable to lie to him about what they had just shared. "I don't regret it."

"Good." A wealth of satisfaction deepened his voice.

"Come here." He turned her in his arms and tilted her face up. He kissed her, hot and hard—urgently—as if they hadn't just lain together. And, Spirit help her, she wanted to mate with him again. She felt bereft when he pulled back.

"We'll work through this together," he promised, his eyes dark with passion. "Come back to bed with me, little one. Let me love you again."

She hesitated, desire battling fear.

"If the energy surge happens again, we'll deal with it," Jarek reassured her. "With practice, you'll learn how to control it." He grinned, a mischievous glint dancing into his eyes. "And we'll practice as much as you want, until you master the energy."

She wanted to refuse. But, oh, she wanted this . . . wanted him. She rationalized that perhaps the energy surge had just been a fluke. It had never happened to her before.

He kissed her, and her magnasteel grip on her fears wavered. It wouldn't happen again, she told herself. She'd keep the energy tightly contained. Now she knew what to expect.

She didn't object when Jarek removed her tunic and carried her back to the bunk. And, like a ship being sucked into a black hole, she found herself hopelessly lost in a vortex of emotion and passion.

Eirene stood next to Jarek, watching while he bartered for weapons. Turlock's men had helped themselves to virtually everything on his ship—suspensions for the food replicator, weapons, medicines, various other supplies.

Fortunately, the gold for the equipment on Aldon had been hidden in the concealed compartment in the galley.

Still, Jarek now had to delve into his precious stash of miterons to replace necessities.

As he argued with the vendor—thankfully, not the foul Jaccian who'd sold Eirene the stunner—she gazed out over Saron's main square. The kaleidoscope of color and movement and sound from the masses of beings moving through the marketplace was no longer so overwhelming. Neither was the emotional bombardment, as she was learning to block much of it out. She found little comfort in that accomplishment.

She did not have control over the activation of her powers.

When she'd mated with Jarek the second time, again reaching a planet-shattering completion, her energy had surged. Even with her aware of it, even with her trying desperately to contain it at the peak of pleasure, she'd been unable to do so. The surge had been even wilder this time, giving Jarek several strong jolts. He claimed most of the energy had enhanced the pleasure. She wondered what the rest of it had done.

And once again, she'd linked telepathically with Jarek. It was an eerie sensation, having another person's voice in your head; knowing that your own thoughts would be broadcast to another—no matter how private or intimate.

She didn't like it at all. Despite Jarek's reassurances that she'd develop the skills to maintain control, she was unconvinced. She had no idea what to do at this point. She didn't see how she could avoid traveling to Aldon with him, but after she convinced him her powers were useless, what then? She knew she couldn't stay with him forever. There were no commitments binding them together, and his people needed him too badly. Yet, for now, she intended to enjoy every moment she had with Jarek.

She sighed, scanning the many stalls and carts with their bright displays of goods, and the hawking vendors trying to draw customers. Her attention fixed on a nearby cart that caught her interest. Herbs. Medicinal herbs, from the looks of them.

Under Rayna's tutelage, Eirene had studied herbs for many seasons. Even though she'd refused to attempt using her powers for healing, she'd hoped she could at least be a conventional healer, like Darya. So she had studied hard and learned all she could about natural and synthesized medicines.

Wondering if the vendor might have some herbs she'd never seen before, or might be able to impart some new knowledge, Eirene stared longingly at the cart.

She turned back to the weapon transaction. "Jarek."

"That's space piracy!" he declared to the dealer. "Thirty miterons for the blaster. That's my final offer." He looked at Eirene. "What do you need, little one?"

She pointed toward the cart. "I'd like to go look at those medicinal herbs."

He hesitated. "I'm afraid I don't have enough gold for you to purchase anything."

Guilt twinged through Eirene. She still had many of the jewels from her daggers, which were in her satchel. She should offer them to Jarek, to help replenish his supplies and buy the equipment on Aldon. And she would, she decided, after they reached Aldon. If his gold wasn't enough for the Shens, then she'd offer the jewels. At least she could give him that.

"I don't want to buy anything," she assured him. "I just want to see what the vendor has."

"Sure. Go ahead. Just stay nearby. Turlock or his men

might be around. We'll get out of here as soon as I have what we need."

Eirene nodded and hurried over to the cart. Moments later, she was engrossed in studying several new herbs, while the female vendor enthusiastically extolled their amazing medicinal powers. Smiling to herself, Eirene discounted most of the woman's extravagant claims.

As she reached for another container, a buzz of voices and emotions drew her attention. She felt an unusually high level of curiosity and excitement, even for Saron. Curious, she glanced toward the square's center and saw a regiment of Anteks shoving through the crowds. She'd seen Anteks a few times, when they'd come to Travan to trade on behalf of the Controllers.

They were ugly—hulkish in build, but with small heads, and snouts instead of noses, and little beady eyes. Spiked bristles covered their heads and their necks, and rows of sharp teeth created their slash of a mouth. The evil-looking laser rifles they carried, and brandished freely, ensured a wide berth as the crowds hastily moved back.

Not certain she wanted to know their purpose, Eirene returned her attention to the herbs, then froze as a unique energy assaulted her senses. The energy was strong—unusually so for the average being—and radiated incredible fright.

Trapped. Terrified. Fully aware that a horrible fate awaited.

The feelings, gyrating in an unstable pattern, were overwhelming. She battled not to give in to the sense of utter panic stirring inside her. Sweet Spirit, who—or what—was broadcasting so strongly?

Giving in to the morbid pull, she turned back toward the Anteks. They yelled and shoved a few hapless beings out of the way. Then she saw him. A young man, slight of build, with pale skin contrasting sharply with the midnight hair that flowed halfway down his slender back. Stumbling along behind the Anteks, he kept his gaze on the ground. His hands were shackled in front of him. More Anteks closed the ranks behind him.

He was the one generating the bombardment of emotional energy, either too frightened or too inexperienced to control it.

He, too, was an Enhancer.

Eirene knew that with intuitive certainty. The energy felt too strong—too familiar—for there to be any other explanation. Her own undisciplined energies must have been broadcasting, allowing him to sense her presence. He lifted his head and looked directly at her.

Another Enhancer. This was another Enhancer.

Unable to look away, Eirene pushed closer to the progression of Anteks and their prisoner. Drawing abreast, she moved sideways with them, staring at the young man. He watched her, turning his head to keep her in sight as she dropped behind, hampered by the crowd.

She could see his eyes now, a deep blue, much like her own. Despair and resignation, an incredible sadness, all swirled in the depths of those eyes. She tried to push closer, and he shook his head in warning.

An Antek shoved him from behind, and he stumbled forward. Falling back even further, Eirene scrambled to keep up and see where the soldiers were taking him. Her mind reeled with shock. Where had this man come from? How many other Enhancers were out there in this vast quadrant? And, more crucial right now, where was he being taken?

She got her answer moments later, when she shoved through the crowd just in time to see the young man being led into a large, iridescent-stoned building on the east side of the square. Moving closer, Eirene read the viewboard, which videovised an upcoming auction of an extremely rare item. The message didn't state specifically what the item might be, but Eirene knew.

With nausea roiling in her stomach, and a heavy heart, she knew. This was the auction of an Enhancer to the highest bidder.

Of their own accord, her legs carried her up the shimmering, multi-hued steps to the huge Variana marble doors. She didn't know what she'd do when she got inside, only that she must see the man.

Two Anteks flanking the massive entry pointed their rifles at her. "Where's your pass, lady?" one snorted, drool hanging from his mouth.

He smelled awful. She struggled not to gag. "My pass?"

"This a private transaction. Not open to public. Get going before I shoot."

Eirene stepped back, the full impact of the situation hitting her. There was nothing—absolutely nothing—she could do to help that young man inside. At least ten Anteks lined the front of the building, and she'd seen more than that go in with their prize.

Sick to her soul, she turned away and slowly descended the steps. Spirit, how could she have forgotten the dangers to those of her kind? Here it was, clearly laid out before her—the horrific fate befalling any Enhancer who was discovered.

Discovery might be very close at hand, if she couldn't control her energy flare-ups. Unfortunately, her mating with Jarek had proven she was unable to maintain *any* control. A psychic tracker could pick her up easily.

Worse, if she was caught, she would drag Jarek down

with her. She could never allow that to happen. He was too important, his people needed him too desperately. And she cared greatly for him, couldn't bear the thought of him being captured because of her.

She wasn't willing to sacrifice Jarek because of her own selfish desire to be with him. He already had a huge reward on his head, and bounty hunters scrambling to track him down. Her presence would draw attention to him, putting him at even greater risk.

The only way to protect him was to distance herself from him. Permanently. She couldn't wait until they reached Aldon. There might be bounty hunters there. She had to act now—to protect him and the Shielders. It would be best to make the break quickly. Anguish swept though her at the thought of never seeing him again, never again lying in his arms, or talking with him, wrapped in the warmth of his smile, nurtured by his understanding and wisdom.

This was why Rayna had warned her to avoid any involvement with men, Eirene thought. Because it caused too much pain. But no matter the cost, it had to be done.

This time, she would be certain her escape didn't fail.

A hand on Eirene's shoulder spun her around. "Where the blazing hells have you been?"

She looked into Jarek's eyes, seeing fear and concern. "You took ten seasons off my life," he ground out. "I thought Turlock or some other lowlife had gotten you."

He didn't appear worried she might have tried to escape. Why should he, when she had returned to save him from Turlock's men? He was beginning to trust her, just as she trusted him. But now she was a danger to him.

She stared at him, memorizing every millimeter of his face, the deep, rich brown color of his hair and eyes, the broadness of his shoulders. Her chest tightened. Very soon, she'd be gone.

He grasped her shoulders, shook her gently. "Eirene! What's wrong?"

"Nothing," she managed to answer. "I tried to walk to another cart, and I got caught up in the crowd and pushed over here. I was on my way back."

His eyes narrowing, he turned and looked toward the herb cart, as if gauging the distance. Then he looked over her shoulder at the iridescent-stoned building. "What were you doing up there?"

He must have seen her come down the steps. He was far too perceptive. Eirene was tired of lying, but knew she must convinced him one last time.

"Once I was this far down, I saw the doors on that building, and wanted to look at them. I've never seen stone like that before."

His sharp gaze seemed to pierce right through her. "Do you know what that building is?"

"No," she answered truthfully, although she knew one event that was hosted there.

"Trust me, you don't want to know." He exhaled slowly and took her arm. "Come on. I have what we need. Let's get off this hellhole."

Numbly, Eirene walked with Jarek to their landing bay. She felt battered on every level. Her body was sore from mating with him, her face ached from the pounding she'd taken from Derian, and her heart was heavy. She knew what must be done, and she had an idea how to do it.

Pulling a wheeled container holding their purchases with his left hand, Jarek kept his right arm around her shoulders. They talked very little. His attention was focused on the area around them. He scanned the crowds continually, always on the alert for danger.

It would be a terrible to have to live that way every single cycle. Eirene hoped he would find a place where his people would be safe. She wished she could be with him when he found what he sought.

They reached the ship, and he said, "I'll put these things away and then we'll take off."

"Okay. I need to get something from my cabin." She watched him wheel the container down the corridor, then walked to her cabin.

She pushed all feelings aside, forcing herself to think only of what she must do. Quickly, she packed her few belongings into her satchel, making certain the daggers were still there. Then she picked up her discarded robe and pulled the stunner from the pocket. She'd slipped it there after shooting Derian on Turlock's ship. Jarek probably thought the weapon had been left behind.

Oh, Spirit, she hated doing this to him. Hated shooting him and leaving him stunned. But she couldn't see any other way to escape him. He was able to pick up her energy, was too good a tracker. If she simply slipped away, he'd find her before she could get on a transport.

Eirene checked the charge on the stunner, finding it still had enough power to do the job. She set the stun level fairly high, hoping to buy a few hours lead time. Her heart heavy, she reminded herself it was for Jarek's protection. If any psychic trackers picked up her presence, she'd lead them directly to Jarek. She couldn't bear the thought of him being captured and killed.

Praying the stunner wouldn't hurt him too badly, she clutched it in her right hand, picked up her satchel with her left, and stepped into the corridor.

She saw Jarek a few panels down, arranging supplies in the main storage compartment. Perched on his shoulder, Rani chattered happily. Keeping the stunner behind her back, Eirene moved towards them. Rani saw her, and the little animal's pitch went up with excitement. Jarek turned, smiled.

Eirene slid the stunner from behind her and trained it on him. His smile disappeared. The realization of her betrayal dawned in his eyes, hitting her like a physical blow.

"Eirene, don't."

She drew a deep breath. No time for hesitation.

"I'm sorry, Jarek."

She pressed the discharge pad.

Chapter Twelve

Eirene studied the departure boards and chose a destination. She walked to one of the automated ticket lines and waited, feeling very vulnerable out in the open. Jarek should be unconscious for at least two hours, she told herself. He couldn't overcome the effects of a stunner as readily as he had overcome her clumsy attempt to put him into an a deep sleep state. She had time.

A tremor ran through her, and suddenly her throat was choked, her eyes filled with tears. She'd never see Jarek again. Spirit, how could she stand it? *You knew this time was only temporary*, she told herself. She realized Jarek was committed wholly to his people, had a destiny that didn't include her. And, more importantly, her presence endangered him. She must leave.

She forced herself to shuffle forward as the line moved. When she reached the automation, she purchased a ticket to Odera, well aware of the holocorder focused on her face. She had no intention of going to Odera, but she hoped to create a false trail that Jarek would follow— one that would lead him away from the threat she posed.

After completing her purchase, Eirene walked a few hundred meters back into the marketplace, out of the range of the holocorders. She quickly twisted her hair up and put on a hooded robe she had just purchased. The hood was deep, casting shadows on her face, and would hopefully make it difficult to identify her on the HC.

Returning to the ticket line, she purchased passage to Elysia. It would be the most obvious place for her to go, and she hoped Jarek wouldn't consider it for that very reason. Elysia would also provide the best hiding places, because it was so large and so many beings flowed through its marketplace on a regular basis.

Jarek might check Elysia, but she could only try to shield her energy and hope he couldn't track her so easily anymore. She would lie low on Elysia until he had likely given up his search. Then she would be free to study healing. She would devote herself to helping others, to make up for what she had done to Rayna, and for not being able to help Jarek and the Shielders.

The remorse and sadness again tried to edge into her heart, but she resolutely forced all emotion away. She wouldn't let herself think about her feelings for Jarek, not now. Now she must focus on doing what was necessary. With her ticket chip, she returned to the boards to verify the time and departure lane for her transport.

A powerful arm snaked around her chest with stunning swiftness, and she was yanked backward against a large body. Just as quickly, she was spun around and her hood jerked off. For a millisecond, all she could see was a stocky chest.

"Well, well, niece," came a chillingly familiar voice

above her head. "I thought you were long gone from Saron. What a surprise."

Shock evaporated rational thought. Slowly, she tilted her head to face her uncle.

A sneer slashed across Vaden's cruel face. "You've led me on quite a chase, girl. You probably thought I had given up."

He dug his fingers painfully into her upper arms. Wincing, she bit her lips together. She wouldn't cry out, no matter what.

"But I never give up—especially when I've been cheated," he hissed.

He jerked his head, and four men stepped out from behind him, weapons gleaming in their hands. The cold fist of fear squeezed Eirene's heart, as she recognized them as Turlock's men—the ones she had stunned. She had never wished for death, but right now, it might be preferable to the alternative. Her chest heaving, she battled to stay calm.

"You made me look like a fool, niece," her uncle growled. "And you ruined an important trade deal. Traitorous bitch. You'll pay, I promise."

He grasped her chin, turning her bruised face into the light and inspecting it. "Looks like someone already got tired of your treachery. Believe me, what I have in mind will be far more painful than this was."

He brought his face within millimeters of hers. His breath was foul, reeking of strong liquor. "Tell me, girl, are you still a virgin? Or have you lain with san Ranul and half the male population of the quadrant, like some cheap slut? Turlock's men here"—he paused and gestured to the ugly brutes behind him—"claim you were acting like a bitch in heat, but swear they never had you."

227

He tightened his cruel grip and shook her. "The truth. Tell me!"

The adrenaline and utter panic surging through Eirene made it difficult for her to think clearly. She knew she had to calm herself, to focus on what she could do to help herself. She drew a deep breath, reaching for rational thought.

Don't tell him you're no longer a virgin, an inner voice warned. Her uncle might not harm her as long as he thought he could still trade her to the Leors. At least it might buy her some time.

For what? Escape would be virtually impossible. Using her powers, as unstable as they were, could put her in an even worse situation. If her uncle realized she was an Enhancer, then her fate would be worse than death. Better to die than spend a life in slavery.

Yet instinct warned her not to take that final step, to tell her uncle the truth about her virginity, and die—slowly, painfully. "Why would I want to lie with any man?" she shot back.

Vaden raised his arm to backhand her, thought better of it. "No, that will mark you further. I'll have to use an electrolyzer rod on you instead." He pivoted toward Turlock's lackeys. "Webb! Go to my ship. Have Stane contact Gunnar and tell him we found his bride, and to meet us on Saron. Stane also needs to contact Turlock and find out what's holding him up. Then get back here. I might need you."

Webb nodded and strode off.

"What are we going to do with her now?" Balen asked, his bloodshot gaze fixed on Eirene's breasts. It took all her self control to quell her rolling stomach.

"Nothing, until I find out whether or not she's still a virgin," Vaden answered.

Eirene closed her eyes, battling despair and panic. *Spirit, I need a miracle.*

"I'm sure the Leor bastard will insist on his own healer checking her over. He won't trust anything I say," Vaden growled. He yanked Eirene's arm viciously and dragged her toward the marketplace. "Gunnar will be here soon enough. But I intend to find out the truth for myself. Right now."

"So is all of Dukkair desert?" Lani asked, fascinated by Gunnar's account of his home planet.

"Much of it is," he replied. "It is very wild, but very beautiful. I have not been there for many cycles."

The longing in his eyes surprised Lani. Except for his irritation with her, or anger over situations she instigated, Gunnar rarely showed emotion. His black-as-sin eyes were usually inscrutable—which she found quite intriguing.

Even when they debated highly controversial topics, his expression rarely gave away his true feelings. And they discussed something every cycle, usually meeting in his council chamber after the mid-shift meal. Lani adored their discussions; Gunnar tolerated them.

She suspected he humored her to avoid a repeat performance of what had happened when he tried to put her in the brig. Thinking about it, Lani smiled to herself. She normally disapproved of females crying to get their way, although she was quite adept at producing tears at a millisecond's notice. But she had decided being imprisoned in a brig constituted extenuating circumstances and had turned on the tears.

Apparently Leors didn't produce tears, had never seen them. Gunnar had panicked, convinced something must be seriously wrong. The threat of the brig had been withdrawn, the temperature settings turned down, the ship cleaned for the second time in one cycle. And Gunnar had promised—very ungraciously—to visit with her every day. Of course, he didn't call it a visit. It was a briefing, to learn more about her culture.

Ah, it had been wonderful. Lani wished she had a holocording of Gunnar's reaction. Oh, well. It had achieved the desired effect.

"If Dukkair is mainly desert, it must be quite hot," she commented.

"Oh yes, very hot." Gunnar leaned back, his solid legs splayed. "There is a great deal of natural sunlight, which is the best source of heat for us."

Lani's gaze was drawn to his loincloth. Until now, she hadn't been a big fan of hot climates. But there could be advantages, she decided, if the amount of clothing was reduced.

"What do the women of your race wear?" she asked.

"The same as thing as the males."

"Just a loincloth?" she asked, somewhat surprised, although many cultures embraced partial or total nudity.

"Yes. Why should they dress any differently than the males?"

Because the Leors, for all their warlike fierceness, appeared to be prudes. Lani had expected the women to cover up any body parts that signified temptation.

Curious, she asked, "Then Leor men don't consider female breasts sexually alluring?"

Gunnar's gaze dropped to her breasts, as it frequently did, especially since she now wore her lightest fabrics in deference to the ship's hot climate. He quickly looked away. "Unmated Leors do not allow themselves to have sexual thoughts. All focus is on training and battle."

Oh, the man had sexual thoughts, all right. Lani was

beginning to have some of her own. He was an incredible specimen of malehood, and she'd been away from her job a little too long.

"The women don't have any hair, either?" she asked.

"No, they do not." Gunnar stared at her hair, which she'd worn down today. He was obviously fascinated with it, and generally divided his staring time between her breasts and her hair.

Lani slid her hand beneath her long tresses and lifted them towards him. "Would you like to touch it?"

He looked startled at the thought. "What?"

"My hair. Would you like to touch it and see what it feels like?"

The expression on his face was fascinating—an odd blend of longing and curiosity. Hesitantly, he reached toward her. "For the sake of learning more about your culture," he said gruffly.

"Here." Lani leaned forward, deliberately brushing her hair against his arm. Spirit, his biceps were bulging, especially tensed as they were right now. Good. She wanted him to react to her. To her way of thinking, men of stone were basically useless.

"Go ahead," she urged. "Touch it."

He ran his rough fingers along a length of hair, the breath hissing from his lungs. "It is so . . . so soft," he rumbled. "And so blue."

Most men found the color fascinating, and many wanted to know whether it was natural or not. Lani never told. Charmed by Gunnar's fascination, she giggled. "Yes, sweetness, it's blue."

His gaze snapped up, met hers. "You have other . . . hair?"

Oh, this was fun. "You mean pubic hair?"

231

"Pubic hair?" He looked confused, so he must not know the term.

"That's hair around the sexual organs," she explained. She didn't believe in orbiting the moon on sensitive topics.

"Oh." His skin darkened a few shades. This fierce warrior was actually embarrassed.

"Do Leors have hair in those places?" Lani prodded.

"No," he answered quickly. "No hair . . . anywhere, male or female."

He paused, his hand still stroking her blue tresses. She wondered if he was even aware of his action. "But you have other hair?" he persisted.

"Oh, yes," Lani answered breezily. "Most humanoids do."

"Ah," he said, then lapsed into silence.

"Any other questions?" she asked, thoroughly enjoying herself.

"Yes," he rumbled, adorable in his utter seriousness. "Is that other hair blue, too?"

Lani could imagine how it would feel to have him stroke that other hair. She wondered just how difficult it would be to sway him from his celibacy. She leaned back, thrusting her breasts forward, again drawing his gaze there. Crossing her legs, she slowly slid her tunic upward, exposing a generous amount of shapely thigh. She was well aware she had his full, undivided attention.

"Tell you what, big guy," she offered silkily. "I'll show you mine if you'll show me yours."

Pulling himself to his feet, Jarek rubbed his throbbing head. A stunner headache was the worse kind. He tried to move down the corridor, but had to stop and steady himself as a wave of dizziness hit him. Rani scrambled anxiously around his feet, making his progress even more difficult.

Eirene had betrayed him.

By the Fires! He couldn't believe it. He'd been so sure of himself, so sure of her. His instincts were usually unerringly accurate. She'd saved him from Turlock's men. Surrendered sweetly in his arms. Mentally cried out his name, as her body clenched hotly around his.

He'd been blinded by lust—pure and simple. How could he have been so stupid?

He stumbled halfway to the weapons vault, then stopped to regain his equilibrium. There might be more to it, he reasoned. Something had spooked her in the square today. He'd picked up a strange energy, but it had been hard to separate it from Eirene's unique pattern, and he'd been more focused on finding her.

He groaned, battling nausea. He didn't have time to figure out what had made her turn and run; he needed to find her, and fast. Turlock and his men could still be on the lookout for both of them, although Jarek hoped they had decided he'd left Saron. He felt certain Eirene would try to leave the planet quickly, and he knew she had the means, with the jewels in those daggers.

He would have trouble tracking her in his condition, but he had no choice. Swinging around unsteadily, he returned to his supplies. He took a swig of some vile-tasting concoction his brother-in-law, Chase, swore would help offset stun shock to the nervous system.

It did seem to help a little, Jarek admitted, as he made his way to the weapons vault. He checked the charge on the blasters he'd just purchased, and snapped them onto his utility belt.

He stopped long enough to scoop up Rani and put her in his lav. Then he left the ship and began the search for

Eirene. Crossing the marketplace, he picked up nothing. He could be too disoriented from the stun to sense her energy, or she could be on another part of Saron—or she was gone. His heart raced in protest. She couldn't be gone. He hurried to the transport station. Once there, however, he met a dead end.

He didn't sense her anywhere in the vicinity, didn't see her in any of the lines. He was forced to acknowledge the very real possibility that she'd already left the planet. He studied the holocorders, but he couldn't get access to the information on them. Sabin could, by showing his shadower credentials and claiming bounty privilege.

Damn. Jarek needed some help. He returned to his ship and sent a communication to Sabin's craft. As he had hoped, Sabin was on board.

"Travers here."

"Ranul here." They never used their full Shielder surnames when communicating on open airways. "Where are you right now?"

"Headed for Aldon. I've got more gold for you. What's going on?"

"I'm still on Saron. Eirene used a stunner on me and escaped. I've got to track her down. I think she may have taken a transport from here."

"Where the blazing hells did she get a stunner? You're getting careless, Jarek."

"She didn't get it from me. Just outside Risa's airspace, Turlock's men hijacked my ship and flew it to Saron. I hid Eirene in the concealed compartment before they boarded, and after they landed, she managed to get off the ship without being caught. She must have gotten the stunner at the marketplace."

Sabin let out a low whistle. "Turlock's men? Damn. How did you get away from them?

"Eirene. She used the stunner on them to save my hide, then turned around and used it on me."

"Women," Sabin said in mock disgust. "We obviously let Eirene hang around with Moriah too long. Sounds like you could use some help there, friend."

He needed a lot more than that, Jarek thought, gritting his teeth against the relentless ache in his head. He needed a miracle. But for now, Sabin would have to do. "Yeah, you're right. I need you here on Saron. How far out are you?"

"Only about one cycle."

Not bad, but not good, either. "Is Blake with you?" Jarek asked.

"Blake's right behind me in his own ship. I've also got Radd on board."

"Good. We might need him, too. Set course for Saron, then. I'll meet you at Solaris in one cycle."

"Will do. In the meantime, be careful."

Jarek signed off. What now? His hands clenched into fists, he felt like pounding the console. If Eirene had left the planet, there was little he could do but wait for Sabin's arrival to determine where she'd gone.

Deciding to check Saron again, on the slim chance she was still there, Jarek trudged back to the marketplace. He intended to find Eirene, on or off planet—one way or another. He couldn't allow himself to trust her again, though. Why in Hades had she turned the stunner on him?

He didn't think his mating technique had chased her off. She was too inexperienced to fake her responses, and he hadn't imagined those climatic energy surges, or his own super-nova releases.

Just the thought of their bed play sent Jarek's heart rate spiraling. He'd never desired a woman the way he did Eirene, never felt so replete and whole, when she lay in his arms after they found nirvana together.

He knew her lack of control over the energy surges when she climaxed had upset her greatly. Maybe that was part of the problem. Compared to the magnitude of what lay ahead, that could be easily dealt with—assuming he could find her.

He would find her, he told himself again. He had to find her. Just then, he picked up a faint trace of familiar energy. *Eirene.* He whipped around, mentally probing for a fix. Over there—near the south end of the marketplace, and moving away—possibly towards the landing bays.

His head still ached, his equilibrium was still shaky, but he strode rapidly toward the fading trail. He battled his way through the crowds, frustrated with the delay. She was moving at a faster pace, probably more on the edge of the marketplace now. Jarek shoved harder, ignoring the protests and threats as he snaked through the carts and stalls.

He drew closer, as the crowd thinned and scattered to various landing bays and lodges, not to mention the Pleasure Domes. There—up ahead. He thought he saw Eirene's dark hair, but then the person appeared to fall forward, as if she had stumbled. Concerned, Jarek broke into a run. Suddenly, he skidded to a halt, barely avoiding a hazardous situation. He stared at the group directly ahead of him, cursing his luck.

There stood Turlock's men—all four of them, and another man Jarek didn't know. They surrounded Eirene, who was pushing herself off the ground.

"Get up!" the fifth man snarled, grabbing her hair and yanking it. "Get up, you bitch."

It took every ounce of control Jarek had to avoid charging forward and blasting the bastard. But getting himself killed wouldn't help Eirene. Drawing a weapon, he edged sideways to get a better look. None of the beings milling around seemed to care about the drama unfolding.

"You're safe for now, girl, until we find that cursed healer," the man said. "Three hours in that crude hut of his! I can finish waiting on my own ship."

Jarek studied the man. He looked vaguely familiar, but Jarek couldn't place him. One of Turlock's men?

Eirene pushed her tangled hair back from her face with a trembling hand. Jarek's gut clenched. She looked terrified, but there was nothing he could do to help her yet. He was outnumbered, in a crowded area, where the firepower from six sets of weapons could injure a large number of innocent people and get Eirene killed. He dropped back a few paces so Turlock's men wouldn't spot him.

"But when that healer shows up, and Gunnar gets here, we'll know the truth," the man continued. "If you're no longer innocent, you'll be sorry you're still alive. Very sorry. Get going."

He shoved her hard, and she stumbled, almost falling again. Jarek clenched his blaster until the metal bit into his palm. He had to stay calm, focused. The man was most likely Eirene's father, or some other relative, probably the one who had made the trade with the Leors. But what was his connection with Turlock?

"Balen," the man barked out. "The healer's woman told us he likes to hang out at Solaris. Get over there and keep a watch out for him."

"But Vaden, I don't know what he looks like," Balen protested.

"You son of an Antek!" the man called Vaden roared. "Ask someone. The bartender will know who he is.

Don't come back without Healer Drake. I'll use you for disrupter practice if you do."

Balen's florid skin paled a few shades, and he turned and stumbled back toward the square. Jarek hastily ducked away as Balen passed him, the reek of cheap liquor lingering in his wake.

Jarek followed the group ahead of him at a safe distance, barely suppressing his rage as Vaden taunted and shoved Eirene. He would pay for his treatment of her, Jarek vowed.

They entered a landing bay, and Jarek was forced to weave between ships to avoid discovery. He crept along, on a parallel course with the group, until they entered a ship. The hatch closed behind them with a foreboding thud.

He stepped into the open and studied the ship. It was a star-class runner, the sort of ship a private supplier—or smuggler—might use. Sleek, fast, well-armored. It also had a sophisticated, high-security hatch. Radd could handle the hatch.

Jarek battled the urge to find some heavy-duty explosives and blast the hatch open and get Eirene out of there. He could well imagine what the vicious Vaden might be doing to her. But forcing the hatch would alert the men within, and he'd be entering a death trap. He couldn't do a damn thing about it until Sabin and the others got there.

He tried to tell himself that Vaden wouldn't kill or maim Eirene as long as he thought she might still be a virgin, and thus a tradable commodity. However, once he found out the truth. . . .

Shuddering, Jarek realized what he could do to keep Eirene safe and alive until help arrived. He could eliminate one of Turlock's men—permanently. And he could make damn sure a certain healer was put out of commission for the time being. There was no telling if the Leor had been contacted, or when he would arrive. Or when Turlock might show up. Jarek could only hope it wouldn't be for at least another cycle.

He glanced at the ship one more time. *Don't give up, Eirene,* he channelled, hoping she could pick up his broadcast. *I'll get you of there. I promise.*

He headed for Solaris to take care of Balen and Healer Drake.

Eirene sat beside her uncle in his meeting chamber, one wrist shackled to the chair arm. Webb, Derian, and Keraat sat around the massive table, along with Stane, Vaden's personal lackey. The men were drinking Elysian liquor—a lot of it—while they waited for Balen to return with the healer.

Vaden had always been a surly drunk, and his mood grew more foul with every drink he took. He held an electrolyzer rod in his left hand, and he shocked Eirene from time to time, just for his own enjoyment. She bit her lips until they bled, refusing give him satisfaction by crying out.

She was exhausted, mentally and physically, her body battered from Vaden's cruel physical torments. It took great effort for her to remain upright in her chair, when she wanted to collapse into a heap. She had difficulty thinking clearly, stunned by all that had transpired. But she tried to force herself to stay alert, to come up with a plan to help herself. Despair quickly intervened. There wasn't much hope to be had.

Turlock's men watched her with a mixture of lust and wariness. She eyed them coolly, refusing to let them see her fear. As her gaze settled on Derian, he drew back in alarm.

"Don't let her give me the evil eye!" he screeched. "Remember what she did to me earlier? She cast a spell that set my balls to burning."

The other men laughed raucously. "Superstitious son of an Antek, ain't he?" Webb snorted. Rubbing his scratched face, he leered at Eirene, an evil glint in his watery eyes. "But she's a wild kerani all right. If she doesn't go to the Leor, I want a chance at retribution for what she did to my face."

Keraat downed his drink. "Hey, maybe Derian's right," he said, his words slurred. "My chest hurt when I tried to touch her. Maybe she's got magic, like one of them Shens."

"She's just a simple female," Vaden scoffed. "Worthless to me if Gunnar doesn't want her." He thrust the electrolyzer rod against Eirene's leg, giving her a nasty jolt.

She gasped, digging her fingers into the chair arms, as agony singed every nerve ending in her body. She wouldn't cry out, she wouldn't. But the shocks were weakening her badly. If Vaden decided to use the rod again, she feared she would pass out.

"See?" her uncle crowed with a mocking smile. "She's no sorceress. I've known her all of her twenty-six seasons. She's weak and worthless."

Eirene released her breath as the agony receded somewhat. Spirit, maybe she should have used her powers while she had the chance. Yet, as inept as she was, she couldn't have controlled five men, then gotten away. They were already suspicious of her, at least Derian and Keraat were. If the others ever suspected the truth . . .

The image of the young male Enhancer's face flashed

into her mind, and she shuddered. No. Virtually any fate was preferable to being sold into slavery and forced to use her powers for evil gain.

Soon Balen would return with Healer Drake, and the pretense would be over. What then? She closed her eyes, seeking refuge from the terrifying probabilities. She thought of Jarek. Where was he now? Would he understand why she'd run? Hot tears filled her eyes. She couldn't have helped him, but they had shared such wondrous intimacies, if only for a short while.

She held on to those memories, and to the ones of Rayna, reliving them, savoring them one last time.

"Keraat!" her uncle bellowed, startling her from her reverie. "It's been hours since Balen went to Solaris. Go see what's keeping the slimy bastard. And don't either of you come back without the healer."

With a grunt, Keraat heaved to his feet, hitching up his pants, and moved unsteadily to the panel. Vaden watched him go, then shook his head in disgust. "Idiots. Blathering idiots, all of 'em."

His attention fixed on Eirene. "Especially you, girl. You thought you could run away, and I'd never find you. No female has ever made a fool of me. You'll get yours. Balen and Keraat will be back any time with that damn healer, and we'll know the truth for sure, won't we?"

They'd know all right, she thought, despair returning in great waves. She wondered what it was like to die.

Chapter Thirteen

A fist pounding on the table startled Eirene from her restless dozing. "Webb, Derian, wake up!" Vaden roared. He heaved to his feet, apparently just awakening himself. He kicked Stane, who was slumped over the table to his right.

Groaning, Webb, Derian, and Stane raised their heads from the table, and stared at Vaden. "Get up!" he ordered. Swiping a beefy hand across his bleary eyes, he looked at his chronometer. "Keraat's been gone fourteen hours. Where in the Abyss is he? And Balen—where's that son of an Antek? Get up, all of you."

The three men stumbled to their feet.

"We'll have to take care of the matter ourselves," Vaden growled. He turned toward Eirene. "I know you'll be eager for our return," he sneered. "In the meantime, some shackles on your legs ought to ensure you can't get away. Stane, get another set."

Eirene, hold on. Jarek's voice suddenly sounded inside her head with startling clarity.

She looked around the chamber. Nothing but the wretched, leering faces of Vaden and the others. She must have imagined hearing Jarek, just as she'd thought she heard him some hours ago, promising to free her. Desperate wishes, when her time had almost run out. Stane moved around the table, toward the entry panel.

Radd's almost got the hatch open, Jarek's voice came again.

Tension ramrodded through her body. It wasn't possible! Surely Jarek wasn't telepathically communicating with her.

We're getting you out of there.

She halfway bolted from the chair, but the shackle halted her reaction with a vicious shock. She fell back, momentarily stunned.

"What, getting scared, girl?" Vaden taunted. "Your Leor master is on his way, should be here in a few hours. I expect you're getting nervous."

A series of tones sounded in the chamber. "Ah, that must be Balen and Keraat," Vaden turned from Eirene. "They'd better have Healer Drake along if they know what's good for them."

Stane opened the panel and stepped into the corridor. Immediately, there came two blasts. Stane crumpled to the ground. Jarek and Sabin barrelled into the chamber, weapons raised.

Webb and Derian fumbled for their guns but were too slow. Several lightspeed shots sent them sprawling. Jarek and Sabin swung toward Vaden and Eirene.

"Drop your weapons, or she dies," Vaden snarled.

Eirene had been so caught up in the unfolding scene,

she hadn't realized her uncle had slid behind her and now pressed a metal object against her head.

Jarek and Sabin both paused, and Vaden's grip on Eirene's shoulder tightened painfully. The metal gouged her scalp. "This is a disrupter, at the highest setting," Vaden said. "She'll die a slow, agonizing death. And I'll still have a good shot at both of you, with her body for a shield."

Jarek threw down his weapon. Scowling, Sabin did the same. Eirene stared at Jarek, drinking in the sight of him. As glad as she was to see him, she was horrified she'd drawn him into danger. He stared back, his dark gaze roaming over her.

"No woman is worth a man's life," Vaden sneered. "I'll wager one of you is san Ranul."

Jarek stepped forward. Fury sparked in his eyes, but his tone was neutral when he spoke. "I'm san Ranul. Take me instead of Eirene. I'm wanted by the Controllers. I'm worth a lot more to you than she is."

"As if you're in a position to bargain," Vaden scoffed. "I don't make deals with any man stupid enough to put his life on the line for a mere female."

Ducking more securely behind Eirene, he shifted his weapon from her to Jarek. "Wait," Sabin said quickly. "The Controllers want san Ranul alive. They'll pay a lot more for him if he's turned in alive."

Vaden shifted the weapon toward Sabin. "That so? Well, I happen to know there's a reward even if san Ranul is dead. Not that it matters to me which one of you I kill first." He slowly swung the weapon back and forth between them. "You, or you. Which one first . . ."

Eirene's heart pounded, and the lack of oxygen in her chest left her lightheaded. This horrible nightmare couldn't be happening. Vaden fixed his aim on Jarek.

"You're the one who helped Eirene evade me. You can die first."

No! Without conscious thought, she sent a surge of energy into the weapon, sparking the charged power source inside it. The disrupter exploded in Vaden's hand, and he screamed in pain. She pivoted her chair around and kicked him backwards.

Jarek was on him in an instant, pounding him in a frenzy of fists. Vaden fought back, but Jarek had the upper hand. Eirene watched, aghast, as he delivered one punishing blow after another to her uncle. She cringed with every bone-crunching thud. She'd never seen Jarek this furious or savage. Never considered the people he might have killed in the line of duty to the Shielders.

"Stop!" she screamed. She held no fondness for her uncle, but he was her only family. She didn't want to see anyone die, and this glimpse of Jarek's violent side upset her greatly.

Her chair was suddenly spun around and she faced Sabin. "I've got to get you out of here," he said, slapping a sequencer on the shackles holding her to the chair. "It might take a few moments to find the sequence."

The sound of fists and grunts of pain came from behind, tearing at her. "Jarek's killing him," she gasped.

Sabin shrugged. "Nothing less than the bastard deserves."

"Please," Eirene begged. "Stop him."

"Relative of yours?"

How she could be a blood relation to someone like Vaden galled her, but she couldn't deny it. "Yes."

Sabin rolled his eyes and shook his head. "Hey, san Ranul. San Ranul. Jarek!" He yelled the last word, but couldn't get Jarek's attention.

Sabin moved around Eirene. She turned the chair and

watched him forcibly yank Jarek off her uncle. "Don't kill the bastard. He's a relation of Eirene's."

"Son of an Antek," Jarek swore, wrenching away and getting to his feet.

Vaden groaned. He started to get up, then collapsed on the floor, his face a bloody pulp. Horrified, Eirene couldn't bring herself to look away.

The sequencer clicked, and the shackles opened and fell to the floor. Then Jarek was lifting her into his arms with startling swiftness. "Let's get out of here," he said roughly.

She was so weak, she could barely hold on to him, but he felt solid, safe. Yet she couldn't leave without knowing about Vaden. She twisted, trying to see her uncle one more time. "Will he live?"

"Most likely. I didn't stop to think you might have feelings for this— For him. I guess I lost it, after seeing how he had treated you." Jarek carried her toward the panel. "Is he your father?"

Before she could answer, Vaden called out, "San Ranul."

Jarek turned toward Vaden. Sabin stood nearby, a weapon trained on her uncle.

"What?" Jarek asked.

Vaden pulled himself into a sitting position, spat blood. "I heard you killed someone, some seasons back. I want to know if it's true."

She felt the tension radiating from Jarek, sensed he didn't want to discuss such matters around her. "Who might that be?"

"Galen Kane," Vaden rasped, his breathing labored.

Her chest constricted, and panic roared through her. *Galen Kane? My father? No, surely not—*

"Heard you blasted him in the back of the head, like

the coward that you are," Vaden persisted. "That true?"

It couldn't be true! Her uncle was lying.

Jarek blew out his breath. "It's no secret," he admitted. "I shot Kane, six seasons ago, on Saron. I'm not surprised he was a friend to the likes of you."

No, no! It wasn't true. She refused to believe it.

"So you admit to murdering Galen?"

"I just told you I killed him." Jarek turned to go. "And I do it again if I had the opportunity."

Eirene's whole world, already careening out of control, seemed to collapse right then and there. Jarek had killed her father. A man she'd only seen a few times in her life, but had always hoped would come for her, would take her away from Travan. She'd fantasized he wasn't like the other males on Travan. Outside her uncle and Rayna, he'd been the only family she had.

Her lover had killed him.

"Hear that, Eirene?" Vaden crowed, a twisted triumph ringing in his voice. "This man you've been traveling with, probably fornicating with, shot your father in the back of the head. Murdered him in cold blood."

Eirene looked at Jarek, her horrified expression etching itself on his soul. The pain in her eyes, the betrayal—the revulsion—stabbed him like a dagger through the heart.

"You killed my father."

Damn! He'd had no idea Galen Kane was her father, had seen no reason to lie about something that was well-known and had happened over six seasons ago. He couldn't rescind his confession at this point. Besides, it was the truth.

"Eirene, I didn't know—"

"Put me down," she demanded, struggling against him.

"No. You're too weak to walk." He continued carrying her from Vaden's ship.

Sabin had used a stun gun on Vaden to give them time to get off Saron. The other men were only stunned, as well. Not that Jarek had an aversion to killing lowlifes, but he'd been afraid of Eirene getting caught in the crossfire and insisted they use stunners.

Jarek looked over his shoulder. Sabin, Radd, and Blake were right behind him. Radd had sprung the mechanism on the hatch, then he and Blake had searched the rest of the ship, ensuring there would be no surprises. They'd entered the meeting chamber just in time to hear Vaden's dramatic pronouncement that Jarek had killed Eirene's father. Which he had. Blazing hells.

"Put me down," Eirene insisted again, her voice rising. "Now! Put me down."

"I don't blame you for being upset. But I am not putting you down. I'm going to take you to my ship. Then we'll talk about this, and I can explain—"

"Explain shooting someone in the back of the head?"

Jarek's chest tightened with frustration. What could he say? She had saved his life a third time. He'd felt the energy flare right before the disrupter exploded in Vaden's hand. She'd come to his aid once more, only to discover he had killed her father.

Desperation washed over him, as he wondered if this wedge between Eirene and him could ever be removed. Her *father*, for Spirit's sake!

She stopped struggling, but she refused to look at him, or listen to him. He entered his ship and carried her to her cabin. Laying her on the bunk, he tried to brush back her hair and assess her injuries. She slapped his hand away and slid to the end of the bunk.

"Don't touch me," she hissed, her eyes flashing blue fire.

"You're distraught right now," Jarek tried to soothe her. "You've had a rough experience, and you're exhausted. I need to be sure you're not hurt."

The fire faded from her eyes, replaced by glistening tears. "It's a hurt you can't fix," she whispered. "Go away. Just go away."

She drew up her knees, wrapping her arms around them and burying her face against them. The dejected slump of her shoulders said it all. Any faith she'd had in him, any trust, any feeling for him, had been destroyed by the fact he'd killed her father.

"All right," he said, feeling the weight of the universe crushing him, as his heart quietly shattered. "I'll leave you alone."

He stepped into the corridor and leaned against the wall in utter desolation.

"How is she?" Sabin asked.

Jarek looked around at his friend. "How would you expect her to be? She won't talk to me. She won't let me touch her, or see how badly she might be injured. And she sure as hell isn't going to cooperate with any of my plans. *I killed her father.*"

"You and I both know that's not the whole truth," Sabin argued. "Let me talk to her. Let me explain what actually happened."

Jarek thought back to that day, six seasons ago, on Saron. Galen Kane was a vicious criminal who had sold the Controllers information on the location of a Shielder colony. His action had resulted in the murder of over two hundred Shielders, and Sabin and Jarek had been determined to seek retribution.

They'd gotten their chance when Galen tried to hijack

one of Moriah's shipments. He'd murdered one of her women, and seriously wounded Lionia. When Sabin confronted him, he'd tried to kill Sabin. Sabin beat him to the draw, with a blast to the heart. Jarek, standing behind Galen, had acted instinctively to save his friend, and blasted Galen in the back of the head.

Each was a kill shot. So, in effect, both Sabin and Jarek had been responsible for Galen's death. Jarek had no regrets. Galen was a mad animal, and had to be put away for society's sake.

Remembering this, Jarek shook his head. "What are you going to tell her? That I only half-killed her father, and you did the other half? Are you going to tell her what sort of man he was? I'd be willing to bet she doesn't know. Nothing you say will change the truth. I shot Galen Kane in the back of the head. I did it to defend you, but the fact remains that I did it."

"We *both* did it," Sabin protested.

Jarek sighed and ran his hand through his hair. "That won't change how she feels about me. Besides, if she doesn't know about your part in Kane's death, she might continue to talk to you. Would you go to her? Make sure she's okay, that Vaden didn't hurt her too badly. Please."

Sabin looked at him a long moment, indecision in his ebony eyes. Then he relented. "All right. I'll go check on her."

"Don't do me any favors. Don't try to explain," Jarek requested. "It won't help anything."

"If that's what you want." Sabin strode to Eirene's cabin and sounded the tone. "It's Sabin," he called out. "May I come in?"

She must have refused his request, because Jarek saw Sabin's eyebrows draw together and he said, "I'm coming in anyway, so make yourself decent." He glanced at Jarek and shook his head. "Women."

Jarek couldn't even muster a smile in return. He watched his friend enter Eirene's cabin, and cursed fate. *He* should be the one comforting her, not Sabin. *He* should be the one to see to her welfare, to treat her injuries.

He should be in there with her now, should be able to hold her in his arms when she slept. And when she awoke, he should be able to love her and replace all Vaden's cruel touches with tender caresses.

But he wouldn't be. Clenching his hands into fists, he paced the corridor until Sabin came out. "Well?" he demanded impatiently. "How is she?"

"She'll be okay. Vaden didn't hit her, or let Turlock's men at her, because he thought there might still be a chance he could trade her to Gunnar. But he used an electrolyzer rod on her. Shocked her five or six times, she thinks. She has a lot of soreness and a headache. She hasn't had anything to eat or drink, so I suspect she's dehydrated. Her state of mind is pretty rocky."

Vaden used an electrolyzer rod on Eirene? His rage returning, Jarek wished he could be alone with the man. He'd show him just how much an electrolyzer shock hurt.

"Are you sure she's not seriously injured?" he asked Sabin.

"As sure as I can be. Hell, I'm no physician. But her color is better, she's coherent, and she's moving around pretty well. No apparent injuries, just that large bruise on the side of her face."

"Derian did that to her when she got me off Turlock's ship. I tried to get her to heal it, but she refused. I suspect she's frightened of her abilities." Jarek paced a few steps, turned back to Sabin. "Do you think she'll talk to me?"

Sabin shook his head. "I'd give her more time."

Jarek felt like the sun had permanently set. His world, always heavy with responsibility, now seemed even darker and bleaker. He trusted Sabin's judgment, though, and yielded to it.

"All right. I'll leave her alone tonight. I've got Chase's concoction for stun trauma, and something for the headache. I'll replicate some broth, too. You can take those to her, and get her to drink some water. She should be feeling better by morning shift."

Sabin nodded. "Sounds like a good idea. So, what are you going to do now?"

Nothing had gone right so far, and Jarek knew he couldn't count on Eirene's cooperation, not now, probably not ever. His theory was full of holes, and the gold he had couldn't possibly purchase the equipment he needed. All the odds seemed against him. But he couldn't give up. Something inside, an inexplicable force that seemed to come from beyond him, wouldn't let him surrender.

"I'll head for Aldon as soon as Eirene is settled," he replied.

If Sabin thought Jarek was deranged for continuing on, he showed no sign of it. His eyes grave, he clasped Jarek's shoulder. "Spirit go with you."

Jarek hoped Sabin's benediction held. Because now, more than ever, he needed that miracle.

Jarek sat by Eirene's bunk, watching her sleep. Even with the bruise on her face, and the dark smudges of fatigue beneath her eyes, she was lovely. He could look at her forever; lose himself in her pale, silky skin, and her dark, glorious curtain of hair, flowing down over perfect breasts. But he knew when she opened her eyes, her loathing would impale his heart.

He had to let go of his personal feelings. He should never have allowed his involvement with Eirene to go this far. Duty came before all else. Duty had brought him to her cabin now, when she probably needed more time to heal than he could give her. They'd arrive at Aldon in two cycles, and he needed to find a way to reach her and gain her cooperation.

He'd been up most of sleep shift, pacing and thinking. He had decided to try and explain his part in her father's death, without revealing Galen Kane's true nature. Not only would Eirene refuse to believe such information about Kane, but there was nothing to be gained from telling her that her father had been a monster. She appeared to have cared for Kane. Why hurt her further, when it would accomplish nothing?

Under normal circumstances, Jarek wouldn't have attempted to justify his actions. He couldn't defend killing Eirene's father. But the fate of his people could hinge on her cooperation, so he had to try and make her understand. He figured his best chance was when she first awakened, when her defenses were down.

"Eirene," he called softly. "Wake up. We need to talk."

She stirred and shifted, her hair falling over her face. He reached out to touch her, thought better of it and withdrew his hand. "Hey. Wake up."

Her eyes opened slowly, and she shoved the hair away from her face. Her gaze shifted to him, quickly going from sleepy to wary. "What are you doing here?"

"I just want to talk."

"Get out."

"I will, as soon as we discuss a few things."

She sat up, pulling the cover over her chest. "I don't want to listen to you."

Jarek ignored her protests. "Thank you for saving my life yesterday. That's three times you've come to my aid."

Her hands clenched the cover. "There won't be a fourth."

"But for what you've done, I thank you," he said gravely. "I wanted to explain to you about your father."

"No," she said vehemently. "There's nothing to explain. You admitted to shooting him in the back of the head. I didn't realize you were so capable of violence. But I guess you proved it again yesterday, when you nearly killed my uncle. Get out."

Jarek held on to his patience. "Your father drew a weapon on Sabin. I was standing behind your father, and I thought he was going to kill Sabin. I reacted without thinking, to save my friend. Please believe me—it wasn't in cold blood."

She closed her eyes, her energy fluctuating wildly. "I don't want to hear any more. I can't . . . listen."

"I'm sorry this is painful, but I swear I would never kill anyone without just cause, or at least, what I believed to be just cause."

Eirene didn't move, didn't react in any way. It took all Jarek's control to keep from taking her into his arms and evoking the most primal of reactions. He leaned back in the chair, sighed.

"I'll admit, I've done some things that might seem questionable, but always with good reason. I've never lied to you, not even when it would have made things easier between us. I've been truthful about the Shielders and my plans. I didn't kill your father in cold blood, but in Sabin's defense. I'm just a man, with failings and shortcomings, but I try to live by a code of honor. I hope you know that."

She opened her eyes, but didn't look at him. Desperately, he searched for the words to reach her.

"*Shamara*. Do you know what that is, Eirene?"

Silence. He hadn't really expected her to answer. Her expression was cool and distant, as if she'd withdrawn from the conversation. From him.

"Shamara means sanctuary. Everyone should have a sanctuary, don't you think? A haven, a refuge from the ugliness of our universe. *Shamara*. A place to seek the light of the Spirit, to live in peace. That place might be calm oasis on a desert planet, or a shrine in a temple, or a quiet space within ourselves. Or for some of us who are more desperate, it could lie just beyond our reach, in another universe."

He rose and paced to the portal. Endless stars glittered against a midnight infinity. "*Shamara*," he repeated softly. "That's all I'm seeking for my people. I know you hate me. I can't change that. But I need your help to find it, Eirene."

He turned back to her. She stared straight ahead, her slender body rigid. He wasn't getting through to her. He'd said all he could say, and he hadn't dented her emotional armor. The chasm between them gaped too wide, fraught with pain and doubt.

"Think about it." He walked to the panel and left her cabin. He'd lost her—completely and irrevocably. No way in the Fires would she help him locate and navigate the worm hole now.

That should have been the most crushing setback. Yet just as painful was the knowledge that she'd shut him out of her life. That he was alone again, cursed forever to a solitary existence, as he upheld the duty that had been entrusted to him.

A duty to his people that he would never forsake— even at the sacrifice of his own life.

Eirene berated herself for foolishly allowing Jarek to get close to her. So close, in fact, that he was now able to communicate with her telepathically. Hadn't Rayna warned her about the dangers of her powers, as well as the evil nature of men? Hadn't her experience with the selfish, cruel males of Travan taught her *anything*?

She should have followed her instincts, respected her fears about her powers. Ignoring her inner warnings, and those of Rayna, had caused her this hardship.

Even now, she felt the pain of the Shielders, felt the lure of Jarek's words. *Everyone should have a sanctuary . . . a haven, a refuge from the ugliness of our universe.* His words had touched her, moved her, despite everything that had transpired. The man could seduce a stone carving with his visions and his charisma.

Eirene rolled over, battling tears and pounding her pillow. She was far from being made of stone. She'd let herself be charmed by Jarek, by his beguiling smile, his boyish good looks, and his magnetism. She'd tried to convince herself he was a different sort of man. Safe. Secure.

Oh, she realized he was a far cut above the men of Travan. He truly cared about something outside himself, and he lived by a code of honor, even if it was based on his own laws. He was dedicated to the Shielder cause, unswerving in his convictions, and probably an excellent leader.

But that type of unyielding strength had its negative side. Jarek had displayed his violent nature when he brutally beat her uncle. He might have killed Vaden, if Sabin hadn't halted him.

Until then, she hadn't thought of Jarek taking lives. But now that the infatuation had cleared, she realized killing would have to be a necessary part of his existence. Warranted or not, he had murdered Galen Kane.

Thinking of her father brought a new wave of tears. She hadn't known him well, but he'd been decent enough the few times he'd visited her at the women's compound on Travan. One time he had brought her an elaborately carved comb. He hadn't traded her when she reached puberty, as many fathers did their daughters.

Because of that, she'd always hoped he would allow her to leave Travan and study healing. But he'd left on one of his many jaunts six seasons ago and never returned. Her uncle had informed her of his demise, but offered no details. Now she knew the truth about her father's death.

She had also discovered Jarek's true nature. In her naiveté, she hadn't realized how ruthless he was, just how far he would go to achieve his goals.

Rayna had been right. Eirene must learn to depend only on herself. She must put aside her feelings for Jarek, must distance herself from him. She wanted to be a healer, to uphold the sacredness of life—not destroy it. A man like Jarek san Ranul could never honor that philosophy, not when he deemed killing necessary.

Eirene curled up on the bunk and lay there a long time, trying to deal with the reality and the pain.

When Jarek came to her cabin later in the day, her emotions betrayed her logic, surging to life at the sight of him. Her feelings for him were uncontrollable, just like her wretched powers.

He stared at her, and for the briefest moment, she

thought she saw the flash of pain in his eyes, before his face hardened into that mask of implacable resolve that she despised.

"We'll arrive at Aldon in one and a half cycles," he said quietly.

Then he turned and left, leaving her with her grief and fears and—far worse—the ludicrous longing to fling herself into his arms, in search of the comfort and protection she'd known there—if only for a few moments in time.

She forced that crazy urge from her mind, but the one word Jarek had shared kept haunting her. *Shamara.* The word resonated inside her, touching a chord deep within her soul.

Shamara. Sanctuary. Spirit, was there a sanctuary somewhere in the universe for her?

Chapter Fourteen

Lani was standing by the hatch when Gunnar entered the ship. He didn't acknowledge her, but strode past, whipping off his cloak. Clearly, he didn't want to speak to her. Of course, he'd pretty much avoided her ever since she had suggested they play show-and-tell. The man had absolutely no sense of humor—or of sensual adventure.

Not one to put up with such rudeness, Lani followed him, her high heels clicking down the corridor—a clean one, at that.

"Commander," she called. "A word with you, please."

"Not now," he growled, handing his cloak to Karr and entering his personal cabin.

Well, really! Pursing her lips, Lani followed right behind him, slipping inside before the panel closed and he could secure it. He turned, glaring at her.

"I said, not now."

She wasn't the least intimidated by his fierce scowl or

his massive body towering over her. Tilting up her chin to see him better, she put her hands on her hips. "Well, it has to be now. I need to talk to you before this ship takes off."

"Is it important enough for you to abandon the *courtesy* you insist upon?" he demanded, unbuckling his utility belt. "These are my private chambers, and I did not invite you here."

Lani smiled to herself at his mocking of her insistence on good manners. During their time together, Gunnar had displayed high intelligence and quick wit, traits she greatly admired. But he still didn't have a clue about the workings of the female mind, so she figured she held the advantage.

"Yes, it is," she answered. "I understand we're on Saron."

He tossed his belt onto a nearby console and sank into a large leather chair. "Not for much longer."

My, she loved the way the man occupied a chair. And the way he dressed for forays into outside societies—his high-gloss black boots and skin-tight leggings, which enhanced his masculinity to perfection. With an effort, she forced herself to focus on the matter at hand.

"Saron is my home," she explained. "I've enjoyed my visit on your ship—for the most part, anyway—but now I'd like to get back to my life, and my career."

"No." He began pulling off a boot.

Lani's mouth fell open in an indignant huff. Quickly regaining her composure, she scooted over to the chair. "What do you mean, *no*? I can't put my life on hold indefinitely while you cling to the silly idea that Celie Cameron lied to you and that your honor has been compromised."

Gunnar leaned back, his expression completely calm.

Lani had the sudden insight that he was becoming accustomed to her little strategies to get him stirred up.

"Help me with my boots," he ordered.

"What?" she shrilled. "I am not your personal servant, Commander."

He remained unperturbed. "Is that a no?"

"It certainly is."

"And it is not negotiable?"

Lani narrowed her eyes. What was he up to? She took another tack. "Oh, it's negotiable, Commander," she purred, running a blue-tipped finger down his bare chest, "if I get something out of it."

He scowled and pushed her hand away. "I do not know what you are up to, woman, but I will tell you this—you are still my hostage, and *that* is also not negotiable. You will not leave this ship."

He yanked off the boot, tossed it to the side, and started on the second boot.

"Why not?" Lani demanded. "I've been your hostage for fifteen cycles. I think that's more than enough. Surely by now you believe Captain Cameron was telling the truth, that she knew nothing of your bride's whereabouts."

Gunnar tossed the second boot on top of the first. "After today, I am more convinced than ever that Captain Cameron knows something."

So Lani's suspicions were correct. The sudden change of direction to Saron had something to do with Eirene. "You got information about your bride?" she guessed.

Gunnar's expression darkened. "It is nothing that concerns you."

"Of course it concerns me. I'm a hostage because of your missing bride. I have the right to know anything that affects how long I'll remain your hostage. The Intergalactic Humanities Act from the Varian Summit of the fourth millennium states that prisoners of war have the right—"

"You are not a prisoner of war!" he roared. "This is not about war. It is a trade deal in which I have been cheated. I tire of your ceaseless chatter about that Intergalactic gibberish, of which I have every intention of ignoring. Leor law dictates my decisions."

"As does Leor honor," Lani reminded him. "The honorable thing would be to tell me the truth. I deserve to know."

"I can see it would be the expedient thing to do," he growled. "If I want you to go away and leave me in peace."

Lani shimmied triumphantly. "So tell me, what happened? Did you get word of Eirene?"

Gunnar threw himself back in the chair, legs splayed wide. "Lady Eirene's uncle caught up with her on Saron. He took her into custody. But before a healer arrived to confirm the status of her virginity, Jarek san Ranul attacked Vaden and his men, and made off with her. There is no trace of either of them."

Oh, this was so exciting—and so romantic. Lani furrowed her brow, mulling things over. "Just because Eirene and Jarek are together doesn't mean Captain Cameron knew about Eirene."

"Captain Cameron was seen with san Ranul on Saron immediately after she arrived there from Travan. Her ship was the only one departing Travan when Lady Eirene disappeared. I believe those events to be related."

Lani thought of Eirene in the Pleasure Dome, and how Jarek had been her first client. Her instincts told her it was a chance meeting. "It could be a coincidence."

"I do not believe in coincidence. I prefer to leave nothing to chance." Gunnar rose and began to remove his leggings.

With a sigh of feminine appreciation, Lani watched him skim them off his well-muscled legs, leaving him in his usual loincloth.

"So, is virginity all that important in a bride?" she asked casually.

"Absolutely."

Lani rolled her eyes. The man had archaic ideas about morals and sex. "Why? Why should Leor men and women deny themselves the pleasure of sex?"

"Because abstinence shows we have total control over every function of our bodies, including sexual urges. Leor men want a woman who has proven she is mentally and physically strong, able to master her baser urges."

"Do you have sex after you're mated?"

"Of course we do," he said stiffly, returning to the chair. "It is necessary for procreation."

"Oh, I see. Repress all sexual desire for Spirit knows how many seasons, then suddenly, contact!—turn on the heat."

A mocking grin curved across his striking face. "That applies for those of us capable of control and self-discipline."

Oh! He was too smug for his own good. Lani braced her hand against the back of the chair and leaned towards him. "I've got news for you, Commander. Sexual urges are not any different from hunger or the need to sleep. They're natural and normal. You don't turn them off and on like running water."

"They can be totally controlled," he insisted.

She moved forward until she was standing between his legs. "Prove it."

His eyes narrowed. The sudden stiffness in his body

indicated his discomfort at her nearness. "It is not something that can be proven."

"Oh, but it is. I can show you just how wrong you are."

"I will not play your games."

"Are you afraid I'm right and you're wrong?" Lani challenged.

That got him. He sat straighter, pride in every magnificent millimeter of his body. "Certainly not."

"Then I challenge you to a battle . . . of the senses."

Before he could object, she ran her hands over his shoulders and down his magnasteel biceps. He didn't react, but she felt the tension radiating from him.

"Does that bother you?" she asked.

"No."

She trailed her fingers down his chest, swirling them around his dark brown nipples. They hardened into tight nubs. "How about this?"

His fingers dug into the arms of the chair. "No."

Just keep fighting it, big guy. She sank to her knees, letting her hands drift lower, and stroked his muscular thighs. His tension increased, as did the bulge beneath his loincloth.

"Is this affecting you?" she purred.

"Absolutely not," he said, his voice strained.

Lani did what she had wanted to do ever since she'd seen Commander Gunnar of Dukkair. She slid her fingers beneath the loincloth, pushing it to the side, and uncovered the masculine jewels of the chief of the Dukkair clan.

Oh, my. The loincloth had been deceiving, masking the true size of him. He was . . . *so* . . . *enormous*. And very aroused, despite his insistence to the contrary.

Lani's respirations and heart rate were becoming very rapid, and other parts of her anatomy were very much affected. She took him in both hands and expertly stroked him. He grew even larger, if that were possible.

"How . . . about that?" she said breathlessly.

"No . . . effect . . . at all," he groaned, shifting in the chair.

Well, so much for finesse. Her big barbarian was about to meet his match. Deciding to take matters out of her hands, Lani leaned down and let her very capable mouth take over.

As for Gunnar, he had very little to say after that. At least not anything coherent.

"I don't understand it," Jarek muttered, punching key pads. "Based on the information Celie gave me, we should be approaching Aldon. The radiometric readings showed our exact location just a moment ago. Now I'm not getting any readings at all."

Offering no response, Eirene stared out the portal. The easiest way for her to cope with all that had transpired had been to withdraw from Jarek as much as possible, a difficult feat in the face of his dynamic presence. She spoke to him only when absolutely necessary. She'd spent most of the past two cycles in her cabin, recuperating from her physical injuries.

Those injuries were fading, but the emotional wounds were still fresh, amplified by her complicated feelings for Jarek, and her lack of control over her wayward emotions. Even as she mourned her father and cursed the untenable situation in which Jarek had placed her, she still experienced the compelling attraction towards him, the desire to touch him, to seek refuge in his strong arms.

Her only haven was withdrawal, attempting to barricade herself from the powerful emotions bombarding her. Trying not to feel anything at all—and failing miserably.

"If I didn't know better, I'd think my navigational system was malfunctioning," Jarek's frustrated musing drew her attention back to the cockpit. "And now the transceiver is jammed. But there's no indication that either the nav or communication systems are down. All the test checks are normal. Son of an Antek!"

Eirene glanced at the console, not really concerned about system breakdowns. The longer the arrival on Aldon was delayed, the better. Suddenly, an odd frisson of energy shot through her, jolting her heart to a faster rhythm. It hadn't come from Jarek, or the ship, which meant . . . Her gaze darted to the portal. It had to be from somewhere out there, in space.

The subspace transceiver beeped, and she started. She forced herself to take a deep, calming breath. *Just nerves*, she thought, willing herself to settle down. She couldn't deal with Jarek if she didn't get better control of herself.

"Now communications are working. Very strange," Jarek said. "And that's my personal frequency." He turned on the videoviewer. "Ranul here."

"Greetings. We've been expecting you," came an odd, hissing whisper.

The viewer flashed onto a face shrouded in a purple cowl. The hood was so deep that no features were discernable, just an indistinct facial image.

Jarek leaned forward, his expression one of confusion. "And you are . . . ?"

"I am Eark. Celie advised us of your coming."

Eirene watched, totally riveted by the presence on the screen. Celie had told Jarek he didn't need to contact the Shens in advance—they would know when he arrived. The coordinates the Shens had provided were extremely vague, with the promise of later instructions. It seemed the Shens had found them, rather than the other way around.

"Greetings, Eark," Jarek replied. "I'm glad you contacted us. I wasn't certain how to reach you."

The hood inclined toward the screen. "She is with you?"

"I have a female passenger on board. Her name is Eirene."

"Yes. Very good."

Eirene's eyes widened in amazement. Why would the Shens be interested in her presence?

"You have another life form, as well."

"Another life form?" Jarek's brows drew together as he considered Eark's statement. "Oh. I have a small animal, a lanrax."

"That is acceptable." The hood leaned closer. Shadows and angles lurked inside the dark oval, as Eark's raspy whisper drifted into the cockpit.

"There are a few requirements before you will be permitted to visit Aldon. You will leave all weapons on your ship. Be advised they won't operate on Aldon should you disregard our wishes. No physical or emotional violence is tolerated at any time. You must agree to abide by our laws and our judgments. You will not reveal anything you see during your visit."

Jarek hesitated, and Eirene wondered if he was willing to go anywhere without a weapon. But he finally nodded. "Those are fair terms. We agree."

"Good. If you will provide a comm link, our computers will transmit the necessary coordinates to your system."

"That could be a problem. My navigational equipment seems to be malfunctioning."

"It will work, Captain," came the strange, whispery voice. "We just need the link."

Jarek gave him the information, then tried to activate his navigational screen. The screen remained blank, but the ship began a descent. He turned to the main console, punched some pads, but the ship continued downward.

Eirene felt a surge of the same powerful energy she'd sensed earlier. It was a very positive energy, not threatening in any way. However, Jarek's tension was palpable. He whirled to the videoviewer.

"Eark, something's wrong. My nav isn't working, and my ship isn't responding to manual commands."

"All is well," the Shen answered calmly. "We will guide your ship from here. I will soon greet you in the physical. Peace of the One be with you."

Eirene sank back, wrapped in reassuring vibrations. She didn't feel at all concerned, although Jarek obviously was not in control of the ship. He gripped the edge of the console, staring at the screens. Then he stood and strode to other panels. He punched more pads, but the ship continued its descent.

Moving back to his chair, he ran his hand through his hair. "I don't have a damn reading on a single screen," he grated. "The ship is not responding to anything."

"It's okay," Eirene said, oddly moved to reassure him. "I sense—I think the Shens are controlling it."

Giving a long sigh, Jarek shook his head. "Well, Spirit has brought us this far. Looks like it's out of our hands."

Just then, the ship inclined even more sharply. He stumbled forward before regaining his balance. "I guess we're going down." He slid into his seat and fastened his harness, looking over to be sure Eirene was strapped in. "I assume there's a planet down there—somewhere."

The ship moved smoothly at a steep angle. Soon they

were in atmospheric clouds, but the ship kept a rapid speed straight down. The monitoring screens remained blank. Finally, the ship leveled out until it was flying horizontally over a seemingly endless carpet of white clouds. On and on they went, nothing but clouds to be seen.

With startling abruptness, the clouds disappeared. Eirene gasped, her heart leaping at the sight below. They were directly above a massive waterfall, with only a few meters between them and the high cliffs. Dark pink water barrelled over the edge, falling hundreds of meters below.

"Damn," Jarek said. "They like to get your heart pumping, don't they?"

Eirene forced air into her constricted chest as the ship flew on, crossing the wide chasm of cliffs. It dropped lower, moving over thick, lush grasslands—purple in color. The carpet of purple extended in all directions as far as the eye could see. Then, up ahead, the outlines of buildings began to materialize, sprawled around a very tall structure.

As they drew closer, Eirene saw the structure appeared to be a multisided tower, rising to a point way above the other buildings. Blinding sun rays reflected off the top of it like a starburst. The energy she had sensed grew stronger as they approached the tower, until it seemed to resonate inside the cockpit.

Eirene realized the tower's entire tip was a huge, multifaceted crystal. It was the crystal reflecting the sun and creating the starburst effect, and the crystal also appeared to be the source of the energy now reverberating in every cell in her body.

She looked over at Jarek, wondering if he was affected by the crystal. He was staring at it. "That must be their main power source," he commented. "I've never seen anything like it." He glanced at Eirene. "I trust you can feel the vibrations from it?"

So he could sense the energy. Not surprising, since she was certain he could track her at will. Not that it mattered at this point. She didn't have much hope of getting away from him.

The ship slowed as they approached a spacious landing pad. The hoverlifts surged on, and the ship set down gently. The screens didn't come back on, but the ship responded when Jarek cut off the lifts and the engines. He shook his head, looking completely baffled. "Okay. I don't want to know."

He unhooked his harness, then rose and offered his hand to Eirene. "Ready?"

She looked at his calm face, into the dark eyes that seemed able to read her every thought. She had discovered the ultimate pleasures of womanhood in his arms; he had killed her father.

The old fears and doubts snaked through her. It wasn't her intent to punish an entire people because of the conflict between her and Jarek. But she couldn't help *anyone*. Despite that, she was being dragged deeper into Jarek's plans.

"No," she whispered. "I'm not ready."

He leaned over and unsnapped her harness. Taking her arm, he pulled her to her feet. His touch was light yet unyielding. He stared down at her as his hand slid up to rest against her cheek.

"There is very little chance for my people, Eirene. But I refuse to give up even the tiniest atom of hope. It's all I have. I must move forward with my plans. I have to pray to Spirit that your heart will guide you to do the right thing."

So much sincerity in his beautiful voice, so much doubt

in her soul. Her feelings towards him were too ambivalent, her grief over her father too recent. She shook her head, unable to answer him. He sighed, and brought up his other hand. He framed her face, his intense gaze boring into her.

"Eirene, about my personal feelings for you—I care for you, very deeply. I don't know if you can ever forgive me for your father's death. And even if you could, I can't give you what you deserve—commitment and stability. But I want you to know I will always cherish the memories of our time together."

She would never forget what had passed between them, either. Yet it upset her that she couldn't banish her feelings for Jarek, or at least keep them repressed, in light of all that had transpired. She turned her face away before he could see the truth of her feelings for him. There was a long moment of silence, then he took her hand, his touch infinitely gentle.

"Come on. Eark is expecting us."

He ushered her down the corridor and out the hatch. Four Shens stood waiting to greet them. Varying sizes and heights, they ranged from shorter than Eirene to taller than Jarek. All wore full-length robes with the deep hoods shielding their faces. As with the heights, the robes varied in color, although they were all rich jewel tones.

As Eirene stepped off the ramp, a potent energy enveloped her, tingling along her skin. It rolled through her, and overwhelmed her with its intensity. She tried to block the energy, but it was invasive. Her heart raced as panic edged her attempt to remain unaffected. Jarek slipped his arm around her. She was too disoriented to protest.

"I feel it, too," he said quietly. "Don't let it get to you."

"Yes, Lady Eirene," came a soft voice. "Be calm, and accept the energy. It is very good."

The tallest figure, cloaked in royal blue, bowed to her. "I am Phylos, the leader of this colony." He waved a graceful, slender hand toward the other three. "This is Eark, Neron, and Zailm. You have already spoken with Eark."

Eark, the shortest Shen, stepped forward. "Greetings," he rasped. "Welcome to Aldon, friends of Moriah and Celie."

"I return the greetings," Jarek answered, dropping his arm from around her, "and I thank you for allowing us admittance to Aldon. I'm not familiar with your customs, so I apologize if I offend you in any fashion. But I'd like to get down to business as soon as your ways will permit."

"Very direct, just like the Cameron ladies," Eark said.

"Yes. I'm afraid the seriousness of our situation necessitates that we be direct and transact our business quickly."

"We are well aware of your situation, Captain," Phylos replied.

"Then you can understand why we need to get down to business immediately. Especially on the matter of price—"

"And we sympathize with the plight of your people," Phylos continued, as if Jarek had not spoken. "However, you must understand that the universe works in ways which are mysterious to those of us who are merely the One's lowly servants. We cannot give you what you seek or discuss terms until all who are involved are ready."

The dark ovals of all four Shens turned towards Eirene. Battling to remain unaffected by the intense energy generated by the crystal and to follow the conversation at the same time, she stood there stiffly. Phylos was talking about her, she realized. *She* was the one who wasn't ready. Therefore, she was apparently the one who would keep the deal from moving forward.

Her heart felt heavy, weighed down by a tremendous burden. They didn't understand; they couldn't possibly. She had grappled with the issues involved, cycle after cycle. She felt deeply for the Shielders, knew in her soul she couldn't wish destruction upon them simply because of her tumultuous relationship with Jarek.

But she couldn't help them. Everyone seemed to think she could channel her powers to perform miraculous and amazing deeds. They seemed to think a mere, insignificant woman could save an entire race. They didn't know how little control she truly wielded, how ineffective she was.

Or that she had killed a woman she greatly loved and admired.

Because of her inability to use her powers, the Shielders would continue to be massacred. Stricken, she looked at Jarek. His expression was neutral, but the tension in his stance, his clenched hands, clearly showed his unhappiness with the situation.

"When all is ready," Phylos repeated. "Then, and only then, we will talk further about that which you seek, Captain san Ranul. In the meantime, you may stay here with us. We offer you our hospitality."

"Thank you, Phylos," Jarek said. "We accept your offer and hope that our negotiations will soon move forward."

He shifted his gaze to Eirene. She saw no censure there, no judgment or pleading, simply a quiet resignation. He knew he couldn't force her, that events were now out of his hands.

"We will show you to quarters where you may rest and renew your spirit," Phylos said formally. "Then you may join us later and replenish your bodies with the bounty of our planet. Lady Eirene, will you allow Zailm to escort you?"

"Of course," she answered.

Zailm, robed in deep emerald green, moved forward and offered a formal bow. He was slightly taller than Eirene, and a little more round in girth than the others. "Come with me, Lady," he rasped.

She followed behind, surprised to realize the landing pad was composed of some sort of pink stone, marbled with crystal. They stepped onto a pathway of purple grass, which felt like a cushion beneath her feet. Still battling the energy pressing in on her senses, Eirene tried to take in everything around her. They passed brilliant gardens alternating with pristine, crystalline buildings.

Zailm halted and turned to face her. "Do not resist the energy, Lady. It is not separate from you, but actually one with your own life force. Only your physical body makes it seem apart from you. Accept that the energy is a part of your being, allow yourself to flow with it."

Eirene stared at the shadowed oval fixed on her, sensing only sincerity and peacefulness from Zailm. Could it really be that simple? Just accept the energy and allow it within herself? She knew so little about how energy really worked.

"All energy comes from the One," Zailm explained, as if reading her thoughts. "Therefore, all energy is good."

Janaye had said basically the same thing. Drawing a deep breath, Eirene forced herself to relax, dropping her mental shields and no longer resisting. Immediately the oppressive sensation eased, and she felt considerably more relaxed. A tingling warmth flowed through her body, calming and revitalizing at the same time.

"Ah. You do well," Zailm rasped approvingly. "Are you ready to continue?"

Eirene nodded, and they moved forward. Zailm kept pace beside her. "You are especially sensitive to the energy," he explained, "because the One blessed you with the innate gift of channeling the energy."

She wasn't surprised that he knew about her powers, having realized the Shens were a highly advanced and intuitive society.

"Perhaps it is a gift," she conceded. "But I don't know how to use it. It should have been given to someone else, someone strong enough to handle it."

Zailm tsked and shook his head. "You must not think that, Lady Eirene. The One does not give us gifts without also giving us the capability to use them. You will meet with Phylos later, and perhaps he will be able to allay your concerns. He is a highly advanced soul, better qualified to offer guidance than a humble servant such as myself."

Eirene held her silence as they moved along the path. Aldon was truly amazing, and the Shens obviously highly advanced. But they couldn't possibly know everything. Phylos might be able to tell her more about the Enhancers, but he couldn't make her competent in the use of her powers.

Nor could he take away the pain that would always be a wedge between her and Jarek.

Chapter Fifteen

Jarek watched Zailm and Eirene moving away. He didn't like being separated from her, but didn't want to challenge the Shens over it. He knew the intense energy bombardment from the crystal was adversely affecting her. She was highly sensitive to all forms of energy, and didn't possess the natural mental shields that he did. Her own energy was fluctuating erratically, and he wanted to stay close to her, in case she needed him.

He scoffed at that last thought. Eirene had shut him out emotionally since she'd learned he killed her father. Nothing could undo the damage that knowledge had wrought. Worse, Jarek worried nothing would overcome her reluctance to use her powers. Fear might be a more accurate description than reluctance. Eirene didn't have a selfish atom in her body, but he knew she was afraid of her powers, convinced she couldn't control them.

Unfortunately, he didn't know if her fears were

grounded or not. He didn't have enough information on Enhancers to understand how their abilities worked.

"There is a creature in distress on your ship." Phylos' calm voice broke into Jarek's thoughts.

He forced his attention back to the Shen leader. "I beg your pardon?"

"The other life form on your ship. It is very distraught at being left behind."

"Oh. That's Rani, a lanrax. She has bonded with me and doesn't like being separated from me."

"We can wait while you retrieve her."

Jarek didn't miss the subtle command behind Phylos' gentle words. Rani must be broadcasting her unhappiness, and apparently the Shens disliked sensing any creature in distress.

"I'll be right back." Jarek strode up the ship ramp, shaking his head over the oddness of the Shens.

He returned moments later with the knapsack slung over his shoulder, Rani peering through the small opening he'd left. When she saw the Shens, she popped her head through, hissing and shrilling and snapping at them.

Phylos raised his hand toward her. Her fussing ceased immediately, changing to the contented chattering she normally reserved for when Jarek or Eirene petted her. Jarek wasn't surprised, not from what he'd witnessed so far. The Shens obviously had powers that went far beyond that of any other beings in the quadrant—with the possible exception of the Controllers.

"There now," Phylos said. "Your little Rani is no longer upset. All is well."

Jarek felt an almost hysterical urge to point out that all was *not* well. His people were being systematically massacred. Their only hope lay in a crazy scheme to locate a wormhole that might not even exist, a woman who despised their leader and didn't believe in her Spirit-given abilities, and a very strange race of beings.

Phylos turned and gestured toward the purple-robed figure. "Eark will see you to your quarters."

"Would you mind if I view the equipment first?" Jarek asked. "I'm fully aware we can't come to any agreement on purchasing it yet, but I'd like to look it over."

The hooded figure nodded. "I have no objection to that," came the whispery voice. "But be warned that seeing the equipment might be more unsettling than you think."

Jarek nodded, not certain how to take the cryptic comment. "My thanks, Phylos."

He followed Eark toward a path that led away from the direction in which Eirene had been taken. He observed everything around him, impressed with the gardens and the pink crystal buildings, and the calm, peaceful manner in which the numerous Shens moved through the city. From the knapsack, Rani watched the passing scenery, her maroon eyes bright and her nose twitching at the various scents. She didn't hiss at the nearby strangers, which was unusual for her.

"You are not so affected by the energy as Lady Eirene," Eark commented as they walked along a path of purple grass.

"No, I'm not. She is unusually sensitive."

"And yet, you're not acknowledging your oneness with the energy."

"I'm not sure what you mean."

Eark shrugged. "The shields that protect your people from the Controllers might also be a detriment when the energy of all must come together as the energy of the One."

Jarek mused over the Shen's words. "I'm certain you

speak words of wisdom, Eark, but I still don't understand."

"Then I will trust in the One to guide you in what you need to know."

The man spoke in riddles as Janaye often did. Jarek pushed back his frustration, knowing his anxiety and impatience would make no impression on the implacable Shens. Spirit had brought him here, and now all he could do was continue forward, pretty much on faith alone. He held his silence as they turned off the path and walked toward a tall building with five massive bays along one side.

"The machinery you seek is in here," Eark said, leading the way to one of the bays.

The huge panel raised as they approached, with only a whisper of sound. They entered an immaculate bay made from the same pink, crystal-laced granite composing the landing pad. The only items in the bay were seven large silver spheres, which lined the three full walls.

Jarek's heart skittered in his chest as he approached the nearest sphere. Here—at last—was the equipment he'd been striving to find. Hopefully, equipment that could locate a wormhole entrance and open that entrance long enough for a ship to pass through. *If his assumptions were correct.*

He stopped before the first sphere. It was large, approximately four meters in diameter. It would barely fit into a storage bay on a standard scouting ship, which was the most common craft in the Shielder fleet.

The sphere appeared to be perfectly round, and made up of a mirror-like silver alloy that Jarek had never encountered before. He saw his reflection as he touched the alloy, finding it extremely hard. The surface was not cool as expected, however, but surprisingly warm, as if it had an active power source within it. Which it did, Jarek realized, sensing the energy pulsing from the sphere.

He studied the surface and ran his hands over it, looking for lines in the metal, or niches, or mechanisms of some sort for opening the sphere. He couldn't feel anything. Nor did he see any panels, controls, or pads for activating the sphere. Nothing . . . nothing at all, but smooth, shiny alloy, completely unblemished.

Jarek exhaled a long slow breath, disappointment riding him hard. He looked at Eark, who had been standing patiently nearby. "I don't suppose you know how to get inside this or activate it?"

Eark shook his head. "This is not of our creation, Captain san Ranul. These machines were created by the Enhancers, and operated solely by them. I can share one bit of information with you—they are directed telepathically."

Jarek was not surprised to hear this, but it wasn't good news. "You mean they are operated by mental power."

"Yes. By Enhancer mental power."

It was what he had expected all along. Only Eirene or another Enhancer could activate these spheres. The despair he'd been holding at bay spread across his soul like a dark stain. He didn't think things could get any worse.

"Captain, I must tell you something else," Eark rasped. "We will not allow you to force Lady Eirene to do anything she does not choose to do of her own free will. Nor will we allow you to take her anywhere without her consent. We are offering her *shamara*. If she does not wish to see you again, we will honor her decision."

No, Jarek had been wrong. He had only imagined he'd hit rock bottom a moment ago.

Now he was facing the worst possible scenario.

*　　*　　*

Eirene sat in Phylos' official chamber, drinking tea with the Shen leader. The circular chamber was a surprise, as it held nothing but two plush sofas. It was encased entirely in glass and overlooked a stunning garden that bordered the outside perimeter. A soft breeze fanned through the room, sounding the chimes that hung from the pyramid point of the ceiling. It was a most unusual chamber.

But then, everything about the Shens was astonishing. At the meal earlier, levitated platters of food had drifted up and down the tables, stopping whenever someone desired a serving. Eirene had watched in amazement, unable to eat anything.

After the meal, Phylos asked with grave courtesy if she would accompany him to his official chambers so they could visit. Now they sat facing each other, drinking a delicious, unfamiliar tea from crystal cups.

"I sense you have many questions," Phylos began. "I will be glad to give you answers, if possible."

"I haven't seen any women among the Shens. Why is that?" Eirene asked, having wondered about that throughout the meal.

"Shens are androgynous. We have double souls within our bodies, containing both fully actualized male and female components. This enables us to procreate from within ourselves, while avoiding carnal desire and keeping our higher spiritual channels open."

Having experienced carnal desire first-hand, Eirene could see how that might cloud rational thinking and spiritual growth. It had certainly blinded her where Jarek was concerned. He still continued to haunt her thoughts. Resolutely, she forced her attention back to her questions for Phylos.

"And the levitation at dinner—was that some form of magic?"

"If you wish to consider explaining creating a reality as magic, then yes. However, it is a simple matter of visualizing that which you wish to create, then combining the energy of One with the will of self. Whatever the mind can conceive can be created."

"Most beings can't do that," Eirene protested, amazed at the concept.

"All beings have the capability to create, Lady. We are all co-creators with the One. But many have become enmeshed in the physical and have lost touch with their spiritual birthright."

"Are you telling me I could levitate things?"

"You could, if you learned how to tap into the energy."

"What about my Enhancer abilities?" Eirene asked, finally reaching the crux of the matter. "Could I learn to properly control and channel them?"

"Absolutely. It would help if you understood more about your people. Will you allow me to enlighten you?"

A part of her longed desperately to know more about Enhancers. Another part dreaded facing her own terrible shortcomings. Yet, she had often wondered about her ancestors. She took the plunge. "Yes, please. I've known so little about my heritage, and I'm confused about many things."

"Like the Shens, the Enhancers were a peaceful race who were more spiritually advanced than the majority of beings in the quadrant. As you know, Enhancers had the ability to tap into the universal energy and to direct it by their will. Because of their advanced spirituality, they chose to use their abilities in positive ways, such as healing and promoting peace. They were also technologically superior, and created equipment for exploring and mapping unknown sectors of the quadrant, and even beyond that."

"Did they really discover a wormhole leading to another galaxy?" Eirene asked.

"They did discover a hyperspace entry, but only to a different quadrant of our own galaxy. They created special equipment to enable them to navigate that wormhole."

So Jarek had been right. "Does that equipment still exist?"

"Yes, it is here on Aldon. The Shens and the Enhancers co-existed together quite harmoniously. Unfortunately, the Controllers learned of the unusual Enhancer abilities, and decided to harvest that power for their own evil purposes. They captured great numbers of Enhancers and attempted to force them to use their powers against the Controllers' enemies. Most Enhancers refused, and were tortured and ultimately executed for their non-cooperation. The Controllers simply hunted down more, but they, too refused to channel energy to achieve evil means."

Phylos sighed. "Eventually, all but a handful of Enhancers were gone. The few remaining went into hiding, never revealing their unusual powers. They crossbred with other races, passing their genetic codes down through many generations. Once in a great while, two people carrying the special genes will mate and produce an Enhancer. Such as you, my lady."

A great sadness engulfed Eirene. The Enhancers must have been incredibly strong in their spiritual convictions, and very brave to refuse to give in to the Controllers in the face of torture and death. She felt insignificant in comparison. And she felt intense anger that the Controllers wielded such cruel power in the quadrant.

"How could Spirit allow this to happen?" she demanded. "Is there no justice? I don't understand how Spirit could stand by and watch innocent people be murdered."

"There is always justice," Phylos answered quietly. "Spiritual justice, which we call karma. It works in accord with the universal plan. Often, we can't see the entire picture, so we can't see karma at work. But the Controllers will face a spiritual destiny that will involve a long and arduous path back to the Light. Their souls will ultimately pay a heavy toll for their choices."

Rayna had often talked about karma, so Eirene understood the concept. She nodded, accepting that there was a reaction for every action in the universe.

"Why haven't the Controllers come after your people?" she asked. "Your race is also highly advanced, and you have impressive powers. Why aren't you hunted and persecuted?"

"We have many abilities in which the Controllers would be interested. But we were more powerful than the Enhancers. They had been in the physical existence longer than we had, and thus had grown more enmeshed in the flesh. Their souls had split into separate male and female entities, making them more vulnerable to carnal desires. They could not mask their presence or evade Controller agents."

Phylos finished his tea. The cup and saucer vanished, and he folded his arms across his chest. "We have the ability to change our appearance, and to block all evidence of our existence. No one can find Aldon unless we wish it so.

"When it appeared the end of the physical experience was near for the remaining Enhancers, we agreed to safeguard their artifacts and equipment here on Aldon, in the hopes there would be a re-emergence of the Enhancer race. Now here you are, Lady Eirene."

"My presence means very little," she said dejectedly. "I have no control over my abilities, Phylos. I must be spiritually weak."

He leaned forward and touched her for the first time, gently patting her knee. Odd sensations sizzled through her. Looking down, she saw that the skin on his hand was translucent, glowing with energy. Maybe his altered appearance was why he kept his face shielded.

"It is," he said, obviously reading her thoughts. "The brightness of our bodies would be disconcerting to you. It is easier to communicate with others if they are not constantly distracted by our appearance. We can make ourselves look humanoid, but choose to wear robes instead.

"Now, let us discuss your powers," he continued. "Although you doubt yourself, you are completely normal for an Enhancer."

"That can't be," she protested, the memory of Rayna heavy in her heart.

The pain was as fresh as if it had just happened. Eirene had a vivid vision of Rayna lying on her crude pallet, gray and unresponsive, her life force draining from her.

"I find it hard to believe that it's normal for Enhancers to kill someone they're trying to help." Tears welled in her eyes, and she looked away, battling for control. "Even if it's accidental."

A whisper of a touch grazed her right temple, issuing a gentle flow of warmth and reassurance. Eirene blinked, suddenly realizing Phylos' palm was pressed against her face. Feeling no alarm, only love and acceptance, she remained still.

After a moment, he drew back with a soft exhalation

of breath. "I have observed your troubling memory. I apologize for the intrusion, but I felt your distress and sensed it was holding you back from your heritage."

"I don't think I should be using my powers if they cause harm," Eirene told him.

"It would be impossible for energy that is channeled with love and the desire to heal to cause harm. However, even the strongest, most positive energy cannot hold a soul which is ready to leave the physical plane."

She drew a trembling breath, trying to calm herself. "I don't understand."

"Your memory showed me your great love for Rayna. You tried very hard to heal her. But her time was at an end. Her body was worn down and her soul ready to depart. It had already lingered much past the call to be united with the One, because she was unwilling to leave you."

He was right about Rayna lingering. She had held on for cycles, with a tenacity incongruous with her frail, diseased body. Eirene had been reluctant to use her powers at first, knowing she didn't have good control of them. But Rayna's suffering had spurred her to try. Then, the unthinkable had happened. Moments after Eirene channelled energy into Rayna's body, her mentor drew her last breath.

"You did not kill Rayna," Phylos insisted gently. "Your energy gave her the strength she needed to accept the inevitable and release herself from the body. You could not have halted her passing, no matter how skillfully you might have applied your powers."

Could he possibly be right? For the first time, a tentative hope bloomed inside Eirene. "How can I be sure?" she asked. "I know so little about energy and healing."

"All young Enhancers need time and practice to learn

how to properly channel energy. But there is more to it than that. They need to be grounded by other Enhancers."

"Grounded?"

"Yes. Enhancers always worked energy in groups, preferably in numbers of three. They grounded each other and created a circle for the energy, thus giving them much greater control. You see, when you channel energy by yourself, it comes from the universe into you. Then it moves from you to the object of your channeling. As it leaves you, it can become dispersed, and thus much harder to focus.

"With two other Enhancers, the energy is drawn into one person, flows through a second person who can temper it if necessary, goes into the object of the channel, then back into the third Enhancer, who returns it to the universe. It can't become diffused, and should there be excess energy drawn in, it is harmlessly redirected by the three workers. There is always more strength in numbers."

His words made sense, and with startling clarity, Eirene could see how some of her attempts to use her powers had resulted in too little or too much energy. For the first time since Rayna's death, the huge burden of guilt eased from her soul. Eirene felt a tremendous rush of relief. Maybe she wasn't truly inept. Maybe she just needed more experience and grounding. But that could never be achieved, since her kind were virtually extinct.

"Then I still can't safely use my powers," she mused, "because I have no way to ground myself with other Enhancers."

"This is a valid concern," Phylos agreed. "But it still might be possible for you to help Captain san Ranul. You see, the spheres that will open the wormhole and navigate it are operated by Enhancer mind energy, which amplifies the internal power source already in the sphere. The sphere will act as a ground for the Enhancers using it, so that the energy can move in a continuous circle, thus creating the power the sphere needs for operation."

"So you're saying the sphere will ground me?" Eirene asked, her excitement rising. "I can safely operate it and help the Shielders?"

Phylos hesitated. "Yes, the sphere will ground you. But it was designed to be operated by three Enhancers. I am not certain if a sole Enhancer can activate it."

"I could try, couldn't I?" she persisted. "I couldn't blow up anything or cause any serious damage, could I?"

"No, with the circular pattern of energy between you and the sphere, there could be no overflow."

"Then I have to try. I need to help the Shielders find that wormhole," she said, more to herself than to the Shen leader. "If Spirit gave me this ability, it would be wrong to turn my back on such need."

"You are very wise, Lady Eirene, that you recognize such an important truth. However, I fear you won't be able to fully utilize your powers on behalf of the Shielders until you resolve your feelings toward Commander san Ranul."

"I don't know if that's possible, Phylos."

"Because he killed your father?"

She was no longer surprised that the Shen knew so much. "Not completely. I truly don't believe Jarek is a cold-blooded murderer. But ... my father ... I feel so wounded inside. I'm not sure I can forgive Jarek, at least not yet. I need more time. Yet I can't blame an entire race of people for the actions of one man. Isn't it enough to want to help them, if the equipment will balance my powers and ground me?"

"Negative emotions require more energy than positive ones. I'm afraid your feelings toward Jarek will be a strain on your powers."

Eirene felt like she was navigating a mine field, trying to balance her need to retreat and heal against the desperate plight of Jarek's people. Why did this have to be so complicated?

"I can't make the pain I feel go away, Phylos."

"You might be able to change your perceptions, Lady Eirene."

"How can I change my perceptions about the fact that Jarek killed my father?"

"Are you willing to face the truth?"

She hesitated, fear edging in. She wasn't sure she could handle any more emotional surprises. "I don't know."

Phylos rose. "I think you are stronger than you realize. Come with me to the temple. We will meditate together in the Chamber of Truth. Perhaps you will get your answers."

She almost refused. But then, that nagging inner voice chided her for her cowardice. She was tired of not being in control, of not moving ahead and creating her own destiny. It was time to take charge of her life. She'd already proven she could withstand pain. Facing the truth couldn't possibly be any worse.

Could it?

The energy in the Chamber of Truth was even more intense and unsettling than it was in the rest of the community. Large granite half-spheres mounted along the walls of the chamber resonated with power.

"They are magnetic, and conduct the energy of the One," Phylos explained, again sensing her thoughts.

"That is why we use this chamber to seek guidance, as all truth comes from the One."

Eirene's heart beat rapidly, and her breathing was shallow. But she'd come this far, and she was determined to learn as much as she could. She settled on the crystal bench beside Phylos and followed his instructions to close her eyes and breathe deeply.

"Focus on your breathing," came his curious rasp. "In your heart, hold the questions to which you seek answers. Think of nothing but your breathing, your questions, your breathing, your questions . . ."

Breathe in, breathe out . . . What answers did she seek? Breathe in, breathe out . . . *Spirit, I'm so confused, I don't even know what to ask. Please show me what I need to know.* Breathe in, breathe out. In, out . . .

Her surroundings blurred, and the bench and the chamber faded away. White wisps swirled in a gray mist. Energy tingled up her spine, then spilled over onto her forehead. There was a burst of brilliant white light, then—

Screaming. Awful, horrible screaming. Utter terror, spurred on by the explosion of weapons, the stench of burning flesh, the blood, and—Spirit help her—the screams. People running everywhere, women scooping up small children and tiny babies, men brandishing small, ineffectual weapons against rocket launchers and laser rifles. Antek troops moving forward, blasting in a wide arc, killing everyone, everything—men, women, children, and animals—in their path. Except for the women they raped—before they killed them. But eventually, every living thing was cut down like morini grass. Until the screams finally stopped . . .

No, no! She didn't want to see this, didn't want to know who these people were. Eirene struggled to block out the scene before her, then blessedly, it changed. Oh, thank you, Spirit, thank you . . .

Turlock—it was Turlock, the same man who had attacked Jarek's ship outside Elysia. He strode down a corridor of what appeared to be a ship and entered an ornate council chamber. He tossed a large bag onto the table. Coins clinked inside the bag—the unmistakable sound of gold.

"Here it is, Kane," Turlock snorted, slobber drooling from his snout. *"Part of the five thousand miterons the Controllers paid. The rest are in the corridor."*

"So they verified it was indeed a Shielder settlement?" said a smooth, cultured voice.

The man's face came into view—unlined skin, almost youthful in appearance. But the neatly trimmed gray hair and beard betrayed his age. The cold, emotionless eyes hinted at the lack of a soul. He looked strikingly like Vaden, only more polished and sophisticated.

Galen Kane. Her father.

"Oh, yeah, they verified it, all right," Turlock chortled. *"They've already destroyed the entire colony. Gave us an extra miteron for every Shielder they killed—two hundred and twenty more miterons."*

Eirene tried to pull back, to cry out her denial. This was her father. He'd never do anything like that, never! She didn't believe it. She didn't want to see any more.

The scene moved forward, inexorable, unyielding to her denial and her attempts to withdraw . . .

Jarek was standing in a clearing, his blaster trained on Turlock and another man, both lying wounded on the ground. It was as if Eirene were inside Jarek's mind, knew all that he was thinking. He could easily kill either man, but his objective was simply to keep an eye on them, while Sabin dealt with Kane.

Galen stood facing Sabin san Travers, his back to Jarek. Although she could only see the man from behind. Eirene knew it was her father standing there. Jarek's thoughts told her that. He waited watchfully, observing the conversation between Sabin and Galen.

"You sorry son of a bitch!" Sabin said furiously. "You didn't have to hurt these women. You enjoy killing, don't you?"

Eirene's father shrugged. "Self-defense."

Self defense? Her father had shot women, and was claiming self-defense?

Just then, a shout came from the woods behind Jarek. "Hey, Travers! Thanks for holding my bounty for me."

Eirene didn't recognize the voice, but it didn't seem important. What mattered was that her father took advantage of Sabin's momentary distraction and swept up a laser rifle lying on the ground. He swung the weapon toward Sabin and fired. Sabin dropped and rolled, raising his weapon toward Kane. Jarek reacted instinctively, bringing his blaster around and discharging it toward her father.

No, no! Father!

Sabin had gotten off a round as well. Her father lay face down on the ground, a wound from Jarek in the back of his head. Sabin rolled him over to reveal another wound to his heart. Either would have killed him.

Jarek felt no sense of triumph, no joy in what had just transpired, only the grim knowledge he'd done the only thing he could do, under the circumstances.

Her father was dead. Eirene sank to her knees. Her father . . .

"Lady Eirene! Are you all right?" A hand on her shoulder shook her back to reality.

She found herself kneeling on the granite floor in the

Chamber of Truth, tears on her face. Phylos' hooded figure knelt opposite her. "Are you all right?" he asked again in his odd voice.

No, she wasn't all right. If she'd thought learning Jarek had killed her father was the worst blow she'd ever received, she'd been wrong. It was far worse to be shown her father had been an uncaring monster who facilitated the slaughter of innocent people for his own financial gain.

It couldn't be true. It was just a nightmare, the deepest darkest fears of her subconscious brought to the surface by the electromagnetic force field in this horrible chamber.

She scrubbed her palm over her face, trying to force away the vision, along with the tears. "Phylos," she gasped. "Is everything seen here the absolute truth? Couldn't it just be my fears?"

He made a slight movement, and suddenly she found herself on the bench again, with him beside her.

"It is truth, Lady Eirene," he said gently. "The power from the spheres in this chamber comes directly from the One. We always come here when we have questions and need guidance."

It felt as if a cold fist wrapped around Eirene's heart and squeezed. It couldn't be true, it couldn't be . . . But then she remembered what Jarek had told her—that he had shot her father in order to defend Sabin.

"Maybe what I saw was only something I heard, and it got stuck in my mind," she said, desperately grasping for some explanation.

"I'm sorry you are upset. But I promise you, whatever you saw is truth."

The problem was, it *felt* like what she'd seen was the truth. She'd known deep inside, although she'd refused

293

to admit it, that Jarek was telling her the truth. He was an honorable and decent person. She knew that, had known it almost from the beginning. Overwhelmed by her grief and fear, she had tried to deny it.

Jarek had never lied to her. He just hadn't told her everything—like the fact that her father was the cold-blooded murderer, not Jarek.

As she accepted the bitter, painful knowledge about the true nature of her father, new concerns inundated Eirene. She raised her gaze to the dark oval focused on her. "Phylos, since Spirit speaks through these spheres, surely It can show me what the future will bring."

"That is not possible."

"It must be possible!" she cried. "Spirit knows everything."

"The One does not know the future, my lady. We have been granted free will, and it is our choices which will mold and create the future, not the wishes of the One."

"But—"

"What you choose to do next will shape your karma, and your existence from this time forward. The future is up to you, Lady Eirene."

Her head suddenly began throbbing. Pressing her face into her hands, Eirene rocked back and forth on the bench. She didn't know if she could bear the emotional torment raging within. Without knowing there was hope for the future, she wasn't sure she could go on. She must have done something terrible in a past life to reap this karma . . .

Karma. She bolted upright, a flash of insight galvanizing her. *Karma.* Of course! Her father had committed an outrageous atrocity toward the Shielders, resulting in hundreds of deaths. Nothing could bring those lives back, nothing could truly make amends, and yet . . .

And yet, she could contribute towards the healing of the Shielder race. She could give of herself, offer her powers to operate the sphere and lead the Shielders to a new life.

To shamara.

Fate had brought her here, to Aldon, to learn about her abilities, and about her destiny. And that destiny lay in helping Jarek realize his dream of finding shamara for his people.

Jarek. The thought of him had her on her feet and moving toward the entry.

"Phylos, I must find Jarek—now. Do you know where he is?"

The Shen showed no surprise at her sudden urgency. "Reach out with your mind—and your soul, Lady Eirene. Seek that which you need. You will find it."

She did, visualizing Jarek, and mentally searching across Aldon. In a startling optic burst, she saw him, as if she were watching a holocorder. He was alone, a solitary figure sitting on a bench beneath a dark sky, staring out across the water. His expression was grim, the look of a man who had no options left.

With a great heave of his chest, he slumped forward, burying his face in his hands. Despair and anguish radiated in every line of his body. So much sorrow, so little hope.

Eirene's heart wrenched. Here was a man who had witnessed the ongoing, systematic destruction of his people. A man who stood firm in his convictions despite insurmountable odds, living his life totally alone. A man in great pain, with no one to ease that pain.

She couldn't stand the suffering any longer—for either of them.

Jarek! she mentally called out to him.

His head snapped up. *Eirene!*

Jarek, I need to see you.

He rose and turned toward the city, concern etched on his handsome face. Her pulse raced faster.

His answer came back to her, his familiar voice clear in her mind. *Eirene, what's wrong?*

I have to talk to you. Where are you?

He started forward. *I'm by the water, near the equipment bays. I'll come to you.*

So easily they communicated, the words flowing telepathically between them. The bond had been there all along, Eirene realized.

No, I'll come to you, she returned.

The visual faded, but she knew she could find him. She ran through the temple entry and into the darkening night, racing toward Jarek.

Racing toward her destiny.

Chapter Sixteen

Eirene ran toward the water, taking the path to her right. She could sense Jarek's energy from that direction. She'd never been able to track his life force before, yet the inexplicable bond between them now guided her unerringly toward her goal.

Night had fallen, but the lights of the city reflected off the water, and the heavens, awash with stars, illuminated the path. The thick carpet of grass cushioned her steps as she ran, moving away from the settlement. The pure, balmy air rushed around her, whipping her hair out behind her.

Her thoughts tumbled inside her mind. Thoughts of Rayna, of her father, of Jarek, all pounded at her. She was mentally and physically drained from the emotional shock she had received, but she needed to see Jarek. She needed to tell him she knew the truth about her father, and what she'd learned from Phylos about her powers.

But most of all, she needed *him*—his calm strength, and his strong convictions. He was her stability in a universe gone nova.

All at once, he was there, coming up the path to meet her. He looked strong, steady . . . and wonderful. "Jarek!"

He opened his arms and she hurled herself against him. He absorbed the impact, staggering back a step, then steadying both of them. His arms closed around her, a welcoming haven to keep the demons at bay.

He was warm and solid, a beacon of security. Inhaling his masculine, woodsy scent, she burrowed against him.

"You're trembling. What's wrong, little one?"

His deep voice, filled with such concern and compassion, resonated through her soul. It released the emotional maelstrom inside her. Feelings, emotions, pushed into her chest until she feared it would explode. Tears pooled, then overflowed, tracking down her cheeks.

"J-J-Jarek," was all she managed before the sobs wrenched free.

"Ah, sweetness," he murmured, gathering her closer.

She grabbed the front of his flightsuit, only vaguely aware of being lifted and carried. Her pain and her grief were too great, the rush of feelings overwhelming. Yet, on some instinctive level, she knew she was safe, even in this emotional storm. Jarek was there, and he was her anchor.

The movement stopped, and she realized he was lowering her to the soft carpet of grass. She had a brief glimpse of tree branches swaying overhead, before he settled against the trunk and pulled her onto his lap.

He tucked her against him as if she were a child, curving her legs beneath her and settling her next to his chest, her head cradled against his shoulder. Then he just held her and rocked her, his voice washing over her in reassuring waves.

It didn't matter that she was too caught up in the storm to hear what he was saying—the tone of his voice, his touch, his concern—all flowed through her like a healing balm, soothing and comforting.

She knew—with every cell in her body—that this man would never hurt her. Nor would he murder anyone in cold blood. He was a trained soldier, skilled in weapons and fighting. He had incredible determination, and a magnasteel will. But he was also a man of honor and integrity.

A man who would hold a weeping woman in his arms with incredible tenderness, and nurture her soul with his touch and his words.

And she let him, soaking up his care like a starflower absorbed water. Gradually, the tears slowed, then stopped. Utterly exhausted, she rested against him, thinking about all Phylos had told her, and about what she'd seen in the Chamber of Truth. She shuddered at the memory.

"Hey," Jarek said softly. "Are you okay?"

"I think so." She shifted, tilting her face to look at him.

The shadows cast by the tree obscured his features, but she could tell he watched her intently.

"You came to me," he murmured. "You were in pain, and you came to me."

"I needed you." As she said the words, she knew they were true. She'd known intuitively Jarek was the only one who would understand her feelings, the only one who could ease her sorrow.

He rubbed his cheek against her hair. "I'm glad. Spirit, I'm so glad you're here."

The tears had given her a release from the emotional

shock, but the pain was still there, soul deep. "Oh, Jarek, why does the truth have to hurt so much?"

His hand slid up to cup her cheek. "Not all truth is ugly." He gently wiped the moisture from her face. "There is a lot of goodness in life."

"I know the truth about my father. At least, I think I do."

His fingers stilled on her face. "What about your father?"

She took a deep breath. "Did he really sell information about the location of a Shielder settlement to the Controllers?"

"Does it matter now?" he asked quietly. "You can't change the past, Eirene, and there might be things you really don't want to know."

He was putting her well-being before all else, she realized, when the truth would clear his actions.

"Yes, it matters. I don't want this between us, Jarek. I want to understand what happened with my father. Please tell me the truth."

He was silent a long moment. "All right. To the best of my knowledge, your father turned in a Shielder colony to the Controllers. Sabin and I witnessed the results of the carnage. We were able to rescue one young boy."

Eirene closed her eyes, renewed pain spiraling through her. Only one survivor—out of hundreds. And her father had been responsible for those deaths. A sound of distress rose in her throat.

Jarek pulled her against him. "I'm sorry."

"You didn't do it. *He* did." Resolutely, she shoved away the pain. "Phylos took me to a place in the temple called the Chamber of Truth. I had visions there. I saw you shoot my father."

Jarek's arms tightened around her. "Eirene—"

"You told me the truth about his death," she rushed on, needing to deal with what had happened. "I saw my father pull his weapon on Sabin, saw both you and Sabin shoot my father. You acted on instinct to save your friend. I know that."

"I'm still sorry—"

"No!" she interrupted vehemently, pushing away and pressing her fingers against his lips. "Not another word. My father was a monster. A monster! You had to do what you did."

He took her hand, touched his lips against it. Sudden, startling heat swirled through her. "I regret you had to discover this," he said quietly.

"I should have believed in you, Jarek. I know I hurt you."

"Shhh. It's over and done."

She cuddled closer to him. "I learned much more tonight. Phylos explained many things."

Jarek relaxed back against the tree, easing her against his chest. He tucked her head beneath his chin, began stroking her hair. "Tell me about it."

She closed her eyes, oddly soothed. She could stay this way forever, she thought, surrounded by Jarek's warmth and strength, lulled by his fingers gliding through her hair.

"I found out more about the Enhancers, and my powers."

She sensed the sudden surge of interest, knew she had his undivided attention. Yet his hand continued its sensuous stroking, and he merely said, "What did you learn?"

"That it's normal for an inexperienced Enhancer to have trouble controlling energy. Enhancers usually did energy work in groups of three, to stabilize and channel the power. Phylos called it grounding."

"That makes sense," Jarek said slowly.

Eirene could almost hear the thoughts whirring through his mind. He was probably connecting that with whether or not she could help him. However, she no longer felt resentful. She knew now that Jarek cared for her, but she also realized saving his people came before all else. She accepted that, even admired his unwavering dedication.

"I also learned that I probably didn't kill Rayna. At least, I hope that's true. Phylos said I wasn't responsible for her death."

His hand halted its stroking. "You want to run that by me again? Who is Rayna?"

Thoughts of her mentor brought a fresh rush of grief, but Eirene wanted to share this with him. She took a deep breath. "My mother died when I was a baby. Rayna raised me, and I grew to love her greatly. She was very wise, and highly skilled in healing. She recognized my unusual powers early on, and urged me to keep them hidden. She feared what would happen if I was discovered."

"And well she should have," Jarek commented.

"As I became older, my powers increased in strength. I experimented with them some, but the results were always disastrous. I set a tree on fire, healed a broken bone unevenly in a kerani, leaving the poor creature with a limp. Awful things like that."

"That's not so terrible. All skills must be practiced and learned."

"I guess," Eirene conceded. "But Rayna cautioned me against using my powers. She said I could acquire healing skills without drawing on them. I learned a tremendous amount from her. I was content, being with her, and watching her work. But then she grew ill." She paused, emotion clogging her throat.

"She—she was quite a bit older than my mother, had seen many seasons. I prayed to Spirit for her to recover, tried every healing technique I knew. Nothing seemed to help. I thought she would . . . would pass on, but she didn't."

Eirene closed her eyes, the memory of Rayna's illness burning like an open wound. Jarek resumed stroking her hair. "Watching a loved one grow old and ill is tough," he said gently.

Wiping away threatening tears, she nodded. "It was horrible. Rayna kept lingering, and she was in terrible pain. I couldn't stand it any longer, so I tried to channel healing energy into her body. She died almost immediately, which I took to be a sure indication of my incompetence."

"No," Jarek said decisively. "It sounds like the will of Spirit to me."

"That's what Phylos said. He told me that the strongest healing energy in the universe can't hold back a soul that's ready to leave the physical plane. But all this time, I believed I killed Rayna. I've been afraid to use my powers."

"Ah, sweetness, how could you think that? You could never kill anyone. You're too good, too caring."

The absolute conviction in Jarek's voice touched Eirene's heart. Not even Rayna had ever displayed such confidence in her.

"Not intentionally," she replied. "But I might hurt someone if my powers backfired. I short-circuited your hatch alarm when I just wanted to turn it off. I didn't mean to explode the disrupter in Vaden's hand, only to disable it. You see the problem? I'm can't handle my powers."

"You healed me in the Pleasure Dome. You're obviously able to pull in the energy. All you need to do is learn how to channel it. Perhaps you can find a way to ground it without another Enhancer. Just being aware of the erratic energy surges might help with controlling them."

That hadn't worked at all when she and Jarek had mated. "I'm not so sure of that. What about when we . . . you know . . ."

Eirene faltered, embarrassment heating her cheeks, as she thought of the shattering pleasure she'd found in Jarek's arms. A spark of desire leaped to life inside her, fanned by those memories.

He shifted, cupping her face and tilting it upward. "You mean when we make love?"

The husky timbre of his voice sent heat pooling in her lower body. Her heart speeded to an irregular beat. "Um, yes, that's what I was referring to."

He stared at her a long moment, and she wondered if he could sense her physical response to his nearness, to the memories of him touching her, filling her, claiming her. She was probably broadcasting her desire loud and clear, since she seemed to have no control over that, either.

He lowered his face near hers, and even in the shadows, she could see the flash of his teeth, the glitter in his eyes. "You mean when we're flesh to flesh, with me buried so deeply inside you, I think I'll die from the pleasure of it?" he whispered hoarsely. "And you make those sweet little sounds that drive me over the edge?"

She made sounds when they were mating? Mortified,

Eirene tried to push away, but his hands slid downward and gripped her arms.

"And then we both explode, and the energy hurls us to the stars in the most incredible ecstasy I've ever experienced in my entire existence? Is *that* what you're talking about?"

He hadn't even kissed her, or touched her intimately, but already her body was going up in flames. What was it between them? It was madness, a physical weakness. She should control it, should resist it, but . . . she didn't want to. She wanted to rediscover the nirvana she'd found with Jarek.

It was more than just a physical need. She craved the emotional closeness they shared, along with the mental bond that formed between them when they mated. She wanted to meld with Jarek, spiritually and physically. She wanted to find healing and peace within his arms.

By the Spirit, why deny it? Deliberately, she created sensual, erotic images of what they had shared in her mind.

"Eirene!"

So she *was* able to broadcast to him. "What?" she asked innocently.

"You have some very suggestive thoughts in that pretty head of yours, lady. I'm shocked."

But his body said otherwise, springing to life against her side. Sexual tension radiated from him as he lowered his mouth towards hers. She turned her face away, determined to be an equal partner this time.

Mating had been something Jarek had done *to* her, because she'd been inexperienced, and totally caught up in the reactions he'd wrung from her. Now she wanted to participate fully.

"First off, stay out of my mind," she said with mock

severity. "And as for my . . . thoughts, are they really so shocking? You seemed willing enough before."

"Sweetness, for you, I'm always willing." With a sigh, he released her and leaned back. "But I understand if you're not up to this. You haven't slept for almost two cycles. You've just had a very upsetting experience and—"

"Hush." She grabbed his head and pulled him down. "This is not the time to be noble."

She sealed her lips over his. He groaned, sliding his fingers up through her hair. She demanded entry to his mouth, and he gave it to her, his tongue mating hungrily with hers. He tasted so good, so familiar, so . . . right. Fire raced through her bloodstream, molten lava into her abdomen and lower.

She twisted on his lap, trying to get closer, to ease the demanding ache. His hand slid down, cupping her breast and teasing the nipple through the fabric. She pressed against his hand, desperately needing the contact.

"Sweetness," he gasped, trying to shift her off him. "Let me move and—"

"No!" she said fiercely. "Stay right where you are. I want to do this my way."

His chest heaving, he leaned his head back, his heated gaze melting her. He held his arms out in the universal gesture of surrender. "Any way you want, little one."

"That's more like it," she muttered, turning so that she straddled him.

She slid her fingers beneath the seam of his flightsuit, and slowly undid it, parting it to press kisses along his firm flesh. His chest was beautifully delineated, so masculine. His nipples were dark beaded nubs.

Wondering if they were as sensitive as hers, she stroked them. His quick inhalation gave her the answer, and she leaned forward to swirl her tongue around one nipple. The breath hissed from Jarek's lungs, and she decided she liked the feminine power she wielded over him.

Except that desire went both ways, she discovered, as she explored the flat planes of his belly, then let her hand trail down over the bulging evidence of his arousal. Her heart was pounding against her rib cage, and her breath was coming in short spurts.

She opened the front of his pants, aware of the new level of tension seizing him, of the sudden tautness of his thighs. She slid her hand inside, amazed by the feel of him—smooth skin over molten magnasteel, throbbing in her hand.

"Oh, Spirit," Jarek groaned.

His hands moved over her, slipping inside her robe and cupping her breasts. It was her turn to groan, as he stoked the flames, and she felt a rush of liquid heat in response.

"That damn robe is in the way," he muttered.

"So are your pants," Eirene said shakily.

She didn't want to wait any longer, wanted only to feel his bare skin against hers. She rose and stepped back, slipped her robe off her shoulders.

His gaze locked with hers, Jarek hurriedly tugged off his boots and tossed them aside. He shrugged out of his shirt, then came to his feet. She let the robe drop to the ground. His heated perusal moved down her body, setting off nuclear reactions inside.

"So beautiful," he murmured, then shoved his pants down and off.

He took her in his arms, pressing her tightly against his scorching skin, his blatant arousal. She tilted her head back as he kissed her face, her neck. She ran her hands over his back and buttocks, shuddering as he leaned her backward to kiss her breasts.

It was madness, all right—a heady, potent mix of pleasure. They sank down onto the soft grass together. Jarek urged her to lie down, but she refused.

"No," she told him, pushing him back against the trunk.

He complied, and she straddled him again, leaning forward to kiss him. He smoothed his hand along her thighs, then between them, seeking her heat.

"Two can play this game," he whispered seductively, sliding a finger inside her and stroking deeply. Pleasure arced through her, leaving her needy for more. She felt her body's hot, moist response, felt herself clenching around his finger. Trembling, she grabbed his shoulders to steady herself.

He dragged her forward with his other hand and lowered his mouth to her breast. Madness, sending them both into a vortex of need and sensation. Touching, caressing, each feeding the flames, until Eirene thought the inferno would consume her.

"Jarek," she groaned. "I can't wait any longer."

"Then don't," he grated out, lifting her over him.

His hands splayed over her hips, he guided her down. She gasped as he filled her, far more deeply than she'd ever thought possible. Then deeper still as he rocked against her.

He guided her movements until she picked up the motion on her own. It was . . . the most . . . incredible . . . sensation, she discovered, moving on him, slowly at first, then more quickly. His touch was were everywhere on her, her breasts, her belly, between her legs, tantalizing, urging.

Jarek!

That's it, sweetness. Come with me, he demanded telepathically, grasping her hips and taking over the rhythm.

Faster, more urgent, until everything blurred, except for the building crescendo of pleasure, and the final explosion that sent them both hurtling into a wild free fall.

Somehow she knew that only Jarek could bring her to the brink of such ultimate fulfillment, then hurl them both over the edge. And only Jarek's hold on her kept her from spinning into total oblivion. It seemed to go on and on, waves of energy arcing between them, around them, wild and primitive. The swells of sensation finally slowed, ebbing away gradually, and leaving her totally drained.

She collapsed over him, too weak too move. He slid his arms around her, held her close. She felt the solid beat of his heart beneath her cheek.

"You make sounds, too," she couldn't resist pointing out.

His laughter vibrated in his chest. "Sweetness, with you, it feels so good, I can't hold back. I don't care if we wake every Shen on Aldon."

Cringing at the thought, Eirene raised her head and glanced around. Fortunately, they appeared to be well out of the city, and she didn't see any robed figures lurking nearby. The poor Shens—they didn't engage in the mating act. What a shame. They were missing out on one of the most wonderful experiences in the universe.

As if reading her thoughts, Jarek said, "That was pretty amazing. You okay, little one?"

The old frustration returned. "I couldn't control the energy. Jarek, I can't control it no matter how hard I try."

"I'm not sure it's realistic to expect control during

something so wonderful. You might start with trying to manage the energy at a less . . . frantic moment."

He sounded so calm, so unconcerned. She wished she could share his confidence.

"I want to help you find the wormhole," she told him. "I intend to use my powers to operate the sphere. But I'm afraid I won't be able to."

He gave a short exhalation, then pressed a kiss against her hair. "Thank you for trying. We'll work together and find a way to ground your powers. First thing in the morning, we'll look at the equipment, and maybe you'll learn something from it."

"I'm willing to try," she said, but doubts still plagued her.

Jarek stroked her back, sliding his fingers through her hair. "I thank you for tonight. I will hold this memory in my heart always."

Tenderness and warmth flowed through her. She lifted her head and kissed him, then collapsed with a tired sigh. "I might never recover."

"Oh, I'll make certain that you do. I have some ideas on how we might channel that energy of yours, but it might take quite a few tries to get it right."

Eirene punched him, and he laughed. She finally felt at peace. She was going to help Jarek find his wormhole. This time, she knew for certain she'd made the right decision.

It was cool and quiet inside the massive bay that housed the Enhancer spheres. Eirene felt the energy the moment she and Jarek stepped through the entry, accompanied by Phylos. It was far different from that broadcast by the giant crystal or the magnetic orbs in the Chamber of Truth. Instead, it was similar to the energy the young male Enhancer had transmitted; more *specific* somehow, as if it was directed solely at Eirene.

Enhancer energy. It reverberated through every cell in her body, hauntingly familiar. It was her own energy, mirrored back to her, at a vibratory rate she recognized on some deep, subconscious level.

Astonished, she looked at Jarek. "Can you feel that?"

"I sense a source of energy coming from inside the spheres, but it doesn't affect me in any way. What do you feel?"

Eirene glanced towards Phylos, who stood a courteous distance away. She could see nothing but shadows in the hood's opening.

"It's just . . . very strange," she murmured, drawn toward the closest sphere. "I'm not sure."

She approached the orb, her body tingling as she drew near. The sphere looked huge to her, its diameter almost twice that of Jarek's height. Her heart speeded up, and she felt winded, as if she'd run a great distance. A vibration hummed through the air, coming from all seven spheres. It was as if they were *singing* to her, although that seemed an odd thought.

Touch me . . . touch me . . . touch me, the sphere chanted, drawing her inexorably to the mirrored surface. As she reached out to it, the hum increased to a higher intensity, and pinpoints of light flashed in the metal.

"By the Fires," Jarek murmured.

The moment she touched the sphere, she felt a powerful drag on her energy, as if an invisible vortex were sucking the life force out of her. Adrenaline-laced panic surged through her, sending her pulse to lightspeed, constricting the air flow in her chest.

Jarek! she cried out mentally, too impeded to speak.

"Eirene! Move away from it!"

But then energy surged back into her from the sphere, in a rush that almost pitched her backward. It flooded her body, with flashes of light exploding behind her eyes, electricity sparking through every nerve ending. It jarred her, leaving her momentarily disoriented. She could barely catch her breath.

"Eirene!"

Wait. Gasping, she raised her free hand and motioned Jarek back. *Don't come any closer.*

Like a mighty undertow, the energy was sucked back into the sphere, draining her, leaving her weak and shaking. She placed her second hand on the surface, felt an even greater pull. The sphere's vibration increased, rising in pitch. The lights sparking off its surface changed from white to blue.

"Eirene, I want you to stop the moment this becomes too much for you to handle. Do you hear me?" Jarek demanded.

Yes. Just a little longer.

She was beginning to understand the pattern now. The sphere was feeding off her life force, along with the outside energies she was pulling in, using them to enhance its own stored energy. The combined energy was circling back to her and then to the sphere, back and forth between them, growing in strength with every surge, fueled by outside energy she was continually drawing.

Three Enhancers. Phylos had said they worked in groups of three, to stabilize and control the energy, especially in the operation of the spheres. Now Eirene understood why. The power the sphere would ultimately generate, the amount of outside energy it would demand to do its intended job, was far greater than one being could handle. It would take the combined strength of at least three Enhancers to control a sphere.

With enormous effort, she wrenched her hands away from the sphere, and stumbled back. Her legs gave out and she collapsed onto the granite floor. Jarek was there in an instant, slipping his arms around her. "Are you okay?"

Gasping, she nodded. "Just . . . give me . . . a minute to catch . . . my breath."

"I don't like this. You're as white as the glaciers on Atara."

"Really, I'm fine."

Closing her eyes, she leaned against him, savoring his warmth and strength. She wasn't even close to being okay. She was weak and trembling and badly shaken up. Now she understood how the spheres worked, how they interacted with the Enhancers using them.

They required massive amounts of energy to be drawn into the Enhancers and then channeled into the sphere itself. The circulating energy pattern the sphere created was immensely powerful, requiring a solid buffer. Which meant at least three Enhancers, and possibly more, were necessary to maintain stability and absorb the strain so no one Enhancer would be totally depleted.

She wondered if the huge drain on one Enhancer would disrupt the grounding and cause the energy to go wild. Her eyes flew open at the thought, the familiar panic flaring. She looked toward the robed figure.

"Phylos, could you tell if the energy remained grounded?"

He nodded. "It did, my lady."

"No spillage or stray surges?"

"No. You kept it controlled."

"I could have told you that," Jarek said, concern harshening his voice. "I can feel when your energy fluctuates. You held steady."

So he could clearly sense her energy, as she had long suspected, although that fact no longer bothered her. Now she had a far more pressing concern.

Three Enhancers were necessary to safely operate the sphere. But there weren't three Enhancers available. There was only one—her. She finally understood why she was here.

Karma.

She was convinced now that fate had brought Jarek and her together because of her father's heinous crime against the Shielders. She'd been given the opportunity to make amends for her father's actions. She had the ability to operate the sphere, to guide Jarek and his people to shamara.

She knew now what her destiny was, and she intended to fulfill that destiny.

Just as she knew she would die in the process.

Chapter Seventeen

From the beginning, he'd been drawn to her when she was asleep. She had a special beauty then, an innocence and purity unmarred by worldly concerns. Jarek sat on the edge of the bed, watching Eirene, wrapped in the spell she wove around him, even in slumber.

But the wonder was tainted by a nagging worry that refused to go away. She was far too pale, and had been since yesterday's episode with the sphere.

After her collapse, she'd had difficulty standing, until Phylos placed his oddly glowing hands on her and chanted something in a strange language.

Even after that, Eirene had been unsteady on her feet, requiring Jarek's support more than once during the walk to his quarters. She claimed it was because she wasn't used to working with the sort of energy the sphere generated, but that she would become proficient at it. Phylos had made no comment. The Shen leader's silence worried

315

Jarek as much as anything, although he couldn't say why.

He felt certain something had gone wrong when Eirene activated the sphere. It should not have left her so weak. She'd climbed on his bed and dozed off and on the rest of the cycle. She'd roused to go to the evening meal with the Shens, but had fallen asleep across the bed as soon as they returned to Jarek's quarters.

She hadn't even been aware of him sliding off her leggings and placing her beneath the covers; nor of him getting into bed with her and holding her close through the night. Rani hadn't been too happy with the arrangement, but had finally settled at the foot of the bed, near his feet.

Now it was well into the new cycle, and Eirene was still asleep. Jarek couldn't decide whether to wake her. She could just be suffering from sheer exhaustion after so little sleep and the emotional trauma she'd been through, but his instincts told him differently.

He suspected the sphere was the culprit, and that it might be dangerous for Eirene to activate it again. Fear tore at him. He didn't want to place her at risk, yet he needed that cursed sphere. She was the only one who could operate it. And, despite his feelings for her, his people must come first.

"Hey." Her soft voice drifted over him like a warm Elysian breeze.

Drawn from his dark thoughts, Jarek gazed into her eyes, falling headlong into those blue, beckoning pools. There was no longer accusation or pain there, only a welcoming acceptance. He thanked Spirit for the miracle that had turned Eirene around, garnering her forgiveness and sending her back to him.

"Hey, yourself. It's about time you woke up. How are you feeling?"

"Ummm." She stretched sensuously, her breasts pressing against the thin fabric of her tunic, and his breath caught. "Pretty good. What time is it?"

"I'm not sure, because the Shens don't keep time like we do. But they rang the bells for the midday meal about an hour ago."

"Midday?" Her eyes widened. "You let me sleep the cycle away." She scrambled upright, tumbling Rani, who had been curled against her. The lanrax chattered in protest. Eirene frowned at Jarek, her hair falling over her shoulders and chest in soft tangles. "Why didn't you wake me?"

"Because you needed the rest. You sure you're okay?"

"Of course. Would you move?" She shoved at him playfully, and he slid over to give her room.

She stood and stretched again, pulling her tunic taut against her shapely little rear. And her legs . . . damn, but they were great. Jarek's body came to full alert. He had no control where she was concerned.

"Where are my pants?" she asked, looking down at her bare legs in bewilderment.

"I thought you'd be more comfortable without them." He'd been tempted to remove the tunic as well, but had decided against it. Too much strain on his libido. "Tell me how the sphere works."

She paused, a wary look flashing into her eyes. He didn't miss the sudden tenseness of her body, or her hands clenched into fists. She turned, tossing her hair over her shoulder, and headed toward the lav. "Give me a chance to wake up, okay?"

Jarek let her go, but he had every intention of discussing the sphere and its effects on her—in great detail. She took her time, and he heard the hum of the cleansing stall. He remained on the edge of the bed, waiting. Rani settled into his lap, vibrating with contentment.

When Eirene returned, she wouldn't make direct eye contact with him. Before he could ask her anything, she launched into rapid conversation.

"Do you think the Shens can levitate or create—or whatever it is they do—some food for me? I'm starving." She looked around the room, her ebony brows drawn together. "Where did you put the rest of my clothes? I'll get dressed and we can go—"

"Eirene, I want to talk to you. Now."

She turned toward him, her expression apprehensive. "I'm really hungry."

"I'll find you something to eat after we talk." Jarek patted the bed. "Come here, please."

She came slowly, reluctantly, but she met his gaze this time. He took her hand and pulled her down beside him. "Bear with me, little one. I need to understand about the sphere, to know how it affected you."

She exhaled softly, her eyes unreadable, but he felt the fluctuation in her energy. "What is it you want to know?"

"How does the sphere work?"

"It has an internal energy source, enough to spark it to life when an outside spark is provided."

"Enhancer energy." He said it as a statement of fact.

She nodded. He wondered if she realized how tightly she was gripping his hand. "So the sphere drains your physical energy?" he asked.

Her eyes flared. "Oh . . . no. I channel outside energy into the sphere."

"What do you mean by 'outside energy?' "

She looked down at their clasped hands, her hair falling like a curtain across her face. "Phylos explained to me that everything is composed of energy, basically the energy of Spirit. That energy can be restructured in various ways, take on many forms."

"So you pull energy from the environment around you and feed it to the sphere, as a sort of fuel?"

She looked up at him, her eyes a startling blue. "Exactly. And the sphere grounds me, so the energy stays between us and doesn't get scattered."

"How does it ground you?"

"It feeds the energy back to me, and I pull in more to feed back to it, and everything moves in a circle between us."

Jarek considered this. "It sounds like the energy cycles . . . so you're getting it returned, and it's not draining you."

She hesitated, and he felt her life force surge again. Something was upsetting her. "Yes," she said. "That's what happened yesterday."

"Then why the blazing hells did it leave you so exhausted if it's returning the energy to you?"

Eirene gave a little shrug. "I have very little experience, and I'm not used to working with energy. I suspect most of this sort of work is tiring. I'll get used to it."

Jarek wasn't convinced. "Did Phylos tell you that?"

"He said all young Enhancers have trouble at first, that they have to gain experience." She placed her hand against the side of his face. "You know what? You worry too much."

He sighed in frustration. "There's too damn much that can go wrong." Curving his arm around her, he drew her closer. "I don't want anything to happen to you."

She suddenly twisted into him, winding her arms around his neck and holding on tightly. Rani squealed indignantly and leaped from his lap.

"Nothing will happen," Eirene insisted, her breath soft

and warm on his neck. "I just need to learn to control the power better."

Then why was she trembling? Jarek rested his face against her hair, inhaling its freshness. He felt her breasts pressed against his chest, their enticing fullness making it hard to think clearly. He needed to bring his attention back to the discussion of the sphere and its possible threat to Eirene, but damn, he was having difficulty concentrating.

She lifted her face to his, and he couldn't resist those lush lips. He bent his head and tasted her, his blood pounding through his veins when she slid her tongue into his mouth.

Heat, as intense as a solar flare, rose swiftly. His body hardened, his skin heating to a feverish pitch. He relinquished any hope of continuing the discussion—for now—but still, he battled for control. He didn't want Eirene to think their joinings were based solely on lust. He wanted to show her how he felt about her, even if he couldn't give her the words or the commitment she deserved.

Deepening the kiss, he pushed her back on the bed. He opened her tunic, sliding his hand inside to caress her breasts. She arched against his hand, and he obliged her silent demand, teasing her nipples into taut peaks.

He could spend a lifetime doing this, getting drunk on the taste and feel of her. He left her lips, feathering kisses down her chin, then paying homage to her graceful neck, the curve of her breasts. Eirene moaned when he drew a nipple into his mouth, and impossibly, his body hardened even more. Spirit, she was sweet. He intended to savor every millimeter of her silky skin.

Moving lower, he kissed his way down her midriff and flat abdomen, lingering to dip his tongue in her navel, entranced by her exquisite responsiveness. Lifting his head, he shifted lower still.

He ran his hands along her slender thighs, spreading them to give him complete access to her feminine secrets. So beautiful, so alluring. He kissed the dark curls, trailing his fingers lower to explore those secrets. He stroked her gently, finding her hot and ready for him.

"Jarek," she said, her voice low and husky, her legs moving restlessly. "Come to me."

"Not yet, little one." He settled between her thighs, inhaled her special scent.

He felt incredibly possessive of her, experienced a fierce, primitive need to brand her as his. He wanted to claim her in every way a man could claim a woman. He wanted to give her so much pleasure, she'd never crave another's touch.

He lowered his mouth to her, kissed her intimately, tasting and teasing.

"Jarek!" Shock reverberated in her voice, and her fingers dug into his hair. "What are you doing?"

Do you like this? He nibbled, trespassed a little further.

He heard her breath catch, felt her rising tension. "Oh, I don't think—"

That's right, don't think. Just feel, Eirene. Feel me loving you this way.

He gave her no chance to object further, grasping her hips to hold her for his sensual invasion. Her little, breathless cries, the feel of her writhing beneath him, the fragrance and taste of her, were a heady, potent elixir that sent his senses reeling. He would never get enough of her, could never begin to give her all that she deserved.

Blazing hells, he couldn't give her anything. He had no right to bind her to him, emotionally or physically. Angry denial roared through him, fueling his passions even higher. By the Spirit, he *could* give her this, could create memories for them both.

Memories to sustain him in the lonely times ahead.

He felt her muscles tighten, the beginning internal tremors, the energy building. He grabbed her hands and clasped them tightly.

Eirene, when the energy surges, direct it back to me, he mentally commanded. *Back to me.*

Jarek—

Just do it. With that, he sent her spiraling over the edge. Felt the pitch of her body into free fall, the soaring of her soul in the throes of climax.

Energy broadsided him with a rush of sensation, pouring through every nerve ending. Pleasure surged, so sudden and intense, he almost believed he was buried inside Eirene, finding his own release. Through the maelstrom, he forced himself to focus on the energy, to marshal it and channel it to her.

It's coming back to you, he thought. *See if you can circle it around to me.*

She jolted against him, her fingers digging into his hands. He felt a new tension seizing her. *Oh, Spirit. Jarek!*

Just go with it, sweetness. He maintained the mind link, reminded her, *Send it back to me.*

She did, and the pleasure hit again, wrenching a groan from him. He let the energy dissipate some, returned it to Eirene with less force. She seemed to know now what he was doing. She absorbed the impact, sent it back, now greatly diluted. He felt only a frisson of sensation this time.

Releasing the remnants of energy, he collapsed against her, resting his head on her belly with a ragged sigh. He hadn't achieved an actual physical release, but during the energy burst, it sure as hell felt like he had. "Damn. I don't think I can move."

"I . . . know I can't," she gasped, her chest rising and falling rapidly.

He found enough strength to crawl up beside her and draw her into his arms. "Do you realize what just happened?"

She nestled her head beneath his chin. "We circled the energy between us."

"I would say we grounded each other. What do you think?"

She lifted her head, her eyes wide in astonishment. "But how is that possible? You're not an Enhancer."

"I might not be able to pull in energy and manipulate it the way you do, but I can sense it, and apparently I can channel it to a certain extent. I've been able to communicate telepathically for most of my life, and there are other Shielders who are the same way. I'm not convinced a person has to be an Enhancer to manipulate energy.

"Phylos did tell me that all beings have the ability to learn how to use energy," Eirene mused, raising herself onto an elbow to look down at him.

She still wore the tunic, although it was completely open and had fallen off one shoulder. Her skin was flushed from achieving the ultimate culmination—fulfillment *he* had given her. Spirit, she was sexy.

Jarek reached up and brushed her hair away from her face. "I wanted to show you that you can learn to handle the energy, that you don't have to fear it."

He shifted, feeling the clamoring of his unsatiated body. They could finish this conversation later. Sliding from away from Eirene, he rose and hurriedly removed his flightsuit. He came back to the bed, stripping off her tunic, and rolling her beneath him.

Her eyes grew wide, smokey, as he pressed his blatant need against her. Cupping her face, he lowered his head. "As I said, there's nothing to fear," he murmured, hovering a mere breath from her lips. "Especially when we're doing this."

He kissed her, hard and urgent. She kissed him back, matching his passion. The feel of her hands skimming over his skin again sent the blood pounding and the fever rising. He slid into her in one smooth stroke, enslaved by her inarticulate cry of pleasure, by how she tightened around him.

He felt as if he'd found his own personal shamara. Staring into the infinite blue of her eyes, savoring the welcoming warmth of her gaze and her body, he began moving inside her.

"But just to prove it, I think we need to practice grounding the energy some more," he whispered before he lowered his mouth to hers, before the madness seized them again.

They sat in Phylos' chamber, drinking delicious tea. Overhead, the chimes jingled melodically, and exotic floral scents drifted through the air. Peaceful, lulling vibrations flowed through the chamber, yet Eirene sensed the tension emanating from Jarek. She knew the source of his anxiety—concern about how much gold the Shens would demand in exchange for a sphere. He had asked Phylos about the price several times, but each time the Shen leader had evaded the question.

Her own terrible tension hovered around her, but it had a different basis. And it was fueled by entirely different emotions.

She loved Jarek.

Lying in his arms earlier, exhausted but incredibly satiated, she'd admitted the planet-shattering truth to herself. She loved Jarek san Ranul, had loved him ever since he'd hidden her from Turlock's men, offering his life for hers.

Now she faced the possible sacrifice of her own life so that the man she loved, and his people, could live. The universe was testing her, demanding steep lessons in this lifetime. Lessons she had no intention of shirking. Spirit had clearly shown her the path she must take. If necessary, her life for Jarek's. Her life to atone for her father's grievous crimes against the Shielders.

While one part of her reached for the resolve to see this through, possibly even reveled in the opportunity to right a horrendous wrong, another part of her was terrified. She didn't want to die, didn't want to leave Jarek. She didn't intend to give up without a fight. She would hold on as long as she could, but she didn't know if she could withstand the drain of the sphere.

Jarek's words jolted her back to the negotiations. "We'd like to purchase at least one of the spheres," he was saying. "More than one, if possible. But we have yet to discuss your price."

"There are many prices in the universe," came Phylos' raspy response. "Not all of them involve gold."

Jarek set down his cup and leaned forward. "There is certainly truth and wisdom in your words, Phylos. But I would appreciate it if you could answer me in terms that I deal with."

The blue hood turned towards Eirene. "Have you reconciled your misgivings, my lady?"

She clasped her shaking hands together. "Yes."

"Have you resolved the emotional concerns, those issues of the heart?"

Eirene looked at Jarek, found herself trapped in the

depths of his dark eyes, in the memories of his body joined intimately with hers. *Issues of the heart* . . . She loved Jarek. It was that simple. And that complicated.

Forcing her gaze away from him, she turned towards Phylos. "I have resolved the issues which we discussed. I'm willing to acknowledge my birthright, and use my powers for higher spiritual purposes."

"Is it your intent to help Captain Ranul in his quest?"

She intended to give her all for Jarek's quest—even her life, if need be.

Unclenching her hands, she let out the breath she'd been holding. "Yes, to the best of my ability."

The shadowy visage remained fixed upon her. "The spheres are not Shen property, Lady Eirene. They belong to you and your people. Oh, yes, there are other Enhancers in the galaxy, small in number and scattered across the vastness."

He turned to Jarek. "You may have all the spheres, if Lady Eirene so wishes. But I suggest that you only take one when you depart. I do not believe your ship could accommodate more."

"Thank you, Phylos," Jarek said sincerely. "But the price—"

"There is no material price, Captain. However, we hope that the spheres will be used with the highest intentions, those of helping all in need."

Jarek's expression indicated his shock, but Eirene wasn't surprised by Phylos' announcement. She was beginning to understand the principles of cause and effect in the universe.

"I thank you from the bottom of my heart," Jarek replied. "I promise the equipment will be used for a good purpose."

Phylos rose with a graceful swish of his robe. "The

sphere is being loaded onto your ship as we speak. Your belongings and the small creature have also been returned to your ship. Your supplies have been restocked, and all is in readiness for departure. There is no further need for you to remain on Aldon. The plight of the Shielders is most critical, and we know you wish to proceed with your plans as quickly as possible."

He started toward the entry, and Eirene felt a flash of panic. Phylos had so much knowledge and wisdom, radiated such calm and acceptance. He had helped her find balance, reach inside to uncover answers. She hated losing his guidance. She had some last burning questions for him, a desperate need for answers before they left Aldon.

"Phylos, may I have a few moments of your time?" she asked.

He halted and turned. "Of course."

"I'd like to speak with you alone." Eirene looked beseechingly at Jarek. "Please."

He reached out and cupped her cheek, a reassuring warmth in his eyes. It wouldn't have surprised her to know he was aware of her emotional attachment to Phylos, and her distress at leaving Aldon. "Don't take too long, little one. We need to depart as quickly as possible."

She nodded, placed her hand over his. "I won't be long."

"I'll get the ship ready for takeoff." He nodded to Phylos. "You will always have my gratitude, and that of my people." He strode through the entry.

"What concerns you, Lady Eirene?"

She looked into the dark oval. "I have been thinking about the wormhole, and what might be on the other end."

"There is another part of the galaxy on the other side.

I can assure you there are habitable planets there."

That wasn't what concerned Eirene the most. What bothered her was the possibility that Jarek would be stranded in this new and unknown territory. She believed she could activate the sphere and start the process of opening the wormhole, but she didn't know how long she could endure operating the sphere. She feared Jarek would be trapped—with no way to return.

"Are there other Enhancers in that part of the galaxy?" she asked.

"You have fears for your survival," Phylos said knowingly. "Yet you plan to continue."

No sense denying what the astute Shen already knew. "I intend to operate the sphere to help the Shielders, and I'm not certain I can survive the process. I want to know if there are Enhancers on the other side of the wormhole."

The dark oval nodded. "We believe there are, Lady Eirene. An unknown number of Enhancers traversed the vortex before the Controllers nearly decimated those remaining in this quadrant. We pray that those who navigated the hyperspace have flourished."

His answer wasn't an absolute guarantee, but it gave Eirene hope that if anything happened to her, Jarek might be able to find Enhancers to operate the sphere. They could bring him back so he could begin evacuating Shielders from the quadrant.

"We will monitor your progress in your quest," Phylos said. "And we will assist any way we can. The rest will be in the hands of the One."

"Thank you, Phylos," Eirene said, emotion constricting her chest. "You have done so much for me. I will never forget you."

"Nor I you," he replied gravely. "The One be with

you, Lady Eirene, and endow you with light and guidance."

He stepped back to let her pass. She walked by him, her heart heavy. "One more thing, my lady."

She halted at the entry and looked over her shoulder. "Yes?"

"Do not fear the energy. And do not discount the power of love. Love is the true essence of the One, and the greatest force in all the universe."

Love. She understood it was spiritual, non-selfish love to which Phylos referred, just as she was beginning to understand its amazing power. Love for his people had motivated Jarek to devote his life to their salvation. Love for Spirit and for doing what was right had given the Enhancers the courage to defy the Controllers.

Just as Eirene's love for Jarek gave her the determination to do what must be done to save him and his people. No matter the personal cost.

It was the damndest thing. Jarek sat back in his seat, staring at the blank screens on his console, as his ship hurtled upward through Aldon's atmosphere. Once again, he had no control of his craft, and all his systems appeared to be malfunctioning. But his ship was moving smoothly toward deep space, directed by the Shens.

Finally the ship cleared the planet. The screens blinked on, and the console hummed to life. All equipment was back on line and functioning fully. Shaking his head, Jarek entered the coordinates that would take them into the heart of the twelfth sector, towards the black hole.

He glanced over at Eirene. She stared out the portal, her hands gripping her armrests. He could feel her energy spiking, knew she was upset over something. Reaching out, he took her cold hand, gave it a squeeze. She turned toward him with a wan smile.

"Feeling sick?" he asked.

She gave a small shake of her head. "Just thinking."

"What about?"

She turned her head back toward the portal, but not before he saw the flicker of unreadable emotions in her eyes. "How long will it take to get to the wormhole?"

"Not very long. Fortunately, Aldon is on the outer edge of the twelfth sector. We can be in the approximate vicinity in less than three cycles."

"Three cycles," she said, almost to herself.

Her hand trembled beneath Jarek's grasp. "Sweetness, what's wrong? I know something is bothering you."

She released her breath on a sigh. "I don't want to fail you." She turned towards him, her eyes darkening to the deepest blue. "I want you to find shamara for your people. But I'm afraid I'll let you down."

He had his own doubts and fears, but they no longer centered around her willingness to help him. He knew firsthand how much heart and spirit she possessed.

"I know you'll do everything you can to help," he reassured her. "I believe in you, Eirene. You could never disappoint me or let me down."

Her eyes glistened suspiciously, and he swiveled toward her, wanting to comfort her, to discover and exorcise whatever demons were plaguing her. "Please tell me what's—"

The alerts went off, blaring an ominous warning. Jarek swerved back to the console. A ship approached on the port side, fully armored, weapons already primed.

"Damn!" he muttered, reaching toward the weapons console.

He never made it. A strike shook the ship hard.

They were under attack.

Chapter Eighteen

Jarek switched on his laser cannon as he scanned for damage. He cursed even more when he saw his main thruster had been disabled. The transceiver beeped. Locking his laser on the approaching ship, he punched the receiver pad.

"Who the blazing hells is this?"

"Just returning the favor, san Ranul. How you like having your main thruster destroyed?"

"Turlock," Jarek snarled.

"Didn't really think you would get away from me, did you, Shielder? Could never happen. One of my men spotted your ship on the other side of Saron, just as you were taking off. I tracked you to this area, then lost you."

Frustration roared through Jarek. He was close—so close—to his goal, only to fall prey to this vicious lowlife. Fear for Eirene's safety followed in the wake of shock and anger. He'd let her down again.

"Wasn't about to let you get away, especially seeing as how the Controllers doubled the price on your head. Been hanging around this area and waiting," Turlock snorted. "Figured you'd come out of your hole sooner or later. I intend to collect that reward."

Jarek quickly weighed his options. He would choose the destruction of his ship over capture, but he had Eirene to consider—and an irreplaceable sphere that represented his people's salvation.

He muted the transceiver and turned to Eirene. "Our main thruster is gone. We can't possibly outrun them. Hell, we can't go *anywhere*. They have more firepower than we do. Our only chance is to for me to surrender. I want you to hide in the galley again."

"No. You can't do that, Jarek. It will mean your death."

She was right—the odds for his survival were grim. "We don't know that for certain. I might be able to escape, like before. But if we don't surrender, if we fire on them, they will blow us to debris. Then we'll both be dead."

Just then, the alert went off again. Another ship was approaching. Jarek whirled back to the console, scanned the data. It was Sabin's ship. Relief rushing through him, he disconnected Turlock and signaled Sabin.

"You could have gotten here a little sooner, Travers."

"I've been trying to contact you for three cycles now. Where the blazing hells have you been?"

"It's a long story. We need to deal with Turlock first."

"Got my accelerator beam locked on him. I see your laser cannon is active. Let's blast him."

The alert went off again. Yet another ship approached. "Damn," Jarek muttered, reading his scanner. It wasn't a Shielder ship, or anyone he knew, and it was heavily armed.

"I think we'd better find out what's going on here," Sabin growled.

"I'm going to conference the calls through the comm." Jarek made the connections and hailed the new arrival.

A battered face appeared on the videoviewer, and Eirene gasped. "I found you, san Ranul," Vaden said, "thanks to Turlock's surveillance. I assume my treacherous niece is with you. You won't escape me again. Especially since I know something the Controllers might find very interesting."

"We'll get away," Jarek said, shifting his laser cannon from Turlock to Vaden. "After I blow you into the fires."

"Can't be done, san Ranul. My ship is too well-armed. Besides, I've already shared my discovery about my beloved niece with Turlock, and a few of our associates. Maybe you'd like to know it, too, san Ranul, if you don't already. How does it feel to mate with an Enhancer? Is it better with her than other females?"

"Yeah," snorted Turlock, now conferenced. "I heard those Enhancers turn on the heat."

Eirene's panicked burst of energy speared through Jarek. He wondered how Vaden had discovered the truth. Jarek patted her arm reassuringly, determined to find a way to get her to safety.

"You're a deluded fool, Vaden," he scoffed. "Everyone knows Enhancers are extinct."

"Everyone knows *most* of those freaks are extinct," Vaden retorted. "But a few show up from time to time. Keraat and Derian told me about the strange things that happened when Eirene was around. She exploded my disrupter—I'm certain of it. She's an Enhancer, all right. Legally, she belongs to me and I intend to have her."

"You're wrong on all counts, Kane. Eirene is not an Enhancer, and she doesn't belong to you. You won't get her."

Jarek's sensors indicated Vaden was activating his laser banks. "Travers, keep Turlock covered," Jarek ordered, preparing to fire on Vaden's ship.

"Now I'm terrified," Vaden taunted. "You and your cohort don't stand a chance. We have better weapons. And you're disabled, san Ranul. You can't run."

"Eirene is no good to you dead, and neither am I. If you disintegrate us, you won't even have my body to turn in."

"Then we'll destroy your friend's ship and board yours." Vaden's weapons switched to Sabin's ship.

The alert beeped again.

"Who in the Abyss is that?" Turlock snarled.

Scanning the readouts, Jarek was amazed to see Chase McKnight approaching. Chase had formidable weaponry, already activated, which he trained on Vaden's ship. Jarek immediately switched his laser cannon to Turlock's ship.

"Thought I'd come along to keep you out of trouble," came Chase's deep, calm voice. "Looks like you need some help with these lowlifes."

"Stay out of this!" Vaden roared. "We're tracking these people on the behalf of the Controllers. Get away, citizen, before we're forced to arrest you for obstructing the law."

"That would be very difficult, Chase replied. "Since I am also a Controller agent."

"Then you understand our rights," Vaden said, his tone now friendly and persuasive. "We are claiming bounty privileges on the two people in the ship on your starboard side. Remove your weapon lock and allow us to proceed."

"I don't think so," Chase said.

"Looks like we're at a standoff, you bastards," Sabin cut in. "Three ships against two. I don't think the odds are in your favor."

Jarek held his silence, waiting to see how things shook down. He looked at Eirene. She was deathly pale, her hands clenched in her lap. Muting the comm, he leaned over and pressed his palm against her face.

"Vaden and Turlock won't blow us up," he reassured her. "They want the gold they could make on us too badly. And they're outnumbered."

"My uncle knows the truth now," she whispered. "He won't stop until he has me in his possession."

"Where we're going, he won't be able to follow." Jarek turned back to the comm. The alert sounded again.

"I don't believe this." He studied the scanners.

A Leor warship bore down on them, weapons activated. Jarek felt like he'd been punched in the gut. It didn't seem matters could get any worse—yet they just had.

"Blazing hells," he muttered, cursing this run of incredibly bad luck.

"What?" Eirene asked.

Jarek looked at her, wishing he could absorb her into himself, could keep her safe. "Eirene, remember that whatever happens I—"

"Kane, Turlock, you summoned me here. This had better be worth my time. I tire of futile chases," a harsh voice rumbled over the comm.

"No false alarm this time, your Lordship," Vaden crowed. "San Ranul and my niece are in the craft on your port side. Their ship is disabled. They can't escape."

"What are these others doing here?"

"This is Sabin Travers," Sabin cut in. "Commander Gunnar, I assume?"

"You assume correctly. What is your purpose here, Travers? Is Moriah with you?"

"Yes, Moriah is on board. Chase McKnight is on the other ship. We're here to defend our friend."

"You mean san Ranul? The man who stole what is rightfully mine?" the Leor challenged.

Jarek decided it was time to speak for himself. "San Ranul here. I had no idea who Eirene was when I met her, your Lordship. It was never my intention to take from anyone."

"Ignorance is not an acceptable excuse," Gunnar growled.

"Yeah," Turlock snorted. "Blow 'em up, Commander."

They didn't stand a chance against a Leor battleship, even if they could dispatch Vaden and Turlock first. Jarek gripped the console, cursing his helplessness, his inability to keep Eirene safe.

"Destroy Travers and the one claiming to be a Controller agent," Vaden said, "but don't harm san Ranul and my niece. We can make a huge amount of gold on them."

Gunnar ignored Vaden. "Turlock, I heard some highly upsetting news. I spoke with an associate of yours—Rafar was his name. I was most interested in what he had to say."

"Can't this wait?" Vaden interjected. "Help rid us of san Ranul's allies. After we have san Ranul and Eirene in hand, I have a proposition which might interest you."

"Silence!" Gunnar roared. "I will decide when we conduct business. Right now I have questions for Turlock."

"D-don't believe anything Rafar has to say, your Lordship," Turlock stammered. "He's a lying bastard."

"And what are you?" Gunnar asked softly.

"I'm your business partner. I'm going to—"

"You told me the irridon shipment had been confiscated by the Controllers, that you were working on acquiring more," Gunnar hissed ominously.

"Th-that's true!" Panic edged Turlock's voice. "I—"

"Yet according to Rafar, you sold that shipment to the Jaccians, for twice the amount you and I agreed upon."

Jarek noted the sudden energy surge from Gunnar's ship. The Leor was priming his laser canons. Turlock apparently also noted that fact. His voice quavered with fear.

"No! Rafar lied. The Controllers took that irridon. I swear it!"

"I went to Orlan and personally verified Rafar's story. You betrayed me, Turlock."

"No! Listen to me, your Lordship! It wasn't good irridon. It was cut with other minerals. You wouldn't have wanted it—"

Three laser cannons simultaneously discharged from Gunnar's ship, burning massive holes into the hull of Turlock's ship. There was no way Turlock could seal off that kind of damage. He'd be dead in moments. His final bellow of terror and pain reverberated over the comm link. Then silence fell.

Sitting on Gunnar's lap at his weapon console, Lani drew back from the discharge pad and clapped her hands in glee. "Oh, that was too fun!" she shrilled. "Who else can I destroy? How about that awful Vaden? He's despicable. Selling his own niece for personal gain. Really!"

"Bloodthirsty female," Gunnar chided indulgently.

"Would you disintegrate everyone you do not like?"

"Absolutely," Lani declared. She looped her arms around his thick neck and kissed his chest. "Violence stirs my passions."

He shuddered, and growled in that primitive way she adored. "We must finish with the business at hand. Then we will see about these 'passions' of yours."

He would, too. Lani sighed, her toes curling in anticipation. Gunnar had the most amazing stamina. Even *she* was hard-pressed to keep up. But she would give it her best attempt.

"Just don't keep me waiting too long," she urged. "And please go easy on Eirene and Jarek, sweetness. They can't help it that fate threw them together. I'm sure if Eirene had met you first, she would never have looked at another male. I'm lucky she met Jarek instead."

Lani swirled her tongue around Gunnar's nipple and stroked his thigh to emphasize her point. The loincloth bulged against her, and she smiled in satisfaction.

The bigger they were, the harder they fell.

Only she was falling just as hard herself.

Jarek could only stare at the scanners in amazement. Sabin and Chase were watching and waiting along with him, but there didn't seem to be anything prudent to say. Gunnar was in control of the confrontation.

Jarek figured he was next on the firing line, since he'd kidnapped the Leor's intended bride. Reaching out, he took Eirene's trembling hand. He intended to plead for her life, and prayed Gunnar had a modicum of mercy beneath that tough exterior.

The Leor commander didn't keep them waiting. "I have no further desire to do business with you, Kane.

338

You did not deliver my bride as agreed upon, and thus forfeited your trade route."

Kane? Why was he turning on Vaden Kane, when Jarek was the one who had taken Eirene from Gunnar?

"Of course you wouldn't want my niece now," Vaden agreed quickly. "She's probably tarnished. Certainly not to your liking."

He *would* say that, Jarek thought, still confused over this turn of events. Eirene's uncle hoped to gain a lot more than a single trade route on her, now that he believed she was an Enhancer.

"But we have many beautiful virgins on Travan," Vaden continued, growing bolder. "Surely we can still reach an agreement."

"I no longer wish to deal with you, or anyone from Travan."

"But, I—" Vaden sputtered to silence, as Gunnar's laser canons locked onto his ship.

"I suggest you abandon this sector immediately. Do not approach me again, or I will send you to your Fires."

There was a long pause, then Vaden snarled, "You won't get away, san Ranul. Neither will you, niece. I'll track you down to the ends of the quadrant. You can be sure of it."

He nosed his ship around and the thrusters surged, taking him away. Jarek tensed, awaiting Gunnar's next action.

"Commander, we thank your for your assistance," Sabin said, as if matters were settled.

"Do not make the mistake of thinking it was an act of mercy," Gunnar responded. "San Ranul, you are seeking an entry to another part of the galaxy?"

How could he possibly have known that? Stunned, Jarek replied cautiously, "I don't know what you're talking about."

"Do not play games, Captain. We have heard that you were looking for special machinery—equipment that could navigate hyperspace. Now you have traveled to the twelfth sector, the location of a black hole. It is easy enough to conclude you are seeking other territories for your people."

Jarek paused. He'd heard much about the Leors and their intelligence and shrewd bargaining abilities. He could see the stories about them were well founded, and he had no desire to reveal anything to Gunnar.

"Commander, if my plans were common knowledge, my people would be in even greater danger. I'm sure you can understand my reluctance to share those plans with anyone."

"I can, Captain, however I believe you are now indebted to me. I would claim first negotiating rights on any trade routes that come out of your explorations."

Jarek was amazed the Leor commander didn't plan to seek retribution for losing Eirene. Still reeling, he took a moment to consider the surprising conversation that had just occurred. Damned if Gunnar wasn't turning the situation to his advantage.

Elation swept through him as he realized the full implications. Gunnar intended to let him and the others go, to continue on with their plans—as long as his demands were met.

Jarek didn't have to think about the Leor's request very long to conclude he had no choice but to cooperate. Besides, it wasn't money from trade routes the Shielders were seeking, but shamara. The Leors could have the routes, for a vow of secrecy. Their word was good. It had been honored as far back as he could remember.

"If the Shielders find any unclaimed trade routes, the Leors will have the first chance to bid on them," he told Gunnar. "However, we would have to insist on total confidentiality."

"I will consider that a binding agreement," Gunnar replied.

"You have my word on it, Commander."

"Then you and the others are free to go. May the goddess shine a thousand suns upon your endeavors."

Jarek couldn't believe this stroke of luck. "Thank you, Commander."

"Gunnar, sweetness, are you done yet?" came a high-pitched feminine voice over the comm. "I'm waiting."

"Signing off," Gunnar rasped. The communication was abruptly severed.

"Well," Moriah's husky voice said after a moment of surprised silence. "That's very interesting. I was going to ask Gunnar what had happened to Lani. I guess we don't need to worry about her anymore. Radd was right."

Sagging back in relief, Jarek squeezed Eirene's hand. She looked at him, her eyes enormous with shock. He managed a wink and a grin.

"See? The good guys always win."

She returned a shaky smile. "You're pretty sure of yourself, aren't you?"

"Always." He turned to power down his lasers.

"What do you say we go find ourselves a wormhole?" Chase interjected.

"*We?*" Jarek asked.

"We'll take my ship," Chase said. "It's better-equipped for medical emergencies."

"What are you talking about?" Jarek demanded.

"Nessa and I discussed it, and we're coming with you. You might need our help."

"I can't let you do that. It's too dangerous. What about your children?"

"Raven is eighteen now, and Brand is thirteen, and the others are old enough that they don't need constant care any longer. We left them on Risa, in Janaye's capable hands."

"It's too risky. All I need is a ship. I don't want you and Nessa placing yourself in danger."

"Mori and I are coming, too," Sabin interjected.

"No. I can't allow it. Moriah is pregnant. We don't know what lies ahead."

"True, but we do know there's no hope remaining if we don't forge onward," Moriah chimed in. "We don't want our child living in fear every waking moment, and always struggling to survive. We *are* coming with you, Jarek."

"If you want a ship, you'll have to agree to take us along," Chase said.

Jarek ran his fingers through his hair, wanting to refuse, but acknowledging they had him in a bind. His spacecraft was completely inoperable.

"I don't even know if we can move the sphere," he said finally.

The comm link crackled with static, then a whispery voice said, "Captain san Ranul, is there a problem?"

Jarek took in then let out a deep breath, not at all surprised that the Shens appeared aware of all that had transpired. "Just a slight change of plans, Phylos. My ship is inoperable and we need to move to another one."

"I am sure you are concerned about the sphere," Phylos replied. "Allow us to assist you. Open your cargo bay and have Captain Mcknight do the same. We will transfer the sphere for you."

"Who is Phylos?" Chase interjected. "And how in the

universe is he going to move equipment from your ship to mine?"

"He's the leader of the Shens," Jarek explained, heartened by this turn of events. "Aldon is nearby, although you can't pick up any readings. Just open your cargo bay. Transporting objects appears to be a Shen specialty."

He watched the scanners as the sphere drifted, seemingly of its own accord, to Chase's ship. Then he sealed off his cargo bay. "Again you have come to our aid, Phylos. We thank you."

"It is always a privilege to serve. The One be with you." The odd voice faded, leaving only static on the transceiver.

One more problem dealt with—in a most surprising manner. Accepting that matters were out of his hands—and had been all along, Jarek resigned himself to the new traveling arrangements.

"Ready to initiate docking, Chase."

He looked at Eirene. "Then we'll be on our way."

It was time. The instrument readings indicated they had come as close to the black hole as they dared without crossing into the event horizon and being sucked to ultimate destruction. The instruments also had picked up a gravitational lens effect, the bending of light due to gravity, and an indication of a probable wormhole. They hoped the wormhole was running through the black hole at a perpendicular angle, with its entry and exit well clear of the event horizon.

They had discussed the wormhole at length during the three-cycle trip, speculating on how the sphere would actually work. Eirene had limited scientific knowledge, but her contact with the sphere convinced her it was ultra-sophisticated, highly advanced equipment. She sensed it would do everything that was necessary—locate the wormhole entry, turn the ship that direction, open the vortex, and guide them through.

All the speculation was simply that, anyway. None of them knew for sure what would happen. But Eirene suspected what the personal cost might be to her.

She glanced at the faces surrounding her in the cargo bay: Chase, Nessa, Sabin, and Moriah. She'd come to genuinely respect these people during their short time together, to appreciate their courage and determination in the face of impossible odds.

She was grateful they would be with Jarek, that he wouldn't be completely alone and isolated if . . . if something happened to her.

"I want everyone to leave the cargo bay," she said. "I don't know how the equipment might affect observers, and I'd feel better if I was alone."

That was true—she was still afraid of energy spillage, or someone being injured. More importantly, she didn't want them around if she didn't survive the drain, didn't want them to try to help her at risk to themselves.

She saw the protest on their faces and headed them off. "Please. I won't operate the sphere if anyone is here."

"I agree it would be best for everyone else to stay in another part of the ship," Jarek said from behind her. "But I won't leave you."

She turned and met his determined gaze. Her heart did the odd little flutter it always did whenever she looked at him. She wanted to stroke his wavy brown hair back from his forehead, to run her fingers along the rugged planes of his face.

She'd fallen more deeply in love with him these past three cycles, sharing his dreams and his passions, lying in his arms at night. She would never regret what had passed between them, would cherish the memories through all eternity. Reluctantly, she tucked her feelings away. It was time to focus on the matter at hand.

"I want to be completely alone," she insisted. "I don't want any distractions."

"I won't distract you. But I refuse to leave you here alone. If you're going to help us, then let's start the process."

She saw the implacable resolve in his expression, knew he was determined to stay with her. She didn't like it, but she wasn't going to renege on her promise. She nodded, pushing her hair from her face. "All right."

"Good luck," Chase said. "Don't hesitate to use the comm if you need us."

"Spirit be with you," Nessa said softly.

Sabin slid his arm around Moriah. "You two be careful," he said gruffly.

They filed from the bay, turning almost in unison for one final glance, their expressions both concerned and hopeful. Then they were gone.

Eirene stared at Jarek, drinking in one last look to carry with her, perhaps even into eternity. She wanted to tell him she loved him, but didn't want to place that burden on him. She knew he would feel guilty if anything happened to her and didn't want to complicate it with emotional baggage.

"Ready?" he asked.

She drew a deep breath. "Yes. Let's hope this works."

His gaze remained on her, steady and confident. "It will. It has to."

She started to turn, but he caught her hand and tugged. "But first, come here."

He pulled her to him, crushing her against him. He raised her chin and kissed her gently, then with more hunger. She kissed him back, clinging to him, reluctant to let go.

He drew away, sliding his hand along her face. "For luck," he said, his voice unusually deep. He released her and stepped back. "Better get to it."

Nodding, she turned to the sphere. It hummed and vibrated, familiar, ancient energy calling to her soul. This was her birthright. Her destiny.

Spirit, see me through this, she prayed, then placed her hands on the sphere. Immediately, the sphere reacted, the vibratory pitch increasing, pinpricks of white light flashing across the mirrored surface. The suction came, fast, relentless, terrifying. Her heart pounded as she battled to breathe, struggled to draw in enough energy to feed the sphere's voracious demands.

Then the flow rushed back to her, and she almost stumbled backward. *Stay focused.* She concentrated, trying to absorb the energy and spread it evenly through her body, to pull in enough outside power to feed back to the sphere.

Without warning, the drag began again, a sharp undertow that sucked every ounce of energy she had, then demanded more. *More.* She must pull in more. But the power rushed back to her before she could stabilize, jolting her with tremendous force.

"Eirene, are you all right?"

She was already weakening, and the process was just beginning. She had to hang on. *I'm fine*, she channeled to Jarek. *Just getting the rhythm.*

She dug in, sheer will keeping her upright. The energy flowed in and out, in and out, with every breath, until it seemed to become a part of her, enmeshed in every cell of her body, regulating her heartbeat, her breathing. It was as if she and the sphere had become a single life force. Each surge was more powerful, more of a shock to her body, more draining and debilitating with each ebb to the sphere.

"By the Fires," Jarek said, his voice awestruck. "I've never seen anything like this."

The tone of his voice pulled Eirene from her trancelike state. Forcing open her eyes, she gasped in amazement. Huge panels had unfurled from the sphere, like the petals of a flower. The panels radiated in a circle around the sphere, and protruded through the ceiling, floor, and walls of the bay, apparently stretching out into space. Yet they caused no notable damage to the ship structure.

"Electromagnetic anomaly," Jarek said. "They're not solid matter. They're passing through the ship structure. Amazing."

Eirene sagged against the sphere, too exhausted to comprehend what she saw.

Immediately his attention shifted to her. "Are you okay?"

Fine. But just as she thought that, the sphere exerted its awful demand again, pulling at her, draining, draining, yet insisting on more.

Gasping for breath, she struggled to keep her eyes open. Sparks of a thousand colors flashed from the sphere now, and light rays erupted forth. The mirrored surface glowed, became a solid expanse of brilliance.

Power surged back into her, more than she could assimilate. Darkness began edging her vision. Frantic, she fought to remain viable. *Jarek!*

"Eirene!"

I don't know if I can hold on. The thought was wrenched from her. She hadn't intended to broadcast that.

"You have to hold on. Do you hear me? Hold on. I won't let you go."

She was vaguely aware of motion beside her. Suddenly, the drain eased, and the darkness dissipated. Jarek stood next to her his palms planted against the sphere. He drew a deep breath.

It's time I learned how to channel energy.

No! It will kill you.

So will losing you.

Jarek, no. Don't sacrifice yourself.

But she felt the easing of the strain, experienced a momentary respite from the horrendous, overwhelming power.

We do this together, little one, Jarek insisted.

The undertow came at them, sucking every bit of energy, demanding more, far more than Eirene could give. She felt Jarek shudder, felt the stir of his own power as he met the challenge. Even with the two of them, it wasn't enough. Not nearly enough.

She lost all track of time, unable to hold telepathic communication with Jarek. All she could do was ride wave after agonizing wave of energy fluctuation, feeling herself grow weaker and weaker. The blackness again threatened, but Jarek was too locked in his own battle to help her now.

She drew on her last ounce of endurance, desperation giving her just enough strength to send a final message.

Jarek, I can't hold on any longer. Save yourself before it's too late. Let go of the sphere and save yourself.

With a terrible finality, the blackness descended.

Indistinct hums and beeps edged into the void, irritating, like a small bug that wouldn't go away. Jarek tried to shut out the annoyance, to return to the welcome oblivion.

Something shook him, tugging at him insistently. "Jarek. Jarek, can you hear me? Wake up! Jarek!"

A deep male voice, nagging at him, skirting the edge of his consciousness, and aggravating the blazing hells out of him. "Go away," he muttered, too exhausted to open his eyes.

"Not going to happen, san Ranul," came another male voice. "Can't have you laying down on the job."

Familiar, and cocky. He knew that voice. . . . He felt a sharp sting in his neck, followed by a rush of adrenaline through his body. Even then, he battled the fog, had to force his eyes open. Two figures above him blurred, came into focus. McKnight and Travers.

He stared at them, shook his head to clear it. "Where am I?"

"I think the better question would be, *where are we?*" Sabin answered. "We did it!"

Jarek tried to sit up. The room seemed to spin. "Don't get up yet," Chase said, pressing him back down.

Jarek realized he was in the medical lab, surrounded by an array of equipment. What was going on? Something important nagged at the edge of his memory. "Was I wounded?" he asked.

Chase shook his head. "I'm not sure what happened to you."

Full recollection burst into Jarek's mind with alarming clarity. "The sphere!" He sat up, ignoring Chase's attempts to restrain him. "Eirene! Where is she? What happened?"

The dizziness increased. He gripped the edge of the table until it receded somewhat. His head pounded like it had been inside a rocket coil, and he was horribly weak.

"Tell me what the hell happened. Where's Eirene?"

Chase and Sabin exchanged glances. "We made it through the wormhole," Sabin said. "You were right, Jarek. We're in an uncharted part of the galaxy."

Fierce elation flared at the news, triumph welling inside Jarek. They'd found shamara! But the sense of victory quickly faded, eclipsed by concern for Eirene.

"We came into the bay to check on you, and found the two of you unconscious on the floor," Chase explained. "The sphere continued to operate on its own until we exited the wormhole, then it shut down and closed back up. Astounding."

"Forget that damned sphere. Eirene," Jarek said insistently, panic beginning to take hold. "Where is she?"

Chase clasped Jarek's shoulder, his expression troubled. "She's on the other side of the screen."

"I have to see her." Jarek slid off the table, pitching forward as his legs collapsed. Sabin and Chase caught him and hefted him up. His legs were like rubber, unsteady and weak. That didn't matter. Nothing mattered but Eirene. "Take me to her."

"Jarek, she's not conscious," Chase said. "You need to lie back down."

"Let me go," Jarek growled, wrenching free. "Eirene!" He stumbled forward ripping away the electrodes attached to his chest and the IV strips in his arm. He lunged for the screen.

"She's comatose," Chase tried explain, grabbing his arm again. "She's not responding."

Jarek whirled to face him. "No one is going to keep me from her. Take your hands off me. *Now*."

Chase stared at him a long moment, then released him.

Jarek staggered around, and shoved the screen to the side. It crashed to the floor. Eirene lay on a table, as white and still as death. Equipment surrounded her, monitors flashing rows of data. None of it was decipherable to Jarek. But he didn't need to be able to read it to know she wasn't emanating the familiar energy pattern.

"Eirene!" he cried, lurching to the table, gathering her into his arms. She was cool, her breathing very faint. No life force radiated from her—no Eirene. Fear raged through him, left him sick and shaking.

"What's wrong with her?" he demanded of Chase. "Why can't you help her?"

"I've tried everything in my power. She's nonresponsive," Chase said quietly. "The equipment indicates minimal brain activity. I'm sorry."

"No!" Jarek roared, denial raging through him. He held her tightly, cradling her against him. "Eirene, you can't leave me!"

He listened for the whispering of her life force. He heard nothing but the blasted equipment. Desperation flooded his soul.

You did it, little one. You controlled the energy and activated the sphere, and we made it though the wormhole. You didn't let me down. I'm so proud of you. Don't leave me now.

He buried his face against her hair, prayed for another miracle. *You can't leave me, Eirene. I need you too much.*

Still no flare of energy, no sign of life, as if the spirit had departed, leaving a fading physical body. *No!* Jarek screamed inside, anguish racking him.

Eirene, stay! Stay here with me. I know I never gave you the words, but I love you. I want you to become my mate, for us to be together always. You're brave and beautiful, with a heart as big as Elysia's sun.

He halted, tears tracking down his face, grief shredding his soul. *We did it, sweetness. We're in a new world. We're free now, and the best is yet to come. You can't go. I love you. I love you. . . .*

He rocked her, beyond words, beyond hope. He didn't know how long he stayed there, only that he couldn't bear to let her go. Time ceased to exist. He was aware only of Eirene's fragile body cradled in his arms, of her utter stillness. *I love you*, he told her, over and over.

He almost missed the faint stirring. A slight sensation of energy touched his mind, pulling him from his litany. He felt a movement against him, heard the intake of air. He drew back, too stunned to even comprehend the miracle occurring.

Clear blue eyes stared back at him, a sea of tranquility and redemption. "Hey," she whispered, her voice so faint, he almost couldn't hear her.

Thank you, Spirit! Oh, thank you! "Hey, yourself." His heart was beating so hard, he thought it might burst through his chest. Drawing a deep breath, he brushed the tangled mass of hair back from her face, cupped her cheek. "Have I told you that I love you?"

A smile tugged at her lips. She tried to raise her hand toward him. He took it and pressed a kiss against it. "I think so," she said softly. "I kept hearing those words. They pulled me back to you."

"I've got news for you, lady. You're never leaving me again. I won't let you. I love you too much."

"That's good," she murmured. "Because I love you, too."

Jarek knew that as long as he lived, he would thank Spirit every single day for this miracle. For all the miracles.

At long last, they had found shamara.

Epilogue

"You're not cooperating, Moriah," Chase chided. "Come on. You can push harder than this."

"Oh, really? Why don't you try shoving a cantafruit up your nose? See how you like that, Doctor."

Chase sat back on his stool and shrugged, humor dancing in his eyes. "We can stay here all cycle, if you insist. I don't have any other patients to attend."

"I'm not going through this for an entire cycle! I want this baby out, and I want it out now!"

"Chase, stop upsetting Moriah," Nessa scolded, placing a slender hand on his arm. "She's in a lot of discomfort, and having a baby is very difficult."

"I'm aware of that, my love," he said dryly.

Eirene smiled to herself. She had come to care deeply for these people in their time together. They were like a large family, struggling together to forge a path in a strange, unknown world. She couldn't imagine any event more special than the very first birth of a baby in their new settlement.

"Sweetheart, try to relax and do what Chase asks," Sabin said, squeezing Moriah's hand.

"I'm not ever listening to a man again," she retorted, then tensed. "Oh, Spirit, here comes another contraction."

"Let us help you," Eirene said, leaning forward. "Will you?"

"Y-yes! Anything!" Moriah gasped.

Eirene placed her left hand on Moriah's left shoulder. She felt confident, no longer harboring any fears about using her powers. Jarek slipped next to her, taking her right hand and placing his free hand on Moriah's right shoulder. Nessa stood beside him, touching Moriah's arm and holding out her other hand, palm up.

As easily as taking a breath of air, Eirene pulled in energy and circled it through Jarek, who let it flow into Moriah. Nessa, who had proven amazingly adept at manipulating energy, channeled the flow back to the universe.

In fact, they had discovered that most Shielders had that capability. They could only speculate that the same genetic makeup giving Shielders their innate mind shields and telepathic abilities also enhanced their ability to channel energy.

Working in perfect synchronicity, Eirene, Jarek, and Nessa directed healing and calming forces into Moriah, stimulating her body's natural pain suppressants, and helping her to relax through the contractions.

"I can do this," she muttered, gripping Sabin's hand and trembling with her efforts to bring forth the baby.

"You're doing great, sweetheart," he told her. "I love you."

"The baby is almost here," Chase announced. "One more push, Mori. That all we need."

Moments later, Alyssa Janaye came into the universe. The beauty and spirituality of the birth touched Eirene deeply. She watched Sabin and Moriah cooing over the baby, tears in her eyes. Jarek wrapped his arm around her and pulled her close.

"One day we'll have children of our own," he whispered.

She hugged him back. It never ceased to amaze her how much she loved him, how much that love seemed to grow every single cycle. Thank Spirit for the fate that had brought them together.

After the baby had been cleaned and bundled up, Jarek took her from Moriah. He cradled her gently in his large hands, his expression so tender, Eirene felt a catch in her throat.

"Welcome, little Alyssa," he told the baby. "You are the first Shielder to be born in Shamara, and the first to be born into freedom in over a hundred cycles. Cherish that freedom, little Alyssa, fight for it always."

The baby stared back at him wonderingly, her golden eyes alert and totally unafraid. He smiled at her. "You're going to be just as beautiful as your mother. Come meet the rest of our family. They've been waiting for you."

He tucked the baby against one arm and took Eirene's hand. "I'll bring her right back," he promised Moriah and Sabin.

Nessa followed them outside. A large group of people had gathered, waiting for news. When they saw Jarek with the baby, they surged forward eagerly. Rani, who'd been perched on Raven's shoulder, chattered loudly and leaped down, scampering to Jarek. Eirene intercepted her before she could climb his leg.

An emotional murmur swept through the crowd as Jarek held the baby aloft for all to see. "Here she is— Alyssa Janaye dan Sabin, our first baby born in Shamara. Spirit willing, may there be many more babies to come, and may they always know peace and freedom."

A cheer rose from the crowd. "Yes!" Blake whooped, as usual, at the front of the group.

Eirene watched her handsome mate, pride and love burning fiercely inside her. He was an amazing leader, commanding respect, yet able to inspire greatness in others. His sheer determination and strength of character had gotten them to Shamara. He'd helped plan and build the colony, had made it possible for hundreds of Shielders to start new lives here, with more arriving almost every cycle. They had a lot of work left to do, but Jarek would ensure it got done.

Raven, Chase and Nessa's oldest daughter, squeezed through the crowd to get a closer look at Alyssa, followed by her brother, Brand. Her dark eyes glowing, she fussed over the baby. "Look, Brand, a little girl. Isn't she pretty?"

"Yeah," thirteen-year-old Brand muttered, trying not to act too impressed, but he radiated excitement.

They all did, Eirene thought. Here on Shamara, the birth of a baby was truly a blessed event, instead of the burden it would have been in the old quadrant. Jarek gave Alyssa to Nessa. Smiling down at the baby, Nessa took her back to her proud parents.

"Be sure to tell Lady Meris about Alyssa," Jarek instructed his niece and nephew. "Also, tell her Eirene and I will join her for the evening meal." He took Rani from Eirene. "Here, take this little monster with you."

"Sure." Brand took Rani, carrying her upside down, a position she didn't seem to mind. Life on Shamara was good for lanraxes. Raven and Brand headed toward their grandmother's quarters. Eirene was glad Lady Meris had weathered the trip through the wormhole. She and Jarek's mother got along very well.

The planet on which they had settled was large, with ample room for every known Shielder, and with room to grow, and still not intrude on the Enhancer colony sharing the planet with them. Eirene had been delighted to find more of her own kind. The Enhancers had been more than generous in allowing the Shielders to settle here.

"I think this calls for a celebration," Blake declared. The excited crowd agreed and dispersed back toward the two main halls, where they would celebrate Alyssa's arrival well into the evening hours.

"You two coming?" Blake called over his shoulder.

"We'll be there in a while," Jarek hedged.

"Yeah, right." Blake shook his head, laughing.

Jarek twined his hand with Eirene's and tugged her toward the lake. They had a favorite spot there, beneath a huge tree near the water. The tree's branches bowed to the ground, its thick foliage giving them privacy, their own personal shamara.

"It's a shame Celie and Janaye weren't here," Eirene commented. "I know Moriah wanted them present for the birth."

"Mori didn't even plan on delivering here," Jarek reminded her. "She thought she had time to get back to Risa."

"That's true. I hope she's not too disappointed."

"I don't think so." Jarek pulled her inside the alcove formed by the tree's branches and drew her into his arms. "Did I tell you Gunnar is arriving tomorrow with more settlers?"

The nearby Enhancers had been willing to help the Shielders operate the spheres so they could evacuate everyone to Shamara, the most obvious name to give the colony. Only one Enhancer was needed for each trip, because Shielders could do the grounding. They'd found that one Enhancer and four Shielders were sufficient to safely operate a sphere. After that discovery, they had returned to Aldon to retrieve the other six spheres and begun transporting Shielders through the wormhole as quickly as possible.

When the Leors learned the areas around Shamara had vast natural veins of irridon, they offered their huge ships to transport the Shielders in return for the rare ore, and the evacuation progressed at a much faster pace.

"More settlers," Eirene murmured, wrapping her arms around her mate. "Where are we going to put them? The lodges are full."

"I'm sure we'll make room, little one." Jarek stroked her hair, slid his hand along her face. "We'll build more shelters."

"It will be fun to see Lani. Do you think she'll be dressed in a blue-feathered loincloth, like she was when we visited her and Gunnar on their ship?"

Jarek laughed softly. "That was pretty interesting, wasn't it? Lani has some nice . . . assets."

"What?" Eirene sputtered indignantly. "How could you have looked at those, at her . . . You know what I mean!"

"Sweetness, how could I miss them?" Jarek began opening her tunic. "They're not nearly as nice as yours, though."

"They're not?" she asked, totally distracted as he slid his hand inside and captured tender game. Spirit, every time he touched her, she melted into a quivering mass.

That's as it should be, he channelled, all male smugness.

Stay out of my mind unless you're invited.

I can't help myself. When you look at me with those gorgeous blue eyes, all soft and suggestive, I have to know if you want me as badly as I want you.

He was outrageous, far more playful and quick to laughter than he'd ever been in the other quadrant. And far too potent.

And what do you discover when you so rudely invade my mind? she asked teasingly, pressing a kiss to his sensuous mouth.

That you want me, all right. You're crazy about me.

He deepened the kiss, and molten heat spread through her body. *I don't know about that. I might take some convincing*, she managed to transmit, before coherent thought escaped her.

Much later, lying content in Jarek's arms, with the gentle breeze rustling the tree branches, she thought about Phylos's last words to her. *Do not discount the power of love. Love is the true essence of the One, and the greatest force in all the universe.*

She thought of the love that had created Sabin and Moriah's baby. The love that had motivated Jarek to lead his people here; had made her willing to sacrifice her life for his dream. Then his love had pulled her back from the brink of oblivion.

Phylos had been right. Love was the greatest force of all.

And it had brought them a most precious gift—shamara.

Catherine Spangler
SHADOWER

Sabin has been in every hellhole in the galaxy. In his line of work, hives of scum and villainy are nothing to fear. But Giza's is different, and the bronze-haired beauty at the bar is something special. Not only can she sweep a man off his feet, she can break his legs—and steal his heart. And though Moriah isn't what Sabin had come for, she is suddenly all he desires.

The man is a menace, what with his dark good looks and overwhelming masculinity. Worse, Sabin is a shadower, a bounty hunter, which means he is only one step removed from the law. He is dangerous to a smuggler like Moriah, to her freedom. Yet he draws her as a moth to a flame, and even as she pledges to stay cool, her senses catch fire. Then, in his arms, Moriah realizes that this bounty hunter is different. His touch is gentle, and his kiss sweet. And his love leads to a fantastic freedom she's never known.

___52424-4 $5.50 US/$6.50 CAN

Dorchester Publishing Co., Inc.
P.O. Box 6640
Wayne, PA 19087-8640

Please add $2.50 for shipping and handling for the first book and $.75 for each book thereafter. NY, NYC, and PA residents, please add appropriate sales tax. No cash, stamps, or C.O.D.s. All orders shipped within 6 weeks via postal service book rate. Canadian orders require $2.00 extra postage and must be paid in U.S. dollars through a U.S. banking facility.

Name_____
Address_____
City_____ State_____ Zip_____
I have enclosed $_____ in payment for the checked book(s).
Payment <u>must</u> accompany all orders.☐Please send a free catalog.
   CHECK OUT OUR WEBSITE! www.dorchesterpub.com

Shielder

Catherine Spangler

Unjustly shunned by her people, Nessa dan Ranul knows she is unlovable—so when an opportunity arises for her to save her world, she leaps at the chance. Setting out for the farthest reaches of the galaxy, she has one goal: to elude capture and deliver her race from destruction. But then she finds herself at the questionable mercy of Chase McKnight, a handsome bounty hunter. Suddenly, Nessa finds that escape is the last thing she wants. In Chase's passionate embrace she finds a nirvana of which she never dared dream—with a man she never dared trust. But as her identity remains a secret and her mission incomplete, each passing day brings her nearer to oblivion.

___52304-3 $5.50 US/$6.50 CAN

Dorchester Publishing Co., Inc.
P.O. Box 6640
Wayne, PA 19087-8640

Please add $1.75 for shipping and handling for the first book and $.50 for each book thereafter. NY, NYC, and PA residents, please add appropriate sales tax. No cash, stamps, or C.O.D.s. All orders shipped within 6 weeks via postal service book rate. Canadian orders require $2.00 extra postage and must be paid in U.S. dollars through a U.S. banking facility.

Name_____
Address_____
City_____State_____Zip_____
I have enclosed $_____ in payment for the checked book(s).
Payment <u>must</u> accompany all orders. ❑ Please send a free catalog.
    CHECK OUT OUR WEBSITE! www.dorchesterpub.com

THE
STAR
King
SUSAN GRANT

Careening out of control in her fighter jet is only the start of the wildest ride of Jasmine's life; spinning wildly in an airplane is nothing like the loss of equilibrium she feels when she lands. There, in a half-dream, Jas sees a man more powerfully compelling than any she's ever encountered. Though his words are foreign, his touch is familiar, baffling her mind even as he touches her soul. But who is he? Is he, too, a downed pilot? Is that why he lies in the desert sand beneath a starry Arabian sky? The answers burn in his mysterious golden eyes, in his thoughts that become hers as he holds out his hand and requests her aid. This man has crossed many miles to find her, to offer her a heaven that she might otherwise never know, and love is only one of the many gifts of . . . the Star King.

___52413-9 $5.50 US/$6.50 CAN

Dorchester Publishing Co., Inc.
P.O. Box 6640
Wayne, PA 19087-8640

Please add $2.50 for shipping and handling for the first book and $.75 for each book thereafter. NY, NYC, and PA residents, please add appropriate sales tax. No cash, stamps, or C.O.D.s. All orders shipped within 6 weeks via postal service book rate. Canadian orders require $2.00 extra postage and must be paid in U.S. dollars through a U.S. banking facility.

Name_____
Address_____
City_____ State_____ Zip_____
I have enclosed $_____ in payment for the checked book(s).
Payment <u>must</u> accompany all orders.☐Please send a free catalog.
CHECK OUT OUR WEBSITE! www.dorchesterpub.com

THE BLACK ROSE

JAN ZIMLICH

Though Lucien Charbonneau was born a noble, he's implemented plans to bring about galactic revolution. He wears two faces, that of an effete aristocrat and that of someone darker, more mysterious. He has subtle yet potent charms, and he plays at deception with the same skill that he might caress a lover. And though Lucien is betrothed, he swears not even his beautiful fiancée will ever learn his heart's secret, that of the Black Rose.

Alexandra Fallon has of course heard of that infamous spy, but her own interests are far less political. When interplanetary concerns force her to marry, the man who comes to her bed is in for a rude awakening. But the shadowy hunk who appears lights a passion hotter than a thousand suns—and in its fiery glow, both she and Lucien will learn that between lovers no secrets can remain in darkness.

The Sorceress & The Savage — Saranne Dawson

He stood amidst the stones, purely male and disarmingly dangerous. Her gaze traveled along his smooth bronzed skin and his strongly muscled torso to the curling dark gold hair framing a handsome, yet savage face. Undeniably drawn to this vision of a man who whispers dark secrets of passion yet to come, Shera knows that he holds the key to the mysteries of her people. She is the one who can redeem her people. When Gar first sees the lovely maiden with the raven-dark hair, when he first touches her alabaster skin, he knows that she is the one who holds the power within her. For after one caress he feels a burning desire within her that matches his own, and knows that only their love can unite their worlds and defeat the evil that threatens to destroy them both.

___52379-5 $5.50 US/$6.50 CAN

Dorchester Publishing Co., Inc.
P.O. Box 6640
Wayne, PA 19087-8640

Please add $1.75 for shipping and handling for the first book and $.50 for each book thereafter. NY, NYC, and PA residents, please add appropriate sales tax. No cash, stamps, or C.O.D.s. All orders shipped within 6 weeks via postal service book rate. Canadian orders require $2.00 extra postage and must be paid in U.S. dollars through a U.S. banking facility.

Name_____
Address_____
City_____State_____Zip_____
I have enclosed $_____ in payment for the checked book(s).
Payment _must_ accompany all orders. ❏ Please send a free catalog.

The CAPTIVE
Amanda Ashley

They gave him a number and took away his name. Took everything that makes life worth living. But they can't take hope . . . and she comes to him looking like an angel with hair the color of silver moonlight and eyes the color of a turbulent sea.

But when her father takes him from the mine to work on his lavish estate, a new torture faces the prisoner. Daily he is forced into contact with the innocent young beauty. Now, instead of his savior, she becomes his tormenter as she frolics in the pool, flirts with other men, teases him beyond endurance. Until one wild night when the world turns upside down and a daring escape makes slave at long last master, and mistress the captive.

___52362-0 $5.99 US/$6.99 CAN

Dorchester Publishing Co., Inc.
P.O. Box 6640
Wayne, PA 19087-8640

A DISTANT STAR

ANNE AVERY

Pride makes her run faster and longer than the others—traveling swiftly to carry her urgent messages. But hard as she tries, Nareen can never subdue her indomitable spirit—the passionate zeal all successful runners learn to suppress. And when she looks into the glittering gaze of the man called Jerrel and feels his searing touch, Nareen fears even more for her ability to maintain self-control. He is searching a distant world for his lost brother when his life is saved by the courageous messenger. Nareen's beauty and daring enchant him, but Jerrel cannot permit anyone to turn him from his mission, not even the proud and passionate woman who offers him a love capable of bridging the stars.

___52335-3 $5.50 US/$6.50 CAN